I0732808

The First Time
I Hunted

JO MACGREGOR

VIP Readers' Group: If you would like to receive my author's newsletter, with tips on great books, a behind-the-scenes look at my writing and publishing processes, and notice of new books, giveaways and special offers, then sign up at my website, www.joannemacgregor.com.

The First Time I Hunted first published in 2020 by Jo Macgregor
ISBN: 978-1-990981-81-4 (paperback)
ISBN: 978-1-990981-82-1 (eBook)

Copyright 2020 Jo Macgregor
The right of Joanne Macgregor, writing as Jo Macgregor, to be identified as the author of this work has been asserted by her in accordance with sections 77 and 78 of the Copyright, Designs and Patents Act, 1988.

All rights reserved. No parts of this book may be reproduced or transmitted in any form or by any means, mechanical or electronic, including photocopying and recording, or be stored in any information storage or retrieval system, without the prior written permission of the author.

Disclaimer: This is a work of fiction. All the characters, institutions and events described in it are fictional and the products of the author's imagination.

Cover design by Jenny Zemanek at Seedlings Design Studio
Formatting by Polgarus Studio

For Edyth, Chase, Nicola and Emily who believe in my writing enough to push me to do my best, even when it nearly kills me.

"I exist as I am, that is enough."

— Walt Whitman

– 1 –

On that early evening in late March, the interior of the Tuppenny Tavern was neat, peaceful, and well ordered — the complete opposite, in other words, of me.

Behind the counter, the barman polished glasses, arranging them in sparkling lines of symmetry — beer, red wine, white wine, cocktail, soda — and a waitress weaved her way between tables, refilling napkin holders, collecting empties, and wiping ketchup bottles. In the corner booth, a young couple sat hunched over their phones. The polished leather seats of the barstools gleamed, the brass fittings shone, and from hidden speakers, Tim McGraw crooned that we should all live like we were dying.

I hear you, cowboy, I thought.

I, too, wanted to get on with my life, make up for lost time, achieve something. I wanted to explore and love and live life to the fullest. So naturally, there I sat in my old haunt in my old hometown, twiddling my thumbs. Or rather, tapping restless fingers on the bar counter. Pitchford was a quaint little town nestled against the foothills of the Green Mountains, in the heart of scenic Vermont. It was where I'd grown up, where I'd run away from at age eighteen, and where, almost four months ago, I had died and been resuscitated back to life.

That evening, I wasn't alone; Ryan Jackson sat on the stool to my right. As usual, the stool to my left remained empty. Then again, depending on what you believed about the world and the possibility of life after it, the stool might not have been empty at all.

Feeling Ryan's concerned gaze on me, I stilled my fingers.

"What's up?" he asked. "You look kind of …"

"Panicky?"

"Well, I was going to say *anxious*. But *panicky* is probably more accurate."

Perhaps the thoughts racing frantically around inside my head gave off an audible buzz.

I took a long swallow of beer and set the bottle back down too hard. "So … this morning, I got a text from our mutual friend at the FBI."

"Ronil Singh?"

"That's the one."

"And?"

"And I called him back."

"*Annnd?*"

I laughed. Usually, it was me trying to pry information out

of *him*; it was fun to have the tables turned for a change. "He instructed me not to tell anyone," I said piously.

"I'm not *anyone*."

That was true.

Ryan Jackson was the police chief, and most eligible bachelor, of Pitchford. He was thirty-four years old, funny, intelligent, and inexplicably tolerant of my innate prickliness. He was also attractive — a good six feet tall with a lean build, thick black hair, and slate-gray eyes. When he gave one of his charming smiles, a dimple dented his right cheek.

I, on the other hand, had two differently colored eyes, no dimple, and no charm. I was shorter than him by about six inches, younger by six years, and my shoulder-length brown hair lacked the lustrous shine of his. But I liked to think that I could outdo him in snark and sneakiness any day of the week.

We were something more than just friends, a little less than officially romantically involved. Facebook would call us "complicated."

"Well?" Ryan pressed. "What did he want to talk to you about?"

"He didn't *want* to talk to me at all." I traced patterns in the condensation on my beer bottle. "In fact, he couldn't believe he'd contacted me and said I should under no circumstances think this meant he had any confidence in my abilities. It really went against the grain to even consider me, but he wasn't one to ignore any potential leads, no matter how unlikely, and so what else could he do, given the latest development?"

Ryan's eyes lit up with curiosity. "What development? Something's happened?"

"Yup. They found a new body. Or maybe it's an old one, newly found. He wouldn't say."

"Ah."

"Yeah, *ah*."

Special Agent Ronil Singh headed the FBI's investigation into a series of murders of young men in New England that occurred between 2006 and 2009, but which may have started earlier and continued later. Less than a month ago, I'd gone for a walk in the woods and stumbled onto the skeletonized remains of one of those victims. Singh had come to Pitchford to take my statement and, at Ryan's suggestion, got me to touch a few objects, one of which — an old wooden button — had sparked off a series of distressing images in my mind.

This was something that happened to me now. Since my near-death experience, I occasionally got feelings or fleeting visions when I touched objects or visited places associated with strong emotions. My mother, who viewed it as a gift from the gods, called it *psychometry*; I called it freaky and disturbing — as unpredictable and uncontrollable as Boston weather.

Looking up, I caught Ryan's gaze on my mouth where my teeth worried at the rough edge of one of my thumbnails. He didn't like me biting my nails but tried not to mention it. I hadn't yet let him find out about the other ways in which I sometimes attacked my body, and I didn't plan on doing so.

"Come on," he said, taking my hand and pulling me to my feet. "Let's find something for your hands to do."

I glanced at the empty seat as I left. If it *was* occupied, I kind of wished it would stay that way for now — I wanted some alone time with Ryan. He led me to a quiet corner of the bar, where a dartboard hung on the wall with a chalk scoreboard beside it.

"Darts?" I said in disbelief. "I've never played in my life."

He handed me a set of three darts with sharp points, black barrels, and a skull-and-crossbones design on the plastic feather bits. The red arrows of his set sported orange and yellow flames on their plastic ends.

I eyed his enviously. "I think red is a luckier color."

"Do you?" he said, unchivalrously ignoring my hint.

"How come I get the death's head pattern?"

It seemed like an omen; I was dead in the water when it came to competitive contests.

"Because you and death" — he held up two fingers twisted together — "are *tight.*"

I couldn't deny it.

"And you get the ones with fire on their … butts—"

"Their flights," he corrected.

"You get flaming flights because …?"

He flashed me a single-dimpled smile. "Because I'm so hot, *duh.*"

"Right."

I stared longingly at the TV set mounted high up in the corner. I'd much rather watch the news on CNN than reveal the shortcomings of my hand-eye coordination. Ryan, however, muted the volume on the set and had me stand behind the line on the floor, about eight or nine feet away from the board.

"I know you're better at crossing lines than staying behind them, Garnet, but you're not allowed to set a toe over this one when you're throwing."

I stood behind the line and glared at the multicolored dartboard. I reckoned I'd be able to hit it. With a basketball. I sighed. "I'm not going to be any good at this."

"You don't have to be. We're playing for *fun*." At my dubious look, he added, "You get to penetrate a firm surface with small sharp objects. Should be right up your alley."

"Too soon, Ryan," I said, narrowing my eyes threateningly because this was clearly a dig at how I'd taken down a murder suspect in my last "investigation."

Grinning, he wrote our names on the scoreboard. "We both start at five-hundred and one, and what we score each round gets deducted from that. First person to zero wins."

"Five-hundred-and-one? We'll be here all night!" I complained. "Scratch that, all *week*."

"Fun fact: it can be done in just nine throws."

"Not by me," I muttered. "Can I have a practice round?"

"Of course."

With my toes nudging the line, I held a dart in my right hand, gripping it like a pencil. I made to throw it at the board, then dropped my arm and turned to where Ryan leaned against the wall. "How am I supposed to hold this thing?" I asked.

"In any way that feels comfortable or natural."

None of it felt comfortable or natural. I rearranged my fingers and held the dart up, sticking my tongue out of the corner of my mouth for improved concentration. I mimed a few test throws, then turned to face him, trying to mold my features into an appealing pout, though I wasn't convinced I'd nailed it. Scowls, I was good at. Cute pouts? Not so much.

"Ryan, I'm no good at sports. I don't sports well."

"Good thing this is a game and not a sport, then."

"But—" I began.

"Quit whining and throw a dart already."

"*Fine.*"

Spinning around, I fired the dart at the board and burst out laughing at the sight of it quivering in the red circle in the dead center.

"Bullseye!" Ryan shook his head in disbelief. "Were you hustling me earlier?"

"No! I've never played before, I promise."

"Hmm."

I threw my remaining two darts. One hit the no-score zone outside the colored rings; the other bounced off the wall below the board. I retrieved the darts. "See? It was just beginner's luck."

"Want some more practice shots to get your eye in?" Ryan offered.

"Honestly, I don't think it'll help. We may as well get on with it."

"Ladies and bullseyes first." He came to stand beside me and lifted my hand in his own, which was warm and steady. "Here, hold it up to your right eye, like so. That's right. Now, you're supposed to get a double to start your game." My body sagged in defeat, and he added, "But rules were made to be broken, so we'll keep it simple. Just try to hit the board, okay?"

"Okay."

I waited for him to go back to his spot against the wall, but instead, he stayed close to me. Too close.

I waved him back. "Your presence is distracting me."

"It is?" He gave me a sexy grin, which distracted me even more.

"*Move.* I don't want to hit you by mistake."

"I reckon I'm safe here."

"You're very trusting."

"Maybe it's you who's not trusting enough?"

"I know enough not to trust my skill at darts."

He didn't budge other than to move his hand in an impatient get-on-with-it gesture.

I threw my three darts quickly, one after the other, and then danced a little jig. They'd *all* missed the wall, and one had landed solidly in a white wedge-shaped section of the board.

"Well done!" Ryan chalked my score of one on the board. "Only five-hundred to go."

I groaned and stepped aside for him to take his turn, glancing up at the TV news. Death and mayhem were everywhere — deadly protests in the Gaza Strip, prison riots in Venezuela, and a school shooting in Maryland. What a time to be alive.

"So, the FBI thinks this body is a murder victim?" Ryan asked. "And that it was one of his, the serial killer's?"

"The Button Man? Yup."

"Is that what they're calling him?"

"That's what *I'm* calling him."

While most serial killers tended to take small items from their victims as trophies to remember the kills by, this killer had *left* something — a button — with each of his victims. And at least once, according to a vision I'd had, he'd left a button *on* one of his victims — stitched onto the poor man's lips with black twine.

Ryan threw his darts expertly and deducted his score of thirty-five from the opening total.

"Told you the red ones would be lucky," I grumbled.

"Yeah, I'm sure it has nothing to do with skill."

"There's probably a darter's ditty about it, like the old shepherd's caution. Red flights at night, player's delight. Black flights at morning, player's warning."

Ryan snorted and tugged his darts out of the board. "Did you know that 'Button Man' is slang for a hired killer, a mafia hitman? Or for a low-ranking member of the *familia*?"

"I learned that when I was today years old," I said. "Do you think these murders might have been mob hits?"

Ryan considered for a moment, then said, "Nope."

"Me either."

"Based on?"

"Based, as always with me, on impeccable logic and unassailable rationality."

"Just a feeling, then?" he asked.

"Just a feeling."

– 2 –

Ryan indicated that it was my turn. "What did Singh want from you?"

I flung my darts at the board. The first was a no-score, and the second hit a narrow strip of wire — which would've been pretty darn impressive if I'd been aiming at it — and fell to the floor. But with my third throw, I actually scored a double seven. I deducted twenty-five points from my score on the board.

"I think he wants me to touch an item from the body," I said. "He wouldn't give me details — tighter-lipped than a razor clam at low tide, that man — but I gather that they're not sure whether the kill is one of the serial killer's."

Ryan threw his darts, wrote down his actual score of forty-two, and stepped back for me to take my turn. I stood behind the line, but when he turned to greet a friend, I stepped over it, hurried right up the board, and thrust one of my darts into one of the small red sections that he'd explained tripled the score. I scampered back to my starting position and let out a triumphant, "Woohoo!"

Turning back, Ryan saw the source of my jubilation. "Well done! You're improving."

"Amazing, right? I put that dart exactly where I wanted it. So, what's my score?"

"Six."

"*Six?* But you said that the inner circle was triple-score!"

"It is. He tapped the wire number on the outer rim of the board. Two multiplied by three is ..."

This game sucked. I couldn't even cheat successfully. I marched over to the chalkboard and gave myself a score of sixty-six.

Ryan laughed. "You're either awful at math or a serious cheat."

"I just want this humiliation to end sooner rather than later, okay?"

On the TV, the news was running an "On This Day" piece, showing footage of John Hinckley's assassination attempt on Ronald Reagan in 1981 and displaying one of the former president's better quotes: "There are no easy answers, but there are simple answers. We must have the courage to do what we know is morally right."

Ryan joined me at the scoreboard, but instead of correcting my score, he picked up the eraser and rubbed out all the scores.

"How about we start with a clean slate and play just for fun?" he suggested.

"You keep saying that F-word, friend. See if it makes it happen."

Now the news showed visuals of an excited-looking reporter who, judging by the yellow police tape and number of law enforcement officers in the background, was at the site of a crime scene. From the sparse information on the scrolling news ticker, I gleaned that the breaking story was the discovery of a mass burial site where the remains of at least six bodies had been found buried in the Nash Stream Forest area in western New Hampshire, not far from the Vermont border.

"Look at that," I said. "Reckon it's from a spree killing or maybe a family murder?"

"I doubt it. If so many people disappeared in the woods at one time, we'd have heard about it," my favorite cop said. "It's probably a serial killer's dumpsite."

I sipped my beer, frowning up at the TV. "It sometimes feels like the world is full of them."

"Serial killers? Not really. I know Hollywood makes it seem like the country's swarming with them, but they're actually quite rare."

I shot him a skeptical glance.

"It's true. Murders by serial killers make up less than one percent of the US homicide rate. And the overall number is in decline." Ryan tossed his darts, making it look easy.

"Why are the numbers going down?"

"For one thing, they're getting caught sooner due to improvements in forensic science, especially in DNA evidence, and better inter-agency cooperation. Plus, we've got access to national databases, now. That's been a game-changer."

"Like the fingerprint one?"

"Yeah, IAFIS. But also the FBI's national crime database, the NCIC, and ViCAP, which is for violent crimes. And, of course, these days convicted serial killers are getting longer prison sentences."

I threw my darts; one of them actually clattered sideways against the board. "I'm getting *worse*. How is that even possible?"

"Your problem is you're too tense. C'mon. Let me see if I can help." He coaxed me back to the line and, standing close behind me, showed me how to stand with my right foot forward. "Now plant your left foot behind, like so, for balance." When I leaned forward to throw, he placed a hand on either side of my hips, holding me steady. "Keep your body still and relaxed. Just let your arm do all the work."

The warmth of his chest against my back and his hands on my hips made me feel the opposite of relaxed. No surprise, then, that my dart missed the board entirely.

"Breathe," he said, massaging my shoulders. "You need to loosen up."

I sagged into his kneading hands. If I were to spin around in his arms and kiss him, would that distract him from the wretched game? Probably not — he was a persistent man. But maybe I should do it anyway, just because I wanted to.

He held my hand and guided my next throw. That time, I hit the board.

"Stop overthinking it," he whispered into my ear, sending goosebumps up my arms. "The more you think, the worse you perform."

A lot like my life then.

"Just trust your instincts."

Trust my instincts? Was he mad?

I threw my last dart and scored a double nineteen.

Ryan hugged me from behind. "There you go. That's better! A legit thirty-eight."

I snuggled back into his chest but gasped in disbelief as the dart sagged, wiggled loose, and dropped to the floor.

"What the …? Did you see that?" I demanded, pointing at the board.

Ryan, who'd been nuzzling my neck, glanced up. "See what? Oh, that."

"Yes, that. It was my best throw so far!"

"Sometimes they don't stick. It's called a bounce-out," he said.

But I was certain the dart hadn't fallen out of its own accord, a conviction which grew when a sudden coldness surrounded me like my own icy cloud.

Jealous, Colby? I thought.

My high school sweetheart, Colby Beaumont, had died in our senior year, plunging me into a deep pool of grief. But since my near-death experience, I sometimes heard his voice in my head or felt his presence, as I did now. Not being into threesomes, I pulled away from Ryan, grabbed my beer, and perched on a stool.

"Quitting?" Ryan challenged.

"It's your turn. They can all be your turns from now on. And I hope you can multitask because I want you to tell me about serial killers."

He retrieved my darts from the board. "I don't know that much, to be honest; I've never investigated a murder by a serial killer."

"*Never?*"

"I see I've gone down in your estimation."

"Utterly," I teased.

He threw my darts at the board, piercing the narrow green circle that surrounded the bullseye and congratulating me for getting my highest score of the evening.

"I reckon you know more about serial killers than I do," I said.

"Didn't you learn about them in your studies?"

"I studied psychology not criminology. I could tell you about psychopaths but killers?" I shrugged. "So dish. Like, what drives serial killers?"

Ryan flung the last darts into the board and came to sit with me. "Generally speaking, people kill for the sake of love, lust, loathing, and loot. Or any combination of those."

"And is that true for serial killers too?"

"Pretty much. I think they especially like the thrill of the power. I mean, some of them are plain insane, like they think God told them to kill red-haired women, who are demons in disguise. But a lot just use other people as a way to get their kicks, especially sexually. Then you have the sadists who like to torture, and the men who are filled with violent rage and when that spills over from time to time, they kill. Some killers believe they're special, that they have a mission to rid the world of some kind of 'bad' person, like sex workers or interracial couples, or—"

"Or gay men?" All the Button Man's victims had been gay or were thought to be so. "Is that why *he* targets them, do you think?"

"Maybe. But they're generally a vulnerable target. They're presumed to be easier to take down and less likely to put up a fight."

I thought about a guy I'd been at school with, Andy something. He'd had a slim build and an effete manner, and the guys were always picking on him, calling him names, tripping him up, and trashing his locker. I'd been too immersed in my love for Colby, and then too lost in my grief, to be much aware of his pain, but now I felt a pang of shame. I should've done something. I should've stood up for him.

"Fun fact," Ryan said, recalling me from my thoughts, "a surprising number of serial murders are committed for profit or gain."

"Like for money?"

"Yup. Especially by female killers." Ryan finished his beer. "It's probably fair to say that for the most part, serial killers are opportunists who strike when the chance presents itself."

I picked at the damp label on my beer bottle, digging scallops into its edges with my thumb nail. "And their victims?"

"Statistically speaking, they're more likely to be female, from the killer's own race group, and taken from the edges of society." At my confused look, he explained, "Runaways, sex workers, addicts, migrant workers, transients, the homeless, people like that."

"Because police don't investigate those crimes as thoroughly?"

He winced. "Historically, for sure, especially with racial minorities. I like to think we're getting better. But often marginalized people become victims because killers know they won't be missed immediately … or ever. Their families might have cut off all contact because they don't approve of their lifestyle and don't know, or perhaps even care, when they disappear."

"Really?"

"Yeah, it's pretty damn sad," he said. "And also, these

individuals are more likely to take greater chances and engage in more risky behaviors, like hitchhiking or sex work, because they don't have money or support systems. And they often abuse drugs or alcohol, so they don't always make wise decisions." He held up his hands as if defending himself against an accusation. "I'm not blaming the victims. I'm just saying it's easier for a killer to snatch a victim from these marginal groups than from middle-class suburbia. There's even a term for them." He met my gaze and sighed. "The 'less dead.'"

"That's horrible."

"No argument from me."

We sat in silence for a while, Ryan glancing at the TV while I thought about how, in death as in life, we weren't all treated as equal.

I tore off a strip of label from my beer bottle and rolled it into a little paper pellet. "I just wish I knew what all the FBI found." That was putting it mildly. I hadn't been able to get the thought of a new body out of my mind. "Singh's meeting me at my parents' house on Monday morning, and I'm going to ask him if I can read the file on this new case."

"Good luck with that. He doesn't strike me as the cooperative type." Ryan pulled my hand away from its frantic fiddling and held it between his two warm ones. "Garnet, are you sure you want to get involved in this? You know it's likely to be frustrating and upsetting. Possibly even dangerous."

Did I want to get involved? I wasn't sure. I wanted the Button Man caught, but did I really want to be sucked into an investigation which might bring me closer to him, to his deeds? There had been moments when I'd wished I'd never been "gifted" with this ability, when I wondered whether, if I ignored it, it would just go away. But then I'd remember the words of my psychology professor, Kenneth Perry: "Whatever you bank collects interest."

Of course, he'd been talking about the defense mechanism of repression, not troublesome clairvoyant talents, but still, I didn't think much good would come from squashing down this powerful new part of myself.

"I'm *already* involved," I told Ryan. "I want to find out more. I want to know where this goes, where it ends. And I'd really like to help nail this guy. Besides, to tell the truth, I've got nothing better to do."

"Is your thesis finished? Submitted?" Ryan asked.

"Yup. All that's left to do is to graduate."

"What does a master's in psychology qualify you to do?"

I shrugged. "Probably nothing useful or well paid."

A part of me wondered if I could turn my new gifts to good use. My mother thought I should hang out a shingle advertising myself as a "psychic private eye," but my mother thought a lot of things that were absurd and impossible.

"What will you do?" he asked.

"Go back to Boston, I guess."

Ryan played with my fingers. "You could stay here."

I could tell he wanted me to, and knowing that melted a chip of the icy shell around my heart. I compensated with sarcastic bluster. "And do *what*?"

"What will you do in *Boston*?" he countered.

Fair point.

He tucked a stray curl of hair behind my ear. "I think we're going to have to find you a job here."

Return to Pitchford permanently? If anyone had suggested it six months ago, I would've rejected the idea outright. But now it was more appealing, especially with the way things were progressing in my relationship with Ryan. I'd led an isolated life in Boston while I studied and battled my way through grief and depression. I hadn't made good friends, and although I'd had sexual partners, I'd never had *lovers*.

Nothing was stopping me from moving my meagre belongings back to Pitchford. But my heart sank at the thought of returning to my old bedroom at my parents' house. Apart from the fact that it would feel like a total admission of my failure to launch my adult life, my mother and I tended to rub each other up the wrong way. Even my father, now that he'd retired, had a tendency to get too much into my business.

I glanced at Ryan. "I can almost hear the wheels of your brain turning."

He gave me a smile that was almost smug.

"What?" I demanded.

He leaned close and pressed a warm kiss to my lips.

"I may," he said, "just have had a brilliant idea."

– 3 –

Monday, April 2

"Still no sign of him," my mother said, peeping out the living room window for the umpteenth time. "I suppose I should stop checking because you know what they say?"

"I'm sure you'll tell us," I said.

"Watching a kettle won't make it boil any faster." With a last peep at the path and road outside, she sat down and scrutinized my appearance critically. "Goodness, Garnet, it doesn't look like you've even brushed your hair this morning, let alone put on any makeup."

"I'm not going on a date, Mom. I'm just going to try to help him with his investigation."

"But he's an *agent*. A *special* agent. I swear, I haven't been this proud of you since you started first grade. I feel dizzy with excitement!"

My father, reading yet another book about Ted Bundy, gave a long-suffering sigh. "Have you forgotten to take your medicine again, Crystal?"

Her brows drew together. "Oh dear, I think I might have."

"Mom! That's serious. You have to take them the same time every day. Without fail," I said.

Far too often, my mother forgot that she was on a regime of blood thinners and blood pressure meds for a very good reason. She'd suffered a mini-stroke the previous year.

"Yes, yes, I know. I'm just so distracted. It'll be a whole new body for you to investigate, Garnet."

"It's more likely to be an old body," my father said. He, too, seemed keyed up about the impending arrival of Agent Singh.

"Why old?" I asked.

"If the murder happened recently, they'd have a body and lots of forensic evidence to analyze. They wouldn't need to go out on a limb with unorthodox methods like these."

"I guess."

I scraped the nail of my forefinger across my lower teeth, searching for an uneven edge. Unevenness — on nails, on skin — bothered me. It niggled like a task undone, an itch unscratched, a sneeze suppressed. For me, it was impossible to resist. Knowing that I bit my nails, and peeled and picked at my skin — that I had onychophagia and excoriation disorders, to be psychologically precise — did nothing to help me stop the horrible habits, especially when I was very upset or nervous, like now.

"You said they weren't even sure it was one of his — this serial killer's, which makes me think it could be his first kill," my father continued. "And you can learn a lot from that. The first kill, the body itself and where it was disposed of, is always hugely valuable to the investigation."

My father had always been fascinated by murder and especially by serial killers. He had a wall of books on everyone from the Blood Countess Elizabeth Báthory to the West Mesa Bone Collector and could tell you each of their usual modus operandi or victim of preference. It was a surprisingly macabre pastime for such a mild-mannered man, but as I lived in my own glass house of weirdness, I wasn't in any position to throw stones at his peculiar hobby.

"Why's it more useful than any other kill?" I wanted to know.

"Because the first murder is more likely to be spontaneous. The killer wasn't *planning* on killing that person at that time, in that place, or in that way, you see? He might slip up on the first kill and leave behind DNA, fingerprints, or other evidence, especially if it happened before the whole world and his wife started watching CSI. With subsequent murders, serial killers tend to get more careful."

The doorbell chimed, and we all stood up. My mother smoothed her dress, but my father, who wore a serious expression, said, "It's not too late to call this off, kiddo."

"*Da-ad,* we've already discussed this." I sidestepped him and headed for the front door. "Why wouldn't I want to help?"

"There are just so many ways this could turn out badly," he said, following me.

He wasn't wrong. There were a bunch of ways this could flop. Maybe I wouldn't get anything from touching the item Singh was bringing me. Or worse, maybe I *would* get a reading, but it would turn out to be unhelpful or even something that would send the investigators on a wild goose chase, wasting time and resources and allowing the killer to remain undetected.

It wasn't like I knew what I was doing with my psychic ability yet. The visions occurred erratically and unpredictably, and although I trusted my skill more now than I had in the beginning, I still couldn't control it. On the one hand, I wanted to help with the investigation, but on the other, I was terrified of failing miserably. I should probably follow my father's advice and call the whole thing off.

Instead, I opened the front door and greeted Special Agent Ronil Singh of the FBI resident agency in Rutland. He looked as spiffy as the last time I'd seen him, and clearly, he *had* brushed his hair that morning. Dark suit and tie, white-button down shirt, polished black shoes, black briefcase. I half-expected him to slip on a pair of sunglasses, whip out a silver tube, and erase my memory.

"Ms. McGee," was the sum total of his greeting.

"Nice to see you again …" What was I supposed to call him — Ronil, Ron, Agent Singh, sir? None of those felt right. "Come in," I said and stepped back to introduce him to my parents, who were hovering behind me.

"Welcome to our home, Special Agent Mr. Singh. We're delighted to meet you," my mother said, all but curtseying. "Can I get you a cup of coffee?"

Singh shook his head. "No, thank you, ma'am."

"This way." I led him to the living room.

"How about a cup of herbal tea? I have ginger, fennel, ginseng, and ginkgo," my mother offered. "Turmeric too. That's excellent for inflammation, you know?"

"No, thank you, ma'am. I'm fine."

"Have a seat," I said.

"Yes, make yourself comfortable, Agent Singh," my mother said. "My house is your *casa*."

I glanced at Singh to see what he made of that. My mother had a habit of confusing words and phrases, and she could be difficult to understand. But his face remained politely blank.

Determined to be hospitable, she said, "Earl Grey?"

"I beg your pardon, ma'am?" Singh said.

"Would you like a cup of Earl Grey tea?"

Perhaps realizing that she was quite capable of listing every liquid refreshment in the house until he accepted one, Singh said, "A glass of water, if that's not too much trouble."

My mother hurried off to the kitchen, and my father settled beside me on the couch. Singh sat in the same spot he had on his previous visit, directly across from me with the coffee table between us.

"So, how can I help you?" I asked him.

"I've brought an item connected to an ongoing investigation in the hope that you might be able to provide me with information regarding it."

My father made a small sound, drawing the agent's attention. "You understand that … that these are just sort of vague *impressions* Garnet gets. I mean, it's not like they're real records of what actually happened."

"Thanks for the vote of confidence, Dad."

My mother, who'd obviously been following every word of the conversation, called from the kitchen, "You're like Cassandra, dear. Never to be believed in her hometown, that is the sad fate of a prophet."

Singh gave me an incredulous look, but before I could deny any claim to being a prophet, he told my father, "I assure you, Mr. McGee, no one appreciates better than I do that these … visions are not reliable evidence."

"If you're so sure that you can't get anything useful from me, then why the heck are you here?" I demanded. It was one thing for me to consider my visions unreliable. Hearing it described that way by others riled me.

Singh raised open hands. *Perhaps I'm too desperate to rule out* any *possible line of inquiry*, the gesture said, *or perhaps I'm just a fool.*

"What information do you hope to get?" my dad asked.

"Whatever your daughter is able to give us."

I took a breath to speak, but my father wasn't done grilling the agent. I guessed that having discharged his duty in warning law enforcement about the doubtful value of my gift, he now felt free to indulge his rampant curiosity about murder. "Do you have any idea who this killer is? Have you developed a profile on him? Do you know what his motivation is? Is he still active? Do you know if he's even still alive?" he asked eagerly.

"I'm afraid I'm not at liberty to disclose any information about the investigation, sir," Singh said.

"But you do have some theories? Any suspects?"

"*Dad,*" I said and gave him a look that told him to shut up.

My mother returned with a tray bearing four glasses and a pitcher filled with water in which floated a fistful of leaves and set it on the coffee table. "I added some sage for heightened memory, rosemary for clarity of mind, and" — she pointed at what appeared to be a piece of bark lying on the bottom of the pitcher — "cinnamon for intuition."

After pouring a glass that contained more foliage than water, she handed it to Singh. I grinned. I bet he wished he'd accepted the offer of plain old coffee. If Ryan had been here instead of the agent, we would've exchanged a glance and then looked away quickly to avoid laughing. But Singh was a serious fella — he eyed the glass doubtfully. He'd been skeptical of my abilities and perhaps even of my sanity *before* he'd met my parents; whatever must he be thinking of me now? He said nothing, however. Placing the glass on a coaster on the table, he opened his briefcase and extracted a plastic evidence bag.

"Oooh," my mother said, perching on the edge of an easy chair. "Is that it? Is that the thingamajig you want Garnet to lay hands on and get her reading from?"

"Did you find that at the dump site or the kill site?" my father asked.

Singh's only reply was to give my father an assessing look. He handed me the bag, and I became aware of the unsettled state of my stomach. This was it, my chance to impress the FBI agent, to prove I was neither a deluded idiot nor an out-an-out fraud. Trying to calm myself, I took a moment to study the snap button inside the bag. It was small, round, and made of metal with raised lettering around the circumference mostly obscured by rust.

The button Singh had brought me in March had been made of wood and found on the body of Jacob Wertheimer, a young man who'd gone missing in 2009. When I'd touched it, I'd seen a vision of the killer's hands doing horrible things to his victim and, just like when I'd touched a rib bone of the victim,

I'd sensed an abyss of fear, darkness and evil which had left me disturbed for days.

I shuddered at the memory. Sensing that I might again be about to experience something similar, my body rebelled, urging my heart into a faster beat. A deep, primitive part of my brain ordered me to drop the bag, to flee and have nothing further to do with this.

I blew out a steadying breath and pushed the soles of my feet onto the carpet, as if that could keep me rooted in place. Then I opened the bag.

– 4 –

My mother sucked in a breath, my father covered his mouth with a hand, and Singh, unblinking as a cobra, watched as I closed my fingers around the button in my sweaty palm and concentrated. And got only the faintest of sensations.

I opened my eyes, and my mother, positively thrumming with excitement, asked, "What did you see, dear? Did you hear anything? Pick up any evil vibrations?"

"Not really. I just got a vague impression of … anger. And pain, maybe?" I said uncertainly. I met Singh's gaze and shrugged, feeling guilty. Maybe he'd come all the way to Pitchford for nothing. Maybe I'd lost the ability to read objects.

My mother slumped back in her chair in unmistakable disappointment and frowned at the pitcher of water. "Perhaps I should've added a pinch of peppermint."

"I wonder," Singh said, glancing from her to my father, "if Garnet would be able to concentrate better if we were alone?"

My mother stood up at once, regretful but still eager to help. "I'll go upstairs to my bedroom and lay a crystal grid. It's directly above this room, so it should potentiate the vibrations. Amethyst, celestite, and quartz should turn the trick, I think."

Singh directed a look of such complete blankness at me that I knew exactly what he was thinking: *WTF, lady?* I had no answer for him.

Instead, I turned to face my father, who hadn't moved. "Dad, don't you have something else to do, somewhere else to be?"

He stood up. "Yes, of course. I'll go rinse my rods."

A flicker of bewilderment crossed Singh's impassive features.

"He means his fishing rods," I explained. "He was away on a fishing trip until last night."

"If you need me, kiddo, you'll find me in the basement," Dad said, leaving the room with my mother, who was wondering out loud whether it would be a mistake to exclude malachite.

As soon as we were alone, Singh jerked his chin at the button still in my hand. "Can you tell whether that's connected to the killer with the last button I brought?"

I closed my eyes again and, concentrating as hard as I could, tried to feel with the fingers of my mind for any link to the other murder, the other victim. When I opened my eyes, I tried to put into words what I'd intuited. "There's a … a resonance. I get 'the same but different.' Where did you find this one?"

He hesitated, obviously reluctant to give me any information. Eventually, he said, "With a body."

"But not on or in its mouth." It wasn't a question.

Neither confirming nor denying this, he pulled a different

evidence bag out of his briefcase and handed it to me. "Let's try this one."

I placed the first button on the table and peered at the dark-green button inside the baggie. It was about an inch in diameter and made of plastic, with a raised edge around the circumference and a crosshatch pattern scored on its upper surface. Four holes punctured the center. I was about to open the bag when a slight movement in my peripheral vision caught my attention. I glanced up just in time to see my father ducking back around the entrance to the living room, where he'd obviously been eavesdropping.

"*Dad!*" I yelled and heard a mumbled apology and footsteps retreating down the hall.

"Your father is very curious about all this," Singh said.

"Yes, he's very … protective of me." I said nothing about his killer hobby; Singh didn't need to know the full extent of my family's strangeness.

I tugged the ziplock of the baggie open and tipped the button into my hand, then closed my eyes and focused. My palm grew warm, and the skin on my scalp tightened. The image I saw was faint and brief but enough to tell me that this button was definitely from one of the Button Man's victims.

I opened my eyes. "Okay, I didn't see much. And what I did see wasn't very clear."

Singh raised an eyebrow, like he thought I was already preparing excuses for a failure to see anything.

"It was a hand, a male hand, pushing this button into a man's mouth."

Singh's blank expression gave me no clue as to whether I was on the right track.

"Did you find the button in the skull of the skeleton, maybe in the jaw area?" I asked, remembering something my father had once told me. "Did you know that the Greeks used to place copper coins in the mouths of the dead so they would have fare for the ferryman on the River Styx? They had to pay him to take them across the river to the world of the dead."

"Is that so?" His tone could not have sounded less interested.

"I'm just wondering what the button in the victim's mouth could mean to the killer."

"Did you see anything else?"

"Give me a minute."

Holding the button between both my palms, I clasped my fingers, slowed my breathing, and tried to empty my mind of all distracting thoughts and worries. When my full attention was fixed on the curves and ridges pressing into my skin, I re-entered the vision I'd seen moments earlier.

Hands, white as death-lilies in the darkness.
Two hands, left and right.
The left hand touches the stubbled jaw of a young man.
His skin is pale, his eyes closed, his lips slightly parted. A
white object lies beside his head.
No fight, now. No fear left. No problem.
The thumb of the hand pushes between the young man's
lips, pulls out, pushes back inside. Thrusting in and out
of the mouth. Then it pulls down the jaw, holding it
open in a silent scream, while the fingers of the other
hand slide a green button over the teeth and into the
mouth, then push the jaw up, pinching the lips closed

between thumb and forefinger. Tugging them into an obscene pout.

The vision dissolved into formless clouds of gray. Swallowing rising bile, I opened heavy eyelids to find Singh watching me carefully.

"Well?" he demanded when I dropped the button on the table.

"Do you want to know what I saw or what I felt?" I asked, my voice breathy.

"What you saw."

I poured myself a glass of the ridiculous water, and between sips, I told him exactly what I'd seen, no more and no less.

When I finished, he asked, "Can you describe the hands?"

"Male." Whether I'd been able to tell from the appearance or whether it was just a feeling, I was certain those hands hadn't belonged to a woman. "White-skinned. No wedding ring. I would guess left-handed."

"Anything exceptional about the hands? Like a scar or a mole?"

"Nope."

"You said the victim was dead. How could you tell?"

"His eyes were closed, and he wasn't moving."

"He might just have been unconscious."

"Ah, well, that's where my pesky feelings come in." I gave Singh an expectant look, wanting the satisfaction of forcing him to ask about my sensations and intuitions, but he said nothing, and after a few more seconds of silence, I caved. "Since you asked so nicely, I'll tell you," I said. "There was a deadness there."

"A *deadness?*"

"Yes, an absence of life. A deep emptiness, a cessation of all life-emanating vibrations," I said, laying the mystical terminology on thick enough to make my mother proud and Singh exasperated.

Looking like he was suppressing a sigh, he reached for his glass of water, clocked the vegetation floating around inside of it, and set it back down. "The hands that were holding the button, do they belong to the same man in the visions you claim to have had about Wertheimer's death?"

Claim to have had? "You want my gut feel?" I asked.

Singh gave the slightest of nods. It was as much encouragement as I was ever likely to get from this die-hard cynic.

"Well then, gut feel, yeah, it's the same guy." I set my glass back down on the tray. "Do you know when this victim went missing?"

He said nothing.

"I think it wasn't that long ago. Am I right?"

No reply.

Singh was beginning to piss me off. It wasn't fair that our communication here was all in one direction. I had a growing need to rattle his self-assured silence. Placing the tips of my fingers against my temples, I rolled my eyes upwards and lowered my lids slightly, hoping he would see only the whites of my eyes.

In the most ethereal voice I could muster, I said, "I think he went missing sometime in the last two years. What's that?" I asked as though listening to an inner voice. "Twelve and sixteen. Ah, I understand. Thank you!" I opened my eyes and said confidently, "He definitely didn't go missing before December 2016."

Singh's eyes bugged. Too late, he schooled his features back into their usual impassivity. "How did you— what makes you say that?"

"Just a *feeling*," I said, needling him further. "It felt more … fresh than the other visions." Also, the white object lying on the ground beside the victim's head was an Apple Airpod. Those had been released just in time for Christmas in 2016. I remembered because my father had offered to buy me a pair for my Christmas present, but thinking they looked ridiculous, I'd asked him for a donation to a new phone instead. Now, seeing Special Agent Just-the-facts-ma'am Singh at a complete loss for words, I smiled. "I'm right, aren't I?"

He didn't deny it. Running a finger around the inside of his collar, he asked, "Was there anything else?"

I glanced at the two buttons on the table, then picked them up, and holding one in each hand, attempted another reading. I had to push aside the images from the newer button and try to direct my focus to what might lie between them.

I was more certain this time. I slipped the buttons back into their baggies. "There *is* some kind of connection between them. I felt it as a kind of *closeness*. But I couldn't say if that was literal or figurative. I wonder … Was the body this came from" — I held up the baggie with the green plastic button — "found near this one?" I held up the other.

Again, he didn't answer my question, but I had a feeling I was right.

"They were, weren't they? This one matched the pattern of previous victims, but this one didn't. Were there only the two bodies?" I gasped as a sudden thought intruded. "Are these from that new site with all the bodies? The one in the Nash Stream Forest?"

He took the baggies from my hands, his lack of denial as good as a "yes."

"They *are*, aren't they?" I pressed. "What was different about the first one? Did all the others have buttons on them? How many victims did you find?"

He returned the baggies to his briefcase, closed the lid, and clicked the locks shut.

"Let me touch things from the other victims, and I'll be able to tell you more," I said.

"No," he said baldly.

"How about a bone from one of the skeletons?" There was a note of pleading in my voice. "That green button … that murder was recent. Is he still active? You've got to stop him, and I can help you, if you'd just allow me!"

"We don't typically allow civilians to assist us in our investigations, unless they are experts, qualified, legally recognized experts," he clarified nastily. "Or unless they were direct witnesses to the crime."

"Then what was this today?" I challenged. "You've seen what I can do. You know it's legit."

"Why do you even want to be involved? Investigations into serial killers are ninety-five percent brain-rotting tedium and five percent life-threatening danger."

"I'm going back to Boston tomorrow, but you can still get

hold of me on my cell. I'd be willing to travel to Rutland to assist you, if that's what it takes."

"You know, Ms. McGee, law enforcement takes a dim view of people who appear too curious about a particular crime or who are too persistent in trying to insert themselves into the investigation process. Because you know who typically does that?"

"Nice, kind, helpful people?" I suggested.

"Suspects, that's who." He stood up to leave, thanking me for my time.

I trotted behind him to the front door. "I wouldn't tell anyone I was helping you, if that's what you're afraid of. And if you give me more information or more access to the investigation, I'm pretty sure I could give *you* more insights." Lowering my voice a notch, I added, "*Quid pro quo,* Agent Singh."

He turned to give me a look that was equal parts disbelief and derision. "You're quoting Hannibal Lecter at me?"

"Don't make me do the tongue thing," I said.

"I think we're done here."

He left without shaking my hand. Standing in the doorway, watching him stride down the path to his car, I consoled myself with the thought that perhaps he'd been afraid to touch me in case I got a reading off him. I wished I'd been able to stow myself away in his briefcase because I wanted in on the hunt for this killer.

When I'd died in Plover Pond, the same spot where Colby had been murdered all those years ago, I came back from the other side with aspects of Colby now part of me — his dislike of anything too sweet, his taste for beer and black coffee, and his passion for justice. That last part was growing in me, and there was no going back.

Before the day's visions, I'd been curious, like a hungry Lake Herring nosing the bait on the end of one of my father's fishing lines. Now, after what I'd seen and felt and knowing that there were a bunch more victims, possibly recent ones, I was well and truly hooked.

– 5 –

Friday, April 6
Boston, Massachusetts

Professor Kenneth Perry peered at me from across his desk in the psychology building at the university in Boston. "I don't mind admitting I was a tad worried about your thesis for a while there, but you aced it. I was right chuffed with the final product," he said in his strong British accent. Perry was a psychologist and my faculty supervisor. "What's your plan now?"

"I'm going to hand over my job — lock, stock, and admin passwords — to the new departmental assistant."

"Yes, sorry about that. We're gutted to lose you, but the position is reserved for an actively enrolled student. And since you bloody well refuse to do a doctorate, we had to give it to someone else."

"It's okay. I understand."

"It's okay. I understand."

We sat in silence for a few seconds, then Perry cocked his head at me. "So?"

"What?" I asked.

"What are you going to do? With your life?"

Why did everybody keep asking me that? It wasn't like I had an answer, though I *was* sure I no longer wanted to be a psychologist or any kind of counselor. My interest in psychology, I now realized, had really been a desire to understand myself and my catastrophic reaction to Colby's death rather than any vocation to help others with their mental and emotional issues. I had more than enough of *those* of my own.

"You can't sit around doing bugger all for the rest of your life, Garnet."

Since getting back to Boston four days ago, I'd alternated spending my time between watching the news coverage of the mass burial site in New Hampshire and searching online job sites. From the news channels, I'd learned that the remains of eight bodies had been unearthed. Names of the victims hadn't yet been released, but police were confident they knew the identity of half of them. Of the bodies as yet unidentified, one was thought to date back much earlier than the other murders. That must've been the different body that had been found near the rusted metal button Singh had brought me.

From Career Builder and Zip Recruiter and a handful of other job-listing sites, I'd learned that I could potentially apply for positions as a teacher's assistant, tutor, or HR officer, or I could try for a general administrative job in marketing, banking, or health services. None of these appealed to me in any way whatsoever.

My mother, keen to lure me back to Pitchford, had invited me to come work in her new-age store, Crystals, Candles, and

Curiosities. "You could do readings for people, dear. Just think of the customers that would attract!" she'd said.

That option would be an absolute last resort for me. If I had to surrender all dignity and ambition in order to dispense dreamcatchers and divinations for my over-excitable, utterly illogical, and verbally disordered mother, I'd soon be on the scene of another murder, one I would have committed.

"Honestly? I don't know," I told Professor Perry. "I'm not really qualified to do anything appealing or profitable, and if it's not for fun or money, what *is* it for?"

I ran a thumb over the tips of my fingernails, staring out of the window behind him. The last time I'd sat in this office, discussing my future, it had been winter. The trees outside had been bare of leaves, the sky gray with clouds, and the icy grounds empty. Now the sun shone down on clusters of students sprawled on the lawns, the bare bones of maples were studded with scarlet buds and tiny yellow flowers, and a pleasant breeze drifted in through his open window.

"Is there nothing at all that's piqued your interest?" he asked.

I wondered what to say. I wasn't exactly eager to lower his opinion of me. Then again, I might never see him again after today. Did it matter what he thought of me?

"I don't know if you remember," I said, "but back in December, I told you I was getting … images and words in my mind when I touched things that had belonged to my late boyfriend."

"I do remember." Perry scrutinized me carefully from behind his spectacles.

"Well …" I fiddled with the African violet on Perry's desk, breaking off a couple of dead leaves and tossing them into a nearby trashcan. "It turns out those weren't just symptoms of concussion or post-traumatic stress."

"Oh?"

"It looks like I might actually have some kind of ability to get, you know, *readings* off of objects."

"I see." Behind his blank expression, Perry was probably thinking, *Are you off your blooming rocker?*

I poured the last inch of a glass of water onto the violet's parched soil, being careful not to wet the leaves. Wet leaves, according to my mother, killed violets.

"You really should take better care of your plants, Prof," I chided him, even though I was a fine one to talk. I'd never managed to keep a potted plant alive for longer than a month. Even cactuses died on me.

"You were talking about your new … ability?" Perry said.

"I know it sounds crazy, and I don't expect you to believe it, but I've had two visits from an FBI agent to assist them with their investigations." As I said it, I heard how ridiculous it sounded. Believing that I had insight into life beyond the veil and was now being courted by the FBI? No doubt Perry thought I was diagnosably delusional. I waved a hand in the air as if to erase any lingering lunacy. "Forget what I just said. The point is that I'm very interested in the case of a New England serial killer."

I expected Perry to challenge me or maybe insist on conducting a mini-mental-state examination to check whether my cognitive functioning and reality testing were intact.

Instead, he said mildly, "Didn't you tell me that your father had an interest in serial killers? Perhaps you've caught his bug?"

I nodded. By all means, let Perry think that I was just following in my father's homicidal hobbyist footsteps. "Anyway, I figure I should learn more about serial killers in general." I gestured to the heavily laden bookshelves that covered three walls of his office. "Can you point me in the direction of some good books on the subject?"

"I can do better than that."

"*You* can help me?"

"No, not my field of expertise at all. But I can connect you to the resident expert." He picked up the receiver of his desk telephone and dialed an extension. "Hi, Brad. I've got a soon-to-graduate master's student here who'd like to know more about serial killers. Do you have a moment? Excellent! Should we come to you or— Wonderful, thank you." He hung up and told me, "He can give you twenty minutes, and he'll be here in five."

The expert arrived almost immediately. He was middle-aged and had milky-white skin, small eyes, and a tonsure of dark hair running around his otherwise bald head. With his thin face and narrow nose, it gave him the look of an aesthetic saint, or perhaps a fanatical monk. I recognized him at once. He'd done a lecture on homicide in one of our psychopathology courses. I didn't remember much of what he'd said about serial killers except that they sometimes went back to the decomposing corpse to have sex with it. That fact had been gruesome enough to penetrate the fog of my depression and lodge in my distracted brain.

"Brad, I'd like you to meet Garnet McGee. She's developed a …" — there was the smallest pause as Perry searched for an appropriate phrase — "a special interest in a New England serial killer and is hoping to assist the authorities with her … insights. Garnet, this is Professor Bradley Deaver, who happens currently to be in the process of writing what will no doubt be a seminal text on American serial killers."

Deaver's hand, when I shook it, was cold, but his gaze was friendly enough as it flicked between my brown left eye and my blue right one. My own gaze, as it so often did recently, automatically dipped to his hands. Pale skin stippled with a few age spots, watch on the left wrist, no wedding ring — unexceptional in every way.

Deaver settled into the chair beside mine and held up the flat Tupperware container he'd brought with him. "I hope you don't mind if I eat my lunch while you pick my brain about death and desire?"

"Well, about serial killers, yes," I said.

"What would you like to know?"

"A general overview would be great. I mean, I know some theories about them, but like, what are the rules?"

Deaver smiled. "First rule of serial killer club — there are no rules."

– 6 –

Professor Deaver opened his lunch container. The contents were organized into subdivisions of different foods — small blocks of chicken, shredded lettuce, chopped carrots, sliced beetroot, a buttered bread roll — and no one type of food touched another.

He leaned over the container and sniffed deeply then said, "The serial killers themselves do have rules, of course — sometimes — but they're rules that make sense only to themselves. Take Israel Keyes, for instance, one of the most intelligent and meticulously prepared serial killers ever to operate in this country. The eleven murders attributed to him — and a great many more are suspected — comprise men, women, single victims, and pairs, including a middle-aged married couple killed right here in Vermont in 2011. His victims were young and old, different ethnicities, killed at night and in daylight and in a variety of states across the country. And he got away with it for at least fourteen years," Deaver said, sounding almost impressed. "He shot, strangled, and asphyxiated. On some occasions, he tortured and raped his victim first, on other occasions, not. In short, he had no preferred type of victim, no discernable kill zone, no favorite killing method, no common way of dumping the bodies. No 'wheelhouse,' as they say."

"The pattern was no pattern, I presume?" Perry said.

Deaver removed a plastic-wrapped disposable fork from his shirt pocket and pointed it at Perry. "Rather presumptuous this time, I'm afraid. You see, Israel Keyes *did* usually kill far from home and never in the same place more than once. He made sure he had no connection to any of his victims, didn't kill during the three years he served in the military and, after his own daughter was born, never again killed children — or so he claimed. And he had a rule that 'Canadians don't count,' whatever *that* means. My point is, he had his own personal set of rules."

"Though this be madness, yet there is method in it," Perry said.

I thought the quote might be from *Hamlet*. He'd seen ghosts, too, and it had driven him crazy.

"Ha-ha, indeed!" Deaver said. "The variety and the lack, or oddity, of rules is what makes it such a stimulating subject to study. But it's an enormous field, young lady, so you're going to have to narrow your question down a bit for me to give you any useful answers."

I pulled my gaze away from the container, where the ruby juice oozing out of a stack of pickled beetroot slices trickled dangerously close to a mound of cubed pineapple. "I guess one thing I'd really like to know is what you can deduce about the perpetrator from the crime scene."

"I believe you mean *induce* rather than *deduce*," Deaver said. "And when you say, 'crime scene,' do you mean the place where the victim was abducted, the spot where the murder was executed, or the site where the body was left?"

"Oh, right." I didn't know whether the cops or FBI knew where the victims had been snatched from or where they'd been killed. "The place where he dumped the body."

He removed the fork from its wrapper, winding the clear plastic around the first joint of his index finger. "The body or the bodies?"

"*Bodies*," I said, aware of Perry's gaze on me.

"You're looking at a specific case, then? I'd need to get more details before I could generate any useful hypotheses." He looked at me with an eager, hopeful expression.

"Sorry, I don't know any specifics."

Not for the first time, I wished I knew more details about the Button Man's murders. Just about the only thing I did know was that the killer had left a button with at least some of his victims' bodies, and I wasn't going to tell Deaver that.

He made a low frustrated sound. "I suppose, speaking in general terms, you can usually tell from the dump site whether the killer is of the organized or disorganized type."

"Organized?" I said, imagining a killer with a planner and a to-do list.

"It's an old classification system but still, I believe, a useful one." He peered down into his lunchbox and used his fork to edge the pineapple away from the beetroot juice. "The kills of the disorganized type are usually impulsive. Typically, the perpetrator is suddenly overcome by rage, or the voices in his head get too loud. Or perhaps the victim just walks blindly into his hunting ground like a juicy insect drifting into a spider's web. He's not prepared, so he just uses what he has on hand to commit the murder and then usually" — Deaver held up an admonitory finger — "*usually*, but not always, he then either leaves the body right there where he did the deed or else somewhere nearby. The disorganized ones aren't *careful*."

"What would the scene of a disorganized killer look like, then?" I asked.

"There might be some real craziness — bizarre or surreal elements that make sense to him but to nobody else. It might look messy or hurried," he replied.

"Right." That didn't much sound like the Button Man to me.

Deaver stabbed the fork into a piece of chicken, examined the meat closely for a second and then ate it, chewing so slowly that I had to fight the urge to tap my foot in impatience. "Now, the organized killer, on the other hand, tends to operate with premeditation and often exquisite planning." Deaver's eyes glinted; clearly, he approved of systematic preparation. "He takes immense care when getting rid of the body. He might, for example, leave identifying pieces of it, like the hands or the head, in different spots from the rest of the body so as to slow down identification of the victim, or he might bury the body properly in some deserted spot in the hope that it will *never* be discovered. He's cautious. He'll use a condom in a rape and wash down the body afterward, even cleaning under the fingernails to minimize the evidence he leaves behind. Overall, the scene will feel less … chaotic."

A bee flew in through the open window and landed on Professor Perry's hand. He gently blew it off and said, "If I translate those two categories into psychological diagnoses or psychopathologies, then it sounds like disorganized killers would tend to be psychotic — schizophrenic, delusional, or paranoid. But organized killers sound more psychopathic, like they'd probably be diagnosed with antisocial personality disorder."

Deaver, who'd moved on to the little heap of chopped carrots, beamed at Perry as if he was a star student. "Right on the button!"

Startled at the word, I blinked and stared at Deaver.

Still smiling, he nodded at me. "Oh, yes. Unlike most disorganized serial killers, the organized ones tend to be sane, in the legal sense, anyway. They know the difference between reality and fantasy, but they are still very disturbed individuals indeed."

I let go of my surprise at Deaver's use of the button phrase and focused instead on the essence of what he was saying. From how he'd explained it, the Button Man sounded "organized." He'd planned at least enough to take a button, and sometimes a needle and thread, along on his hunting trips. But for all I knew, the dump sites could have been very chaotic indeed. Damn Singh for not sharing more information with me, for not letting me visit the latest site with all the bodies.

"Of course," Deaver continued, impaling the last carrot on the tines of his fork, "there are scores of ways to classify both the killers and the killings, and the types overlap. What's more, a killer may evince aspects of more than one type at various times in his career."

His *career*?

"I've found that the more you try to narrow down the categories, the more exceptions you have. Nothing truly fits neatly, even though 'experts' in the field of profiling want you to believe that it's a science rather than a combination of intuitive hunches and educated guesswork based on past experience."

While I pondered what to ask next, Deaver ate two more pieces of chicken and dabbed at his mouth with a paper napkin also taken from his pocket. I wondered what else might be stashed in there. Packets of salt and pepper, some ketchup, dessert? The bee, meanwhile, flew circles around Perry's head until he shooed it out the window with a piece of paper.

"Would you be able to tell from the dump site what the killer's motive was?" I asked.

Deaver considered this for a moment. "Not necessarily, although the body itself can give you clues. For example, killers who want to exercise their sadism are more likely to bind and torture their victims, while the hedonistic killer motivated by lust is more likely to rape or to pose the body in sexualized poses."

An image of that thumb penetrating that mouth, thrusting in and out, flashed across my mind's eye.

"And if the killer took, or indeed *left*, something distinctive, that could provide insight into their motive," Deaver continued.

I glanced up to find him staring at me expectantly. "Um, there isn't much to go on in terms of the remains," I said, even as I wondered if that was true for the latest site.

"Ah!" Deaver rubbed his hands together in pleasure like an old timey detective considering a fresh clue. "So there are only partial remains. Perhaps just skeletons? Then these would be old deaths. How do the police know they're murders?"

"I— I'm not sure." Deaver looked ready to pelt me with more questions, so I quickly steered his attention back to the part that most interested me. "Can you explain what you meant about things taken or left at the scene and the murderer's motive?"

"Taking or leaving something would be a feature of a killer's signature." At Perry's questioning glance, Deaver clarified, "His distinctive style. His *stamp,* if you will."

"Such as?" I asked.

Deaver contemplated the remaining contents of his lunchbox. "A lot of things contribute to the signature. His choice of victim, for example, or his *modus operandi.* The killer might leave his mark — literally, sometimes — by carving a symbol onto the body or painting a message on a surface or inserting an object into an orifice."

My ears pricked at that, and a flashback of a button sliding over teeth and onto a tongue, hovered at the edge of my attention. I dug the edge of a nail under a cuticle and pushed hard, welcoming the pain that kept me anchored to where I was now rather than letting me drift into what had happened back then.

"Or they might *take* a trophy, like a driver's license or a piece of jewelry, some such small item belonging to the victim."

I nodded. Ryan Jackson had told me a bit about trophies when I got involved in the last murder investigation.

Deaver stared up at the ceiling, thinking. "They may even take a body part."

Perry tucked back his chin in surprise and said, "Come again?"

"Oh, yes. Often," Deaver said. "Ted Bundy kept the decapitated heads of some of his victims in his apartment. Jack the Ripper made off with a victim's kidney."

"Bloody hell," Perry said faintly. "Why?"

"To eat it." Deaver chuckled, stabbing a chunk of beetroot and popping it into his mouth, leaving his lips bloodied by juice.

"Bugger me."

"And Charles Albright, who killed three sex workers in Texas in the early nineties, carried their eyeballs off with him." Deaver pointed his fork at my mismatched eyes and said, "He'd have loved to have collected *yours*, my dear."

$$- 7 -$$

I winced at the idea of a killer scooping my eyeballs from their sockets. "Why did the killer take their eyes rather than any other body part?" I asked Deaver.

"Your guess is as good as mine," he replied. "Perhaps he didn't want his victims looking at him, judging him. Or perhaps he did, ha-ha!"

I imagined a killer keeping that particular type of trophy in a bottle on his desk, where he and his victim could eyeball each other, and shuddered.

"Had someone in his history always said they'd be keeping an eye on him? Or did he perhaps believe that his victims were demons who could be destroyed in that way?" Deaver said. "This is psychology, not math; multiple interpretations are always possible. From what was learned subsequently in Albright's case, it seemed he'd been obsessed with eyes since his work as a taxidermist. Perhaps he'd originally intended to stick his victims' eyes into some of his stuffed animals." Deaver ate the rest of his beetroot with gusto, the gruesome details of these murders seemingly not sufficient to kill his appetite. "Whatever the reason, Albright spent the years of his incarceration endlessly sketching female eyes, so clearly he hadn't quenched his *idée fixe*."

"But why take anything?" Perry asked.

"As a memento of the murder. A little keepsake, you see?"

From his expression, Perry didn't see at all.

"They often keep a whole collection of souvenirs and pore over them, touching them" — Deaver rested the fork against the side of his lunch container and stretched out pale fingers as if reaching for a pair of earrings — "remembering the touch, the *feel* of the victim. Masturbating to relive the sexual excitement of the kill." He closed his hands as though throttling an invisible throat and made a squelching noise.

This man was creeping me out. He seemed to enjoy the details of the crime and the violence of the killers entirely too much. Where was the respect for the victims? I cleared my throat. "So why would they *leave* an object at the scene?"

"What kind of object?" Deaver asked quickly.

"I can't say."

"Who swore you to silence? The police? FBI?"

I gave the sort of half-nod and shrug that could mean yes or no or anything in between.

"You can't expect me to hazard an opinion unless I know the details of what the authorities found," he said, sounding pissy.

"I'm sorry. I really can't say," I repeated.

"Can't you give me a hint? Just a little one?" His beetroot-stained lips stretched into a smile. "I'm a psychologist, you know, a colleague. Your secrets are safe with me."

When somebody doesn't hear your no, they're trying to control you. Where had I heard that? "No," I said bluntly.

Deaver sniffed, looking both disappointed and miffed. A loud buzzing underscored the sudden silence. The bee was back, circling the African violet this time.

"Could you perhaps tell us, in *general* terms, what it would mean if you found something left with the body?" Perry said, giving me a look that clearly advised me to be more conciliatory.

"Yes, Professor Deaver," I said, softening my tone. "I'd be very appreciative of anything you can tell me, even if only in general terms."

Deaver looked mollified. "Are they even sure *he* left it? It could be something that was already there, or subsequently left by someone else."

"They're pretty sure he left it, I think."

The bee lifted off the violet and drifted closer to Deaver; he batted it away from his food. "It might mean nothing; it might be something he dropped at the scene accidentally. *Or* it could be his 'calling card.'"

That wasn't enough of an answer for me. "And what could you hypothesize about him — the killer — from the *type* of item left at the site?"

"Again, I can't tell you without more detail." He cast me a sidelong glance, but I said nothing. "I suppose if it's something that has a general symbolic meaning — a crucifix, a peace sign, or a heart — we could make some guesses. If he were to leave a red rose with his victim, for example, that might symbolize love for the one he killed or for all women like her. Or that he killed her as a proxy because in some way she reminded him of his true love."

So what might a button mean? Connecting things, maybe? Fastening separate pieces?

The bee circled back and landed on Deaver's little mound of pineapple. He frowned and fanned it away then closed his lunchbox. "But often the meaning of the object is more subjective, *privately* symbolic rather than *generally* so."

Perry leaned forward, curious. "You're saying it could mean something to him because of his personality or history?"

"Exactly," Deaver said, his gaze following the path of the thwarted bee from over his head to a resting spot on Perry's desk, where it paused to wipe its antennae. "Perhaps his mother once ripped his back to shreds by beating him with a bunch of thorny red roses or his father made him work in the family garden center instead of letting him party with his friends. Or he might just want the media to christen him the Red Rose Killer."

So basically, a button could mean literally anything. Wonderful.

Deaver half-rose from his chair and leaned forward slowly. Then quick as a flash, he upended the empty glass over the bee, trapping it inside. "Hah!" he said in satisfaction and sat back down.

Perry squinted from the glass to Deaver and looked set to challenge this incarceration, but while I felt sorry for the bee, I was running out of time to pick Deaver's brain, so I quickly asked, "What sorts of things are commonly left behind?"

"Again, it could be anything," Deaver replied, watching impassively as the bee furiously dashed itself against the walls of the glass. "Keith Hunter Jesperson, the so-called Happy Face Killer, always left a sketch of a smiley face. The Beltway Snipers in Virginia left tarot cards."

My mother would be interested to hear that.

He reopened his lunch box and took out the bread roll. "Sometimes, of course, it's not an item *per se*. Killers might leave bitemarks or a distinctive knot in the ligatures or cover the victim's face with her own clothing." He took a big bite of the roll and chewed it meditatively. "Henry Ramirez, the Night Stalker, would use the victim's own lipstick to draw an inverted pentagram on walls or mirrors at the scene, sometimes on the victim's own skin. But he didn't always leave one. Why not?" Another bite. More chewing. "And why an *upside-down* pentagram? Did that mean something to him personally? Was he making a statement of some kind, or did he perhaps have dyslexia and not know which way was up? And why use lipstick? These are the things that keep the machinery of my mind turning when I should be sound asleep." Chuckling, he popped the last piece of roll into his mouth, dusted crumbs from his shirt and jacket into the Tupperware, and closed its lid, leaving the pineapple uneaten.

"If they want to evade detection, why leave anything at the scene?" Perry asked.

"Some theorists argue that they *don't* want to escape detection, that they have a subconscious wish to be caught and stopped. I, however, tend to believe that they simply want to take credit for their kills. It's at least partly that age-old desire to stamp your presence on a place, or in this case, a person or scene." Deaver placed his lunch container on the desk, beside the overturned glass where the bee raged silently against its imprisonment. "The teen rebel paints graffiti on a wall, the impassioned lover carves a heart into a tree, the big game hunter wants a photograph with his foot on the lion's neck." There was a slight smile on Deaver's lips as he contemplated those images. "It says, 'I was here. I did this. I exist.'"

"I kill, therefore I am?" I said.

Deaver nodded and winked at me.

"I don't know how you can immerse yourself in this awful stuff, Brad," Perry said. "It turns my stomach just thinking about it."

"I find it fascinating. But" — Deaver turned to me — "our time's almost up. Any last questions?"

"Yes," I said. "Do serial killers typically have only one way of killing?"

"For the disorganized type, there's a wide range of variability, but organized killers generally favor one *modus operandi*, although not *necessarily*. No rules, remember? Additionally, the method usually evolves over time because they tinker, reiterate, and refine, always aiming for the perfect kill that matches their fantasy."

I frowned. "Their fantasy?"

"One theory about what finally tips disturbed individuals into killing is that they've invested huge amounts of time and emotional energy into dreaming about catching and killing and torturing a victim. They frequently use pornography, especially of the nastier paraphilias, to fuel this process. And one day, dreaming about it is no longer enough. They want more. The real thing rather than a pale imitation. They want to experiment with bringing their monstrous fantasy to life. So they kill. And initially, it's *wonderful*," he said, rolling the word around in his mouth like a sweet, firm grape. "They feel excited, aroused, ecstatic!"

I stared at Deaver, whose face was alight with a kind of manic intensity. Perry's gaze was fixed on the poor bee, which was now crawling in circles under the glass on his desk.

"But," Deaver said, "after the frenzy and the climax, disappointment sets in because the real-life experience never quite matches the fantasy. Well, it *can't*, can it? It's never perfect, and so it's never completely satisfying. The thirst, one could say, is not quenched."

"That's why they go on to do it again?" I guessed. "It's a cycle?"

"Indeed, an addictive cycle. There's rising tension and excitement as they fantasize, the joy of finding and snatching precisely the perfect victim, the prolonging, perhaps, of the thrill of power and control by keeping the victim imprisoned for days or even months at a time, watching, touching, toying, torturing … Then, finally, comes the orgiastic high of the kill and the *petite morte* recovery period of quiescence." Deaver sighed. "Discontent inevitably follows, leading the killer to refine the fantasy. The urge to do it again mounts. This time, he wants to make it better, to bring the perfection of the imagined to reality."

I was repelled by the way he described murder in the language of lovemaking, but I understood what he meant. The killer couldn't stop until he got it right, and it was impossible to get it right *enough* to match the fantasy, so he kept going.

Deaver glanced at his watch. "I need to make my escape, I'm afraid. My class commences in precisely eight minutes."

"Thank you for your time," I said. "I really appreciate it."

"I'd be most interested in hearing more about this case or in consulting with any and all law enforcement agencies," he said. "What wouldn't I give to be inside an active FBI investigation team? Particularly of a serial killer whose career covered multiples states and spanned many years."

"I didn't say any of that." I said worriedly.

If Singh found out that I'd somehow let slip some details, he'd … he'd … I didn't quite know *what* the agent would do. I couldn't imagine him ever losing enough control to show real anger. He'd probably just scowl and give me a *look*, but coming from him, it would feel like a death ray from Darth Vader's mother ship.

Deaver smirked. "You didn't have to. You" — he inclined his head to Perry — "said the serial killer was operating in New England, which implies more than one state. And if the murder occurs in different states, jurisdiction passes from local police to the FBI. You also said that Ms. McGee here was hoping to help the authorities, which would tend to suggest an open investigation with recent developments. And you, Ms. McGee — may I call you Garnet? Such a pretty name — said there wasn't much in the way of remains, which implies skeletonization, which in turn implies these murders happened many years ago."

"Oh," I said. I really needed to watch my mouth, especially with such a clever man.

"But if that's so, what's making you want to find out more *now*, eh?" Deaver cocked his head, keeping his gaze fixed on me as if wishing he could cut open my brain and peer inside. "It makes me wonder if there's been a recent development. And putting two and two together, I come up with last week's discovery of multiple bodies up in New Hampshire." He waggled his eyebrows and chuckled.

"I don't— I couldn't— Please don't assume I have anything to do with that."

Deaver stood up. "May I leave you with a 'calling card' of my own in case you'd like to contact me?" With a smile so wide it bordered on a leer, he handed me his business card and, with a little wave of his fingers, stepped out of the room.

"Wait!" I called after him. "Your lunchbox."

My fingers prickled as soon as I grabbed the plastic container. No images filled my mind, and I felt no emotions, but strong sensations flushed through me. *Order. Control.* Those were the words that most closely matched my disturbance. The feeling faded as Deaver took the lunchbox from my grasp.

"Thank you," he said and left.

I rubbed a hand over my breastbone, staring at the empty doorway.

"Funny sort of a fellow, isn't he?" Perry said.

"That, he is." I lifted the glass and freed the bee, which made a direct bid for freedom via the window. "I'd better be going too. I've taken up enough of your time. Thanks for everything."

"Come and visit anytime, Garnet."

Outside his office, I pressed my fingers against my eyes, trying to push back images of buttons on tongues and heads on mantlepieces and mismatched human eyes staring out of dead ferrets, and then I left, walking away from the psych department and the part of my life that went with it.

– 8 –

Back in my tiny Boston apartment, I saved Professor Deaver's details as a contact in my phone in case I needed to chat with him again and made myself lunch — a bacon-and-peanut-butter sandwich and a cup of coffee. The neighbor's baby trumpeted the start of his late-afternoon colic with loud wails and, from outside, the discordant city symphony of rush-hour traffic rose up to my window.

The four walls of my apartment — and of my life — were closing in. It was time to make a decision. The lease was up for renewal, and my father, who'd been paying the rent while I studied, had told me in the nicest possible way that if I wanted to keep it, I'd need to get a job to pay for it myself.

Did I want to keep it, though? I wasn't sure.

I grabbed a pencil and made a pros-and-cons list of staying in Boston on the blank scratchpad beside the crossword puzzle in the day's newspaper. On the upside, I loved privacy, and here in my apartment, I had it. At least, I had privacy from my parents and people I knew, even if not from the neighbors behind the paper-thin walls and the pot-bellied guy in the building opposite who regularly stood stark naked at his window, showing the world how he could hang a Red Sox cap on his erection. *Look, ma. No hands!* His baseball team was the only thing I knew about him, and he knew nothing about me. That was the pleasure of big-city anonymity.

In Pitchford, everybody knew everybody. And they knew everybody's business.

Bostonians were a cool breed, with their dry sarcasm and hardy, stoic approach to life. I noted this as a point in the pros column, even though I knew that the New England mentality stretched through Massachusetts and New Hampshire, all the way to Vermont. Another pro: Boston had a great pace and vibe. I enjoyed being a nobody watching from the edge of the crowd at the St Patrick's day parade and at the Boston Pops concert on the Fourth of July. There were amazing coffee shops and pubs filled with students and man-bunned hipsters sounding off on politics and global warming, and the night life buzzed with burlesque, ballet, stand-up comedy, and live theatre. Admittedly, I never attended any of those, but the point was, surely, that I could if I ever wanted to. Life *happened* in the city, and I could feel part of things without having to *be* a part of them, which suited me just fine. People were hard work, and I was about as good at socializing as I was at darts.

I bit down on the pencil, sinking my teeth into the soft wood as I tried to think of more advantages to living in Boston. *Food.* If I left, I'd totally miss the vodka-sauce pizza from Santarpio's as well as the amazing ice cream parlors, especially the one three blocks down that served a flavor called Mexican Chocolate. Just the thought of that super-dark chocolate mixed with cinnamon and hot pepper in cold creamy deliciousness was enough to make me drool.

On the other hand, there were loads of things I didn't like about the place: the noise, the ugliness of city living, and the lack of a beautiful view. Grabbing my list and coffee, I relocated to my window. In Pitchford, my view would be of endless trees and distant green mountains still frosted with snow, but here, my apartment faced another apartment complex.

In the parking lot below, a couple was having a fight. A woman in an open-topped convertible wagged her finger at a man who threw his hands in the air and stalked off to his car. Backing out of his spot, he lowered his window to get in a last yelled word and with spinning tires spitting gravel, sped out of the lot. The woman gave him a one-fingered salute. Crazy — I would have thought she'd be happy to get his parking spot; they weren't easy to find in this part of town.

Also on the cons side of the list was the fact that I hated the long brutal winters here. Yes, Pitchford had freezing winters with plenty of snow, but snow in the city was different, nice for five minutes, and then it became a filthy, muddy mess with rivers of slush and pelting ice shrapnel that made walking a misery. I also wasn't wild about the vitriol-spewing, bone-deep, take-no-prisoners fundamentalist religion that was sports in this city. For someone who had no clue about ball games, and even less interest, it could be hard, even isolating.

Isolation. That hit home because in Boston, I was deeply and profoundly alone. I didn't feel *lonely* precisely, or at least didn't feel it very much. I'd been flying solo for a long time, and I'd been emotionally and mentally disconnected from others for even longer. But recently, I'd become aware of an increasing tendency to navel-gaze and talk to myself. On Wednesday, I caught myself muttering out loud about the limp serrano peppers at the local Stop and Shop. I was at definite risk of turning into a mad cat lady — minus the cats, of course. I didn't even have pets for company.

The cost of living in Boston was crazy — that was a definite disadvantage. If I was being honest, it was probably the killer blow. I couldn't imagine landing the sort of job I'd need to pay for even this tiny apartment. Thanks to my parents, I had no student debt, but even so, money was a big factor in my decision. Then there were the other biggies: no job, no prospects, and no real network to help me out.

Also, no Ryan.

I missed him, no two ways about it. I missed his sense of humor and his hugs and his solid presence beside me when we went for walks in the woods or snuggled on the couch. I missed his kisses. It was time to admit, if only to myself, that I liked him. A lot. And he liked me. I could tell. And we could get together and do a whole lot of mutual liking *if* we were in the same place at the same time. The tip of my pencil hovered over the line between the pros and cons columns, unsure where to catalog this point. Part of me thought that a relationship with Ryan, a real relationship, might be wonderful, that with him, the juice might just be worth the squeeze. But another part of me — a raw, vulnerable, weak part — lived in fear of loving and losing again. I didn't trust life not to betray any faith I placed in it.

I finished my coffee, black and bitter, the way I'd preferred it ever since my near-death experience back in December, the way Colby had always taken it. I'd spent ten years mourning the loss of him, but in the last few months, I'd grown up a little and healed a lot. I'd emerged from my cocoon of numbness, and I felt like I might just be ready to move on from the past, possibly even from Colby. I had a feeling I'd need to if I wanted to deepen my relationship with Ryan because juggling two boyfriends — one in this world and one in the spiritual plane — was bound to get all kinds of crazy.

I tallied up the pros and cons of my balance sheet. There were equal numbers on both sides, and only one that really tugged at me emotionally. Awesome. I was absolutely no closer to making a decision.

I flung myself onto the sofa and stared at the light fixture in the center of the ceiling. Two of its three bulbs were dead, and I couldn't figure out whether the black mark on the ceiling beside it was a stain or a roach. I narrowed my eyes, squinting for better focus. Had it just moved? If so, it was bolder than me, stuck and stagnating here, pinned in place by the fear of failing or getting hurt again. The daily horoscopes printed beside the crossword puzzle in the newspaper caught my eye. Feeling like I was becoming more like my woo-woo mother by the day, I checked mine on the off chance that the stars would have some guidance for me.

You can't swim to your future paradise if you're still clinging to the shipwreck of your past.

Irritated, I flung the paper up at the ceiling, hoping to hit the black spot and answer at least one question of the many that were bugging me. Instead, the newspaper made it a scant two feet into the air then rained loose sheets down on top of me. I unearthed myself from my paper-and-ink shroud and checked the ceiling. The black spot was now on the other side of the light. I mentally added *roach infestation* to the right-hand column of my list.

There were now officially more cons to staying, but if I went back home with my tail between my legs, what on earth would I do with myself there? With a sudden burst of clarity, I realized that my problem wasn't about having to choose between Pitchford and Boston; my real crisis lay in figuring out how to move forward with my life. I was almost twenty-nine years old and had nothing to show for it. No career, no savings, no home of my own, and no husband or kids, which according to my mother, were shortcomings indeed. I felt like such a failure. Worse, I felt like a cliché. I might as well be lurking in the basement of my parents' house, playing Fortnite and hanging out on Reddit because I was little more than an overgrown teenager whining about my life while having no idea how to kick it into gear.

My phone rang. Startled, perhaps from the loud sound intruding on my morose meanderings or perhaps from seeing who was calling, I tapped the answer button.

"What's up?" the upbeat voice on the other end said, and without waiting for an answer, continued. "Good news! I've found you a job."

– 9 –

Saturday, April 7
Pitchford, Vermont

The woman who opened the door of the large brick house wore a hopeful expression. In her late thirties with neatly braided blond hair and wearing skinny jeans and a white linen shirt, she managed to look casually elegant in a way I could never pull off.

"You must be Garnet McGee," she said.

"That's me."

"I'm Gwyneth Fletcher, Henry's daughter." She stepped out of the house, closing the front door behind her. "Come on. I'll take you straight to him. He's in his playroom with all his babies."

His *babies*? I'd been told that Henry Mason, attorney-at-law, was in his seventies.

As we walked around the house to the back of the property, I snuck a look at my phone. That morning, I'd texted Agent Singh, once again offering to help with his inquiries, telling him I was even willing to drive down to Rutland and meet him at the FBI office there or at a coffee shop if he didn't want to be seen with me at his workplace. Seeing no reply message, I shoved my phone back into my bag.

At the back of the Mason property, cedars, ash, and alders reached the bare bones of their branches up to the sky, but the maples sported a rash of red buds, the only spot of color against the dull grays and browns of the early spring day. Located in the center of the backyard, surrounded by the stumps of trees — felled to give it more sun, presumably — was a large greenhouse about twenty feet long by fourteen feet wide, with sides and a roof of opaque glass.

"This is where you'll usually find my father," Gwyneth Fletcher said.

"That's his playroom?" I asked, skirting a muddy puddle in the grass; it wasn't for nothing that spring in Vermont was known as "mud season."

"Yup." She opened the door to the greenhouse and went inside, telling me, "Close the door behind you. *Always* close it behind you unless you want to see my father blow his stack. He needs to keep the temperature and humidity just right for the babies inside. Plus, he has to keep squirrels, rabbits, mice, and insects out."

I stepped inside, shutting the door as directed, and almost reeled backward from the onslaught of color and fragrance. Orchid plants of every size, shape, and hue rested on every surface, hugged the walls, and peered down from hanging baskets. Gray roots fingered their way out of pots and stretched for the ground as though the plants longed to escape this tame confinement and return to wild, steamy jungles. I rotated on the spot, gazing in wonder at saucer-sized white blooms with acid green leaves, tiny florets of deep rust with frizzled orange beards, fuchsia blossoms with lemon hearts, buttermilk petals veined with scarlet, and violet tongues protruding below mottled black flowers.

Gwyneth grinned at me, and realizing my mouth was open, I closed it, even though breathing through my nose verged on unpleasant. The humid air held a heady mix of fragrances — raspberry, vanilla, lilac, jasmine, coconut and citrus — with a faint underlying odor of rot and decay.

"It's kind of overwhelming, isn't it?" Gwyneth said.

I gestured to the plants crowded around us. "These are his babies?"

"Yup. I sometimes think he's more of a father to them than he ever was to my brother and me," she said without rancor.

We threaded our way through the greenhouse, between double-tiered wooden benches stacked with a seemingly endless variety of orchids, and past a central workbench cluttered with bags of potting mix, spades, secateurs, a spray bottle, a watering can, and dozens of tiny plants growing in old cream cheese and yogurt pots.

"The temperature is kept steady with gas heating, and there's an automatic system to maintain the correct humidity too. Those" — Gwyneth pointed to a couple of electric fans situated at either end of the greenhouse — "keep the air and moisture circulating, and if it gets too hot in summer, we can open the vents." She pointed to the flaps at the top of the glass walls.

"Why's the glass painted?" I asked.

"The whitewash helps to soften the light. Direct sunlight would burn the plants, especially in summer."

I expected to find my potential new employer clipping leaves or perhaps crooning lullabies to his plants. Instead, he was lying fast asleep on a leather recliner in a small clearing at the back of the hothouse. He had sparse gray hair, a build that could most kindly be described as portly, and a deeply lined face.

"Dad. Dad?" Gwyneth said, gently shaking his shoulder.

Henry Mason startled awake, blinked in bewilderment, and glared at his daughter. "I wasn't sleeping," he said fiercely. "I was just thinking about the possible permutations of a bifurcated divorce process."

"Sure, you were," she said. "Dad, this is Garnet McGee, the person Ryan Jackson recommended to help you with your practice. Garnet, this is my father, Henry Mason."

Her father pressed a button that moved the chair into a more upright position while he assessed me with eyes the color of an arctic iceberg. "I'd get up, but my foot is recalcitrant." He flicked aside a tartan blanket to reveal a swollen foot in a thick sock and added laconically, "Gout."

I stepped closer and shook his hand. "Pleased to meet you, Mr. Mason."

He gave a *harrumph* that could've meant anything. "Well, don't stand there hovering over me. Sit down, both of you."

Gwyneth and I pushed aside a few plants — "Gently!" Mason growled — and perched on the closest bench.

"So, you're a psychologist, are you?" he said.

"Nope. Several thousand hours of supervised professional experience, state and national Board examinations, and an official license stand between me and that title."

"So what are you then?"

I gave him my brightest smile. "Looking for a job."

He stared at me for a long moment. "Your eyes are different colors," he accused.

I conceded the point.

"Were you born that way?"

"*Dad*," Gwyneth chided at the same time as I said, "No."

Before her father could ask any more personal questions, she continued quickly, "As Ryan probably explained, my father is an attorney, but he's semi-retired."

Mason gave a grunt of disgust. "I wouldn't be if Meredith hadn't abandoned me."

"Meredith was my father's secretary and assistant for many years and—"

"For over *forty* years. And then one day, she got it into her head to pack her bags and jet off to Wales, where she intends to squander the meager remainder of her years in some Podunk parish with an unpronounceable name. Left me all alone. Wales!" He thumped a hand on the armrest of his chair. "What's Wales got that we haven't, eh? Tell me that, if you please."

"Her children and grandchildren, Dad. And if you don't want to live alone, come and live with us already!" Gwyneth said. From her tone, I could tell they'd had this discussion many times before. Mason grumbled something unintelligible, while she told me, "The point is, her retirement leaves my father without administrative help. Even though he doesn't have a full workload, he still needs someone to do his transcription and filing and run the odd errand. He has a weekly cleaning service, so you wouldn't need to do anything like that. Mostly, he needs help digitizing his files and doing anything that requires the computer. I'm afraid Dad is a bit of a Luddite."

"Don't think I don't understand the meaning of that word, young lady. I probably taught it to you," he snapped.

"I'm assuming you can use a computer and that you know the basic packages?" Gwyneth asked me.

"Sure." What I didn't know, I could learn quickly enough.

Mason scowled at my confidence. "I could accomplish it myself if I put my mind to it. But what I can't do is bilocate."

"Bilocate?" I repeated.

"Be in two places at the same time. I like to go on fishing trips, but with Meredith cavorting with the Celts, there's nobody to tend my babies while I'm away."

Hoping to find some common ground with him, I smiled and said, "My father's a fisherman too."

"Bass? Trout? Pike?" he barked.

"All of the above."

In truth, I had no idea what my father fished, only that from time to time, he disappeared to one or other fishing hole in New England and came back a few days later, declaring himself "rejuvenated and restored."

"Catch-and-kill or catch-and-release?" Mason demanded.

"He lets them go." That, at least, was his excuse for always coming home empty-handed.

"Casting rods and reels or spinning?"

"Sir, I'm no expert on angling, but I'm sure I could help you with your admin."

"That's great!" Gwyneth said. "My father also has the occasional case that needs a little investigation. Ryan said you have skills in that area?"

"He did?" I said, pleased by the endorsement.

Mason snorted. "I believe his actual words were that you have a talent for sticking your nose where it doesn't belong."

Now *that* sounded more like the sort of thing Ryan would say about me.

"Which does not sound like a positive character trait to me. How can you be sure you aren't foisting a light-fingered miscreant on me?" Mason asked his daughter. "Have you checked her references?"

"Yes, and they were excellent."

Silently thanking Professor Perry for coming through for me, I said, "Can I ask what you're offering as a salary?"

Mason stated a figure so low that I laughed, earning myself a dirty look from under his beetling brows.

"Dad, that's not even minimum wage," Gwyneth said, but then she suggested a figure that wasn't a whole lot better.

"That's …" What? Damned disappointing, a joke, a nope from me? "That's lower than I was hoping for," I said, surprising myself with my unusual tact.

"Kindly bear in mind that it's a part-time position. Just some light paperwork and typing now and then, hardly anything to raise a sweat. How much could you possibly expect to be compensated for such light duties?" Mason blustered.

"It's just that I'm looking for a job that will allow me to pay for a place of my own rather than living with my parents."

"Been a sponger, eh?"

I opened my mouth to retort — his barb had struck a nerve — but Gwyneth clapped her hands together and said, "I've just had a fantastic idea! Why doesn't Garnet move into the loft room?" Turning to me, she added, "It's a small apartment really, above the garage. If we threw that in, would it sweeten the deal?"

"You bet it would," I said.

The job might not be the most high-flying position in the world, but the income and flexible hours would allow me to investigate the Button Man, and with free accommodations thrown in, I'd be able to avoid moving back to my parents' house.

"I'll take you there now, if you like, so you can see it for yourself before you decide, but I'm sure you'll love it. I used to live in it before I got married. All the furniture's still there, though it'll need a good clean, of course." Gwyneth stood up and dusted the seat of her jeans. "We'll be back in ten minutes, Dad."

"You're not fooling me, Gwyneth!" her father said crossly. "You came up with this notion before now. You want someone residing on the property in order to snoop on me!"

She merely laughed, and I followed her out of the hothouse, eager for a breath of fresh air.

"I *do* want someone here," Gwyneth admitted as we walked across the soggy lawn. "Someone responsible, someone I can trust to keep an eye on him."

Uh-oh. It was one thing being responsible and trustworthy

when it came to filing and spreadsheets; it was a whole other thing if I was secretly expected to be a live-in caregiver.

"Keep an eye on him?" I said.

"He doesn't look after himself properly. Too much sugar and not enough exercise. I wish I could care for him personally. I truly do. We all miss him so much. But my husband and I both have jobs in Albany, and our kids are settled in school there. We've asked Dad again and again to come live with us, but he flat out refuses, says he values his independence and wants to be here for his clients. I think he's secretly afraid of becoming a burden on us." She sighed. "Having someone live on the property is a compromise I can live with"

She gave me a pleading look — a good daughter wanting to spend more time with her father, making plans for someone to look after him. It was admirable and even kind of inspiring. Gwyneth the Good made me want to be a better daughter.

"I don't want him living alone. He has heart problems," she said.

"The thing is, I'm not a nurse," I warned.

"Oh, I don't *expect* any problems. I'd just feel more at ease if there was someone here. You know, just in case."

"And I can't guarantee to always be here." Mason wasn't the only one who valued his independence.

"Of course. Just let me know if you're going to be out of town, okay?"

"Sure." That much I could commit to.

"And maybe you could keep an eye on what he eats, encourage him to cut down on junk and eat his five-a-day?"

Crap. I was no role model when it came to eating healthily.

In fact, I was the very last person who should be put in charge of anyone's diet. I needed to warn her that her expectations of me were entirely too high. As my father would say, an ounce of prevention was worth a pound of cure.

"Look, I don't—" I began.

"Over here," she said, tugging me to the massive garage where outside stairs led up to a door on the level above. As we climbed the steps, she said, "I think he's lonely too. He'd deny it with his last breath, of course, but he could really use some company, someone to chat with over a cup of coffee now and again, you know? I think, deep down, he'd welcome that."

I raised my eyebrows. Mason hadn't struck me as the sociable type, and he didn't appear to have taken an instant liking to me either.

"Well, at the very least, he'll welcome someone to spar with — a good argument always energizes him. And Ryan says you're no shrinking violet."

Nosy *and* sassy? I wondered what else Ryan Jackson thought of me.

– 10 –

Gwyneth Fletcher was right — I *did* love the loft apartment above the garage. Yes, it was filled with spiderwebs and dusty boxes of old books, but within five days, I'd cleared it out, cleaned it up, and moved in. I was delighted with my setup and with Ryan, who'd gotten me the gig. He'd helped me pack and move my stuff from Boston, too, and I'd appreciated the help as much as the sight of his muscles bulging under his sweatshirt as he lugged heavy boxes down to our cars and up to the loft.

A tiny galley kitchen ran along one side of the space, with a narrow bathroom adjacent to it. In the middle of the loft, a worn leather couch faced a table with two chairs. I placed the TV set from my apartment in Boston on one end of the table, set up my laptop on the other, and managed to cram most of my clothes into the corner closet. Once I'd added a few decorative touches — a landscape painting in muted grays, a braided rug for the floor, and a free-standing oval mirror —

looted from my old bedroom at my parents' house, it looked more homey.

It was basic, but it was mine. Plus, it had great Wi-Fi.

When my parents came over to inspect my new digs, they gave it their stamp of approval. My father, ever practical, brought bags of groceries and a potted plant as housewarming gifts. He took in the arrangement of furniture and insisted we swap the bed and chest of drawers around so that I didn't wake up with sunlight shining into my eyes.

My mother, ever mystical, brought a collection of crystals, which she set up in a grid on the kitchen countertop, and then walked around the entire space, waving a burning bundle of sage. "It's White Californian, dear, and the smudging will clear out any negative energies."

The woodsy smoke made me cough, and the crystal grid took up precious surface space. But knowing she meant well and inspired by Gwyneth's admirable example, I waited until they left before I swept the stones into a bowl along with the apples and bananas from my father's groceries and placed the dish on top of the refrigerator. I found a home for my new plant, a small Venus flytrap that my father ought to have known better than to leave with me, on the windowsill.

That afternoon, sprawling on the amazingly comfortable couch, with throw pillows behind my head, I sighed with pleasure and raised my glass of pinot noir in a toast to my new space and job. My father had been delighted that I now had what he called "a proper job" and told me it was high time I settled down. The words "and grow up" hovered unspoken in the air.

My mother, who'd been hanging onto the hope that I would set up shop as a psychic private eye, was less thrilled. "It's all very well to want to earn a living, Garnet, but for goodness sake, don't throw the baby in the bathwater! You've been given a gift, and if you don't use it, you'll lose it. That's how the universe works."

I didn't know *how* to use it. That was the problem. There I was, sitting pretty in my cozy pad and drinking wine, while out there in the darkness, a monster who'd ended multiple young lives and left families destroyed by grief had literally gotten away with murder. He might even now be hunting for more prey. And what could I do about it? What had it helped to get visions of hands and buttons? Singh hadn't replied to any of my texts — I'd already sent three — or returned either of my two calls. I reckoned he regretted ever consulting me and, not wanting his colleagues to find out about it, was determined to ignore me.

I'd no sooner had that thought than my phone chirped with an incoming message. *Finally,* I thought, but it wasn't a reply from Singh. It was a series of texts from Professor Deaver.

Dear Garnet, I enjoyed our discussion last week very much! I've been keeping an eye on the news, and it seems your serial killer is targeting gay men. If you'd told me that, I could've shared more information with you at the time, but better late than never, not so? I thought you might be interested to know about anti-LGBTQ murders.

I did, indeed.

Unfortunately, there's scant research in that area in general and for gay male victims in particular.

Big surprise. I bet the net was full of articles, research, statistics, and theories for the murder of pretty, straight young coeds.

But what there is supports my theory of no hard and fast rules when it comes to methods or motives. A significant number of gay individuals are targeted simply because they're viewed as easier or more vulnerable targets. Many are targeted because their sexuality is seen as abhorrent or offensive. Murdering them could be thought of as a homicidal extreme of "gay-bashing." And as for the perpetrators who target gay men, they might be gay, straight, bisexual, or undecided. If you'd like to pick my brain further, it would be a great pleasure to meet with you again. Warm regards, Bradley

I sent him a thank you for the information, wondering what the news had reported about the victims. I'd been so busy with my move that I'd had no time for watching TV. I read through the details of his message again while finishing my wine. Maybe my father was right. Maybe I should just settle down, date Ryan, try to be a good daughter to my aging parents, and stop chasing the darkness. Setting my empty glass down on the floor beside the couch, I closed my eyes.

Sometime later, I woke up from my nap with a jolt, dream images still vivid in my mind. A white orchid in a hothouse had morphed into a Venus flytrap closing its teeth around a fly, squashing it to a bloody pulp. The teeth became black stitches piercing lips, and a hand, *my* hand, placed pretty buttons over staring eyes and onto the sewn mouth. I didn't need my years of training in psychology to understand the message from my subconscious: if I didn't help catch the killer, I'd feel complicit in some way.

Struggling to shake the dream images, I went to the bathroom to splash my face with water. In the mirror, I saw that my cheek was creased with indentations from one of the cushions on the couch. Four lines imprinted by raised seams met like the crosshairs of a rifle sight at a central circle made by the button that had pushed into my skin. I touched that red circle, pressing my button.

At seven o'clock that evening, I drove over to my parents' house. My father had invited me for supper, telling me that he had a real treat to show me. I asked him what it was as soon as I got there, but he merely said that all good things come to those who wait and eat their vegetables.

When we finished supper, he said, "Did you see the *Stakeout* special on the Gay Slayer?"

"The who?"

"That's what the media is calling your killer."

"Oh, for goodness sake!" I said, shaking my head. "And no, I didn't. When was it on? I wish you'd given me a heads-up to watch it."

"Follow me," he said, looking pleased. "I recorded it so that we could watch it together."

All three of us got comfortable in the living room, and then my father hit Play on the *Stakeout* special, which promised both an in-depth look at New England's worst serial killer and fascinating information about serial killers in general. It started with a summary of what had been found at the burial site in New Hampshire. Over footage of the taped-off crime scene, a female voice said that a total of eight bodies had been found, all of them belonging to men. Five of them had now been identified as young men who'd gone missing between 2011 and 2017.

"So recently!" I said. "They thought the murders stopped after 2009."

A police spokesman confirmed that two sets of remains were, as yet, unidentified and one of these didn't appear to fit the profile of the other victims either in terms of age or the date of killing. Tests to confirm the date of death had not yet been finalized, but it was thought to have occurred at least ten and possibly as many as thirty years previously. The shot cut to the anchor, a woman with gray-blond hair who wore a serious expression and an even more serious skirt suit. She said that an "anonymous source" had informed *Stakeout* that the remains of this body had also not been disposed of in the same way as the others.

"Interesting," I murmured.

"Authorities have not confirmed that this body is in fact even related to the others," she continued. "But what are the odds that the killer coincidentally chose a spot where an older corpse just happened to be buried?"

"Good point," my father said at the same time as my mother said, "There's no such thing as coincidence. *Everything* is connected."

– 11 –

I commandeered the remote control and turned up the volume on the TV in time to hear the anchor say, "It's bad enough to think of seven or eight people dead at the hand of this killer, but it seems there may be many, many more. Our researchers have been digging deep, and we now have reason to believe that the bodies found in the Nash Stream Forest are only the most recent victims of a serial killer who's been operating in New England for the last two decades. Our researchers have identified twenty-nine unsolved murders where the victims were young men between seventeen and twenty-seven and a further two hundred and two missing males in that same age range during the last twenty years."

My father gave a low whistle at the shockingly high number which, the anchor explained, was "probably an underestimation since some disappearances are never reported to police," though their estimated number did include several victims whose remains were never claimed or even identified.

"Of course, not all of the murder victims will have been killed by the Slayer," the anchor pointed out. "And the missing persons statistic includes people who purposefully go missing, like runaways and those wanting to escape abusive or unacceptable circumstances or perhaps join a cult, as well as those who wander off due to mental illness or those who die from natural causes far from home. And since the FBI has not released a comprehensive list of murders attributed to this killer, it's impossible to say how many of these older murders and missing person cases were young men who ran afoul of the Slayer, but one thing is certain: the number is horrifyingly large."

"But can't they tell which ones are his victims by the buttons?" my mother asked.

"The FBI will have withheld that detail so they can distinguish true from fake confessions," my father said. "The press probably doesn't even know about the buttons."

"But from our long list of possible murders, an inside source has identified several as confirmed victims of the Slayer," the anchor said.

"A leak? Singh's going to be furious!" I said as my phone chimed an incoming message.

Hoping it was from Ryan, who hadn't been able to join us for dinner because of some problem at the station, I checked my phone. The text was from Deaver. He was just following up on our chat in Perry's office last week, he said. Were there any new developments on the case? Did the FBI need him to help compile a profile? Could I put in a good word for him with the investigative team?

I sent back a polite message reminding him that I wasn't part of the FBI investigation and that they didn't share information with me (very true), that I had a new job which would be sucking up a lot of my time (true), and that I'd be sure to let him know if there were any definite developments in the case (a rotten lie). Then I returned my attention to the TV, where the anchor was saying, "Let's take a closer look at who these young men were."

I grabbed some paper and a pen from the writing desk in the corner so I could note the names and dates of disappearance as the victims were listed. A photograph of a white man with flyaway fair hair and a shy smile appeared on screen. His name was Dylan Floyd, and he'd been a librarian from Greensboro, Vermont. In 2001, his body was found dumped in a culvert near Caspian Lake.

"Dylan's sister still remembers him well," the anchor said.

The shot cut to a fair-haired woman. "Dylan was my younger brother, and I loved him. He was an introvert who would rather spend the night in bed with a good book than go out partying. He was gentle. Really good with animals." A photograph of her brother having his face licked by two Labradors appeared. "When he died, our family just … it was terrible for a long time afterward. We're okay now, but for a long time, it was bad. Our hearts were broken, you know?"

The next victim highlighted — Todd Ennis from Springfield, Massachusetts — had been a twenty-year-old gymnast who'd hoped to make the US team for the 2004 Olympics in Athens. He went missing in January 2003, and his body was found three weeks later beside Route 91 outside of Northampton.

Eric Zhang, originally from California, disappeared in

2005. He'd just finished high school and was visiting family in Rhode Island when he vanished. His remains, buried in a shallow grave near someplace called Nooseneck, were discovered by land developers only in 2012.

"Oh, dear," my mother said. "This is very sad."

"Yes, one forgets that behind the statistics are real people," my father added.

I was feeling much the same way, and the next victim's story had my eyes prickling with tears. A photograph of a black man roasting a giant marshmallow over a campfire appeared. Antoine Marshall, a twenty-two-year-old electrician's apprentice from Meredith, New Hampshire, disappeared in May 2006. According to his family, he'd loved to play the guitar and had dreamed of starting his own rock band.

His mother, her face creased with lines of suffering, appeared onscreen, dabbing her eyes with a tissue. "Antoine was adopted. But we couldn't have loved him more if he'd come from our own bodies. In the year before he went missing, he grew very curious about his biological family. He wanted to find out who they were and to meet them. So when he disappeared, a part of me always wondered if he'd gone looking for them, if he'd preferred them to me, and that's why he never came home. Then a year later, they found his body, and I knew he hadn't. But sometimes, I still pretend that's where he is, living safe and sound with another family, making good music."

"This is heartbreaking," I said, my voice rough in my constricted throat.

"Yes, I think it might be a bit much for me. I'll just go wash the dishes," my mother said and left.

A yearbook photo of a smiling white guy was displayed. "Sean Walton, most likely to become president," the inscription read. The voiceover said, "Famously the hometown of crime writer Stephen King, the city of Bangor, Maine, was also home to one of the victims. Twenty-two-year-old law student Sean Walton went missing on August eighth, 2006. His body was found two days later, buried in an overgrown embankment of the Penobscot River."

Ewan Grady was nineteen years old when he was murdered in April 2007. He'd been a runaway who worked intermittently as a sex worker and was squatting in an old hunting cabin just outside Manchester, so no one was sure of the exact date he went missing. Based on the state of decomposition, the medical examiner estimated he'd been dead around ten days by the time he was discovered in an abandoned building site on the last day of the month.

In an interview segment, his father described him as "smart and real funny but not the easiest kid to raise." Then a sad expression came over the father's face, and he added, "He, uh, he came out to me. That's the phrase, right? He said he was a homosexual, and I … I reacted badly. I was just so shocked, you know? I never saw it coming. But I would've come around. I *would've* come around." The heavyset man on the screen sighed and looked down at his knees. "But he just ran off, and I never saw him again. He died thinking I was angry and disappointed in him. And I have to live with that every day of my life."

Anger rose in me at the killer who'd ended the lives of those young men and left so many broken people behind. I imagined shockwaves of pain, despair, and grief radiating out from the murders, rippling through time and touching hundreds of lives. I wanted to get away from the TV, to go outside and suck in a breath of cool night air, but the name of the next victim riveted my attention.

"Jacob Wertheimer, twenty-four, went missing in November 2009." Familiar footage of the turnoff to the quarry outside of Pitchford filled the screen, and my father gave me a worried glance. "His skeletonized remains were stumbled on just last month by a hiker in the woods outside of Pitchford, Vermont."

I was the hiker, though technically it had been a dog who'd found the remains.

"Jacob was a barman in a restaurant in Randolph with hopes of saving enough to start his own nightclub."

I stared at the onscreen photograph of the young man whose rib bone I'd held in my hands. So Jacob had had black hair, blue eyes, and a smattering of freckles over his nose and cheeks, which made him look younger than he was. He wore a Kings of Leon T-shirt and was laughing at the camera, pointing at whoever'd been taking the shot.

The TV footage cut to a sandy-haired man in his mid-thirties, and the camera zoomed in for a close-up of his face with its sad brown eyes. "Who was he?" the man — Doug Piccolo, according to the title at the bottom of the screen — said. "He was my best friend and my lover. He was fun and daring and really brave. He didn't care when people judged him or his lifestyle. He used to say, you only get one life, and you should live it being true to yourself. He wanted to take up skydiving as a hobby, but I begged him not to. I told him it was way too dangerous." The man gulped back a sound that was half laugh, half sob.

My own throat closed, and the tears began to spill for Jacob, who'd laughed and loved and listened to Southern Rock, who'd tried to live life fully and honestly and had wound up with a garotte around his neck and a button stitched to his mouth.

Onscreen, Piccolo was still talking. "For almost nineteen years, I lived in limbo, waiting to hear what happened to him. I was stuck. Stuck in the past. Stuck in doubts and regrets, never knowing what happened to him. I couldn't seem to get on with my life."

I felt this man so hard. That was what it had been like for me after Colby died, but at least I'd known almost immediately that he was dead. It must've been excruciating to have lived in uncertainty for so long.

Piccolo said he hadn't been taken seriously by the cops investigating Jacob's disappearance. "As soon as I told them we'd had a fight, they wrote it off to him ditching me after a lover's tiff and didn't put much effort into searching for him. I hired a couple of private detectives, but they got nowhere."

Maybe I should try to contact some of the friends and relatives mentioned in the TV show. I had their names now. Then again, I wasn't really sure what that would achieve. I'd find out more about the victims but probably not about the killer. Maybe I should reach out just to Jacob Wertheimer's partner, to give him some comfort since I knew firsthand the pain he must be going through. But I killed the impulse when

I heard his bitter account of the "so-called psychics and charlatans" who'd taken his money and delivered nothing but false hope.

"One of them said Jacob was alive and well and living in Seattle with a new partner and had adopted a baby girl," he said. "And all that time he was dead and buried."

No, Piccolo would definitely *not* welcome a call from me.

$$- 12 -$$

After an ad break, the program switched to an interview with a clinical psychologist who was apparently an expert in the field of serial killers.

"How did the killer get away with it for so long?" the anchor asked him. "How is it possible he still hasn't been apprehended?"

"Good question," I murmured, leaning forward with interest.

"Everyone thinks they'd know a serial killer the minute they met one, but that's just not how it is," he said. "Many of them are extraordinarily ordinary. They hold down jobs, marry, and have children, all the while committing murder after murder on the side. They can be like chameleons, taking on whatever camouflage necessary in order to fit in and fool those around them. The friendly married man on the bus next to you, the cute guy who pats your dog in the park, the man at the bar everyone calls Santa because of his jolly laugh? Any one of them could be a killer. They wear a mask of sanity over their deviancy and often seem normal, pleasant, polite, and even charming. Under that façade, however, they're cunning, callous, manipulative, exploitative, incapable of real love, and utterly self-serving. Many, if not most, serial killers are psychopaths."

"Is that scientifically true?" my father asked me.

"Yeah, though some of them are psychotic."

"I've never been entirely clear on the difference between those."

I paused the TV and explained about the psychotic's loss of contact with reality. "Psychopaths, on the other hand, aren't insane. They know what they're doing is wrong and illegal, but they simply don't care. And while most serial killers are psychopaths, most psychopaths aren't serial killers. Many are conmen or other criminals, but some make a great success of their lives because their personality make-up is an asset in a bunch of careers."

"Such as?" my father asked.

"Being a surgeon, for example, or a sniper in the armed forces. Those require you to stay cool under pressure. And if you're willing to cut corners or bend the rules, you're likely to do well as a salesman or politician. If I remember right, the careers with the highest proportion of psychopaths are CEOs, lawyers, and journalists."

"That doesn't surprise me," my father said. "Which careers have the lowest?"

I smiled wryly. "I can't remember exactly, but I do know that therapists were near the bottom of the list." I turned back to the TV and hit Play.

The psychologist onscreen said, "Psychopaths are apex predators of other humans because they lack empathy and are largely insensitive to fear due to their underactive autonomic arousal systems."

"*Ohhh*," I said.

My father frowned. "What's that mean?"

I gave him the CliffsNotes version. "Psychopaths don't scare easy."

It made sense. I knew psychopaths usually had chaotic childhoods. It sounded like that rewired them neurologically, so they developed a physical tolerance for the sort of extreme thrills and danger that would turn your average Joe Schmoe into a quivering sack of nerves. It explained why, as adults, they got bored and restless easily and tended to be sensation-seekers who got a kick from lying, cheating, stealing, and of course, killing. It took a big thrill to move the needle on their excitement gauge.

"When we return," the anchor said, "what makes a serial killer?"

I fast-forwarded through the advertisements and pressed Play in time to hear the anchor ask, "Are serial killers natural-born killers, or are they made?"

"It's probably a combination of both nature and nurture," the psychologist said and went on to explain that the repeated experience of trauma and abuse — physical, sexual, or emotional — was a common theme in the childhoods of serial killers.

"Not always," my father said. "Ted Bundy had a reasonably happy childhood with no abuse. Jeffrey Dahmer was wanted and deeply loved by his parents."

"But most victims of childhood trauma don't grow up to be

abusers, let alone serial killers," the psychologist continued. "Apart from possible genetic influences, other common factors we see in their backgrounds include being abandoned or neglected in childhood, prolonged bedwetting, early use and subsequent abuse of drugs and alcohol, head injuries, and the use of pornography, which gets increasingly more graphic and violent as they grow older. As children, they tend to be loners who struggle to make friends, and that isolation increased their withdrawal into an inner fantasy world. They have more brushes with the law at a young age for things like molesting other children, vandalism, arson, cruelty to animals, shoplifting, and Peeping Tom activities."

My father chimed in again. "Not always. The BTK killer, Dennis Rader, seemed like a normal kid; he was active in Boy Scouts and the church. And Jeffrey Dahmer's classmates remember him as an oddball — the class clown who often played pranks — rather than as a juvenile delinquent."

I nodded. "A professor I spoke to said there are no hard and fast rules when it comes to serial killers."

Onscreen, the interviewer asked the psychologist, "The real question, I suppose, is can they be treated?"

"There's no cure for psychopathy," he replied.

The interviewer looked shocked. The general public, I'd discovered, believed that therapy could fix pretty much everything. The general public was dead wrong.

"Well, for one thing," the psychologist explained, "they take no responsibility for their own actions and usually feel no remorse, so they don't volunteer for treatment. And because they lack anxiety for the most part, they're motivated more by the reward of indulging their desires than the fear of punishment, so they aren't easily stopped or reformed."

"And why," the interviewer asked, "does *this* killer specifically target young gay men?"

Perhaps she hadn't gotten a nice, simple soundbite from the psychologist because the program now presented us with another sort of "expert," a man whose sole qualification appeared to be that he ran a website about serial murder.

"The killer is probably gay himself," he said, tossing his head to shake his bangs out of his eyes. "He's a lust killer who gets his kicks from killing men after satisfying his sexual urges with them. Or he could still be in the closet, a repressed homosexual who envies them their freedom to be who they are and who punishes them for it."

"The professor I spoke to — and he's a *real* expert — said the killer could just as easily be straight," I told my father.

"Up next," the anchor said, "the New Hampshire bodies, plus a shocking new revelation!"

"You've read hundreds of books on these guys. If you had to do a profile of this killer, what would it be?" I asked my father.

"From what I've read," he said, gesturing for me to pause the program while he gathered his thoughts, "your *average* American serial killer is male, from a lower-to-middle-class background, with little education, and of low or average intelligence. He's most likely to be white, although in recent years, black killers have taken the top spot."

"The FBI profile was very similar," I said, remembering the details Ryan had once shared with me. "They also said he'd probably have a job where he travels a lot, like a salesman or a truck driver."

"Moving around gives them access to a bigger pool of victims and makes them harder to track down," my father said. "Let's see, what else do I know? They're impulsive, likely to abuse substances — oh, and they often have a fondness for bitter foods."

"That's bizarre. Do you know why?"

"No idea. I do know that most of them operate alone, though some work in pairs. I even read a post that speculated about a syndicate of connected killers who might be kidnapping and killing young college-aged men."

"I'm glad I'm not the cop investigating that one," I said and pressed Play.

"While the Slayer's earlier victims were disposed of in a variety of locales around New England," the anchor said, "it seems that his most recent kills were all buried in a single spot in the Nash Stream Forest in New Hampshire. Why? What prompted the change?"

Apparently, nobody had a good answer for this. She went on to list the names of the five newly-identified victims who'd all gone missing since 2010: Denzel, a ski instructor who'd disappeared from a resort near Stowe; Rory, an accountant who'd longed to get into acting; Zack, who'd just been awarded a scholarship to study chemistry at Boston U; Benjamin, who'd painted portraits of cats; and Nathan, the most recent victim.

One by one, I took in the stories of the young men, the achievements of their short lives, their photographs, the painful statements made by their grieving families. Each of them had been a unique individual whose life was cut brutally short, leaving dreams unfulfilled, hopes ended, and loved ones empty armed. The family and friends they'd left behind tried to keep the memories of them alive, but the truth was that people tended to remember the names of killers rather than those of the victims. I felt a moment of unprecedented charity toward Singh. I might not like the man, but I gave him credit for not giving up on the investigation, for doing his best to bring the victims and their families justice by tracking down the monster who'd killed them.

To a soundtrack of somber music, a collage of eight blocks filled with the photographs of the recent victims appeared. Each block was labelled with the victim's name and date of disappearance, while the two unidentified victims were represented by a blank profile with a question mark.

"Hey!" I said, noticing something. "Look at the dates."

"Sharp-eyed viewers will have noticed a startling pattern," the voiceover said. "While the victims of earlier years seem to have been killed on random dates with multiple murders occurring in later years, the recently discovered victims were killed at a rate of one per year. And each of them went missing and was presumably killed on May sixth."

My father and I exchanged a shocked glance, and I said "But that means ..."

"The clock is ticking for the FBI to find and apprehend the Gay Slayer before he strikes again in just three and a half weeks," the anchor said.

The show ended, but I sat staring at the credits, feeling weighed down by what I'd learned about the victims. Wanting to solve this case was no longer an academic challenge for me. Now that I knew who the victims had been, it was much more real and urgent. It was personal. But the problem was, I hadn't learned much more about who the Button Man might be or how he operated.

When I was about six years old, I'd gone through a phase of being terrified of the boogeyman. Part of that fear, perhaps the worst part of it, had been that the monster could be anywhere or anything. Anyone. He could be slender enough to secrete himself in the folds of my dressing gown hanging behind the bedroom door or as flat as a toppled gravestone lying under my bed, watching for the moment I dropped my guard and let my foot hang over the edge. He could be the shadow behind the shower curtain, patiently waiting until I could no longer hold it in and had to run to the toilet at night, terrified to go in the dark and yet too scared to switch on the light because who knew what I might see? Maybe he could shape-shift himself to look like the mailman, a teddy bear, my father. Unknown and invisible, he loomed huge in my imagination.

That was how I now felt about the Button Man. In my mind, he was a nebulous cloud of darkness, a murky shadow that resisted my attempts to define him. I wanted to reduce him to what he was: a mere mortal. I needed to contain his presence in my mind by giving him a form, a face, a name. When I knew him, I'd be able to find him. And when I found him, I'd stop him.

Watch your back, Button Man. I'm on your trail.

− 13 −

I woke up early the next morning, determined to get going as soon as possible. After what I'd learned about the Button Man's victims on the television program, I was determined to give the investigation my all, not to impress Singh or to convince myself that my gift had value but to do right by the victims. I would do it for Jacob Wertheimer, Antoine, Denzel, Rory, and Zack and all the other young men whose lives had been extinguished so brutally. I would do it to spare another man from being killed in less than a month's time. I would hunt the Button Man, and I would find him. I vowed it.

And the first item on my to-do list was a visit to the FBI field agency in Rutland. As my mother would say, "If the mountain won't come to Muhammad, then Muhammad must go to the mountain." Then again, knowing her habit of confusing words and mangling expressions, she'd probably say, "If the mountain won't come to Muhammad, then faith as small as a mustard seed must move it."

I set out at eight o'clock sharp, which gave me enough time to drive down to Rutland, buy a big box of doughnuts — Singh would be a hard nut to crack, and I hoped fried dough and sugar would soften his shell — and present myself at the FBI resident agency office by five past nine.

Even though the address was freely available online, it wasn't easy to find. Google Maps directed me to a nondescript building located between a Wendy's and a tire dealership in Rutland's small commercial district. The roadside signage indicated the two-story office complex housed a realtor and a dentist's office, but there was no indication of an FBI presence. Not even a flag flew outside the building. I parked my Honda in the small lot and went to check whether I had the right place. Inside the building, a small sign on a door at the end of a corridor indicated that I did, as did the fisheye camera mounted above it.

"Here goes nothing," I muttered and pressed the buzzer.

After about a minute, during which I assumed someone on the other side of the door was checking me out and assessing my potential risk, the door clicked open, and I stepped into a small room. I'd been expecting a reception area, but the room was empty except for a ceiling-mounted camera and a big potted plant in one corner. I recognized its variegated crimson and emerald leaves. My mother had one of those plants in her living room and claimed it was called a "crouton plant." Directly facing me was a wall made of thick glass, inset with an intercom and a door, presumably for staff to gain access to the offices beyond. To my left, was a small empty office with an open door.

On the other side of the glass barrier, safe from any attack I might launch, stood a man wearing a neat suit, striped tie, and polished shoes. He wore his hair short at the back and sides and longer in front, and although he wasn't young, he had the fresh, enthusiastic face of a rookie. I stepped up to the glass and greeted him, showing him my driver's license when he asked for ID and opening the doughnut box to show it hid no weapons.

"I'm Special Agent Tyler Washington. How can I help you today?" he asked in a surprisingly deep voice.

"I'm here to speak to Special Agent Ronil Singh."

"*Senior* Special Agent Singh is out of the office this morning."

"Ah, no," I said, disappointed.

"He didn't mention expecting anyone. Did you have an appointment with him?"

"Yeah, I do," I lied. "And I drove all the way over from Pitchford to see him."

The agent rubbed a hand over the full beard that failed to disguise his cherubically round cheeks. "I'm his colleague; perhaps I can assist you. What's it in connection with?"

My father would've told me to back off and not make a nuisance of myself. But making a nuisance of myself was something I was good at, and I wasn't one to overlook my talents. Plus, I suspected it would be a whole lot easier to pump this young man for information than to face off with Singh again.

"I'm … er … a confidential informant on one of his cases, and I'm here to assist with your recent discovery," I said.

"Oh." Washington sounded more interested now. "Hang on. I'll just get the magnetometer."

A minute later he was with me in the anteroom, which he called the "mantrap," running a security wand over my body and the doughnuts. When nothing beeped, he shook my hand, indicated the side office, stepped aside to let me enter first, and shut the door behind us. Good. With any luck, I'd get what I came for and be gone without Singh being any the wiser, or at least without him being able to stop me until the deed was done. I sat in one of the chairs around the central table. Washington pulled out the chair to my left, hesitated, and then went to sit on the other side of the table instead. Was he looking to create more formality through distance, or had he intuitively sensed in some primal part of his brain that the spot to the left of me was already taken?

"So," he said, "what case is this in connection with?"

"The New England serial killings. The ones the media is calling the Gay Slayer."

His eyes widened. "I see. And you have new information for us?"

"Maybe. I'd need to touch some of the items recovered from the latest scene to be sure, though."

"Touch them? Why?"

I'd hoped I would be able to get what I wanted without having to explain in too much detail, but I could see that wasn't going to happen. I opened the Dunkin' Donuts box and offered him one. When his mouth was full, I said, "I don't know whether Ron's told you about my involvement with this case. How I've given him feedback on the objects left at the dumpsites?"

"Not a word."

"Well, you know Ron," I said, making it sound like he and I were old buddies. "Always plays his cards close to his chest, am I right?"

Washington grinned and began nodding then checked himself.

"Thing is, I have a certain … skill." This was always the hard part, trying to make it sound real. Trying *not* to make myself sound as though I had long since parted company with my right mind. "I can kind of *read* objects. When I touch them, I sometimes get images and memories associated with them."

"You're a *medium*?"

"No, no, I don't speak to departed spirits." Often. "I use post-cognition and psychometry." I deliberately used the scientific-sounding terms in an attempt to sound more legitimate, but judging from the frown crumpling Washington's sweet face, they meant nothing to him. "I'm a psychic and clairvoyant."

He laughed. "And Ron consulted *you*? No way!"

"How else would I know that your killer has left a button with each of his kills?"

His eyes widened, then narrowed. He munched his doughnut, assessing me, while I arranged my features into the sort of benign expression I imagined an innocent and trustworthy person would wear and tried not to stare at a yellow sprinkle nestling in his black beard.

"You don't trust me? Test me. Let me touch something that might have an emotional memory associated with it, and I'll tell you what I get." When he hesitated, I added, "Come on,

Agent. What've you got to lose?"

He tilted his head as if acknowledging the point and handed me his pen. I closed my fingers around the glossy black-and-gold Sheaffer and pulled my attention away from the office and the agent across from me and my worry that at any moment Singh might storm in and catch me.

A few seconds later, I opened my eyes. "I saw a young man, clean-shaven. He's someone significant to you. A brother or partner? He has a mole right here." I tapped a spot on my chin.

Washington's eyebrows rose in surprise. "That sounds like Darnell, my husband."

"Darnell, yes. That's his name. I sensed it clearly." I'd sensed no such thing.

"Wow," he said, definitely intrigued even if not yet convinced.

"He gave you this as a gift," I said. "It was in a flat box wrapped in black paper with a silver ribbon."

Agent Washington's eyes bugged out. "It was his gift to me when I graduated the academy."

"Yes." I nodded as though I'd seen that too. "Yes, it was. So special. So, as you see, I'm pretty accurate. If you have an item collected from the latest site — or from any of them, really — I could probably give you some very useful information."

Washington chewed on his lip, considering.

I dug into my well of therapy skills and added, "It must be tough wanting to crack this case but having no leads to work on." He nodded. "You investigators must feel so helpless and powerless, so frustrated!" He nodded again. Two agreements and they're more likely to acquiesce to the third suggestion. It was called a *yes-set* and was one of the few things I remembered from a lecture on the theory of hypnotherapy. "Maybe I could just see if I get anything? It might give you a useful direction to explore."

He studied me for a long moment then said, "Wait here," and left.

Like taking candy from a G-man baby.

– 14 –

I picked at a cuticle, staring at the blank walls and wondering whether the camera eyeing me from above was recording this. Whether Singh would watch it later.

Washington returned within minutes, bearing a manilla envelope. "This is all I have access to right now. The only reason I've got them at all is because I've been researching whether they're unique or special in any way. Did you know there's a button collection in the Smithsonian?" He fished in the envelope and pulled out two small plastic bags; each contained a button that I recognized. One of them was the metal snap button Singh had brought me ten days ago. The other, a wooden button he'd brought me back in March, had belonged to Jacob Wertheimer.

I pointed at the bags. "I've already read those two and told Ron what I got off them."

Disappointed, Washington started to drop them back into the envelope.

"Hang on," I said. "What's that in the bag with the wooden button?" Leaning closer, I saw that it was a short piece of frayed black twine. When I'd touched the button previously, I'd seen black thread in my vision, but Singh hadn't shown me any twine, let alone allowed me to try get a reading off it. "Can I touch the thread?" I asked.

He nodded. "Yeah, all of this has already been through forensics."

"Get any fingerprints or DNA?"

"Nope."

"The killer's a careful one, isn't he? Organized."

Washington nodded, confirming one of my hypotheses. I took the baggie, opened the seal, and extracted the piece of nylon twine. Bracing myself for what might be coming, I closed my hand and my eyes and felt the familiar ripple over my scalp. The image, when it came, was faint but still visible.

Tomatoes.

Red and green tomatoes hang on a vine. A rotting wooden trellis sags under the weight of the plants.

A split tomato lies on the dry ground. Insects burrow into it, squirming through the soft, ripe flesh and the blue-white fur of mold on its skin.

I opened my eyes to see Washington waiting expectantly. "I saw tomatoes growing on a vine on a trellis."

The agent's mouth formed a perfect O.

"That mean something to you?" I asked.

He took the piece of black nylon back. "We had this analyzed. It's tomato twine, the kind of cord usually used to tie tomatoes to stakes and trellises." Judging by the wonder that permeated his voice, Washington's conversion to Team McGee was complete.

I stared at the wooden button in the baggie for a moment then held out my hand for it. I'd learned more about how my ability worked since I'd last touched that button. It was possible that if I read it again, I might be able to get more. Again, I closed my fingers and my eyes and concentrated. At once, a darkness swamped me, stealing my breath and pulling me down toward a black hole of pain. I pushed back, dragging my mind away from the edge of that abyss, sending it instead to my hand where the button was hot against my palm.

Blue eyes wide with panic stare out from a young man's pale, terrified face. A face surrounded by black hair and sprinkled with freckles.

A man's hand, a left hand with a ring on the third finger, moves over the young man's stubbled jaw and bloody lip then trails down his neck where a wire garrote bites into the flesh. The hand brushes aside an open red-and-blue-plaid shirt and touches the naked chest, circling bruises with a forefinger.

"You like that?" the voice, rough with emotion, says.

The only answer is a strangled sound.

The hand moves lower, opens jeans, presses hard into the flesh beneath with fingers and knuckles, and rubs. "Huh? You like that?"

The hand moves back up to the throat and tightens the garrote.

I gasped awake, panting. Immediately, I forced myself to try re-enter the vision, but what I saw when I shut my eyes again was a different scene.

The young man's face, skin pinpricked with red dots, is empty of life, now. The blue eyes are stippled with red and stare fixedly upward, seeing nothing.

Two hands wearing latex gloves thread a wooden button with black twine, secure it with a double knot, then thread the other end of twine through the eye of a large curved needle. One hand pinches the bloodied lips together between finger and thumb, and the other begins sewing, setting stitch after neat stitch until the mouth is tightly closed with the button fastened in the center of the lips.

I opened my eyes, took a few deep breaths, and told Washington exactly what I'd seen. He nodded, asked a question or two, and then sat back in his chair, apparently processing what he'd just heard. I returned the button to its baggie, aware of the creeping fatigue that always swept through me after a vision, but Washington wasn't done yet.

He pulled another evidence baggie out of the envelope and handed it to me as he took back the button. "I think you should give this a go too."

Inside the evidence bag was a scrap from the cuff of a long-sleeved shirt. The disintegrating fabric was stained a reddish brown and a shard of cracked button still poked through the buttonhole. I took it out of the bag and held it between both palms. Even as I closed my eyes, my lids began to flutter, and my scalp tightened. A tingle woke my fingers, and lights flickered at the edges of my dark field of vision.

The sleeve of a shirt. Blue.
Blue as the sky above the arm held up, thumb extended.
A car approaches. Hope.
The car passes by. Disappointment.
Walking backward. Willing another car to appear on the deserted road.
A car draws near, and the thumb goes up once more.
The car slows. Stops.
Excitement. The hand punches the air. At last!

I blinked several times as the vision faded.

"This fabric was once baby blue," I said. "And it wasn't his — the killer's, I mean. I think it was a victim's. A young man, white."

"You saw him?"

"No, just his arm and hand. But I can sometimes tell more from the feel and the energy, you know? Which victim did this come from?"

"One of the old unidentified ones," Washington said.

"He was hitchhiking," I said. "And a car stopped to pick him up."

"Wow. You saw that? What kind of car was it?"

"A dark sedan." I tried to remember exactly what I'd seen. "Dark blue or green, maybe? I can't be sure. It was an old model, from the seventies or eighties, I think, and there was an emblem on the front." I closed my eyes and pictured the scene again. "It looked like silver wings."

"Wasn't that what old Fords used to have? Or was it Chevys?" Washington said excitedly. "Could you see the plates?"

I shook my head. I'd seen it from the hitchhiker's point of view, and he hadn't been looking at those.

"Anything else? Could you see where this happened?" the agent asked.

"Not really. Only that it was a highway running through a forest."

That described half of New England. Why couldn't I have seen something useful, a road sign, for example, or the car's plates?

Washington chose another doughnut, but before biting into it, he asked, "How far can you see? Can you tell if we'll catch the killer?"

"Sorry, I can't see the future. At least, I haven't so far." As I was giving him back the fabric cuff, a thought crossed my mind. "Can I try holding all the items together?"

Maybe holding multiple objects that the killer had touched would potentiate the effect, or something they had in common might strike me. Of course, it might give me a big blast of nothing — the separate items could just as easily cancel out each other's effect as increase their impact — but there was no harm in trying. I took the buttons, twine, and cuff and held them between my palms. Shutting my eyes, I doubled over my hands in concentration. My eyelids fluttered and series of images swarmed through my mind.

A handful of buttons fall onto a floor. The buttons, metal and wood and plastic of all colors, bounce and roll to a stop on the worn wooden boards. The protruding loop of a brass button with an embossed anchor motif on the front wedges itself into a crack.

A man. He's tall and thin, and his eyes are filled with derision and hate.

A house. A white house with a porch out front and the weathervane-topped roof of another building behind. A tall tree to the side casts deep shade onto the house.

Beyond the tree, there is a pool of darkness more intense than the absence of light. It pulls me to the core of itself where death lies, old and silent.

I was in so deep that I yelped out loud when a hand clamped down on my shoulder. Shaking my head to clear it, I glanced up. Oh, crap. Singh.

"*What* are you doing here?" He spoke softly, but the icy tone carried the power of a shouted demand.

I dropped the items on the table. "I, er, I was just chatting with Agent Washington."

Singh directed his icy gaze at the poor agent who wore the expression of a little boy caught stealing cookies. "I'll talk to you later." Grabbing the box of doughnuts with one hand and my elbow with the other, Singh hoisted me out of my chair and steered me out of the room. "You, Ms. McGee, will stop interfering in this investigation effective immediately. Is that understood? You will not call me. You will not text me. You will not come to this office and attempt to extract confidential information from a federal agent under false pretenses. Are we clear?"

"But I can help!" I cried as he propelled me down the corridor toward the entrance. "I saw—"

"Are we *clear*?" he repeated as he pushed me back into the mantrap.

I returned his glare with one of my own. "Yes."

He nodded curtly and opened the outer door. I stepped outside but kept a foot wedged in the doorway like a persistent salesman. Speaking rapidly, I said, "I saw a bunch of stuff! Tomatoes and twine and that the victim was hitchhiking and—"

"Nothing we didn't already know."

"But there was—"

He thrust the doughnut box into my hands. "*Goodbye*, Ms. McGee."

"—much more," I finished. But I was speaking to the closed door.

– 15 –

Face flaming, I stormed back to my car. How dare he? Where did he get off treating me like that? He'd all but grabbed me by the scruff of my neck and tossed me out like a pesky little kid. Screw him and his condescending, disdainful attitude. I'd show *him*. If he didn't want my help, if he didn't value my contributions or respect me enough to include me in his investigation, fine. I'd go it alone.

I slammed the car door shut and searched for a piece of paper and pen, in a hurry to capture what I'd seen and felt before it faded. I found a half-dry Sharpie and an old receipt under my seat and quickly drew the tomatoes hanging on the sagging trellis, as well as the arm with the hitchhiker's thumb and the car in the background.

Was Washington having his ears singed by Singh even now? Poor guy. I hoped I hadn't gotten him in too much trouble. I was seriously tempted to go back and give him the rest of the doughnuts *and* to give Singh a piece of my mind while I was at it, but I didn't want to make things worse for Washington or give Singh the pleasure of detaining me in the mantrap and arresting me for some ridiculous reason. Plus, what mattered most was what I'd just *seen*.

I needed more paper to draw the three separate images that had followed each other in quick succession when I'd held all the objects together but couldn't find anything. Making a mental note to buy a notepad — essential equipment for any investigator, surely — I resorted to using the inside of the doughnut box lid and quickly sketched the buttons on the floor, the man, and the house with the darkness nearby, trying to include the details of what I'd seen and felt.

The man was middle-aged and thin, with a stern face and patchy graying beard. Recalling his contemptuous, angry expression sent a ripple of fear and horror through me. I might have just seen the killer. I warned myself not to leap to conclusions. The man was connected to the case, but that didn't mean he was the Button Man. Perhaps he was the father of one of the victims. My limited artistic skills couldn't capture the emotion in his gaze, so I wrote the words next to the picture. *Hate. Rage. Contempt.*

The house I'd seen was free-standing and a bit rundown, with a huge tree to the left of it. I hadn't seen any other houses alongside it, but just visible behind had been the roof of a building with some kind of chimney or turret topped by a cow-shaped weathervane. What had struck me most intensely was an ominous feeling, something I couldn't see but that I *knew* was at the side of the house, beyond the tree. I didn't know how to draw that, except as a solid black scribble. I *did* know that I needed to find the scary man and the old house with that spot of obsidian darkness where death lingered. I knew the house and the darkness were related, but was the man connected to the house or to the buttons? Were the buttons on the floorboards of that house? There was no way to tell.

Still feeling shaken and tapped out by all I'd seen, I started my car and headed home. *Home.* It was the first time I'd thought of my new living space as home, and the thought pleased me. On the drive to Rutland that morning, I'd been so preoccupied that I'd hardly noticed the scenery. Now, I made myself drive slowly, carefully checking both sides of the highway, searching for an old house with a front porch and a tall tree alongside. The image of the man with the cruel, furious eyes was disturbing, but for now at least, it led nowhere. But I sensed that the house with the vortex of darkness churning beside it was connected to the killer, and it was a more solid lead. Searching for it, however, would be needle-in-haystack territory. Short of driving up and down every road in New England, I didn't see how I could find it.

Inside my handbag, my phone rang. Maybe it was Agent Washington calling to crap on me for landing him in hot water. Or just maybe it was Agent Singh calling to apologize for manhandling me and to beg me for the details of my visions. Yeah, right. That would happen when pigs grew wings. Checking my review mirror for traffic — and the sky for flying swine — I pulled off onto the muddy shoulder of the road to take the call.

My phone had stopped ringing by the time I got it out of my bag, and the caller hadn't left a voicemail, but my list of missed calls showed neither of the G-men had tried to contact me. The call was from Professor Bradley Deaver; no doubt he'd wanted to check if there were any updates on the case. Singh must feel about me like I felt about Deaver, wanting to get information but not wanting to share any details in return. I'd sensed when touching the professor's lunchbox how much he valued order and control. Being out of the loop on this must be killing him.

I didn't return the call, partly because I was tired of him bugging me but also because I truly had no new *facts*. I did, however, have new information that might lead somewhere useful if I could get some expert assistance, and Deaver's call had given me an idea in that regard. Finding the number on the university's website, I called the School of Architecture, where a helpful assistant listened to my rambling request.

"We've got a couple of experts in local architecture in the department. I'll put you through to the friendlier one."

Professor Schultz was indeed friendly. "I'd like to help you, but your description sounds like half the houses in New England. I don't suppose you have a photograph?"

"I only have a very rough sketch," I said.

"Well, if you send it to me, I'll take a look."

"Can I text it to you?"

"Sure," she said and gave me her cell number.

I thanked her, photographed my drawing, and sent it to her immediately along with my contact details. Then I drove back to Pitchford and went directly to the police station. Officer Veronica "Ronnie" Capshaw was on duty at the front desk, ready to throw a wrench in my plans on principle, but I had a strategy to subvert that.

I placed the box of doughnuts in front of her and smiled.

"Hey there, Officer Capshaw. These are for you."

"Oh yeah?"

Officer Capshaw was many things: heavy of bone, strong of muscle, no-nonsense in disposition, smart, efficient, and skeptical to a fault. But one thing she wasn't was friendly or gregarious, not to anyone in general and not to me in particular. She had little tolerance for my woo-woo side and, I suspected, resented my influence on Ryan. She opened the Dunkin' Donuts box and peered inside, no doubt noticing the two gaps where doughnuts had been, and then treated me to her best raised eyebrow.

"If it's any consolation," I said, "those two went to one of Vermont's finest law enforcement officers."

Giving me an unconvinced look, Capshaw asked, "And you've brought me these … why?"

Deciding that honesty might be more to her liking than tact, I said, "They're a bribe, Ronnie. I want to see the chief, and I don't want to have to wrestle you aside to do so."

Her lips twitched fractionally, and then with a sniff, she jerked her head back in the direction of Ryan's office.

"Thank you! Can I just—" I snagged one of the doughnuts and a piece of blank paper to carry it on. "It's for the chief." Then I walked through the low swing door beside the front desk only to return immediately. "Sorry, I just need this." I tore the lid off the box and scampered down the corridor before she could say anything more.

$$-\ 16\ -$$

Sticking my head into Ryan's office, I said, "Surprise!"

He looked up from the paperwork covering his desk and smiled. "Hey, you."

I stepped inside, shutting the door behind me, and handed him the doughnut. Then I settled in my usual chair on the opposite side of the desk.

"What've you got there?" he asked, indicating the doughnut box lid that I'd folded up and was stuffing into my handbag.

"Sketches of visions, but that's not why I'm here."

"Yeah?"

"Yeah. I wanted to come say hi and ensure you're getting your proper nutrition." I gestured to the doughnut. Chuckling, he took a bite. "You're looking tired," I said, studying the shadows under his eyes and the droop of his shoulders. "You taking care of yourself, Chief?"

"There was an accident involving one moose and two cars on Route 100 last night. And this morning, I'm stuck with all the admin." He finished the doughnut.

"Anything I can do?"

Ryan sucked sugar off a fingertip and then gave me that slow, sexy smile of his that always did something to my heart. And other parts too.

"You could kiss it better," he said softly.

I stood up and leaned over the desk, noting with satisfaction how his eyes dipped to the V of my blouse. Grabbing a fistful of his shirt, I tugged him closer to kiss his irresistible dimple. Then I moved my attentions to his mouth, licking sugar off his lips before tasting him fully. Ryan made a noise deep in his throat that I took as encouragement, so I stepped around to his side of the desk, moving my hands behind his head as he stood up and lacing my fingers through his thick hair. I pressed my lips to Ryan's, ignoring the invisible cloud of cold air that suddenly enveloped us.

It was a good minute before I realized that the increasingly loud banging was someone knocking on the door rather than the hammering of my heart. Reluctantly, I pulled away from Ryan. "I'd better go," I said, sighing. "Ronnie is never going to let me have my way with you."

"Tonight?" Ryan said, fingers touching his lips.

"I'm pretty beat. Can we do tomorrow instead? My place, and I'll cook."

"I'd love that."

Ronnie must have stashed the doughnuts because I saw no sign of them as I left the station. I drove home, singing along with Norah Jones's "Come Away with Me" on the radio until static killed the song.

"Cut that out, will you?" I told Colby.

As I turned into the driveway at Henry Mason's house, a

grocery store van pulled up behind me. I signed for the delivery and lugged it to the main house's kitchen, where I found the man himself tucking into a late lunch of bacon, eggs, sausage, and pancakes swimming in syrup. When I raised an eyebrow at his plate, he thrust out his chin and glowered at me.

"Don't even think about telling me what I can and can't eat, Missy," he growled.

"I wouldn't dream of it."

Thwarted by my mild reply, he launched another salvo. "If you didn't emerge from the womb that way, how the devil did you wind up with one blue and one brown eye?"

"I drowned, and when I was brought back to life, my left eye turned brown." Henry looked like he didn't believe me. "The doctors said it was a medical mystery." I placed the box of groceries on the kitchen counter. "How did you wind up with gout, assuming *you* weren't born that way?"

"I read up on the subject after I noticed it during that pitiful excuse for a job interview last week."

"What, gout?"

"No, differently colored eyes," he snapped.

I peered inside the box. "Oh, look. Carrots and kale. Yum!"

"They're called dichromatic."

"I think they're called superfoods. And Gwyneth said *these*" — I unpacked a bunch of celery and a huge head of broccoli and shook them like maracas — "are your absolute favorites."

He snorted. "I researched the meaning of your mismatched eyes in folklore and mythology. Very interesting and entertaining it was too."

"Glad to have brought some amusement into your life." I

unpacked skinless chicken breasts, diet soda, and a packet of quinoa.

"In Eastern European pagan cultures, they were believed to be the sign of a *witch*." He said the last word with unmistakable pleasure.

I took the last item out of the box and studied the label. "Carb-free keto cookies! Who knew? My, my, this all looks delicious." My voice was bright with false cheer, but I could feel that my smile was evil, and it must've given me away because he scowled at me.

"I don't for a single moment believe you think that, but if you do, then you're welcome to it. Take it all!" Mason said. "My daughter keeps sending me this … this *rabbit* food. I didn't ask for it, and I don't want it. Some of it's downright inedible."

At my challenging look, he ripped open the package of keto cookies and insisted I try one. Cookies being right up there on my favorite foods list, I happily bit into one. Two seconds later, I spat the masticated mulch out into the trashcan.

"Told ya so!" Blue eyes twinkling with glee, he stacked pancakes on a plate, anointed them with syrup, and handed it to me. "This will clear the taste of them."

"Gwyneth would not approve," I said around the first heavenly mouthful.

"That's because she believes — incorrectly, I need hardly say — that it's preferable to live forever, miserable on a diet of bran and beans, than to head into the afterlife a little sooner with a round belly and a smile on one's face."

"See now, *I* thought it was because she loves and wants the best for you."

"Bah! She fusses too much." He eyed me warily. "You're not going to snitch on me, are you?"

I considered for a moment. "Well, I did promise your daughter that I'd keep an eye on your health."

His bushy brows lowered.

"But I'm not in the habit of ratting out friends," I continued sanctimoniously. "So I'm willing to strike a deal."

"Oh? And what might that be?"

"I won't spill the beans about your" — I pointed at his plate — "fat and sugar consumption *if* you promise to eat some vegetables occasionally."

After a moment's consideration, he gave a grudging nod.

"*And* if you swear to tell me if you're ever not feeling well," I added.

He scowled, but said, "All right!"

"*And—*"

"More conditions?" he demanded.

"You're a lawyer. You should be used to it." I licked maple syrup off my fingers. "And being a lawyer, you will have noted that I said I don't rat on my *friends*. Which means, Henry, that you're going to have to be less ornery and more friendly to me."

His scowl vanished. "You strike a hard bargain, young lady, but it's a deal."

– 17 –

Saturday, April 14

Checking my email the next morning, I was surprised to see a reply from Professor Schultz, but the reason for the quick turnaround on my query was soon clear: there wasn't much to say about the house in my sketch. It was, she said, a wooden structure with a shingled roof and had probably been built around 1900. The tree beside it looked like a beech, but she was no arborist. She was sorry not to be able to tell me more, but there really was nothing distinctive about the building. She didn't know what the black patch to the left of the house was — had I just been scribbling to check my marker worked?

Her email got more interesting toward the end, though.

As to where it might be located, the area looks rural, given that there's a barn in the background. In fact, I think that barn is your best bet for trying to identify the house. What little you drew of the roof is enough for me to tell that it's a round barn, and those aren't very common. That weathervane on top of the ventilation shaft's cupola is pretty distinctive too.

You may not know it, but there are people who are passionate about cataloguing and preserving New England's historic barns. They're called barnologists or barn-spotters. :)

She listed a number of websites for me to explore, wished me luck in my search, and said I was welcome to contact her again if necessary.

I stared at my sketch, amazed. I hadn't even realized the roof belonged to a barn, let alone that it might be round or that the chimney-like structure was actually a ventilation shaft topped by a cupola. What the heck was a cupola anyway? A quick online search informed me that in this context, it was a small pointed roof on top of a ventilation shaft.

I made myself a cup of coffee, grabbed a handful of animal crackers, and parked myself in front of my laptop to research barns in New England. I learned that the round ones were usually dairy barns, most commonly built in the period between the 1890s and 1910s. Although there were different styles, they generally had three levels: a basement for collecting and storing manure, a ground level where the animals and equipment were kept, and a hayloft for storing the feed. There was often a raised drive sloping up to that upper level so that bales of hay could be easily unloaded from wagons and stored in the dry, airy loft. The feed would then be dropped or lowered to the ground floor for the cattle, and when the indigestible remains emerged from the animals' rear ends, it would be swept into the cellar through a trapdoor-covered hole in the floor. The ventilation shafts allowed the stench of manure and the fumes of cattle farts to escape and also helped to keep the barns relatively cool in summer. It was a pretty ingenious design.

Prof Schultz hadn't been kidding about there being people passionate about the barns. Several organizations worked to preserve what remained of the historic structures and to get them listed as protected buildings, while barn afficionados posted photographs and wrote blogs about their visits to different sites, checking them off on lists as bird spotters did with different species. Best of all, one of the sites Schultz had linked to maintained lists of all the round barns in each state in New England, giving exact GPS coordinates. Finally, I had some factual information and somewhere concrete to start my investigation.

Outside, it was gloomy, and rain had started to fall. From my window, I could see Henry's greenhouse glimmering ghostly pale in the worsening weather.

Darkness. Deep darkness.

The furious man with the blazing eyes.

The flashbacks were over almost before they began, but they left me uneasy. That thin man was filled with hate and violence. I just knew it. I checked myself. Did I really know it — like *know* it, know it? — or was I just making assumptions based on his expression and my own intuition? My visions had, so far, proved to be accurate, if not always useful. My *intuitions,* however, had been less reliable.

Was the angry man connected to that vortex of darkness beside the house? The only way to find out was to locate it. And the only way to do *that* was to check out each potential site. I printed off the lists of round barns and studied them, crossing off those with pictures showing them to be located in the middle of fields with no other buildings nearby since the barn I wanted was near a house. That still left scores of sites to visit.

Next, I printed out a map of New England and marked the locations of the round barns on it. I decided to start by visiting the ones nearest to Pitchford the next day. Of course, "nearest" was a relative term; the route I plotted — south to Andover, northeast to Weatherfield, up Route 91 to Hartland, then heading northwest along Route 89 to East Bethel with a sideways jaunt to Tunbridge — would take a full day. What better way to spend my Sunday?

That night, I cooked dinner for Ryan. I found a recipe online promising the best chili in Texas, and it turned out pretty good, even though I probably made it too hot, judging by how much water and then milk he gulped down during the meal. He chatted about work and the mysterious case of Pitchford's vandalized mailboxes. I told him about my visit to the FBI and my most recent visions. Then I brought out my fancy dessert — a giant pack of dark chocolate peanut butter cups — and we moved to the couch.

I started telling Ryan all about the round barns of New England, but I couldn't help noticing that he didn't seem to be paying much attention. His eyes kept dipping to my lips, and I couldn't stop mine from checking out his or sliding sideways to his dimple when he grinned. A heat was building between us; I could all but see it shimmering in the air. My stomach fizzed with anticipation. And nerves. If we slept together — and it was beginning to feel more like *when* than *if* — I'd be opening myself up to the kind of vulnerability and intimacy I hadn't felt since Colby. I'd walled myself off from my feelings, especially the romantic ones, for so long that the thought of that kind of exposure scared me.

"The round ones were pretty rare," I said, my voice sounding breathy.

Ryan claimed one of my hands. With one finger, he lightly traced the lines of my palms and the old, faded crescent of scar. Desire rose, fear ebbed, and chocolate melted between my thumb and forefinger.

"… and some of them are really polygonal or octagonal … rather than …" My voice petered out entirely when he licked the chocolate from my fingertips.

"Garnet?" He looked me in the eye. His were a deeper gray than usual.

"Yes?"

"Come closer."

I moved closer, all the way closer, sitting right beside him so that our bodies touched all down their lengths — shoulder to shoulder, hip to hip, thigh to thigh. I liked the feel of that contact, but now I couldn't see his eyes. Or his lips.

"Like this?" I asked.

In answer, he moved my hand up to his mouth and began sucking the chocolate off my fingers, his tongue licking and swirling, his teeth grazing the sensitive skin. Now I was the one melting. A mewl of desire rose within me. Before it could escape, I swung around, straddled his lap, and slanted my mouth across his, and then we were kissing. My head buzzed, my fingers tingled, my heart thumped, and my head emptied of any thought. Ryan's hands cupped my face, my head, my breasts. He unbuttoned my shirt, placing a hot kiss on each inch of revealed skin. My head fell back, but just as I reached for him, a loud bang and clatter startled both of us.

We pulled apart to see that the painting I'd brought from my parents' house and hung on the opposite wall was now lying on the floor. The scent of cola lip balm — Colby's favorite flavor — was strong in the air. Dammit! I'd been enjoying Ryan, which was no doubt why Colby had made his presence felt. The moment was pretty much ruined for me.

I clambered off Ryan and went to pick up the painting. One corner was damaged; I'd need to get it reframed. Ryan, meanwhile, investigated the wall.

"The nail's still here, so how did it fall off?" he asked, baffled.

"I couldn't have hung it securely," I said.

I didn't like lying to him, but what was I supposed to say? *My dead boyfriend is jealous and determined to keep us from getting too hot and heavy?* Colby had been interfering in this relationship since he first knocked Ryan's gift of a blue teddy bear off my bed in the hospital back when I'd nearly died. It was an issue that I'd have to address soon, and I had no idea how.

"Maybe we could continue this another time?" I suggested.

Ryan looked disappointed, but he didn't try to persuade me otherwise. Perhaps he, too, could feel that the vibe wasn't the same after the interruption.

At the door, he gave me a final kiss and said, "I wish I could come barn hunting with you instead of doing duty at the station. Be careful, will you?"

"Sure, sure," I told him. "You know me."

"I do," he said. "That's why I worry."

– 18 –

Sunday, April 15

Early the next morning, while I was tucking into a breakfast of leftover chili topped with sliced avocado, sour cream, and pickled jalapenos, my mother called to ask if I'd like to come over for Sunday lunch with her and Dad. "I know you're not fond of chickpeas and tofu, dear, so I'll roast a chicken or a ham," she offered.

"Can I get a rain check? I'm going barn spotting today," I said.

Of course, I had to explain what that was and why I wanted to do it, and when she heard I was trying to find something I'd seen in a vision, my mother got way too enthusiastic.

"I'll come with you!" she insisted. "I'd love to hunt a vision barn. It'll be fun."

I groaned internally. A day on the road stuck in a car with my mother sounded like the opposite of fun. I'd rather eat chickpeas *and* tofu.

"I thought I'd just go alone. It's going to be super boring," I warned.

"Don't be silly! Your father will want to come too. I'll bring snacks, and we can stop at a restaurant for lunch — your father's treat."

No amount of trying could convince her that it was more likely to be a boring trek across the length and breadth of rural Vermont than a grand family adventure, so at nine o'clock that morning, I collected her and my father from their house in Abenaki Street, and we headed south. I regretted bringing them even before we reached the first barn in Andover.

My mother, sitting in the back seat, spent the hour-and-a-half drive bending my ear with town gossip. "Poor old Frank Turner passed away last week. Remember him, Garnet? He was the chief of police before Ryan Jackson. But as one goes out, another comes in an open window because guess what? Jessica Armstrong's pregnant!"

I moved into the left lane and increased my speed.

"You don't seem very surprised, dear."

"I already knew she was expecting," I said.

"You didn't tell *me*. And Judy Dillon was in the store last week for a tarot reading. She was *particularly* interested in what the cards said about money, which makes me wonder if the café is struggling financially. I sent her off with an abundance crystal bag, just in case. Ooh, that reminds me! I spent some time last night assembling a collection to help with searching and to boost our chances of finding."

I checked my father's reaction to this; he was rolling his eyes. I was already feeling an urge to bite or pick or tear at something.

"It wasn't the easiest set to put together," my mother

continued. "I know which crystals help you find *love* and your path in life or lost belongings, but it was difficult trying to find stones to help search for a lost *place*. And this barn we're searching for isn't really lost, is it? I'm sure it must be where it always was. We just don't know where that is. I considered moldavite, but that works more for lost *people*. Anyway, I wore my amazonite pendant just in case." She held the blue-green stone to her throat and chanted some incoherent mantra.

"What are you doing, Crystal?" my father demanded. Clearly, I wasn't the only one growing irritated with her prattle.

"Awakening the powers of my throat chakra. I researched it," she said proudly. "Now I'll say the name of the place we're searching for and close my eyes, and in a few seconds, I'll get a vision of where it's at. What's the place called, dear?"

I huffed in annoyance. "We don't know, Mom. That's the reason we're in this car driving around the godforsaken backwoods of Vermont with a Dunkin Donuts box lid in the first place!"

"Oh yes, of course. Well I'll just ... Barn, round barn, roundbarnround barnroundbarn," she intoned.

My father rummaged in the glovebox.

"What are you looking for?" I asked him.

"Headphones. Ear plugs. Cotton wool, in a pinch."

My mother stopped making the awful noise, and for a few seconds, there was blessed silence in the car. Then she said, "Oh dear."

"You *saw* something?" I asked, astonished.

"No, but I remembered that I forgot to take the chicken for tonight's dinner out of the freezer. I wonder ... Maybe it's not working because I'm not the searcher. It might work better if *you* hold it and do the chanting."

"I will not," I said flatly.

"For goodness' sake, Crystal, she's driving!" my father said through gritted teeth. "She needs her hands on the wheel and her full attention on the road."

"Well, at least hang onto these." My mother stretched forward and tossed a silver gauze bag filled with blue gemstones onto the dashboard. "I'm not sure whether it'll help with searching, but it will boost enlightenment, and I think we can all agree that you need as much of that as you can get."

I turned on the car radio and began scratching at a rough patch of skin on my left hand.

"I included angelite to enhance communication with the divine, blue calcite for inner vision and heightened awareness, charoite to stimulate your intuitive abilities—"

"Anything there to calm a temper?" I muttered, digging hard enough into the back of my hand to break the skin.

"And merlinite to strengthen your connection to elemental energies," my mother continued, speaking louder when my father turned up the volume on the radio. "And— Oh dear. Now I'm wondering if I should've included purple obsidian too. What do you think, Garnet?"

"I think it doesn't make any difference because these bits of rock will have zero effect on anything." I wiped the back of my hand on my jeans before either of my parents spotted the line of blood.

"How *can* you say that," my mother said, sounding scandalized at my indifference, "when you *know* how much that purple amethyst quartz you found helped you to get visions? Turn that noise down, Bob. I can't hear myself think. Do you still have that crystal, Garnet? And the lepidolite I gave you?"

"No. I tossed them."

I hadn't. The two crystals were currently nesting in the lint at the bottom of my handbag.

"Garnet!" My mother sounded genuinely distressed. "And the seer kit I made for you?"

"I think I lost it."

The little gauze bag of crystals was also lurking down there between tissues, loose change, and crumpled receipts. Somehow, I hadn't been able to let the stones go, but I felt like a superstitious idiot for keeping them and wouldn't admit I had for fear of encouraging my mother. If I wasn't careful, she'd soon have me lugging around a sack full of rocks.

I *had* gotten a bunch of visions while keeping the crystals with me or while holding them, and although there was no evidence that what I'd seen and heard was in any way related to their presence, I reckoned they couldn't hurt. Plus if I ever needed to wander into the woods, I could leave a trail of colored stones to find my way back out.

"Bob, put those in her purse, will you, before she loses them too. Oh, look. A windmill. Did you know that windmills are symbols of—"

"Garnet," my father said, cutting her off, "how exactly does the barn you ... saw ... relate to the serial killer?"

"I don't know for sure." What I didn't know for sure could fill all the round barns in New England, plus a few grain silos.

"Maybe he lived there once, maybe he killed there once, or maybe it's where he's *going* to kill."

"Hmmm. It seems like so little to be going on."

"Tell me about it." If the TV program was correct, the killer was due to strike in exactly three weeks. My fingers found an old scab on my other hand and began scratching. We arrived at the Andover barn half an hour later, but it was a bust, in no way resembling the barn I'd seen in my vision. The next couple of barns near Weatherfield either didn't have houses nearby or were near houses that didn't match the one I was looking for. We struck out for another site off Route 91 before spotting a promising round roof outside of Hartland. The reason it hadn't been on my list of barns, however, soon became clear.

"False alarm," I said, reading the sign outside the building as we drove past. "It's a Buddhist temple."

"Such an extraordinary belief system," my mother said.

"You're one to talk!" I said.

"Did you know that Buddhism is all about suffering?"

Before she could set off down another rabbit hole, I asked my father to program our next destination into Google Maps on my phone.

"What does the FBI know about this killer?" he asked me when we were on course for the next site, a farm outside Hucknall,

"If I had a dollar for every time they told me something about this case, then I'd have fifteen cents," I grumbled.

"I don't understand what that means, dear," my mother said.

"It means that whatever they may or may not know, they're

not telling me. I'm the one passing *them* information. Or at least, what I've seen in my visions."

Had Agent Washington given Singh a rundown of what I'd seen? If so, how had Singh reacted? I would freaking *love* to tell him something that could be proved true. And I'd really like to help out Washington in some way. It had been nice to be treated with politeness and respect by an FBI agent, for a change. When I got back home, I would send Washington a text describing what I'd seen when I'd held all those items together. Maybe he could use it in some way.

My father was saying something.

"Sorry, what?" I asked.

"What all *did* you see?"

"Tomatoes growing on a vine and rotting on the ground. A house with a round-roofed barn behind it. A hitchhiker — I think he was one of the victims — being picked up by someone in a car."

"What kind of car?"

"An old sedan, dark blue or green. Probably a Ford."

"You used to drive a Ford, remember, Bob? Oh, the good times we had driving around in that!"

"David Berkowitz, the Son of Sam, used to drive a Ford, a 1963 Galaxie, unless I'm mistaken," my father said. "And Ed Gein drove a Ford Fodor."

"I remember once—" my mother began.

"But the vehicle of choice for modern serial killers is a *van*," he said, "especially one of those with the sliding doors on the side because that makes abduction real easy, particularly if there are two perpetrators. One steers the van alongside the victim, the other slides open the door and just drags him or her inside. That's what the Toolbox Killers did."

"I don't even want to know why they were called that." Following Google's instructions, I took the turnoff to Route 80.

"A van provides storage for kill kits. It can be soundproofed, so it's a good place to do the deed — a mobile kill spot, as it were — not just a method of transporting the victim. No one can see the victim once she's inside if you get a windowless one. And once you've disposed of the body, it's easy to clean and rinse out with bleach to destroy any DNA evidence."

I glanced at my father, kind of disturbed that he knew all this, but he must've interpreted my look as interest in murder-mobiles because he continued. "Some of the worst serial murderers in history — Jeffrey Dahmer, Robert Lee Yates, Ian Brady, and Myra Hindley — used vans. There was a petition recently to ban them, but I don't think it got much support."

"Does it ever worry you that this stuff is stored in your head, Pops?" I asked.

Before he could respond, the app told me that we'd arrived at our destination. A row of fir trees screened the property, preventing us from seeing any house or barn.

"Here goes nothing." I turned into the drive marked by an old-fashioned mailbox and studied the homestead that stood about fifty yards down the way. "Now, this is more like it."

$$- 19 -$$

The house was white, with a porch and the winter-tattered remains of a rose garden out front. Clearly visible behind the house was the roof of a barn topped with a ventilator shaft. No weathervane, though. I checked the left of the house — lots of deep shadow but no tree and no sense of death or darkness. It didn't look identical to what I'd seen in my vision. This house was neater, well-maintained with fresh paint and gutters that didn't sag, but that was all cosmetic. The basic structure wasn't too dissimilar.

My mother leaned forward between the front seats of the car. "Is this it, Garnet? Is this the one?"

"It's … it's a definite possible maybe."

My father compared the structures in front of us to my sketch on the doughnut box lid. "I don't think so. The barn looks too close to the house and too far to the right."

"But do you have a *feeling* about it?" my mother asked me.

I hadn't checked my "feelings." I'd been comparing points of visual similarity between this place and my vision. Now I tuned in to my gut. There *was* some vague disquiet there, though it could've been hunger; it had been a good while since breakfast.

I pulled to the side of the drive and killed the engine. "I'd like to take a closer look."

At once, my mother climbed out of the car, but my father stayed put.

"Are you sure you want to do this?" he asked me.

"What are you so worried about?" I asked.

"This is someone's house. It's private property, and we're trespassing."

"I'm not planning on stealing the family silver, Dad."

"If you go looking for trouble, sooner or later, you'll find it," he said, but I was already getting out of the car.

My mother tugged an orange backpack out of the back seat and hoisted it onto her shoulder.

"What is that?" I asked her. "More crystals?"

"A ghost-hunting kit! I've been watching those young men on TV, the ones that yell at spirits — and let me just say I consider that to be downright impolite — and although I don't have their hi-technical stuff, I put together my own collection." She clicked the strap of the backpack around her waist. "I've got a crucifix in case of demons, sage for smudging, a digital thermometer from the first aid kit to measure cold zones, a flashlight in case we have to go into a dark room, and a bottle of holy water. Well, it's not precisely *holy* per se, but it *is* boiled, and I did say a blessing over it, so I'm sure it'll do. A sunhat, in case we have to do field work and, of course, a voice recorder for EVPs."

My mother believed that electronic voice phenomena —

the supposed "voices" of spirits and ghosts — could be captured on old analogue tape recorders, and she'd recently blown a few hundred dollars acquiring one of the gadgets.

"Oh, and some wet wipes in case we get hit with ectoplasm. Or" — she glanced at the muddy patch in front of the house — "dirt."

Shaking my head at her foolishness, I walked toward the house, taking a few steps to one side and then to the other to check the barn roof from different angles. It *did* appear to be nearer to the house than the one in my vision. Then again, maybe I was just bad at drawing perspective accurately.

I headed toward the shadowed left-hand side of the house. Where a tall beech may once have stood, there was now an old tree stump on which someone had marked a tic-tac-toe grid in white paint. I trailed my fingers across the surface of the stump in the far-fetched hope that I might see what the tree had once looked like. Instead, I saw something very different. Faded and fleeting as the image was, I was still able to make out two bodies, naked and intertwined, doing the old rumpity-bump on the stump. *Ugh.* A Folger's coffee can rested on the grass beside the trunk. Wondering if it would contain chalk or game markers, I picked it up and opened it. And nearly dropped it in shock.

Inside were teeth — human teeth, complete with their roots. Five molars and five incisors. The hair on the back of my neck rose as I stretched a finger toward a milk tooth. A sudden rush of movement and noise had me leaping back, arms flung wide, the teeth flying into the air. Slavering jaws, wild eyes, straining muscles — a huge dog, as big as a bear, was charging at me, barking madly. It lunged into the air then fell to the ground with a throttled yelp, pulled up short by the chain around its neck.

I stood as still as a pulled tooth, except for my galloping heart, while the beast leaped and plunged, yanking against its shackles, barking and baying. My father yelled something behind me, and I took one small unsteady step backward. Then another. A shout rang out, and at once, the dog sat on its haunches, eyes fixed on me, a low growl rumbling in its chest. I backed away, supported by knees whose load-bearing capacity now matched that of Jell-O and, at a movement in my peripheral vision, turned to face the porch, where an old man now stood. Tall and slim with snow-white hair and a hostile expression, he held a walking stick in one hand and scratched his chin with the other.

I walked around to the front of the house. My mouth was dry, but I managed a "Hi, there."

The man said nothing.

I forced my lips into a smile. "Quite a watchdog you've got there."

"Gunner doesn't like strangers. Me either."

"A stranger is just a friend you haven't met, yet," my mother said, coming to stand beside me.

I figured a stranger could also just be a murderer looking to add to his kills. I checked the dog. His gaze flicked to my mother for a second then returned to me. *Just give me the order, and her throat is yours, Master,* those eyes said.

"I'm Garnet McGee," I began and at once realized the error of giving my real name. "This is my mother and" — I glanced over my shoulder and found my father standing a few paces behind me — "my father."

"What are you doing on my property?"

"We're—" my mother began, but I cut her off before she could spout anything about a psychic quest for a mystery barn. This man already had us pegged as trespassers; we didn't need him to think we were crackpots too.

"We're barn-spotters," I said, trying for a bright, confident tone. "We love to visit Vermont's best barns. And that one over there" — I pointed to the roof in the distance — "is listed as being one of the best round barns in the state. I wondered if we could maybe take a look?"

"No."

"Just a little peep?" my mother said.

The screen door of the porch creaked open, and a woman stepped out, wiping floury hands on a black apron. She had gray hair, a doughy face and was as wide as the man was narrow. Standing side by side, they looked like Jack Sprat and his wife. Meanwhile, the dog, losing interest in me for a moment, snuffled around in the dirt, picked up something small with his teeth, and crunched it between his powerful jaws. The next time this family gathered to play tic-tac-toe, they'd be short a marker.

"Your house looks vintage too," I said. "Built around 1900, I'd guess?"

No reply.

"And it's in such great condition. Really lovely! Would you mind if I asked you some questions about it?"

"Why, yes, I would mind. You think I've got nothing better

to do all day than answer nosy questions from a bunch of snoopers?"

"Fair enough," Dad said from behind me. "Well, we'll just be on our way, then. Come along, ladies."

While my father was speaking, the woman leaned over and whispered something into the man's ear. A strange smile spread slowly across his face. "My wife tells me I'm not being very neighborly," he said. "Why don't you folk come inside and have some tea with us? She brews her very own blends, special-like. And she's got some still-warm Joe Froggers for you."

An uneasy feeling took root in the pit of my stomach. Something wasn't right here. The feeling grew when the door creaked again, and a man of around forty, wearing denim overalls over a plaid shirt buttoned up to his throat, came out onto the porch. He knocked a dangling windchime with his head, but instead of stepping away or removing his straw hat, he merely tilted his head toward his left shoulder. In appearance, he took after the man, but he had the woman's silence and slack expression. He stood perfectly still, watching us with his mouth open, his head angled and his palms pressed against his thighs.

"Will you join us?" the old man asked, and there seemed to be something more than a simple invitation to tea threaded through his words.

I shivered, chilled by a cool breeze that moved neither the tendrils of hair about my face nor the windchime on the porch. Perhaps sensing the new presence, Gunner bared his teeth in a snarl then released a cacophony of wild barks. Straining at his chain, he bounced on his paws as he backed up and lunged forward over and over again, ignoring his master's commands to sit and stay.

My mother stepped forward. "Well, if you're sure it's not too much trouble, a cup of tea would be lovely. Thank you."

No!

The voice in my head was Colby's.

Go. Leave!

– 20 –

I grabbed my mother's arm, restraining her from waltzing into the house with this creepy family and tossing "special tea" and warm froggers down her gullet. "Thank you," I told the man on the porch. "But we really should be going. We have a long drive back home."

"But what about the house and the barn?" my mother asked plaintively.

"*Mom*," I said, giving her a look filled with meaning, "I really *feel* we should go now."

The words felt true. Even apart from Colby's warning, I felt a wrongness about the place that was almost tangible. My body was willing me to get the heck away from it.

My mother's eyes widened. "Oh!" she mouthed.

I waved at the trio on the porch. "Goodbye, then."

A look passed between the mother and son, then he straightened his head, sending the windchime into another discordant tinkle, and started walking toward us. I spun and half-ran back to the car, my hand clamped around my mother's wrist. Glancing over my shoulder, I saw the younger man tramping down the front stairs of the porch.

"Get in the car," I whispered, unlocking the doors with my remote.

My father, needing no encouragement, pushed my mother into the back before getting in himself, and was buckled up before I could start the engine. The man in overalls continued trudging toward us, undaunted when I threw the car into reverse and backed up the drive at top speed, my engine whining in protest. When we got to the highway, I turned the car around and then had to wait for a line of cars to pass.

My father turned in his seat to look out of the back window. "Hurry! He's still coming!"

Spotting a small gap in the traffic, I shot onto the highway and floored my accelerator. When the needle hit seventy and a glance in the rear-view mirror confirmed no one was following us, I blew out a relieved breath.

"Can I have one of your wipes, Mom?" I asked.

"Of course." She opened her backpack and pulled out an economy-sized pack. "Here you go."

I took one and wiped under my arms, where a cold sweat had broken out.

"Bob?" my mother said, nudging my father with the pack of wipes.

He took one of the proffered towelettes and dabbed at his face. "What in God's name is a Joe Frogger?"

"It's a cookie, dear, made with lots of spices and a little rum. They sell them at the Cakey Bakey in town. Delicious! I'm sorry to have missed out on tasting the ones that woman made. Still, it's always better to be safe than sure," my mother said, unintentionally accurate. "So, Garnet, what did you feel back there?"

"I don't know. It was … off. Like there was a wrongness."

"Wrong like there was something bad about it? Or wrong as in it wasn't the right place?"

"Either. Both maybe?" I said. Was the Hucknall house the same as the one in my vision? I honestly couldn't say for sure. I hadn't felt that evil darkness to the side of the house, but I'd also known — and Colby had, too — that it wasn't a good place. "I'm not sure. I just knew we shouldn't go into that house with those people."

"Well, I could've told you that for nothing," my father grumbled. "In fact, if I neglected to mention while raising you that you shouldn't go off with strangers offering treats, then consider that lesson now taught!"

"And those men — were either of them the man in your vision?" my mother asked.

"Not the younger one."

"Floppy Head?"

"Yeah, not him. But the older one …"

"Grumpy Stumps?"

"He could maybe be a twenty-year-older version of the mean man I saw."

My father checked the doughnut box lid. "I see what you mean. They're both tall and thin."

"And hatchet-faced," my mother said, peering over his shoulder at the sketch.

"The problem is my visions don't freaking well come with time- and date-stamps. What I saw in my vision could have happened decades ago or last month."

My mother sat back in her seat and rooted around in her handbag. "But you definitely got a feeling that something was bad or dangerous there. That's something, at least."

"Yes, but it's entirely possible for there to be more than one bad place or person in the world at the same time," I snapped, irritated more at myself than her. Why on earth had I been given this so-called "gift" if it was impossible to employ it usefully?

"So, bottom line, kiddo, what do you think?" my father asked.

"What does she *think*?" My mother snorted. "You're beating on a dead horse, there."

"Oh yeah?" I said, spoiling for a fight.

"Yes." She handed my father a packet of goldfish crackers, dropped a packet of chili-flavored beef jerky into my lap, and tore open a bag of pistachio nuts for herself. "You're going about this in entirely the wrong way. Instead of trying to think your way through, you should be using your *feelings*, dear. If I've said it once, I've said it over and over again. The appearances of buildings change. People too. My goodness, you should see Michelle Armstrong! She's had another round of fillers and Botox. I hardly recognized her when I bumped into her at the bank on Monday. Then she posted one of those goose-face selfies on her Facebook page, and I commented, 'Lovely pic. Who's it of?'" My mother chortled; she loved getting one over on Pitchford's haughty town clerk. "Of course, everyone else posted raving compliments. The way people pretty-foot around her, it's enough to make you sick. Anyway, my point is you should tune in to your feelings and your gift to *sense* which barn is the right one."

My father turned his head to stare out of the window at the blur of trees and pastures. I tore a strip off a stick of jerky and chewed, thinking. There was no stopping my mother from talking, though.

"Why, when you were a little girl, we had a game where I'd hide a candy in one of my hands and hold them out like this" — she thrust both fists through the gap between the front seats — "and tell you to choose. And you'd always guess right! Don't you remember, Bob? It goes to show you already had the sight, Garnet, even way back then."

"Or maybe she was just smart enough to choose the hand with the bigger fist," my father said.

My mother made a dismissive noise. "Then how do you explain that time with the shell game on the pier at Old Orchard Beach? The fellow had three upside-down shells, Garnet, and one dried pea. He'd pop the pea under one of the shells, then he'd shuffle them around and around faster than anyone could keep track of." She milled her hands furiously in the air to demonstrate. "And when he stopped, *you* knew which shell the pea was under. Every time. He got sick of you guessing right, so he decided to get even more tricky, hiding the pea in his hand or flicking it onto the floor, I guess. And when he stopped moving the shells, you called him a cheat. Quick as flash, you turned over all three shells to show it wasn't under any of them. My word, there was such a fandango with the crowd who'd gathered to watch. They all booed, and he had to pack up his case and vamoose!" She laughed in delight at the memory. "Your dad bought you a popsicle for exposing the fraud, and I bought you a ride on the Ferris wheel for seeing with your third eye."

I gave my father a skeptical look. "Did that actually happen?"

"I think it might have been cotton candy, not a popsicle."

"Seeing through the trick?" I clarified.

He pulled a face and, almost reluctantly, said, "You were a lucky kid."

"So you should go by what you *feel*, my dear," my mother concluded. "There's no two ifs and buts about it."

Going with my gut rather than leading with my brain wouldn't come naturally to me. I liked logic, verifiable facts, and accurate data. Still, in this search at least, I had nothing to lose and nothing better to go on. So when we approached the barns in the sites near Tunbridge and East Bethel, I tuned in to my feelings — and felt diddly squat. Of course, none of the sites much *looked* like the buildings in my vision either.

We stopped for a late lunch at a quaint roadside inn with a cheffy menu. Dad had wild mushroom ravioli, Mom had spring asparagus risotto, I ordered maple bourbon salmon, and we each had a scoop of Ben and Jerry's ice cream for dessert. Dad, who'd polished off two beers over lunch, fell asleep on the way home, leaving me the sole audience to my mother's rambling stream of consciousness until we finally arrived at their house. I shook my father awake, eager to get home to the peace and quiet of my loft. What a waste the day had been. Thank goodness Ryan *hadn't* been there to witness my succession of psychic flops, not to mention the exhausting and eccentric dynamics of my oddball family.

"That was a lovely day, Garnet," my mother said. "Thank you for taking us along."

"Sure, sure."

Taking them had been a bad idea. They'd slowed my pace and revved up my stress levels. Plus, it now occurred to me that involving them in a hunt for a killer was in no way a smart idea. My mother, for all the emphasis she placed on intuition, seemed to lack any of her own. She'd happily have gone right into that house with Floppy, Grumpy, and Lumpy with no thought of any potential danger. From now on, I'd hunt alone.

I lowered my window and told her, "Don't forget to take your ghost-hunting kit with you."

But she insisted on having my father stow it in the trunk of the car. Bending down at my window, she said, "I'll just leave it there for our next barn-hunting trip, dear. See you bright and early next Sunday morning?"

Over my dead body.

– 21 –

Henry Mason's study was pretty much what one would expect for a lawyer: shelves of legal tomes, a gleaming wooden desk forested with piles of paper and files, and a worn Persian carpet on the floor. I was immediately drawn to the abstract painting on one wall. Clouds of color swirled above a hazy gray horizon in a mood that was both hopeful and foreboding, a fitting picture for my first day of paid work for the old curmudgeon.

The man himself sat in a leather wingback, his feet up on a footstool and a blanket thrown over his knees. When I greeted him with a bright "Good morning," he scowled.

"It's overcast, cold, and wet. Nothing good about it."

Recalling Gwyneth's theory that he was invigorated by arguments, I replied, "Well, aren't you a ray of sunshine?"

Beneath his deepening scowl, I saw the strain of real pain in his face. I'd need to take care not to bump his foot as I moved around the room. "What's my first job today?" I asked.

"I've misplaced my spectacles. I last remember using them when I was tending to my babies."

"I'll go check."

"The key is on that rack by the door. Be sure to shut *and* lock the door of the hothouse when you leave."

"Will do."

"And take the garbage out while you're at it. It's collection day," he called after me.

I was going to have to teach Henry how to say *please*.

When I wrestled the garbage can to the sidewalk, it clinked at every bump. Peeking inside, I saw enough empty red wine bottles to explain Henry's flare up of gout. Gwyneth must not know about the wine, or she'd have asked me to monitor his drinking too.

After the chilly outside air, the heat and perfume of the greenhouse was cloying. I didn't much like the place. If I were a superstitious and suggestible sort of person, which I most certainly was not, I might've imagined that the flowers were watching me, resenting my intrusion into their exotic world. And I might have said out loud, "Just passing through. Don't mind me." Instead, I switched to mouth-breathing and hunted in silence for Henry's specs. They weren't on his workbench, but a mud-smeared black apron was. It reminded me of the woman on the porch of that house outside Hucknall with the unfriendly man, the strange son, the fierce dog. The teeth.

I found the glasses inside a book, *The Talented Mr. Ripley* by Patricia Highsmith, lying on the recliner and hurried out of the hothouse so fast I forgot to shut and lock the door and had to go back once I realized. Back in Henry's study, I handed him his spectacles. "Here you go."

Perching them on his nose, he peered over the rim at me. "Did you remember to lock the door?"

"Of course. And you're welcome." Clearly, I was going to have to teach him how to say *thank you* too.

"Hand me that folder over there. Not that one, the blue one," he said.

This time, I held onto the item he wanted until he uttered a grudging "Thanks."

"What's that on your hand?" he demanded, pointing at the scab at the base of my thumb, a vestige of my skin-picking the day before. "Do you have a disease?"

"No. Do you?" I cast a significant look at his swollen foot.

He moved it an inch and winced. "I have an excess of uric acid in the bloodstream."

"I guess that explains your mood," I said but added more kindly, "Chronic pain is enough to make anyone miserable."

"You have chronic pain?" he asked. "Or your parents?"

"Luckily not. My father's fairly healthy, but my mother has high blood pressure."

He checked something in the file, then had me return it to the desk. Next, he asked me to pass him his medicine and a glass of water. "Gout won't kill you, but it will make you wish you were dead. Gout," he said in the tone of someone stating an important universal truth, "is a bastard."

I nodded sympathetically. "It's enough to give anyone a chronic case of PLOM."

"Plom? What's that?"

"It's a common psychological diagnosis. PLOM stands for 'poor little old me.'"

Henry glowered at me and began issuing a steady stream of orders, clearly getting a kick out of keeping me on the hop. The worst part of the job, I soon discovered, was filing the papers that overflowed his in-basket. It should have been a mindless task, freeing my mind to think about serial killers and attractive cops and other fascinating things, but it wasn't.

Instead of arranging his files alphabetically in the cabinet, like any sane person would do, Henry had stored them according to categories — criminal, civil, estates, divorce — and beneath that, he'd put them behind tabs which related to how much he liked the client. These were then arranged with no respect for the virtues of alphabetical order. A bunch of thick folders were filed under A (for "Annoying," according to Henry) and D ("Dreadful"), and shoved into the back of the drawer, while far fewer files were stored under S (for "Sheer delight to deal with") and stowed in the front. All his banking and insurance documents were stored under F (for "finance") and his software manuals, cell phone instruction booklet, and a handwritten list of pins and passwords was filed under U — for "Unpleasantness and confusion."

"This whole cabinet needs reorganizing," I said after a frustrating two hours of asking him where every single paper needed to be filed. "It's chaos!"

"It most certainly is not," he said hotly.

"Then tell me where I found this." I held up a slim bar of Swiss chocolate.

"Under V in the criminal drawer," he said smugly. He was right.

"But why?" I pleaded.

"For *Verboten* and because Gwyneth considers it a crime."

"And this? It's a divorce contract for one Mary-Anne Applequist."

"Under N."

"What's that stand for?"

Henry blushed. "None of your business. You can test me all you want. You won't catch me out, Missy."

"Garnet."

"Garnet," he said. "What kind of a name is that, anyway?"

"You'll have to take that one up with my parents. I didn't choose it. What I want to know is how you expect me to do your filing when you alone know the secret location of every document?"

"You'll learn. It's easy once you get the hang of the system."

"There's a method in this madness?" I swung a hip into a drawer, slamming it shut.

"There's a very sound set of organizing principles that make complete sense to me. I have systematized the raw data so that I have relevant and useful information. What use is it to know that LeBron George's surname starts with G? Instead, his position in that top drawer reminds me that he's particular and pedantic about every last detail of his contracts."

I checked. The third file under P in the top drawer belonged to Mr. L.K. George. Henry's system was an interesting insight into how his mind worked. My own filing system consisted of a tote bin stuffed with every piece of paper I worried I might ever need again. What did that say about *my* brain? Confused and cluttered but reasonably watertight? I made no more complaints about the filing, and when I finished at lunchtime,

I was pleased to see that his office looked a lot neater. Henry had grown marginally less grouchy over the course of the morning, but he got in one last jab before I left.

"Your eyes," he said as I slipped on my fleecy hoodie.

"What about them?"

"In certain Native American cultures, they're called 'ghost eyes.'"

I snorted a laugh. How, with all her speculations on the meaning of my near-death experience and everything that followed, had my mother missed that gem?

"Those who possess ghost eyes are believed to be natural guardians of the tribe because the different eyes can see on earth *and* into heaven simultaneously."

I blinked in astonishment.

"Although," Henry amended, "this belief is primarily attributed to dogs with the condition."

In revenge, I refiled his chocolate bar, telling him, "If you're so smart and your organizing principles are so logical, you should have no problem at all finding it again."

With that, I left, leaving him looking a lot less PLOM and a lot more *I-for-irritated-but-invigorated* than he had been all morning.

– 22 –

The bananas in the bowl on top of the fridge were turning black, and the apples were sagging into wrinkled balls. If my father had bought me wasabi peas and Doritos instead — and why the heck hadn't he? He knew my fraught relationship with fresh produce — the bowl would've been empty by now. I made a cheese and pickle sandwich and sat down at the table with my laptop and the New England state maps I'd printed out.

Henry had been spot-on about the difference between data and information. There was useful and relevant information hidden somewhere in the maps in front of me, but it was lost in the mass of data. I frowned at the circled round barns sites in Vermont, New Hampshire, Maine, and Massachusetts. Like Henry, I needed an organizing principle. Or at least, I needed a better one than merely checking out the sites located nearest to Pitchford because that was easiest.

I didn't know exactly how my visions about the house and the angry man related to the Button Man killer, but I did, thanks to the *Stakeout* TV program, know roughly where at least some of his snatch and dumpsites had been. I plotted those places on the maps, too, scoring deep circles around Randolph, where Jacob Wertheimer had last been seen, and Pitchford, where his remains had been found. Then I studied the maps, searching for any overlap between victim abduction and disposal sites and the locations of round barns. There were no precisely matching correlations, and none of the sites were within a couple of miles of each other. But as I widened the circle of overlap, there were more and more, and I had no clue which ones to check out first.

Damnit, I'd wasted my precious time with Agent Washington. I should've extracted some solid facts out of him when I had the chance. But maybe it wasn't too late. I dialed the number of the Rutland agency office and asked to speak to Special Agent Tyler Washington.

"Speaking." He sounded wary; perhaps he recognized my voice.

"Oh, hi, Tyler. It's Garnet McGee."

After a pause, he said, "Why are you calling me?" He didn't sound nearly as friendly as he had the last time we'd spoken.

"I sent you a text about the other visions I saw. Did you get it?"

"Yes."

"Was any of it helpful?" I asked hopefully.

"Not yet."

"Yeah, I know. It's hard-core vague. But I'm working on it, Tyler, and if I get anything more specific, I promise you'll be the first to know."

"Uh-huh."

He didn't sound overly enthusiastic about the prospect of continued communication between us, but I pressed on regardless. "I wondered if I could ask you a couple of questions? I promise I'll only take a few minutes of your time."

"No, I'm afraid not … Shirley. We're not in the market for a new property."

"Huh?" I said, puzzled for a second. "*Ohhh*, Singh's in the room with you, and you can't talk freely?"

"Yes, that's right."

"And he tore you a new one for helping me before?"

"Oh yeah. You bet," he said fervently.

"Look, I'm *really* sorry about that. I was honestly just trying to help. And I *can* help you if you could just tell me—"

"No, I'm afraid that's out of the question."

"I admire your integrity, Tyler, I do. But we both want to nail this killer, right? Tell you what, I'll narrow it down to just two questions, and we'll make it a quick multiple choice. I'll just say the possible answers, and you tell me yes or no, okay? That surely won't break your code of ethics."

"Okay, but just the two … bathrooms."

"Have you identified any more of the victims found at the Nash Stream Forest burial site?"

"Yes, one."

"Did he go missing in New Hampshire, too?"

"No. We're very happy in our current home."

"Oh, that's a clue, right? Okay then, did he get taken from Vermont?"

"Yes."

"Can you tell me where exactly?"

"No. I'm sorry, I've got to get back to my work now, so—"

"Wait!" I'd just remembered something. "In the original FBI profile, the geographic experts said they thought the killer was from Vermont, too, right?"

There was a second of silence, then Washington said, "You certainly sound like you know what you're doing, Shirley. I'll call you if we decide to sell."

"One more quick question. Is there any evidence the killer had sex with or raped any of his victims?"

"None, yet."

"And — last one, I promise! — this victim you've just identified, did he also go missing on or around May sixth?"

"Yes. Goodbye, then."

"Thank you, Tyler Washington! You're a good man, and I owe you a steak dinner," I said, and ended the call.

So the Button Man had snatched another victim in Vermont and left his body over the state border in New Hampshire. Somewhere in or between those two places, he'd committed the murder. But even if I limited myself to Vermont, or Vermont *and* New Hampshire, that still left me with a lot of territory to cover. This was hopeless. I needed more data points to narrow down my search, especially since the *Stakeout* list of earlier murders was incomplete and quite possibly inaccurate. Their information had, after all, merely been based on a tipoff.

I called Ryan. "I want to ask you a favor, but you can say no if you think it's going to be an issue because of our relationship. I mean, I don't want you to think I'm using you or taking advantage of you."

"Garnet?"

"Yes?"

"If you want to use me or take advantage of me, I'd be happy to submit anytime," he said, his voice deep and playful.

I was glad he couldn't see my blush over the phone. But he could surely hear my giggle. It sounded strange to my own ears — lighthearted and almost girlish. I couldn't remember the last time I'd giggled. It felt … good.

"So what's the favor?" Ryan asked.

"Remember how you told me that when the Pitchford police department was investigating Colby's murder ten years ago, you briefly wondered whether Colby was a victim of the serial killer operating in New England at that time?"

"Yeah."

"Can you tell me the victim names and places of abduction and body disposal that you knew of back then?" He'd told me them once before, but I couldn't recall them.

"I guess, sure. Hang on while I look up my old case notes."

By "old case notes," Ryan must mean Colby's case file. Old memories floated to the surface — the last time I saw Colby alive, the days of waiting and searching, his pale, battered body lying beside Plover Pond — but the images seemed more distant now, more faded. It was easier to recall the times when he was alive, the days when we'd laughed and swum at the quarry and kissed in the rain, the nights when we'd made love. And even those memories were infused with a golden haze that blurred the details. Remembering Colby now felt bittersweet instead of like poking an open wound of raw pain.

"Here we go," Ryan said, interrupting my musings. "I don't

know much, I'm afraid. I wasn't directly involved in any of the serial killer investigations, and the FBI had jurisdiction even then, so this list is far from complete." He rattled off the names of a number of towns and rural locations. "Any reason in particular you want this information?"

"I want to see if there's a correlation between those sites and the location of the New England round barns I told you about, so I can narrow down my search. Else I'll be spending the rest of my natural life visiting barns."

"I could help you," he offered.

"Much as I'd love your company, I couldn't do that to you. Honestly, it's crazy boring and likely a total waste of time. Plus," I added, "it would ruin any faith you have in my abilities if you saw first-hand how often I strike out."

He paused for a moment and then said almost sternly, "Garnet, promise me you won't go marching headlong into any danger, that you'll call me if you need help."

"Aye, aye, chief."

"Promise?"

"I promise."

"Are your fingers crossed?"

I uncrossed them and declared, "No! Sheesh, don't you trust me at all?"

"I know you too well," he said.

That was probably true, and it alarmed me a little. The closer he and I grew, and the more of ourselves we invested in each other, the more devastating it would be if our relationship didn't work out. Knowing I couldn't handle another catastrophic heartbreak, I'd vowed never to risk it. But I was beginning to see that my self-protective strategy kept me in a place of not living fully either. To be alive was to risk pain, and I didn't like it.

"Do you by any chance know the name of that latest Nash Stream Forest victim who's been identified?" I asked in a more businesslike tone.

"I didn't even know they'd made another identification."

"Can you find out? Would it help if I told you that the victim disappeared in Vermont?"

"Singh told you that?" Ryan said, sounding amazed.

"*Him*? Not likely!"

"Then how did you find out?"

"Do you really want me to tell you, or would you prefer to maintain plausible deniability?"

Ryan sighed. "I'll nose around and see if I can find out anything. I don't think there's any point in me contacting Singh directly. He's leery of letting me know anything because he suspects I'd tell you."

"Would you?" I asked.

"Only if you promised to take serious advantage of me," he said, and that warm note was back in his voice.

I was still smiling when I ended the call a minute later.

Some of the information Ryan gave me hadn't been mentioned in the TV special, and from the increasing number of murders in the years leading up to Jacob Wertheimer's death, it seemed like the serial killer had been escalating. I added the new names to my list of victims and marked the places on my maps, then I pored over the information again, looking for a pattern. If I searched within a thirty-mile radius of the victim disappearance and disposal sites I now knew, there were five round barn sites — one in Maine and two each in New Hampshire and Vermont. Were any one of them the place I'd glimpsed in my mind's eye? Another Vermont disposal site was about forty-two miles from the barn in Hucknall, making me wonder if I'd already found the right place — the farmhouse with Grumpy, Lumpy, Floppy, and Gunner the psycho dog.

If she were here, my mother would've advised me to use my "third eye" to identify the most likely site. What the heck? It couldn't hurt, and no one was present to witness my lunacy. I rolled my shoulders then shook out my hands and stretched them over the maps. I tuned in to my gut, but whatever I was waiting for didn't happen. My mother would probably also have advised me to use crystals to "boost my inner vision" or something of the sort. So, feeling like a first-class fool, I fetched the crystals from my handbag — the amethyst quartz that I'd found at Plover Pond and that was supposed to amplify my intuitive abilities: the lepidolite my mother had given me to assist in decision-making, the "seer kit" she'd foisted on me during my last investigation, and the bag of stones from our jaunt around southern Vermont. Deciding I may as well go the whole hog, I arranged the crystals in a circle around the maps, closed my eyes, and stretched out my hands again.

My scientist brain intervened just then, informing me that this was a wildly compromised experiment. My knowledge of how the maps beneath my hands were arranged could easily influence my findings. My subconscious mind might steer me to the places I knew victims had disappeared or been found. Keeping my eyes closed, I scrambled the maps around on the desk and stuck out my hands for the third time. At first, I felt nothing. But after a few minutes, I got two very clear sensations: growing tiredness in my arms and an increasing conviction that I'd lost my marbles. What the hell was I even doing?

"Eeny, meeny, miny, moe," I yelled defiantly and stabbed a finger down onto whatever part of the map lay beneath it.

Opening first one and then my other eye, I saw that my finger rested on a section of Vermont northeast of Montpelier, not far from one of the circled barns in Caledonia county.

It was a complete coincidence. Of course it was. But still, that was where I'd look next.

– 23 –

Saturday, April 21

The moment I saw it, I knew that I'd found the right house.

It sat at the end of a rutted dirt road overgrown with weeds and grass, its windows as dark as the gaps of missing teeth. It had a porch with a broken supporting post and a caved-in roof. A round barn roof peeped out from behind it, and although there was no sign of a fancy cow weathervane, the cupola matched the one in my vision. A massive beech tree shimmering with the vivid lime green of new spring leaves stood guard to the left of the house, where something malignant beckoned me from the shadows.

I parked out front, reasonably confident that no homeowner would emerge from the dilapidated wreck to challenge me and that no hound would appear to rip out my trachea. It was a cool day, so I slipped on my jacket when I got out of the car but left my handbag in the trunk. Seeing my mother's ghost-hunting backpack, I searched inside it for the flashlight she'd mentioned. It turned out to be an old toy one of mine with a cartoon firefly on the side, telling me to light up my life. I checked the beam strength — feeble — and decided to take my phone instead. My mental list for P.I. equipment to purchase now included a strong flashlight, a notebook, maximum-strength antiperspirant, and pepper spray in case of attack by mad dogs or people.

I'd transferred all the crystals my mother had ever given me into my jacket pockets, and as I walked up to the house, I clicked them together like worry beads. Stomach tight with nerves and growing dread, I climbed the steps at the front of the house.

"Hello?" My yell startled a mourning dove from its nest under the eaves, but otherwise, there was no answer.

I shouldered the stiff front door open and stepped inside. Sunlight coming through the open doorway illuminated a small hallway laced with spiderwebs. I moved into the room to my left, which must once have been a living room, and took in the peeling wallpaper, a couch spewing springs and stuffing, an old box-shaped television with a smashed screen, and a naked lightbulb dangling from the ceiling. I flicked the switch on the wall but wasn't surprised when it didn't work; this house had clearly been abandoned many years ago. Spiders had staked out the corners, but judging from the droppings covering the floor, rodents ruled below.

A heaviness pressed against my chest as I walked around the room, touching the walls, the couch, and a crushed cigarette box. I yanked the neck of my T-shirt up over my nose to filter out the musty, decay smell and the dust that stirred from every surface, then crouched beside a little mound of termite sawdust on the wooden floor. As soon as I laid a hand on the boards, an image shimmered to life in my mind. Closing my eyes, I surrendered to the vision.

A polished wooden floor is strewn with buttons. Crimson, turquoise, ochre, mauve. Brass and wood, round and square, domed and ridged.

A young boy with soft dark curls and a face glistening with tears kneels on the buttons. They dig into his knees and shins, bruising flesh and hurting bone.

A man, angry and purple faced, wags a finger at him. How many times have I warned you about that? Stop sniveling like such a sissy. Like a girl. The more you cry, the longer you'll stay there. All night if that's what it takes for you to learn to be a real boy.

A young woman with a white face and worn dress pleads with the man. It was an accident, and he's learned his lesson. Please, Father. He's so little.

He's not little, he's eight! What eight-year-old still does that? It's a disgrace. He's a filthy little shit. To the boy: you're a filthy little shit. What are you?

A filthy little shit, the child says in a whisper.

Another hour for cursing!

The boy's shoulders slump.

The woman steps forward. But, father—

He turns on her. Shut up! You think I care what you have to say? If you had any sense, he wouldn't even be here. You're too soft on him. You're going to turn him into a little fag.

But—
Just button that lip of yours before I thicken it for you!
Please—
His hand lashes out, strikes her cheek, sends her stumbling backward.
The boy half rises. Mom!
That'll be another hour for you, shithead. And as for you, you go clean the mess, and then you do what you need to, to fix my mood.

I opened my eyes and came back to the present, gasping and rubbing my aching knees.

It was the same middle-aged man from my vision at the FBI office. The woman in the worn dress had been his daughter and the boy his grandson My heart went out to the poor little kid and to his downtrodden mother, who was too afraid or too weak to protect him or herself from her father. Was he my killer? He was clearly angry and aggressive enough, and he had a thing about using buttons in his violence, like the killer did, and in his language.

Shuddering at the cruelty this house had witnessed, I got to my feet, dusted off my hands, and continued my exploration. One of three small bedrooms housed an old wire bedstead with a disintegrating foam mattress, and sun-faded pink drapes hung in shreds at the window. In the second room, a thin stained mattress lay on the floor, and pencil lines on the doorjamb recorded the height of a child — that poor boy, probably — at different ages. The last mark, made when he was fifteen, was about my height. Had they left this place, then? Had he run away or possibly even died? Or had his mother merely lost interest in preserving memories? I laid a hand against the markings but got no reading.

In the third bedroom, several bolts of rotting fabric — black-and-white gingham, cream cotton stained with rusty blotches, and gray-and-blue plaid — stood like dunces in the far corner below a sagging ceiling discolored with water marks and black mold. A desk was pushed up against the south-facing window. Had the boy's mother sat there once, sewing clothes and drapes?

The kitchen was at the back of the house. Ducking under a dangling strip of fly paper peppered with the mummified remains of dead insects, I activated my phone's flashlight and shone it around the gloom. Cupboard doors hung ajar, and drawers gaped from their housings. Paint peeled from the walls, and the cement floor was strewn with the dirt and debris of decades of neglect. Loose wires snaked out from behind the electric stove, where some kind of critter had made its nest in the warming drawer. There were no faucets at the kitchen sink, and the doorknobs and cabinet handles were missing. Maybe the same vandals who'd taken the weathervane had stripped this house of anything valuable.

Broken glass crunched underfoot as I walked around the room, touching items: a bread loaf pan scarred with scratches and rust, a blown can of beans, a few mismatched plates still stacked in a cupboard. I trailed my fingers over a dented kettle on the stovetop and a folding chair that lay on its back in the center of the room, and held a dishrag which crumbled to dust between my fingers.

Nothing.

The back door was locked, but a single hard kick took care of that. I made my way through the overgrown grass and weeds of the backyard, tripping over the skeleton of an old wheelbarrow and flushing a ruffled grouse from its cover. The barn, red with a gray roof, was situated about two hundred yards behind the house. Its board and batten siding walls rose from a stone-walled foundation, and it had the three levels I'd read about: a hayloft accessed by a raised drive at the top, the manure cellar at the bottom, and the main barn in between, where the cows would've been kept and milked. Each had its own wide entrance.

I strode up the raised drive and into the hayloft, where light filtered down from the cupola and gaps in the wooden shingle roof. The hayloft was comprised of a circular platform with a large central hole. A thick chain on a pulley dangled down into this space, ending in a pair of big pincers, which rested on the barn floor underneath. This must've been the contraption used to grab and lower bales of hay from the loft to the animals below.

I was tempted to climb down the long ladder that rested against the lip of the loft, but closer inspection showed it to be rickety and missing several rungs. Remembering my promise to Ryan not to put myself in harm's way, I left the loft and walked around the barn to the entrance at the main level. An iron wheel supported a heavy sliding door, which I was able, with much pushing, pulling, and grunted curses, to open a few inches.

Blinking as my eyes adjusted to the dimmer light, I looked

around. Cattle stalls were ranged against the south side, with non-opening windowpanes set in the walls above them. The wooden floor, where grain would once have been threshed, was littered with roof shingles, wind-swirled piles of straw, and old tools — a rusted hoe here, a pitchfork there. The air was thick with the smell of dust and mildew, and rustles from the murkier edges of the barn told me that rats and mice had colonized this structure too.

As I walked over to inspect the hay pincers, a sharp crack of splintering wood rent the air, and I plummeted.

– 24 –

My fall through the floor was halted by my chest and the one elbow I'd had time to fling out. Wedged at the waist with one arm pinned to my side and broken floorboards digging painfully into my ribs, I dangled halfway between the barn and the cellar below. My legs cycled uselessly in the open air, seeking purchase and finding none. Why the hell was I always falling through things?

I stopped moving in case the motion precipitated a further plunge and took a moment to catch my breath and think. I was stuck in a half-rotted wooden trapdoor mounted in an iron frame in the barn floor. I'd read about these in my research. They were the holes through which cow manure was swept into the cellar below. I struggled to haul myself out but couldn't do it with only one arm. Given my feeble upper arm strength, I probably wouldn't have been able to do it with two. Doing my investigating along with others might slow me down, but it was, I admitted to myself as I wriggled like a mouse in a trap, probably safer.

Spitting dust and chaff, I twisted my head around, looking

for something I could grab. The hay hook and chain were out of reach, but stretching as far as I could, I managed to lay fingertips on the handle of the hoe. Once I'd edged it close enough to grab, I lifted it into the air and brought it down, trying to hook the chain with the hoe blade. I missed the first time and spent several curse-riddled minutes wresting the hoe blade free from the floor where it had lodged in the wood too shallowly to support my weight. On my second attempt, I swung the hoe a few inches into the loop of chain puddled on the floor then slowly pulled back, dragging the snagged chain along the floor toward me.

"Yes!" I yelled when I could reach it.

Wrapping the chain around my hand and wrist, I dragged myself upward until I could free my other arm and haul myself out of the hole. Sweating, I lay back on the dirty floor for a few moments to catch my breath. I was learning new stuff about being a private investigator all the time, like that I should get in better shape and watch where I put my feet.

I stood up, dusting ineffectually at my clothes and procrastinating at going down into the cellar I'd almost fallen into. I wasn't exactly claustrophobic or nyctophobic — not diagnosably so, in any event — but I loathed being in small dark places like cellars. Even the basement in my parents' house, crowded with my mother's metaphysical junk and my father's fishing tackle, creeped me out. If I died — again — and was sent to the bad place, it would take the form of a small cellar with no light and no exit.

I lifted the trapdoor frame with its splintered remnants of wood and left it in the upright position so I wouldn't accidentally fall through it again if I came back here. Grabbing the hoe, with some vague idea of fighting off rats, I walked out and around to the manure cellar. Its entrance — closed — was wide enough to allow a wagon or tractor to back into it and load up manure for the fields. I hesitated a moment, then made myself tug the sliding door open a few inches and go inside. If only I'd accepted Ryan's offer to come with me. Together, this would've been a fun adventure. We would've joked about haylofts — maybe even made out in the light, airy one above — and surely he had a proper police-issue flashlight. And a gun. Alone, this part of my investigation was scary and unpleasant.

I directed the beam of my phone's flashlight around the murky space. The cellar was about nine feet high with a floor of hard packed dirt. The damp air still carried a faint, sour stench of manure. In one section, the stone wall had collapsed inward in a rocky pile, making me worry about the stability of the barn floor above. At any moment, it might collapse on me and leave me trapped, pinned facedown in the dirt by beams and boards and stone. Cause of death: terminal stupidity and pig-headed independence.

Gingerly, I made my way into the darker recesses, where my light picked out a wire cage standing against the far wall, its drop-down side raised in the open position. This must once have housed rabbits or chickens, possibly a dog, though whoever had thought it a good idea to store animals down here surely needed his head examined. I was about to leave when a glint of something on the floor of the cage caught my eye.

Getting down on my haunches, I poked the hoe around in the mulch at the bottom of the cage and unearthed a battered old Christmas cookie tin. Pushing aside a flashback to those stomach-turning teeth in the coffee can, I prized the lid open to discover that this tin contained only a toy car, an ancient half-empty packet of Wrigley's chewing gum, a matchbox, a candle stub, and a small true-crime magazine with a lurid cover. This must have been where the little boy hid his toys and treats from his grandfather's sharp eyes. Clever. I pushed myself up and as I leaned on the cage for support, I was felled by a sharp vision.

You know what this means, the man with the furious face shouts at the skinny boy with the dark curls and huge scared eyes.

The boy begs and pleads, promises to be better, to be a good boy. Tears brim in his eyes.

The man points. Go!

Whimpering, the boy crawls into the cage. Crouches in a corner.

And take your useless cat with you. The man grabs a hissing grey cat by the scruff of its neck and hurls it into the cage, then slams down the hatch and padlocks it shut. You can stay there until you learn to control yourself! Control!

The man leaves, and the little boy cuddles the cat, murmuring softly while he strokes its fur, keeping it close for comfort.

Holy hell. Swallowing hard, I stood up, trying to wrap my head around what I'd just seen.

This was yet another awful way the grandfather had punished the boy — by locking him in a freaking cage. And leaving him there for … how long? Long enough and often enough that the poor kid had squirreled away a source of light and something to do while imprisoned like an animal in this dark, dank hole. What kind of monster could do that to a little child? A psychopath, that was who. A stone-cold psychopath with uncontrollable anger and no empathy. The violent man I'd seen in my visions was looking more and more like the Button Man to me. Hadn't he told his daughter to button her lips? That was basically what the serial killer had done with his victims.

I needed fresh air and light. Rubbing my hands against my jeans as if that could wipe them clean of the painful echo they'd detected, I hurried out of the manure cellar and headed back across the farmyard toward the house. Righteous anger swelled inside me — anger at the man who'd abused the boy and at the mother who hadn't protected her son. Sure, she must've been terrified, too, her self-esteem and self-confidence broken down by abuse throughout her life, but parents were supposed to love and protect their children, no matter what. Life on this little farm had been ugly and miserable. I wondered if anyone in the outside world had ever known the extent of it.

I skirted the house, passing the huge beech tree, the only healthy, solid thing still in this place. Its gray bark, wrinkled and scarred as elephant hide, was patchworked with blue and yellow lichen, and above, a canopy of leaves trembled in the breeze. Just beyond the tree, a collapsed trellis lay on the ground, its wooden frame now food for termites and beetles.

When I touched it, the dim glimmer of an image flickered behind my eyes: sunburned hands picking a tomato and passing it to a smaller set of hands marked with raised circles of scaly skin. Ringworm.

My visions, both the actual seeing of them plus the emotional weight of what I'd unearthed, had left me dog-tired. I wanted nothing more than to get away from the place, to drive home and console myself with tea and toast and a hot bath, but I sensed that the hardest part still lay ahead. The darkness beyond the beech tree invited me closer. My feet, obeying the increasing pull, stumbled over rocks and clumps of rough grass. Above the background buzz of insects and the wheezing *oh-oh* of some bird, I could hear the thump of my heart. Somehow, I could hear the darkness too. And feel it. I heard it in my chest, not my ears. I felt it behind my eyes.

The sensations intensified as I drew closer to the structure that sat in the darkness clouding my vision. It was a small brick building only about five feet high, with a rusty tin roof and a low flap door for access. I came to a halt at an invisible border about ten feet away from the hut, fear overtaking curiosity. My mind told me to go on and investigate. My body ordered me to back off and run away. It felt like a strong magnet at the core of that dark place was repelling another inside my gut, yet I felt compelled to go inside.

Taking a deep, uneven breath, I stepped over the line.

– 25 –

Shoulders tense, limbs heavy, feet reluctant — my body protested every step I took nearer to the small brick structure. I hesitated for a moment, listening for any warning Colby might be sending me, but heard only the buzz of insects. Before I could think better of it, I lifted the flap covering the opening, crouched down and crawled inside.

At once, my chest hurt as though it was being squeezed. I couldn't take a full breath, and cold sweat beaded my top lip, yet I could see nothing scary in there: a dirt floor, a low metal roof, a rolled-up rope ladder, a covered tubular shaft sunk in the middle with a hand pump beside. This must be an old well house. I shone my phone's light around the interior, nibbling a fingernail. Then remembering what all I'd touched that day, I dropped my hand.

The bones of some long-dead critter — a raccoon or squirrel, perhaps — lay on an old newspaper against one wall. Wanting to see the date on the paper to get an idea of when the farm had last been occupied, I brushed the small skull aside with the back of my hand.

A cat.
A gray cat hisses and writhes under the booted foot
pinning it to the ground.
A rock smashes down onto its head. It lies twitching and
bleeding on the dirt.
A hand in a dirty work glove holds a bowie knife. The
blade flashes in the light, then plunges down.

I jerked upright, banging my head on the roof and dropping my phone. Flakes of rust rained down on me, and spots of light popped in my vision. Staggering back from the bones, I braced a hand on the lid of the well to keep from falling.

The man shouts, his face mottled red with rage. Idiot!
Look at what you made me do. Can't you get anything
right?
He stares down into the wide well. It's fallen right down
to the bottom! Go get the ladder. You're going to go
down there and fetch it back, you stupid excuse for a—
The metal teeth of a green-handled rake shove into his
chest, once and then again.
The man grunts, steps back, and opens his mouth to yell.
The rake is thrust once more. Harder.
The angry man grabs the head of the rake and tries to
wrest it away from his attacker. But a hard shove sends
him stumbling backward. He tumbles over the edge of
the well and falls into the tunnel of darkness below.
A moment of silence, then a bellow of pain and rage.
Curses echo up from the hole. Orders to fetch the ladder.

Warnings of vengeance and payback.

The person holding the rake doesn't move.

The shouting continues and then a banging rises from inside the well. Next comes the sound of a rock hitting stone over and over again. After a long while, the banging stops, replaced by a scream of incomprehensible fury.

At the top, the presence waits, silent and patient, a spark of joy flickering inside.

The yells subside into pleas for help. The man begs, promises to change, to be better.

Up in the well house, the flame of joy grows.

The cries from the well slow and weaken. There will be no reprisals, he promises. Just let him out, just drop the ladder. Hoarsely now: he's hurt, his hip is broken and maybe a rib. He can't breathe. He's suffocating. It's cold and wet. Get him out of there. Please, please!

When the weeping starts, the presence slides the cap over the top of the well, trapping the sobs inside.

Trembling, I fell to my knees and vomited. When all that was left was empty retching, I wiped my mouth on my sleeve and reached for my phone.

"I told you not to call me" was Singh's greeting.

"And I told you I could find more to do with this case."

"Whatever you think you've found—"

"I have a jurisdictional question. If I'm at the scene of crime — a murder or an attempted murder that I think is related to the Button Man killer — should I notify the local police department or the FBI field office in Albany?"

I could almost hear Singh's inner struggle in the long silence on the other end. He *so* did not want to have anything more to do with me.

"Where are you?" he asked eventually, and I told him.

After the call, I went back to my car, cleaned my hands with the wipes from my mother's backpack, and rinsed my mouth out with water, mentally adding a toothbrush and toothpaste to my growing list of essential private eye equipment. Then I made another call.

"Hey, Garnet," Ryan said. "How are you doing?"

"Hey," I said. "Remember how I told you that I was hunting for a particular house and barn?"

"Yeah."

"Well, I found it."

"The one you saw in your vision?"

"Uh-huh. And I think maybe I found a body too." Had I, though? Suddenly, I had doubts. The body felt both there and not there.

Ryan cursed. "Where are you now?"

"On a farm outside of Crowbury, in Caledonia county."

He cursed again. "I have no jurisdiction there."

I paused, then said, "I wasn't calling you in an official capacity."

"I'm on my way," he said at once.

"No, that's not necessary," I found myself saying, even though I wished he were there to hold me; I couldn't stop shivering. "I just needed to hear a friendly voice, you know? I'll be okay in a minute or two. I'm just a little spooked."

I told him what I'd found and seen in my visions, and I felt calmer afterward. Something about putting it into words helped corral the crazy foulness into a describable experience, and I could feel my heartrate slowing. Of course, that might have been the effect of Ryan's calm voice and empathic responses.

"Are you sure you don't want me to drive up?" he offered again at the end of our chat.

"No, by the time you get here, Singh will already have evicted me." The agent had said he was in Montpelier for a meeting; he'd be at the farm within the hour. "I'll see you tonight?"

"Call as soon as you're back in town, and I'll come over with a pizza and a bottle of wine."

"And a shoulder. I might need to discharge some eye water."

"I'll bring two."

I scratched at my hand, trying to remove a splinter, while my mind raced, attempting to put together the mismatched pieces of what I'd seen. I knew the man who'd been pushed into the well was the same man I'd seen in my previous visions, though he'd looked older and meaner. Strangely, my feeling about whether the body was still down there kept waxing and waning.

I hadn't seen who'd attacked him. The most likely candidate, I figured, was the woman, the boy's mother. I could easily picture a scene where she finally reached a point where she couldn't stomach it anymore and got rid of the man who'd made her and her son's lives a living torment. But could it possibly have been the little boy, several years older and possibly bolder than the timid kid I'd seen in the cage? Maybe he'd done it as revenge for his grandfather killing his cherished cat. I had to concede that it could have been anyone, even a fed-up farm worker or another relative. There would've been many people with a grudge against such a horrible individual.

I felt bone-tired and confused but good, proud of myself for finding something that even *Senior* Special Agent Singh with all his arrogant condescension wouldn't be able to dismiss. After this, he'd have to admit I had a genuine and useful ability, and going forward, he'd have to include me in the investigation. For the first time since I'd been fished out of that icy pond and yanked back from the beyond, I felt like I knew, at least a little, what I was doing. I was a psychic investigator, and whoever didn't like it could suck it.

– 26 –

I was resting in my car, fighting off the flashbacks that came every time I closed my eyes, when Singh arrived. He came alone. Clearly, he wanted to make sure this wasn't a false alarm before he declared it a crime scene and summoned backup. He directed a disparaging look at my scruffy appearance — cobwebs and rust flakes in my hair, dirt on my clothes and face, and mud slimed over my Doc Martins — and wrinkled his nose, no doubt catching a whiff of vomit. While waiting, I'd caught a glimpse of myself in my car's side mirror but could find neither the energy nor the inclination to give a rat's ass about how I looked.

"Where's this supposed crime scene?" Singh asked.

I led the way to the well house, stopped several yards away, and pointed. "In there. In the well."

Seeming to feel no hesitation at that border of darkness *I* could all but see and touch, Singh marched up to the well house, wedged the flap open, and stuck his head inside. Looking back over his shoulder at me, he said, "You'd better not have called me out for a dead possum."

"It's a cat. It was once gray."

He gave me a look. It wasn't an appreciative one. "What makes you think a murder or attempted murder happened here?"

"I saw it. I mean," I added quickly, "I didn't *see* it see it, but I *saw* it."

He rolled his eyes.

"And there are human remains inside the well. At least, I think there are," I said.

"You *think*?" Without waiting for an answer, he went inside the little building and inspected the lid of the well. I knew what he was observing: spiderwebs, a thick layer of dust, and a frosting of rust from the roof.

"How can you possibly know what's down there?" he demanded. "This well cap hasn't been moved in years."

"I *saw,*" I said again. "A man, mid-fifties maybe, was pushed into the well. He was wearing dirty blue overalls, and his hip was likely broken. A rib, too, maybe."

"Is this vomit yours?"

"Yes," I said, bending down so I could see what he was doing. "Sorry."

Singh pulled on a pair of latex gloves, heaved off the heavy well cap, and peered down into the well. "It's black as pitch in there." With a stern warning not to touch anything, he exited the hut, stalked back to his car, and returned brandishing a Maglite as large as a baton. No friendly cartoons on the side of Agent Singh's flashlight, no, sir.

Noticing the pair of handcuffs he was clipping to his belt, I frowned. "He's been dead a while, Agent. I don't think he's going to be resisting arrest."

"They're not for him," Singh said darkly.

Wonderful. So if he didn't find anything in the well, he'd arrest me for wasting police time. And just like that, I was back to biting my nails. Singh, meanwhile, shone the strong beam down into the stygian depths of the shaft then hung the rope ladder over the well wall so that it dangled inside. He climbed over and disappeared from view. When he emerged ten minutes later, he stared at me for several long seconds.

"What did you see?" I asked, wondering if he was going to cuff me or congratulate me.

Neither, as it turned out.

"I'll tell you what I didn't see," he said. "A body."

"No body? Oh," I said, deflated. "Well, maybe that's because—"

But Singh didn't want to hear my excuses or qualifications. "Come with me," he ordered.

I trailed him back to where our cars were parked, puzzling over what it meant that there was no body in the bottom of the well. If the old man wasn't still down there, he must've been rescued. He would've been seriously pissed, possibly enough to murder whoever had put him in the well. That might be why I'd had a strong sense of death. And if the person he'd killed had been his grandson, that would explain why there were no more height lines for the kid after he was fifteen. If the old man was still alive, then he could easily be that mean old man at the creepy house in Hucknall.

When we reached our cars, I slouched against my Honda, pretending to be checking my phone while I eavesdropped on

Singh, who was making a series of phone calls to the local cops, Agent Washington, a specialized recovery and CSI team, and others.

"If you didn't find a body, why the need for all the experts?" I challenged him.

"I saw some … things which might — *might* — be evidence, and I need specialists to check them out," Singh replied.

"Oh!" I said, feeling a little cheered by this. "So there was *something?* Did you find a bunch of animal skeletons down there?" Maybe the killer had slain loads of little animals, and *that* was the reason for the sense of death in wellhouse.

Instead of answering, Singh demanded, "How did you find this place?"

I explained about my visions and the search for the right barn and house.

"Did you touch anything here?" he asked.

I fessed up about all the surfaces I'd touched in the house, barn, and well house. He was seriously annoyed — shocker — and said I'd have to have my prints taken for exclusion purposes.

"Sure," I said. "But what exactly did you see down in the well?"

He ignored me.

"Did you notice the newspaper under the cat bones? Did you check the date?" I pressed.

He answered an incoming call and grunted terse answers. "Yes … Possibly, and a 10-45 … one team should do it. And did you remember to— Good, thanks."

When he ended the call, he took my statement, writing down what I said and recording it on his phone too. I took perverse delight in describing my visions and the accompanying feelings in minute detail, enjoying the discomfort I knew this caused him. Local police arrived first, taped off the scene, and spoke to Singh out of range of my hearing. Then a couple of FBI agents and a crime scene team pulled in and trooped off toward the well house. After getting my fingerprints taken, I crept closer to the action but was blocked by Singh.

To my surprise, he told me I was free to go but warned me to say nothing to the press. "Not a single word! I mean it."

I tried again to get more information from him and to persuade him to let me touch whatever they recovered, and once more, I struck out.

"Ms. McGee, I am under no obligation to give you any details, let alone involve you in this investigation. This is official business, and you are a civilian."

"I'm more than that, and you know it." I couldn't believe he was still dismissing me, still acting like I hadn't just found something really important. "Why won't you let me help you?"

He blew out an annoyed breath. "Why on earth would I trust you with confidential information?"

"Because I found this. I helped your serial killer investigation."

"You found an abandoned house and a well. No body. No evidence of a crime having been committed. And no proof that this is in any way related to my investigation."

"You found something relevant. I know you did. You just won't tell me what it is." Incensed by his refusal to reply or acknowledge the truth of my involvement, I snapped, "Dammit, Singh, you owe me!"

"I owe you *nothing*. You trampled all over a possible crime scene, vomited, and touched everything in sight, contaminating the area with your biological evidence. Then you called me out on the basis of a mere hunch."

A flush crept up my neck. "What will it take for you to trust me?"

"A badge. Nothing less than an FBI or a police officer badge."

"But I don't want to be a police officer or an FBI agent."

"Then stop trying to act like one!" Summoning an agent to escort me off the premises, Singh asked her, "Any media out there?"

"So far, just one reporter from the local rag and a few looky-loos," she said.

"Do you have something to cover your face?" Singh asked me.

Was he being protective of me or just trying to cover his butt by not wanting the media to see me? Either way, it was probably a good suggestion. I put on my sunglasses and a floppy sunhat from my mother's backpack and, before I left, gave it one last shot with Singh.

"No one needs to know I'm helping you," I told him softly. "We could meet somewhere else, like we did before. At my mom and dad's house?"

The mention of that occasion seemed to flip a switch in Singh. He glared at me and, between gritted teeth, said, "Not a chance."

"But—"

"It was an error of judgement for me to have allowed you anywhere near this investigation in the first place, and I am not going to repeat it, especially since I now know that you're related to someone who was a person of interest in this investigation."

"Related to— *What?*" I said, bewildered.

"Didn't see that one coming, did you? A major failure for a psychic who's lived with the man for years."

"Are you— are you talking about my *father*? No way!"

"Get her off my crime scene," Singh told the agent.

"Wait!" I said furiously as she laid a hand on my shoulder. "What did you mean about my father?"

"Ask *him,*" Singh said coldly. "Or better yet, touch his watch or something."

He stalked off, and I gaped after him, my mind reeling.

The agent took my elbow and steered me to my car. "I'll drive ahead of you to the police cordon," she said, "then move the barriers for you to drive through. Don't make eye contact with anyone, and don't say anything to the media. I'll follow you for a couple of miles to make sure you're not followed. Which way are you headed?"

"Uh," I said, trying to gather my teeming thoughts. "Into town. I, uh, I need to grab something to eat before I drive back to Pitchford."

I wanted to speed home and ask my father what the hell Singh was talking about, but I needed to shelve that for now because there was more work to do while I was in this neck of the woods. I wanted to ask around about the farm and the family who'd once lived there. Besides, I *was* starving.

And I could delay speaking to my dad because I knew there was no way he was a suspect in the killings. Yeah, there had been a brief period of paranoia about my father's fishing trips back when I'd been investigating Colby's death, but back then I'd been fresh from taking a couple of knocks to the head and dying. My brains had been scrambled. Now, however, I wasn't going to make the same stupid mistake again. I knew who my father was, and he wasn't a killer, not even of fish.

I got into my car, cracked my neck, which had gotten progressively stiffer and sorer during the course of the morning, and started the engine. As I drove past the cluster of people who'd gathered to watch, I caught a glimpse of a thin white face with a mostly bald head. A reporter stepped up to my window, shouting something at me and blocking my line of sight. When I could see again, the man was gone.

I knew it must've been a trick of my imagination, but for a split-second there, I could've sworn I'd spotted Professor Bradley Deaver.

– 27 –

I found a diner on the main street of Crowbury, took a stool at the lunch counter, and scanned a syrup-sticky laminated menu. There were no fancy risottos or ravioli here; it was all stick-to-your ribs fare. I ordered a burger with extra bacon, a side of fries and a Miller Lite, and then made a pitstop at the restroom. A woman with a toddler gave me an unflattering once-over as I came out of the toilet stall. I scrubbed my hands, washed my face, combed fingers through my hair, and wiped my smudged eyeliner and mascara away as best I could. When I returned to my seat, I downed a good half of my beer in one long swallow.

While I waited for my food, I chatted with the waitress, a forty-something woman with soft features and bad highlights, asking her about the old house with the round red barn outside of town.

"That old wreck?" she said. "It's been empty for years."

"Do you know who used to live there? I'm thinking of a family with a woman and her little boy, and an older man who was maybe her father?"

"Yeah, I remember them. The Kellys, I think." She turned to an old woman nursing a cup of coffee at the far end of the counter and said, "Ruth, what was the name of those folk who lived out on the dairy farm with the round barn?"

"Kehoe," the woman said.

"That's right, Kehoe. The girl was called Mary Kay, like the cosmetics, that much I remember. But her father … Now, what was Mary Kay's father called, Ruth?"

The woman scrunched up one eye and rolled the other skyward as if searching the heavens for the answer. "Might've been Melvin. Or Marvin. Can't say for sure. We always just called him Mr. Kehoe."

"And the little boy?" I asked.

"I'm pretty sure he was called Derek," the waitress said. "I was a grade below him at school. Derek Kehoe," she said, testing the sound of it for recognition. "Yup, that's it."

"Was that the whole family?"

"Was that the whole family, Ruth?" she asked the old woman.

"I think there were some relatives in New Hampshire, but I don't know anything about them."

At the ping of a bell, the waitress fetched my burger from the serving hatch and set it down in front of me. It didn't look half bad, but the knife and fork were smudgy with fingerprints, so I went in with my fingers.

"Do you have any hot sauce?" I asked the waitress after a bite of the burger.

"Of course," she said and brought me a bottle of sriracha.

I squirted a blob onto my plate and taste-tested with a

French fry. Too sweet, very salty, disappointingly tame. "What happened to the Kehoe family?" I asked. "The farm is completely deserted now."

"Oh yeah, it's been empty for years and years," she replied. "I don't remember the whole story. But Ruth will know; she knows everything about this town. And she'll keep talking as long as you keep feeding her. You up for that?"

"Sure," I said.

"Ruth, this nice young lady wants to buy you lunch and pick your brains."

The old woman beckoned me over. I grabbed my food and beer, leaving the mild sauce behind, and walked to her end of the counter.

When I was two seats away, she held up a hand. "That's close enough."

I sat down, taking in her appearance: white hair, black eyes, a sharp rabbit's chin, and the wrinkled lips and stained fingers of a lifelong smoker. I estimated her to be pushing ninety but her gaze, when she studied me, was clear and shrewd.

"Interested in the Kehoes, eh? Why's that?" she asked. "You one of those researchers who writes up the family histories?"

"Exactly right." I grabbed a menu and passed it to her. "What'll it be?"

Waving away the menu, she told the waitress, "Liz, I'll have the meatloaf with gravy, mashed potatoes, and green beans. And you can throw in a side of fried onion rings and" — she considered my food — "another of crispy bacon. Just pile it all up on the one plate. And a short stack of pancakes with blueberries for after."

"And to drink?" Liz asked.

"Just keep the coffee coming."

"You got it."

Ruth rubbed her hands together, either in anticipation of the feast headed her way or the opportunity to gossip, and said, "The old Kehoe place was originally a dairy farm. That's why they had a cow on top of their weathervane. Did you see it?"

"The cow part is gone," I said.

She nodded, seeming unsurprised. "Juvenile delinquents, that'll be. It's getting as we'll all soon have to lock our doors. Last week, they stole my garden gnome and stuck the poor thing headfirst into the mud at the pond. And don't get me started on the timber thieves or the hog-snatchers." She craned her neck to check the food hatch then glanced at the front windows, where a state police car with lights flashing was passing by. "See what I mean?"

I nodded and gave a what's-the-world-coming-to kind of shrug, even though I suspected the police were headed to the farm with the mysterious well house rather than chasing down pig thieves. "The Kehoe's farm?" I prompted.

"Kehoe bought it … oh, that must have been in the late fifties or early sixties. It was a going concern then but not doing too good. Already, the commercial farms were doing it bigger and better, driving the small outfits out of business. Kehoe and his wife — a pretty young thing, she was — tried to make a go of it for many years, but it was a struggle, and then along came Belle."

"Who was Belle?"

"*What* was Belle, you mean." She blew on the coffee Liz

brought her. "Belle was a hurricane. Made landfall down on Long Island before it turned inland. We had floods and drownings and power lines down for days. Bridges and trees washed away, and enough rain to float Noah's boat. President Gerald Ford declared us a disaster area." She sounded proud of the distinction. "Kehoe and his wife were out trying to save the cows from the flood when the river broke its banks, and she was swept away. It got most of the cows too. Kehoe was left alone with a teenage daughter, no more'n a handful of animals, and no money to start afresh. And things just kinda went downhill after that."

"What did he do then?" I asked.

"Kehoe? He got a job in town, at a store that sold all kinds of fabric and ribbons, sewing machines, yarn, and needles, that kind of stuff. He wound up buying that store from the old owner eventually."

Her food arrived then — a great mound that my mother would've called "a dog's breakfast." Deaver, with his preference for obsessively tidy piles of food, would no doubt have fled the diner, traumatized, but Ruth tucked in with relish.

"Where was I?" she asked around a mouthful of meatloaf.

"Kehoe's fabric store," I said. "Did he sell buttons?"

"Oh Lord, yes!" She dispatched a few forks full of mashed potatoes and gravy. "He had 'em stored in tubes with a button stuck on the lid and then stacked on these shelves that went nigh up to the roof. Any kind of button you wanted, he had it. People came from all over the state to buy their sewing paraphernalia from him. And he did well too. Better than he ever did dairy farming, anyway." Loading bacon onto meatloaf, she crowned it with an onion ring, popped it into her mouth, chewed and swallowed. "Well, I guess wool and cotton are easier than cows. They don't want milking at dawn, don't catch blackleg or bluetongue, and don't kick you when you tug their teats too hard."

We both ate in silence for a while, then I asked, "And his daughter?"

"Mary Kay left school early, didn't she? That old man wanted her working in the business, hauling down the bolts of cloth and cutting with those giant scissors, because by then he was already starting to get the arthritis." She paused with a tower of green beans and potatoes loaded on her fork. "You reckon being pessimistic and bitter can put acid in your bones and make 'em grow all crooked?"

"I don't th— … I mean, perhaps?"

"'Cause he was not what you'd call a happy man." She popped the food into her mouth and chewed meditatively. "Kehoe could look out on a sunny field of flowers and see only weeds that needed poisoning. It didn't rain for a week, he'd be calling it a drought and bitchin' about his vegetable patch."

"He grew tomatoes, I think?"

"We *all* did that. Back in the day, we were self-sufficient. Grew our own food and made our own bread and moonshine."

She glanced around the diner, and I couldn't tell whether her deep sigh was one of disgust at the softness of the modern generation or of satisfaction with the enormous meal she'd scored from one of them. She leaned away from the counter, stretching her belly and belching into her hand. Then she tucked back in, hoovering up her food with impressive efficiency.

I ate a few more fries and, when she came up for air, asked, "Anything else you can tell me about Kehoe?"

She twisted her mouth and shook her head, as though saddened by her paucity of information on the man. "We weren't what you would call *friends*. I never could abide a moody man, and he was that all right."

… and then you do what you need to, to fix my mood.

Kehoe's words to his daughter came back to me. He might just have meant she should bake him his favorite pie, but I had a horrible feeling that he'd wanted a different kind of favor from her. Was it possible that Kehoe had been not only Derek's grandfather, but also his father? My stomach turned at the thought.

I finished my beer. I longed for another, but I still had a drive ahead of me, so I opted for coffee instead. The waitress started a fresh pot and above the hiss of the coffee-machine, I asked Ruth, "So, Mary Kay worked for her father in the fabric store?"

"Oh yeah. Well, until she was too far along." Ruth cupped an imaginary nine-months' belly with her hands. "And what a scandal that was!"

$$- 28 -$$

"It was all anyone could talk about for months. You remember, Liz? When the Kehoe girl got herself knocked up the year after her momma died?" Ruth said.

"Well, she was bound to get a bun in the oven sooner or later the way she spread it around," Liz said, bringing Ruth a plate of pancakes.

Ruth clicked her togue in exasperated pity. "She never used to be like that. She was a good girl, quiet, well-mannered, but then her mother died, and I guess the grief changed her. It does that, you know?"

I nodded. I did know. I also knew that it wasn't uncommon for girls who'd been sexually abused to act out sexually.

"Wait," Ruth said when Liz started to clear her plate. "I've still got some bacon and gravy left, don't I?"

At a nearby table, a kid sent a milkshake flying. Liz grabbed a cloth and went to clean up the pink puddle while Ruth drenched her pancakes in syrup and folded one around some gravy-coated bacon, taco-style. Fork halfway to her mouth, she caught my expression. "What? The savory brings out the sweet. Want a taste?"

"I'm good, thanks." I ate the last of my burger and fries, then asked, "How old was Mary Kay when she got pregnant?"

"Fifteen or sixteen, I reckon. Thereabouts, anyway." Another pancake taco followed the first.

"Who was the father?" I asked, trying to keep my tone casual despite my dark suspicions.

"I don't know. I wonder if she even did, poor girl. She just wanted to be loved, you know? They think they've found it with the neighbor's farm hand or the sweet-talking salesman passing through town, but all they get is used," Ruth said and finished the rest of her pancakes.

"How did her father react to the pregnancy?" I asked.

"Not well, I think."

I'd put good money on his reaction having been a lot more negative than that. But maybe he'd only let rip with the abuse in private. It wouldn't have been good to let this town of potential customers know his true nature.

After scraping the last of the syrup off her plate with her fork, Ruth licked it off, looking around as if for the waitress. To place *another* food order? If she kept eating like this, I'd have to pay for the bill by washing dishes; I'd yet to get my first paycheck from Henry Mason.

"He never said a word to me about it," Ruth continued. "And he would pinch his lips up like he was sucking on a lemon if I asked. But I got the sense he thought she was dragging the family name through the dirt even though it was the seventies, and things were changing, you know? Loosening up. And it wasn't like he could've had religious objections. Why, if he ever as much as set foot in a church, I'll eat my hat."

I believed her; this old lady had the appetite of a bird, a pterodactyl.

Another cop car passed the diner. Liz stuck her head out of the door and returned to clear Ruth's plate, telling us that something was clearly happening somewhere but damned if she knew what or where. The old lady watched her plate disappear with the sort of longing look that suggested she'd have liked to lick it clean too.

"And the boy, her son? What was he like?" I asked Ruth.

"Sweet little thing, he was. A bit soft, perhaps, and a little shy."

"How did he get on with others?"

Ruth summoned Liz over and asked, "How'd the Kehoe boy get on with others?"

Liz leaned a hip against the counter, settling in for a good gossip. "Fine. He was a bit quiet — an introvert, I guess — but he had friends. The girls liked him because he was so cute—"

"He looked like a little angel. All big eyes and brown curls," Ruth interjected.

"—and gentle. And the teachers *loved* him," Liz finished.

"Why?" I asked.

"He gave them no trouble, I guess, and he really was very cute."

"And real helpful to his mother and grandfather," Ruth said, smiling fondly. "When he wasn't at school, he was doing all the chores at the homestead or working at the store. The ladies who came in to buy their haberdashery and whatnot used to love to pinch his cheeks and call him cutie pie."

"How did he and his grandfather get on?" I asked.

Ruth thought about that for a moment, sipping on her cold coffee. "I reckon the old man would've liked Derek to be tougher. More of rough-and-tumble boy, you know?"

"He thought the boy was too soft?" I suggested.

She nodded slowly. "He was a little hard on the kid, maybe."

Lady, you don't know the half of it.

"I remember I once went into Kehoe's store to buy a zipper for a dress." A dreamy smile crept over Ruth's face. "Silver satin, it was and tight in all the right places. You wouldn't know it to see me now, but I was once a hot tamale!"

"I can imagine," I said, smiling.

"Anyhow, I was there in the store when what should happen but a bunch of people come in squawking, carrying the boy — limp as a noodle and out cold, he was! He'd been hit by a car in the street outside, see? They said he got catapulted into the air and landed square on his nut."

"How old was he then?" I asked.

Ruth looked at Liz, who said, "Around thirteen or fourteen, maybe?"

"Yup, could be," Ruth said. "Well, his mother took one look at him — as pale as a November frost and bleeding from the head — and she panicked and started screaming. The old man told her to wait in the storeroom because her hysterics weren't helping the situation. I thought that was a bit harsh, I don't mind saying. But she did as she was told. Well, I always thought she was a timid, mousy little creature, but judge not lest ye be judged, as the Good Book says.”

“Did she *ever* stand up to her father?” I asked. “Do you think she might ever have confronted him about being too tough on her or her kid?”

Ruth canvassed Liz’s opinion on this, placing an order for an iced coffee at the same time.

“You knew her better than I did,” Liz replied, tumbling ice cubes into a blender.

Ruth nodded, conceding the point.

“You want whipped cream on top?” Liz asked above the noise of the machine.

“Load her up!” Ruth yelled back. When the racket subsided, she said, “I’m battling to imagine Mary Kay taking on her father, but you never really know folks, do you? They can look like the sort who wouldn’t say boo to a goose, but inside, they could be boiling mad.”

“Folks,” Liz said, setting a tall glass of iced coffee topped with swirls of cream and drizzles of chocolate sauce in front of Ruth, “can be pushed too far.”

“Anyhow,” Ruth said, admiring her towering beverage, “when they laid the boy on the fabric cutting table, Kehoe moved a bolt of cloth away so it wouldn’t get blood on it. Worried about his fabric at a moment like that, can you believe it?”

All too easily.

“I can still see it as clear as if it happened yesterday.” Ruth paused to consider and eat a spoon of whipped cream. “Well, as clear as last year, anyhow.”

“What happened then?” I asked.

Ruth stuck a straw in her drink and slurped up a good third of it at once. "The boy came around and started crying, clutching his head. Well, I reckon it would've been hurting like heck. And Kehoe told him to get control of himself, to be a brave boy and stop crying. As if he didn't want the folks in the store to think his grandson was a pansy. By then, the boy had a goose egg swelling up on his head."

"Did he get taken to a hospital for a head scan?" I said.

"We didn't have a hospital in town, but Kehoe said he'd take the boy to Doc Caruthers to check and see if he was okay."

I wondered if that had ever happened. Based on the visions I'd seen, I doubted it. If these ladies were anything to go by, the townsfolk hadn't known a fraction of what went on at the Kehoe farm. They'd thought Kehoe was just a hard man made bitter by life, that he was a little unsympathetic with his daughter and wanted to toughen up his grandson. But I knew how truly abusive he'd been to both. My heart went out to the gentle little boy who didn't fit his grandfather's ideas of how a "real boy" should look and behave and feel. No wonder he never caused trouble at school — he needed someplace where he could be relatively happy and free from harsh criticism and punishment.

"Was Derek any different after that accident?" I asked the two ladies.

"He had a dent right here." Liz touched the right side of her forehead. "It never filled in or popped out again. He took to combing his hair over it to hide it, though some kids still teased him about it."

"And did he behave differently? Would you say his personality changed?"

Liz laughed. "*All* our personalities changed. We were teenagers! But Derek wasn't brain-damaged or anything, if that's what you're asking."

"What happened to Mr. Kehoe?" I asked.

"Didn't they send him to a nursing home in New Hampshire?" Liz asked Ruth.

Ruth stopped sucking on her straw to shake her head. "Way I heard it, he went to live with family there. He was tired of working in the store and wanted to spend his retirement with his elder brother. Or was it a cousin?"

Had Kehoe died in the well? Or had he left the farm because he was growing frail and was no longer confident he could keep his family in line? Maybe Mary Kay and Derek had insisted he leave. If he was the Button Man, then he might've been happy to go because he would've had even more freedom to drive around, looking for victims. Had he wound up in Hucknall playing tic-tac-toe with teeth?

Liz answered the phone, and her expression grew increasingly surprised as she took down what seemed to be the details of a huge take-out order. I guessed the cops and agents at the Kehoe farm where getting hungry. It wouldn't be long before the news hit the diner; I needed to hurry.

"When did Mr. Kehoe leave Crowbury?" I asked Ruth.

"You sure do want a lot of detail. I wouldn't have thought anyone would be much interested in the Kehoe history," she said, eyes narrowed in suspicion.

"More food?" I asked. "Coffee?"

"In a minute. Just got to let the pancakes settle a bit. Now, what did you ask me?"

"When did Kehoe leave town?"

"Well, it was after my Walter died. I know that, and he passed in 1992. And it was before my youngest got married because he wasn't in the store anymore when we bought the lace for her dress, so I'd say somewhere in the mid-nineties."

"Did you ever see him again?"

Both ladies shook their heads.

"So once Mr. Kehoe was gone, did Mary Kay run the store?" I asked.

"Yes, with the help of her 'lodger,'" Ruth said with another cackle.

Liz drew in an excited breath. "I'd forgotten about him!"

— 29 —

A lodger at the Kehoe place — this was interesting. "Can you tell me more about him?" I asked Ruth and Liz.

"I sure can," Ruth said. "He had dark hair and a big smile, and he was young — a good five, maybe even ten, years younger than Mary Kay. The rumor was that she was more than just his landlady, if you know what I mean? Ah well, a lot of the ladies in town had a crush on him. He wasn't bad looking if you like 'em slicked-back and smooth-talking. A real charmer, as you'd say." She shrugged. "Plus, he was new."

By which I gathered that in an old small town like Crowbury, novelty was in short supply. Ruth turned her attention back to her iced coffee, and Liz weighed in with her opinion.

"He wasn't as handsome as he thought he was, but when you're confident, people don't tend to notice," she said. "When he came sliding into town in that car of his—"

"What kind of a car was it?" I asked.

"A Thunderbird, same as my Aunt Nancy's."

"What color was the car? The lodger's, I mean," I said.

"Something dark, I think. Can't really remember. It sure wasn't white with black racing stripes like Aunt Nancy's." Liz topped off my coffee mug and gave a big sigh. "She wrapped that automobile around a tree two hours into 2000 after celebrating that the world hadn't ended."

I stayed silent for a few respectful seconds while we all contemplated the irony of that, then I cleared my throat and asked, "Was he a white guy or—"

"White. Like most folks around here," Ruth said.

"And did he use to pick up hitchhikers?"

"Now how in the world would we know *that*?" Liz said.

"And why would you want to? It's not even about the Kehoes," Ruth pointed out.

I blew on my coffee and then sipped it, buying time to come up with an excuse. "Thing is, I'm thinking of turning the history into a book, so it really helps to get these little details. Fills in the picture, you know?"

"A writer, huh? Well, that explains it," Ruth said in the tones of someone who clearly believed writers were a strange breed and there was no accounting for their ways.

"Can you remember the lodger's name?" I kept my fingers crossed under the counter. I needed to catch a lucky break here.

"Larry," Ruth said confidently. "I remember thinking of him as Larry the Lounge Lizard, because he was an oily one, you know? And a drinker, you could smell it on his breath."

"And his surname?"

Ruth frowned, tugged on an earlobe, and consulted the ceiling again. "Smith, maybe? Or Jones. Something common like that." I must have looked disappointed because she added, "Sorry, hon. Liz, can you remember his last name?"

"I remember he took his coffee white and sweet," Liz told me. "Some people have a memory for names, others for faces. Me, I got a memory for beverages."

"Would anyone else in town remember?" I asked.

"Some drifter from twenty-something years ago?" Ruth laughed.

Liz said, "If Ruth don't remember, you can bet your bottom dollar no one else will either."

Ruth chased the last of her iced coffee around the bottom of her glass with loud slurps. "Anyhoozle, Larry stayed at the Kehoe place and worked in their store. Supposedly, he was paying room and board to help poor Mary Kay out, but we all wondered if he was just a sponger, you know? Because he had that way about him."

"What way?"

"Too friendly."

Spoken like a true New England native.

"Was he ever *not* friendly?" I asked them. "Ever see him lose his temper?"

Ruth shook her head, but Liz said, "There was one time he got into it with Chuck Robbins from the feed store. Chuck ran a Wednesday night poker game there, and I don't know exactly what happened, but one day, he had a black eye, and I asked who did it." Lowering her voice, she said, "I wanted to congratulate them, you know, because Chuck was a real ass wipe. And he said it was Larry who did it."

"Larry beat up Chuck?" Ruth dabbed at her mouth with a napkin. "That surprises me."

"I was pretty surprised, too, because he didn't seem the type, did he?" Liz said.

"Exactly. He was a lover, not a fighter," Ruth said. "Always touching the ladies on their elbows, complimenting them on their dress or hair, sniffing at them like a dog looking for something to eat, letting his hand dip to fondle their rear ends, and more besides when he got them behind the shelves, I reckon."

Liz tilted her head, considering this. "You know, I always wondered if all that hound-dogging was just an act."

Ruth looked puzzled. "What do you mean?"

"Like maybe he preferred men but didn't want anyone to know?" Liz said uncertainly.

"You think he was a *homosexual?*" Ruth said, sounding flabbergasted. "But … but he was always groping girls. And what about him and Mary Kay? And what about Tiffany?"

"Who's Tiffany?" I asked.

"The young girl he left pregnant when he ran out of town!" Ruth said. "How'd he knock her up if he didn't get it up for females?"

"We don't know for sure it was him," Liz pointed out. "Maybe it was just convenient to blame it on him because he was gone. It would've let the real culprit — and I have my suspicions about who *that* might be — right off the hook." Ruth still looked unconvinced and Liz continued, "My husband always thought so too, and he wasn't the only one. He told me how one of the boys at the bar once made a comment insinuating Larry might be gay, and Larry saw red and went in swinging. He said it took a couple of guys to pull him off! I'd forgotten about that incident," she said to me. "I guess that was another time he was violent."

"Liz, I believe I'm going to need another cup of coffee," Ruth said, looking shocked that, at her age, she was still capable of being surprised by the nature of mankind. But she soon rallied to declare, "Well, one thing I *can* tell you about Larry for sure is that he was always more talk than action. He had an opinion on everything and most of it hooey if you ask me."

"You think he was a liar?" I asked.

"He was one of those people always telling stories about himself. Some of them were sob stories about how bad his childhood was, which just melted the ladies' hearts because there's nothing a silly woman wants more than to fix a broken man. And some of the stories were the kind that made him look grand. Like, he wore this flashy ring on his pinkie and said it was a class ring from his old school."

"Which school?" I asked, desperate for any fact I could actually follow up on.

"A swanky one, ivy league, but don't ask me which. Point is, I didn't believe it for a moment. I figured he'd picked that ring up in a pawn shop somewhere and concocted a story to go with it. Anyhow, next thing we knew, *he* was running the store."

"So he arrived in town only after Melvin or Marvin Kehoe d—" I caught myself and finished, "Departed?"

Liz and Ruth put their heads together to discuss this but couldn't reach consensus.

"Before or after, he was soon the one behind the counter, giving instructions and running the store." Ruth gave a disgusted snort. "Running it all the way into the ground. Pilfering from the register, no doubt, and not buying new stock. There's a fashion in fabrics, you know, same as everything else, and he wasn't staying with the trends. Place got an old, neglected feel. Dusty and dull. Soon the ladies weren't giggling at being sassed; they were taking their business elsewhere."

"Shouldn't Derek have run the store once his grandfather was gone?" I said.

"He certainly would've done a better job of it. But he was still young, maybe eighteen or thereabouts, and didn't have much of a say, I guess. So he worked the farm all day while Larry and Mary Kay canoodled in the store."

Liz looked like she doubted the canoodling part, but she merely said, "That poor woman."

Ruth nodded sadly. "She must've thought the business was going to recover with him at the helm because he talked such a good game, and she probably thought he'd make an honest woman out of her, too, because they'd been bumping uglies for sure" — she shot Liz a defiant glance — "and I daresay she fancied herself in love."

"But he wasn't the marrying kind?" I asked.

"Right in one," Liz said.

"Well, if it has tires or testicles, it's gonna give you trouble." Ruth craned her neck to see what was written on the specials board. "Then one day, he just packed his suitcase and left. He came around town to wish us goodbye and tell us of his grand plans then drove off in his fancy car."

"Did he say why he was leaving?" I asked.

"He said he had a backer for some new business idea, but I figured he needed a new goose to pluck. There wasn't any money left in the business; it had gone under by then. They'd sold everything on clearance and closed it down, and I don't think there could have been much left over after the debts were settled. I could be wrong, though." Leaning closer to me, Ruth confided, "Money and finances and such don't interest me much. I like to know about *people*."

"Me too," I admitted. "Where did he go after Crowbury?"

"Larry?" Ruth said. "Portland, Maine."

"He told *me* San Francisco," Liz said. "Had some offer in a new tech business out in Silicon Valley, he said."

"Well, he definitely told me Portland," Ruth said. "It struck me because I had an old beau living out there who used to send me a birthday card every year. Risqué ones, they were too."

So Larry with the unknown surname had either gone west or east. Great. I'd have no trouble at all tracking him down.

"And a couple of years later, Derek left too," Ruth said. "He must've been around twenty by then and free to seek his fortune."

That pleased me. I was glad he hadn't died at that miserable farm at the tender age of fifteen. I wanted to believe that he'd left this town and never looked back, that he'd shed all the old pain and bad memories like a too-small coat. I hoped with all my heart that he'd built a new and happier life for himself somewhere else and found a terrific therapist to help him deal with the trauma and build his self-esteem.

"And where was Derek headed?" I asked the ladies.

"New Hampshire," Ruth said at the same time as Liz said, "Hucknall, I think."

My ears pricked. "Hucknall, Vermont?"

"Uh-huh. I think his grandmother came from there," Liz replied.

"Not wishing to disagree with you again, Liz," Ruth said, "but I got the idea that he was going to his grandfather's family in New Hampshire."

Liz shrugged. "Well, I guess he could've gone anywhere, but we never saw him again in Crowbury."

"Neither hide nor hair of him," Ruth concurred.

"And he just left his mother behind, alone on the farm?" I said.

"Lord, no! She was dead by then. Didn't I say?"

"That poor woman," Liz said again. "Drowned in the pond on their farm. But *I* heard she had a bottle of vodka in her stomach and rocks in her pockets."

I blew out a long breath. So Derek had lost his mother as well. And in such a difficult way. Having a near relative commit suicide raised his own risk for doing the same, I knew, so maybe the reason no one had ever seen him again was that he'd followed his mother's example. It hurt to consider that possibility.

"If you ask me," Ruth said, "Mary Kay died of a broken heart. Her father had left, the business had tanked, the farm was falling down around their ears, and her *lover*" — another pugnacious look at Liz — "had run off. And what with the money troubles and taking care of the lodgers who came and went, why, she was just used up and worn out. Like an old lady despite she was still young."

"There were more lodgers?" I asked.

"Yeah," Liz said. "They never stayed long, though."

"And the house?"

"It just sat there, crumbling," Ruth said. "I guess what's left of it still belongs to the kid because it never got sold."

She pushed her coffee cup and glass away. Was she finally done eating or just making space for another order?

"There are rumors that farmhouse is haunted," Liz said.

"That's just baloney. There's no such thing as ghosts," Ruth declared, scanning the glass-domed display of pies on the far counter with the kind of serious consideration usually brought to bear on making life-altering decisions. "You can bring me a nice slice of cherry pie, Liz, with two scoops of vanilla ice cream, and then I reckon you can stick a fork in me and call me done."

At that moment, a man with an excited expression came into the diner. "Hi, Liz, Ruth. Did you hear the news?"

That being my cue to skedaddle, I paid the check, thanked the ladies, and hurried out. It was already late afternoon, and I still had a two-and-a-half-hour drive back to Pitchford, so I called Ryan to let him know I'd be too late and too tired to make the date we'd set up earlier.

"Are you okay to drive?" he asked, the real concern in his voice melting another sliver of my heart's frozen shell of protection. "I can drive up and get you."

And I knew he would; it wasn't just an empty offer.

"No, I'll be fine. Really," I said.

"Pull over somewhere safe if you get too tired to drive, and call me, okay?"

"I promise." This time, my fingers weren't crossed.

I drove home, thinking about all I'd learned that day, trying to arrange the pieces into a pattern that made sense. By the time I got home, it was long dark, and I trudged up the stairs to my loft on exhausted autopilot. On the landing outside my door, a bottle of merlot stood beside an insulated bag. I opened the zipper, and the mixed aroma of cheese, pepperoni, and jalapenos wafted out.

"Bless you, Chief," I murmured. A sure way to this woman's heart was through her stomach.

– 30 –

Sunday, April 22

When I woke up late the next morning, I was aware of a distinct lack of rise and shine. If I was a phone battery, I'd have been on about twenty-two percent. All that psychic stuff the day before had drained me, and a night of complicated, distressing dreams hadn't helped. After a breakfast of enough toast and coffee to impress Ruth, I set off for my parents' house, calling Ryan en route to thank him for his thoughtfulness the night before.

"How are you feeling this morning?" he asked.

"Strong as an ox."

"That bad, eh?"

I snorted a laugh. "Pretty much."

"What you need," he said, "is a holiday. A good couple of days at a beach or spa, at least."

"That sounds amazing." The thought of possibly taking a break with Ryan was even more tempting. "But I can't. I've got work to do." The clock was counting down to May sixth, when the Button Man was due to take his next victim.

"Anything I can help you with?" Ryan offered.

"Since you ask ..."

"Uh-oh."

"Could you run a name, a couples of names, through your databases for me?"

"Off the record?"

"Always."

"Sure."

I gave him the names of the Kehoe family, asking him to check possible variations of spelling, and he promised to see what he could do.

At my parents' house, my mother opened the door, delighted by my unexpected visit. "Did you go barn hunting yesterday?" she asked at once. "I bumped into Henry Mason in Dillon's yesterday, and he said you'd set off bright and early."

It was supposed to be me keeping an eye on him, not the other way around. "What was he eating?" I demanded.

"I didn't notice. He said you went alone." There was a definite note of recrimination in her tone.

"Yeah, well," I said, heading toward the kitchen, where I found my father reading the Sunday newspapers over a cup of coffee. "I thought it was going to be another dead end, and I didn't want to waste your time."

"And was it?" my mother asked.

"Was it what?"

"A dead end."

I grimaced wryly. "In a way. I found a site where I think someone was once killed."

That announcement was met with excited exclamations and a barrage of questions, which I tried to answer without giving away too much information. Singh had only cautioned me about talking to the press, but I suspected he wouldn't be too happy if I told my mother and she blabbed to the whole town.

I poured myself a cup of coffee and took a seat at the table. "So, something else strange happened that I wanted to tell you about," I said to my father.

"What was that?" he asked.

I had no idea how to start the conversation tactfully, so I just barreled in. "Is it true that you were a person of interest in the serial killer case I'm investigating?"

"Good heavens!" my mother said crossly while my father tucked his chin back in surprise, saying, "What? Why would— Where did you hear that?"

"Yesterday at that farm. Agent Singh told me."

"I don't trust that man," my mother said. "Did you notice he wouldn't accept any tea or coffee? He didn't even want my water! What's up with that?" She yanked on yellow rubber gloves and began washing dishes.

"He made it sound like you were a suspect," I said to my father

He frowned. "That's not true. I was *never* a suspect. You're not—" My father directed a disbelieving look at me. "You're not thinking I had anything to do with it, are you?"

"No, of course not," I said and meant it. "I was just surprised and curious about it."

He gave me another wary glance. "I happened to be at Lake Winnipesaukee in New Hampshire for a fishing tournament when a young man disappeared in the area. The police went through the campground, taking everyone's details and asking if we'd seen the young man or noticed anything suspicious, that sort of thing. I was briefly questioned — voluntarily, I might add," he said crossly. "And then I was dismissed from the enquiry. I was never a suspect."

I nodded. "I reckon Singh was trying to get under my skin because I've been bothering him."

"Passive-aggressive. I'll bet his star sign is Cancer," my mother said darkly. "Or possibly Scorpio — they can hold grudges for *years*."

I chewed the side of my thumb, tearing at filaments of skin there. I figured that when the agent had come to this house with the button, my father's overly inquisitive behavior had raised his suspicions, leading him to run a check, and the name of Robert John McGee had popped up in some old record of the investigation. Singh couldn't have regarded it too seriously or he'd have been back to interview my father, but it had been a juicy little tidbit to use against me.

"Is that why you've been so interested in this case?" I asked.

He nodded. "That day at the lake when that young man went missing? It was horrible." He rubbed a hand over his face and sighed. "It was that Antoine Marshall. Remember him from the TV program?"

"He was the one that was adopted, wasn't he?" I said.

"That's him."

"So sad," my mother said, stacking a plate on the drying rack.

"I guess the incident was one of the things that sparked my

interest in murder and especially in serial killers," my father said. "But I'm realizing I only ever really read about the killers, not their victims. And now I'm beginning to think that's … a bit off. I mean, it's not entertainment, is it?"

He looked at me with sad eyes, and I reached across the table to squeeze his hand before asking him, "Why didn't you mention it when I had my first brush with this case, back when I found the skeleton?"

He pulled his hand away. "At the time, if you'll remember, you'd been under the misapprehension that I might be involved in Colby's death." He looked really angry at the memory of that, and I felt heat creeping up my neck. "I didn't want to add fuel to the fire of your absurd paranoia. I was hurt, Garnet, hurt that you could even remotely entertain such an awful thought about me."

I could see the pain on his face and felt awful that I'd been the cause of it. I loved and respected my father. We'd always gotten along well, and we'd been each other's sensible refuge from the crazy that was my mother.

"I'm really sorry about that, Dad. I wasn't in my right mind at the time." I got up and went over to kiss him on his forehead. "Forgive me?"

"Of course, kiddo," he said gruffly, wiping a tear from the corner of one eye. "Will you stay for lunch?"

"Thanks, but I need to do some research based on what I learned yesterday."

"I've been doing my own research," my mother told me proudly.

"You have?"

"Yes. Here" — she handed me a dishcloth — "make yourself useful while I tell you about it." Sounding like a quizmaster, she said, "What do you think is the most common star sign of serial killers?"

I exchanged a glance with my father, who grinned. Feeling relieved that we were back on our usual ground, I said, "I have absolutely no idea."

"Pisces!" my mother said happily. "Most serial killers — well, the famous ones in your father's books, anyway — are Pisces. Not *too* shocking, though, because Pisces are never fully in touch with reality, are they? And Geminis are in second place. All that smooth-talking charisma and the ability to live double lives, I suppose. And then Sagittarius. Reckless, you know? They like a bit of danger and adventure."

She rinsed a cup and handed it to me while I stared at her, at a loss for words.

"Now interestingly, the signs of Pisces, Gemini, Sagittarius and Virgo all fall at the end of a season," she continued, "which makes them *mutable* signs. And if you think about it, that makes sense too!"

"Why?" I asked in spite of myself.

"They're the chameleons of the horoscope, aren't they? Unsettled, unpredictable, changeable, adaptable. They like variety — in work, where they live, in lovers. They're not good at sameness. It bores them." She pulled the plug and watched the water drain. "Funny that Virgos weren't at the top of the killer list. But maybe they're just so neat and organized, they never get caught."

"If anybody wants me, I'll be in the living room, reading the newspaper," my father said. Clearly, he'd had enough of this nonsense.

My mother wiped the sink to a shine and hung the gloves neatly over the faucet. "A lot of your dad's killers have aspects in Pluto too."

"Is that so?" I said, polishing a glass.

"A fixation with *death* and repressed urges, you know?"

"Right."

"Do you know the dates of birth of any of the people at that farm you visited?" My mother asked.

"Nope." I dried and put away the last plate. "In fact, I don't know nearly enough, which is why I need to get on my way and start researching."

"Back to facts instead of feelings, are you? Well, off you go then, and don't forget to tell me everything you find out," she said, though her tone made it clear she thought I was unlikely to find out anything much.

– 31 –

I spent the morning working for Henry Mason, capturing his income and expenses into the accounting software he refused to learn and arguing with him about the relative deliciousness of salmon versus trout. It was a topic I had no opinion on, but I made an effort to be downright oppositional by declaring a passionate preference for the taste of cod in order to give him one of the debates he so enjoyed. Or perhaps because I, like him, was also a stubborn, ornery individual. He got his own back, though.

"I've been thinking about your odd eyes," he said.

"*Again?*"

"They say that eyes are the mirror of the soul."

"They do say that," I admitted.

"So does that mean you've got mirrors of two souls?"

I turned away before he could see my startled reaction. The memory of Colby's warm brown eyes surfaced. Whether or not my eyes mirrored two souls, when it came to color, I had one of his and one of my own.

Henry kept me busy the whole morning, but when I clocked out at lunchtime, I hurried back toward my loft, eager to dive into the research I'd meant to do the previous afternoon when I'd instead fallen asleep in front of some mindless television. Halfway up the stairs to my loft, I heard a car pulling into Henry's driveway, so I turned and ran back down, expecting to see another grocery delivery van. But it was a midnight-blue Nissan, and I was shocked to see who climbed out of it. What on earth was *he* doing at my place? How did he even *know* it was my place?

He gave me a little wave and walked right up to where I stood at the bottom of the stairs. "Hello again, Garnet. How are you?"

"Professor Deaver," I said. "This is a surprise."

"I hope you don't mind me coming to visit you unannounced like this?" He took a step closer to me, and I backed up until my heels were against the bottom step. "But I just happened to be in the area, and I thought I'd pop in and we could have another chat about killers and the Gay Slayer investigation."

He was just in the area? *Ri-ight.* "How did you know where I live?"

He gave me a smile that was no doubt intended to put me at my ease but which only creeped me out. "Well, Kenneth told me you'd left Boston and gone home to your parents in Pitchford, and there was only one McGee listed in the directory here."

I drew an indignant breath, but what he said next outraged

me even more. "And your mother — such a sweet, friendly lady — steered me in the direction of your new digs."

I'd be having a word with her all right. "Did I see you on Saturday, outside of a town called Crowbury?"

His eyebrows rose high. "Nope, not me."

"I could've sworn it was you."

"Maybe I have a doppelganger." He chuckled again then pointed at the loft above the garage. "Your mother said you live up there. Are you going to invite me up? I'm just dying to pick your brains about the investigation and find out if you've learned anything new."

The thought of allowing Deaver into my private space, of being alone with him anywhere, made me uncomfortable. Unpleasantly aware of the strong fruity scent of his aftershave, I quickly stepped around him and put more space between us.

"Right, but the only problem is, I … er …" I stammered. "I can't. Sorry. I work for the man who lives her — he's a lawyer — and I'm already late for my afternoon shift."

"When I arrived, it looked like you were on your way upstairs."

Where I'd been going was none of this man's business. "I was just going to fetch my phone." I hoped he hadn't spotted it in the back pocket of my jeans. "But I really do need to get back to work."

Deaver pouted. It wasn't a good look on a grown man. "How about afterward? I'd be happy to wait," he said.

"Oh dear, no. After work, I've got a date with my boyfriend," I said, and added. "He's a cop."

"Another time then, I suppose." He sounded put out.

"Yeah, maybe, but always call first as I'm hardly ever here. Mostly, you know, I sleep over at my boyfriend's. The cop."

"I see." There was no trace of a smile on Deaver's face now. With a curt goodbye, he got into his car and drove away.

I climbed the stairs slowly, unsettled by his visit, and made myself a quick bowl of Captain Crunch for lunch. I sniffed the air, imagining I could still smell Deaver's sweet aftershave, but tracked the smell to the fruit bowl on top of the refrigerator. The bananas were now tight black bags of liquid and the apples as saggy and wrinkled as a witch's face. I tossed the whole mess into the trash, finished my cereal, and sat down at the table beside my laptop.

I started by making a list of everything I knew about the killer, the Kehoe family, and their lodger. Images of the cat and the well and the cage blitzed into my mind every so often, but I pushed them aside and kept going, adding what I knew about the murders and the victims. When I sat back to read through the two pages of notes, I realized that I'd included what I'd "seen" along with verified facts, as if I now accepted my visions as truth. Interesting. When had that shift happened?

The idea that I'd forgotten something important nagged at me. I chewed on my pen for a minute, thinking, then added two new items to my notes: that Special Agent Tyler Washington was a good and helpful man, a real sweetheart, and that Senior Special Agent Ronil Singh was a cynical, passive-aggressive, uncooperative pain in the butt who didn't play well with others. I still felt like I was missing something, and the niggle didn't go away when I added "ungrateful" to Singh's list of descriptors. I ran through my experience at the farm, my exchanges with the agent, and my departure, then made a note that, as unlikely as it seemed, I may or may not have seen pushy Professor Deaver in the crowd at the Kehoe farm. The professor's expression of surprise at my question had seemed just a little too exaggerated.

Was there anything else? I racked my brains. Something to do with a car, maybe? Of course, the *lodger's* car. I ran a search for Thunderbirds online, and the first thing I discovered was that they were manufactured by Ford. A frisson of excitement fizzed inside me. The man who'd picked up the hitchhiker had driven an old model Ford. I found a site that listed every model of Thunderbird ever made, each with an accompanying photograph, and punched the air when I found the exact one. The Ford Thunderbird 1988 had a badge with wings mounted on the front between the headlights, and right where I'd sketched shadows in my drawing of the car's hood, the 1988 model had twin vents. There was no doubt in my mind that this was the right car.

I needed to share the information with the investigative team, so I sent Washington a text message telling him the car make, model and year, as well as the other facts I'd learned about Larry the Lodger and the family he'd stayed with. What the agent did with the information was his business; my conscience was clear.

I logged onto my laptop and checked whether any known serial killers had owned Thunderbirds. Almost immediately, I got a hit.

Samuel Little, a man who'd confessed to crisscrossing the country over a thirty-five-year span while killing ninety-three people, had a Thunderbird and had, in fact, been caught in the act of beating and strangling a woman in the backseat of it. But he was black, and all his victims had been women, so he wasn't the man I was looking for. Pity. It would've been great to solve this case so quickly.

I took a break to make myself a cup of peppermint tea and catch up on the news, checking online sites for any mention of the discovery at the Kehoe place. So far, Singh was keeping a tight lid on it. There was just a brief report by the Caledonian Clarion that the authorities were searching a derelict farm outside of Crowbury in connection with a possible crime but that no further details were available. The media *was* still hyped up about the mass burial site in New Hampshire, and that the Button Man would soon kill again. One channel even displayed a countdown ticker to May sixth when they reported on the "Gay Slayer."

Thirteen days, it said.

– 32 –

Based on my trip to Crowbury, I had a handful of suspects. Logically, there was an infinite number of suspects and the serial killer could easily be someone I'd never heard or thought of. But my intuition told me that it was someone linked to that house, to those people. I wrote down the names from least to most likely.

Assuming he hadn't kicked the bucket in the well or subsequently died somewhere in New Hampshire, Melvin or Marvin Kehoe would now be in his eighties, and that was surely too old to still be killing young men. Then again, maybe that was why the killings had slowed, because he'd become less capable. Was he that grumpy old man on the farm down in Hucknall?

I scratched at a scab on my arm, thinking. I needed to consider the possibility that the odd, middle-aged man there might be Derek Kehoe all grown up. I should probably pay that farm another visit and ask around town about the creepy family. I didn't *feel* a connection between the Hucknall and the Crowbury farms, but I reminded myself that feelings weren't facts and added a follow-up trip to my to-do list.

Derek Kehoe, born the year after Hurricane Belle — which a quick search told me had been in 1976 — would be in his early forties if he was still alive, and might be living somewhere in New Hampshire or Hucknall, Vermont, or anywhere else.

Larry the Lodger, based on what I'd learned from the ladies in the diner, would now be in his late forties or early fifties and might be in Portland or San Francisco or anywhere else on the planet. I wondered if he was still driving the Thunderbird. Probably not. These days, it would be unusual enough to attract attention. If he was my killer, he'd now be behind the wheel of something less obtrusive and memorable. I wondered whether Liz or Ruth was right when it came to his sexuality because that might well be a factor in his motivation for killing young gay men.

I spent another hour researching serial killer motives in more detail and then, without consciously intending to do so, found myself looking for more information on Jacob Wertheimer instead. His profile was still up on Facebook with a picture of a group of friends at a club, all holding up beers in celebration. I scrolled down the timeline back to 2009 and saw his last post: a Halloween party photo of him dressed as Jack Nicholson's crazy character in *The Shining,* complete with plaid shirt, red jacket, axe in hand, and his face stuck though a splintered rectangle of wood. His eyebrows had been sketched into sharp arches and he was grinning like a madman, but I could still see his blue eyes and freckles. I smiled sadly at the caption, which read, "Here's … Jacob!"

The next post, in November, was a frantic appeal from

Doug Piccolo, saying that Jacob was missing and asking if any of his friends had seen or heard from him. I scrolled up through the succeeding posts: messages of shock and concern from friends, more appeals for help, an invitation to a night vigil organized by his family, complaints about the lack of progress in the investigation, and a flurry of posts on the first anniversary of his disappearance. Over the months and years that followed, the number of posts dwindled to the occasional "Keep the faith" and "Missing you, bud" and "Never forgotten."

Doug Piccolo alone had continued to post on every anniversary of Jacob's birthday and the day he'd gone missing. Then, on March 17, 2018 Doug had posted that Jacob's remains had been found. He gave details of a commemoration service, and again, there were a dozen more shocked posts from old friends, but I noticed that after that, it was once again only Doug who posted on Jacob's birthday.

I was looking at Jacob's gallery of photos — heart-breaking when you knew what had ultimately happened to him — when a loud knock sounded at the door. It was my mother, wearing a purple-and-yellow muumuu and carrying a bunch of flowers.

"Here I am, dear!" she said as though I'd been searching everywhere for her.

"I've got a bone to pick with you," I began crossly.

"I know, I know. I'm sorry. Look," she said, thrusting the bouquet into my hands, "blue hyacinths to make peace and white tulips for forgiveness. May I come in?"

I stepped aside to let her pass, but I was far from pacified by her floral offering. "You can't just hand out my address to strange men, Mom."

"Yes, your father told me afterward that I shouldn't have done that, but by then, it was too late. The bus had sailed the train station. And in my defense, he *did* look and sound very professorial."

"Professors can also be very bad men."

"Yes, dear. I won't do it again." She went to my kitchen cupboards and began searching. "I see now I should have brought a vase."

"Why were you even home instead of at the store?" I asked.

"Wyoming does Monday, Wednesday, and Friday afternoons for me," she said brightly. "I can't think why I never hired an assistant sooner. Since you won't come work with me, at least I can come and visit you!"

"Uhm…" I said, not nearly as pleased at the prospect as she was, then I was distracted by my phone beeping an incoming text. Checking it, I saw that Tyler Washington had sent me a single emoji — the open-mouthed "Wow!" So the info I'd sent him the day before clearly matched what the FBI had discovered about the Crowbury crime. Score one for the interfering civilian without a badge.

"I guess this will do," my mother said, filling an ice bucket with water and dropping the flowers into it. She pointed at my laptop. "Learning anything interesting there on the googler?"

I shrugged and rubbed my knuckles into my eyes. I'd spent the whole afternoon staring at a screen, sifting through information, and stuffing my head with facts, but was I really any closer to knowing who the Button Man was or why he'd killed? I was certainly no nearer to actually finding him. Puffing out an irritated breath, I pulled out the maps of New England

and studied them again.

My mother crept closer and peered over my shoulder. "What have you got there?"

"These are the places where I know Button Man victims went missing or where bodies were found." I pointed out the marked areas. "And the farm where I had my visions on Saturday is around here."

"Oh, Garnet, look at your arms and hands! You've been picking at yourself again."

She was right; there were smears of blood and new scabs on my upper arms and the backs of my hands. I often fell into the habit when I was zoned out, like in front of a TV or computer screen, and didn't realize until afterward.

"I swear, one of these days I'm going to buy you a cat scratching post!" she said.

My gaze slid over to my phone, where my screen had just lit up with another message from Washington. This time, it was the emoticon of thankful hands. Somehow, in some way, I'd added something useful to the investigation, and Washington at least, was grateful. I wanted to whoop in delight but settled for sending back a thumbs-up. We were developing quite the relationship, Tyler and me, though I'd put good money on him regularly deleting any trace of our conversations, just in case Singh got nosy.

"What have you found out from all your research?" my mother asked.

"Not a whole helluva lot," I admitted.

She gave me an *I-told-you-so* look. "Then what's your next step?"

"No idea. I have two, maybe three suspects, one of whom looks more promising than the others because he drives the kind of car I saw in one of my visions, but I have no real idea of where any of them went after they left Crowbury, what they might be doing now, or even if they're still alive."

She pulled a chair closer and sat down. "What did they do before they left?"

"They all worked in a fabric store, and one also worked on that farm."

"Maybe they stuck to what they knew. Now, *I'm* no expert private eye," my mother said. As though *I* was. "But I would guess that there are fewer fabric stores in New England than there are farms. Maybe you could check those out first?"

"There must be lots, though. Where do I even start?"

"From Crowbury, of course," she said.

"That's the one place I know those men *aren't.*"

"I didn't mean that. Wait. It'll be easier to just show you. I need some string or thread and one of your crystals. The charoite, I think."

"Mom, I don't think—"

"If only that were more true! You think too much about everything. Analysis paralysis, that's what you've got. And it's getting you nowhere. It's time to try something different."

Since one definition of insanity was doing the same thing over and over again and expecting a different result, I decided to embrace whatever kooky technique my mother had planned. But I owned no sewing supplies or string, so I brought her a length of dental floss and all the stones from my jacket pockets.

"Glad to see you're keeping them on you, dear." She

selected a pretty purple stone and tied it up neatly in a cradle of floss. "Now, you need to take this end and let the crystal hover over that farm on the map. Hold it absolutely still."

I balked at that. "You're kidding, right?"

"Oh, do you have some nice solid facts to be going on with, then?" My mother was capable of dialing up the sarcasm when she chose.

I took the end of the dental floss and suspended the stone directly over Crowbury, about eight inches above the map.

"Now, close your eyes, and think of what it is you want," my mother instructed.

Despite feeling utterly silly, I did so. I concentrated on the thought of where either Larry or Derek might have gone after they left the farm. I got no finger tingles, no tightening scalp, no messages. Good. For a moment there, I'd gone over to the dark side, abandoning all logic to dangle a freaking chip of rock over a map.

"Nothing's happening," I said smugly.

"Open your eyes, Garnet."

"What the hell?" I said, staring at the pendulum, which was swinging in small circles. Was *I* making that happen?

"See how it's pulling slightly to that side?" my mother said. "Move it over toward there, just a little at a time."

I moved my hand fractionally to the right, crossing the border between Vermont and New Hampshire. The pendulum moved faster. Its arcs grew wider. When I moved it a fraction to the right, the movement slowed and shrank. It was like the old getting-warmer-getting-colder game I'd played with friends when we were kids. When I established the area with the strongest movements, my mother put her finger on the spot of the map directly below the pendulum's circle.

"How is this supposed to work?" I asked, dumbfounded.

"The spirits gather their energy from the ethos and direct your inner essence."

While I puzzled over what *that* meant, she lifted her finger and peered underneath.

"Woodbridge," she said. "Is there a fabric store there?"

I did a quick search online and discovered that it was indeed home to a fabric store called A Stitch in Time.

"There you go. That's where you start, then. It's the logical conclusion."

"It's the opposite of logical," I mumbled, still not convinced that I hadn't subconsciously caused the pendulum's movements.

When my mother left, I grabbed my phone and began dialing. Then I hit the red telephone and stood undecided for a minute, rubbing my fingertips over my lips and wondering if I was brave enough to do what I wanted. I weighed potential risks against possible pleasures, and then, with a muttered, "Ah, screw it," I dialed the number again.

"Hey, Chief," I said when Ryan answered. "What are you doing this weekend?"

– 33 –

Saturday, April 28

"So, this is where I'll be staying." I handed Henry Mason the slip of paper on which I'd written the details of the B&B in Halliwell, New Hampshire.

Ryan and I would be starting in Woodbridge, the town the pendulum had seemingly indicated, but we'd take the opportunity to check out a couple of other fabric stores in the general area while we were up there.

"And you've got my number." I'd written that in large print and stuck it to his refrigerator with a *Best Grandpa in the World!* magnet. "Call if there's any kind of problem, okay?"

"You think I'm a kid? You think I've never stayed home alone before?" he growled. "Stop fussing over me, you odd-eyed duck, and get a move on."

"I'll miss you too, Henry," I said. Outside, Ryan called my name. "Coming!" I yelled and paused at Henry's hallway mirror to check my appearance. I finger-combed my hair, applied a coat of lipstick, popped a mint in my mouth, and headed out, leaving Henry still grumbling about smothering women.

Ryan, looking fine in khaki chinos and a white button-down shirt, was waiting beside his Toyota Highlander in the driveway. He held my overnight bag. "This it?"

"That's it." When he made to toss it into the back of his car, I added, "But I'm driving, and we're going in my car."

His black eyebrows drew together in surprise. "Why?"

How to answer that? I could hardly say, "Because we'll be spending the night in New Hampshire and only returning tomorrow, and that's the longest I will have spent in a man's company since Colby and I am excited but also freaking anxious, and if it all gets to be too much, I want to be able to jump into my car and flee." So instead, I just stuck a finger in my mouth like a little kid and chewed on a nail. Real mature.

"My car's faster," Ryan said.

"Oh yeah? Says who?"

"Says the two-seventy-horsepower, 3.5-liter V6 engine."

"If you're hoping to impress me with a vehicle, Chief, you'd be better off with a food truck," I said, walking over to my old Honda.

Ryan dropped my bag and took a few steps closer to me. "But hey, if you *like* slow …"

"I like slow," I said, giving him a naughty smile.

One of his eyebrows quirked. "I'll make a note of that." Another step closer. "How about noisy?"

"Sometimes, you know, when your engine's revved, you can't stop the … purring."

He smiled. "I do believe I have heard that purr," he said,

closing the distance between us. "And what about some real power when the pistons start pumping?"

"Tempting," I said, staring up into those slate-gray eyes and feeling the heat in my cheeks.

"Because you need real staying power for a long … slow … drive. And I've got six cylinders and two hundred forty-eight pound-feet of torque."

I swallowed then whispered, "Okay," committing myself with the word. I was in this, both feet inside the circle. There would be no running away when things got intense.

But maybe some of my anxiety showed on my face because Ryan tucked a strand of my hair behind my ear and said, "We'll go at your pace, Garnet. Just say the word, and I'll hit the brakes, okay?"

"Okay," I said again, and this time my voice was steadier.

At a loud throat clearing, I glanced back at the house to find Henry spectating. I waved a hand between the two of them. "Ryan, have you met Henry Mason?"

"Course I have. How're you doing, Henry?"

"Chief," Henry said with a nod. "Arresting this one, are you?"

Ryan grinned. "Just detaining her for a while."

"See you tomorrow night, Henry." I went to Ryan's car, tossed my bag into the back, and climbed into the passenger seat. Outside, the two men chatted for another minute, and then Ryan got in behind the wheel, chuckling.

As we pulled away, I asked, "What's so funny?"

"Henry. He said to watch my back around you."

I gave an exasperated snort. "Let me guess — my eyes?"

"He said differently colored eyes mean that when you were a newborn, you were touched by a fairy, or so they say."

"Who's 'they'?" I asked, and before he could answer, added, "I can't tell if he actually has an obsession with my eyes or if he just gets a kick from needling me."

Ryan glanced at me, his cheek dimpling in a grin. "He also said that when the wee folk visit babies, they confer great fairylike beauty on them."

"Oh," I said, mollified. No one had ever called me fairylike before, and only Colby had ever called me beautiful.

"But he added that they must have skipped that step in your case."

"That man! I'm going to tell his daughter he lives on chocolate and pancakes. *And* wine."

Ryan snagged my hand and squeezed it. "But I told him that I don't think they skipped any steps."

At that, *I* smiled too.

We took the ramp onto the highway, headed east out of Pitchford, and Ryan turned on the car radio. An upbeat love song thumped out for all of ten seconds then subsided into dull static. Ryan fiddled with the buttons and touchscreen controls for a minute but only got the harsh white noise.

"I don't know what's up with this," he said, finally switching it off.

I did. Radios tended to act up when Colby was near. Was he near now, perhaps coming along to play chaperone?

"So," Ryan asked as he took the turn north onto Route 89, "want to hear about my search for the Kehoe family in the databases?"

"Yes! Did you find out anything?"

"Not much, unfortunately. There was a 1998 death certificate for a Mary Kay Kehoe, listing drowning as the cause of death. I didn't find one for a Melvin or Marvin or even a Martin Kehoe."

"He could still be alive," I said. "But if he did die there on the farm, Mary Kay and Derek probably never reported the death. If they had, some awkward questions would've been asked. I'll bet that's why the farm was never sold. Without a death certificate, they couldn't transfer the old man's estate." I nibbled on a nail. "Find anything for Derek Kehoe?"

"There's a birth certificate—"

"1977?"

"Yup. Nothing after that, though. No criminal record, no parking ticket, no driver's license, no taxes paid, not even a social security number. The man's a ghost."

I shot Ryan a glance. "Do you think that means he's dead?"

"Could be. Though there's no death certificate for him, either."

At a sudden thought, I drew in a quick breath. "What if the Button Man killed *him*, too? He could've been one of the first victims — *the* first victim — and his poor body is lying somewhere undiscovered, and that's why it's like he doesn't exist. Maybe *that's* the connection to the house. It's the victim who's associated with it, not the killer. Or— Or," I said excitedly, "it could be both! Derek was the victim, *and* Larry was the killer." My mind raced, connecting ideas, coming up with theories. "Maybe, after Derek left the farm, he met up with Larry again — they could've kept in contact over the years."

"And Larry just killed him? Why?" Ryan asked.

"Derek's grandfather was really afraid that the boy wasn't straight." I shrugged. "What if Derek *was* gay, and he liked Larry. Maybe he'd once had a crush on him, and then when they met up again, he came onto him. Larry would've lost his temper like he did with Chris, the guy at the store, but this time he didn't stop the assault until the guy — Derek — was dead." I could almost see the scene playing out in my mind's eye. "Larry discovered he had a taste for killing, and went on to murder other men that reminded him of Derek and Chris — men who were the same age and had the same sexual orientation."

"You do know that's all just speculation, don't you?" Ryan said.

"Yeah, I guess," I conceded reluctantly.

My phone rang, and a glance at the screen told me it was Deaver again. I cursed under my breath and rejected the call.

Ryan glanced from my phone to my face. "Someone bothering you?"

"Kind of." I explained about Deaver and chatting to him in Perry's office. "He was helpful, but now he keeps bugging me, wanting to know what's happening. I mean, there's curious, and then there's being like a dog with a bone. And then on Monday, he just showed up at my place uninvited. I didn't like it."

"What's he like?" Ryan asked, sounding serious. "This professor with all the questions."

– 34 –

"Professor Deaver is … strange," I told Ryan. "Creepy even," I said, remembering the obsessive organization of his lunch box, how he'd enjoyed trapping the bee, and that sense I'd gotten about his need for control, not to mention his unexpected visit and the way he'd gotten my address from my mother. "And he's dead set on being involved in an investigation like this."

"An investigation like this, or *this* investigation?" Ryan asked.

"What do you mean?"

"It could be a red flag." His hands shifted, tightening their grip on the steering wheel. "Many perpetrators are obsessed with how their own cases are investigated by law enforcement and covered by the media. They keep newspaper clippings and record the news coverage, and it's not uncommon for them to try insert themselves into the investigation."

"Singh once told me something similar," I said.

"They volunteer for searches, call in helpful tips, even submit witness statements," Ryan continued. "They want in on the action to establish how much the cops know or to find out what the cops think of them or just to have a laugh, knowing they're right under our noses and we stupid flatfoots don't even guess."

"Yeah, I can see how that would feed their narcissism," I said, rubbing a fingertip over the back of my hand and feeling the scabs there from where I'd picked at myself. "A funny thing, there was a moment, and I mean literally just a split-second, when I thought I saw Deaver in the crowd outside the Kehoe place."

Ryan shot me a interested glance.

"But honestly, I think I must've been mistaken. He's based in Boston. What would he be doing all the way up in Crowbury?"

"I don't like it. At all," Ryan said. "Call me if you see him again?"

"Sure."

"Do you like him for this? You think there's a chance he could be the killer?"

I considered for a minute, then said slowly, "No. No, I don't think so. For one thing, he's so fastidious, possibly even OCD. He wouldn't want to risk getting blood on himself."

"That's what gloves and coveralls are for."

"And he's not very big. I can't see him taking down a healthy young man."

"Never underestimate the element of surprise," Ryan said.

"I guess." Anyone could've stunned the victims with a quick blow to the head or some kind of tranquilizer quickly injected. Was chloroform to the nose still a thing for kidnappers? Bottom line, I shouldn't make assumptions based on size. "I just figured he was curious because he knows all the theory but isn't able to apply it in real life. That must be frustrating. Like, he wants to be useful, and he probably also wants his work validated by real-world findings, but he's outside the real world of the investigation."

"Hmmm. What do you shrinks call it when you say something about another person but you're actually talking about your own issues?"

Everyone was an armchair therapist.

"Projection," I mumbled. "I guess he just … doesn't seem like the type."

Ryan tapped his fingers on the wheel. He had strong, square hands with nails cut short and wore a stainless-steel wristwatch, analog with no extra dials or buttons. I snuck a glance at his profile, the firm jaw, the deep line that became his sole dimple when he smiled, the nose with a little bump on the ridge. I liked that small flaw; perfectly straight noses were too much like beaks for my liking.

"What are you thinking?" I asked.

"Back when I was new on the job, I spent a couple of weeks at the Middlebury PD, helping them out with a drug operation they had going. And while I was there, I caught a case."

"Yeah?"

"There was this guy who was a popular high school gym teacher. Everyone thought he was great. Even the *kids* liked him."

"Impressive."

"They told me he was involved in the community too. Volunteered at the local food bank and collected chocolate eggs at Easter to send to a children's home in Montpelier."

"Did he wear a clown suit at charity parties to entertain the kids?" I asked, thinking of John Wayne Gacy, who'd raped and murdered at least thirty-three boys and young men and buried most of them in the crawlspace under his house.

"What?"

"Never mind. You were saying he was this all-around champ."

"Right. So one night, a call comes in. A woman says there's a huge ruckus going on at the house next door."

Ryan glanced out his window, watching the woods flash by, but I could tell he was seeing something else. I wasn't the only one plagued by bad memories. I reached across to squeeze his knee, and he placed his warm hand over mine.

"What did you find?" I asked softly.

"His wife. On the kitchen floor, surrounded by broken glass and plates. He'd broken her jaw and cheek. Her nose was bleeding, and she was bleeding between the legs too. She was pregnant, quite far along, and he'd kicked her in the stomach." His thumb stroked the back of my hand, moving without pause over the scabs. "She lost the baby."

I turned my hand over, threaded my fingers through his and held tightly for a moment. "I don't know how you do the work you do."

"We found the kids in the closet. She'd trained them to hide there when he went into a rage. It happened often, see? But the thing that really got to me is— Who am I kidding? The *whole* thing got to me. But my point is," he said, glancing at me, "you can't judge by appearances. This abusive son of a bitch in

Middlebury, for instance. Outside the house, in public, he was this cool guy, friendly and helpful. Nothing was too much trouble. And when he was out and about with his family, he was apparently the sweetest, most loving husband and father you could imagine. But when he'd downed a few and the drapes were drawn, he was this completely different person. Vicious. Worse than an animal."

"So I shouldn't assume Deaver is as harmless as he seems?"

"Exactly," Ryan said. He stared out at the road, which stretched ahead as straight as an arrow with nothing much to see except trees and an occasional pasture dotted with cows. "I've always wondered how they juggle those two selves. Most of the criminals I deal with, they're assholes all the time, you know? Ask anyone who's had dealings or a relationship with them, and they'll say, 'Yeah, Tom's a real dickhead.' But these psychopaths are a whole other story. I just don't get how the cold-blooded, violent part doesn't slip out during the budget debate at work. Or how Mr. Nice Guy doesn't appear when they're torturing someone."

"The thing is, there *isn't* a Mr. Nice Guy, not with psychopaths, at least," I said. "They aren't capable of feeling real empathy or compassion, though they can often mimic it pretty well. They're experts at reading people, so they figure out what others want or expect to hear and give it to them. It's part of their manipulation skill set."

For a mile or two of highway, we were stuck behind an SUV with three kids in the backseat, all of whom spun around to make hideous faces at us. I treated them to my own best effort: bottom eyelids tugged down, nose pushed up into a snout, and tongue wagging. Ryan and I chatted for a while about other things: family, travel, our opinion on the grave topic of whether pineapple belonged on pizza. Ryan, a purist, insisted that fruit had no place on top of cheese and tomato-basil sauce. I, on the other hand, had no such prejudices.

"I have never met a pizza I couldn't eat," I told him.

As we drew nearer to Woodbridge, we veered back to the topic of the Button Man. Ryan asked what my current working theory was, and I summarized what I knew or suspected about the perpetrator — that he was a lust, rage or thrill killer of the organized type who'd cruised the highways of New England in a Thunderbird, trawling for young men.

"Maybe he wanted to bump uglies with them, or—"

"I'm sorry. What?" Ryan said.

"Bump uglies. That's what the old lady in the diner called it."

He shook his head in amused disbelief. "You learn something new every day."

"And then he kind of got carried away and killed them. The strangling could even have been erotic asphyxiation taken too far. Or maybe the hitchhikers demanded money for services or turned down his advances, and then he felt rejected and enraged, so he killed them."

I closed my eyes and tried again to see past the moment when the Thunderbird had pulled up to the hitchhiker on the side of the highway, but I saw nothing more. It was so frustrating. What was the point of a talent that couldn't be called into use on demand? We entered Woodbridge, and I consulted Google Maps to give Ryan directions to the first fabric store we'd be checking out.

"What do you reckon is the significance of the button with the victim's bodies?" Ryan asked.

"I'm still working on that," I said. "Buttons were a big thing in the Kehoe family and business. The old man used them as a punishment, and the fabric store sold every variety of them. So I'm guessing that's a factor. If our killer is Kehoe senior, then I guess it's a part of his button fetish. He wants to button them up. But I don't think it is Kehoe senior. It's too much of a stretch for a man that old to still be killing. If it's Kehoe junior, then the buttons have got to be connected to his trauma in some way. *He* suffered with buttons, so now *they* have to?"

"And if it's Larry," Ryan said, "maybe he acquired a taste for buttons when working at that store?"

"Association doesn't imply causality," I said like a well-trained scientist. "It could have been the other way around — Larry already had an obsession for buttons and that's why he wanted a job in the trade. Then again, it could just be random. Like when he was killing his first victim, one of his own or the victim's buttons got ripped off in the struggle, and he flung it at the body or shoved it in the mouth in irritation. And then afterward, he just left a button behind every time, like a calling card."

Ryan pulled into a parking bay outside the fabric store and cut the engine. "So basically, it could mean anything."

"Yeah," I admitted. "But I'm going to find out what it is if it's the last thing I do."

— 35 —

Stitch in Time — established in 1990 by the Gifford family, according to the sign over the door — was a cutesy fabric store decorated in vintage style with glass-fronted display cabinets, ancient sewing machines, and an old-fashioned cash register complete with push buttons and a swivel-handle on the side. A wooden rocking horse stood guard beside the door, baring its teeth in an unsettling smile.

At the back of the store, bolts of cloth lay stacked on sloping shelves and on a vast oak table where a man was measuring out a length of fabric for a customer. One wall was a patchwork of shallow shelves stuffed with fat skeins of yarn in every hue, and a huge wooden cabinet housed dressmaking patterns, knitting needles, embroidery frames, pincushions, and haberdashery of every kind, each neatly displayed in its own cubbyhole. Deaver would've approved.

My gaze was drawn to the hodgepodge of odd buttons filling an antique cigar box on the front counter and then to the assistant standing behind it. She wore a denim apron with a black heart stitched on the front, and with her emerald hair, purple lipstick, nose and lip studs, and the leather collar around her throat, she stood out in the quaint store like a bruise on pale skin. When she turned to assist us, I half-expected her to snarl.

Instead, she gave us friendly smile. "What can I do for you today?"

"Um," I said, uncertain where to start.

"We're trying to track down a man who came to this town in the mid- to late-nineties." Ryan said smoothly. "He was in the fabric trade and might have come here looking for a job."

"I wasn't even born then!" the girl said cheerfully, and suddenly, I felt old. "Let me ask my mother. Mom? Mom!"

A tall woman also wearing a denim apron, although hers had a pink heart on the front, emerged from a back office. Her ash-blond hair was immaculately styled, her lipstick was a soft pink, and around *her* neck, she wore pearls. She wasn't nearly as interesting as her daughter or, we soon discovered, as friendly.

"These people want to ask about the last century," her daughter said.

Ryan repeated his question, but the woman shook her head. "That's ages ago, and assistants come and go all the time."

"He would've been in his early to mid-twenties with dark hair," I said.

"Call your uncle," the woman told the goth girl. "Maybe he'll remember." To us, she explained, "He's older than me."

The man who'd been measuring cloth finished with the customer and came to join us. He had a pleasant, open face with brown eyes and hair, and I estimated him to be in his mid-fifties. He fiddled with the edges of the blue heart on his apron while he considered our question.

"That sounds like a guy who worked here for a short while," he said eventually. "Name of Larry."

A frisson of excitement shot through me. "That's him! What was his surname?"

"I don't remember. It must have been nearly twenty years ago."

"Would you still have employee records?" Ryan asked.

"We're only obliged to keep those records for seven years," the woman said, as though we were IRS inspectors finding fault with her paperwork. "Then we shred them."

I wanted to kick the rocking horse in frustration but settled for digging the nail of my index finger under the cuticle of one of the nails on my other hand, tugging back in satisfying pain.

A mother and child entered the store, and the woman said, "I'm afraid we can't help you further. Now, if you'll excuse me, I have *customers* to help."

The man shifted his weight, drawing my gaze. He gave me a significant look and tilted his head a fraction in the direction of the door. I gave him a miniscule nod.

"Thanks, anyway," I said. "Come on, Ryan. Let's go."

"You have a good day, now," the girl said as we exited the store.

Less than a minute later, the man caught up with us outside and introduced himself as Chris. We walked a little way away from A Stitch in Time to where a railing separated the row of stores from a small public park. He leaned up against the bar and said, "My sister doesn't like me discussing this side of my life in the store or in front of her daughter, as though *she'd* care."

"What side of your life?" Ryan asked.

"First, can you tell me why you want to know?" Chris asked, taking a crushed packet of cigarettes and a lighter out of his apron pocket.

I glanced at Ryan, who gave me a small nod. "We're investigating a series of murders and we think he, Larry, might have been involved."

"Shit," he said, pausing in the act of tapping out a cigarette.

"We need to find him for questioning. So we'd seriously appreciate any information you can give us," I said.

"Murder, huh?" He chewed on his bottom lip for a moment, then said, "Okay. I was only twenty-one when Larry arrived, and maybe I hadn't experienced enough of the world, but I thought he was the same as me only he didn't know it yet."

"Know what?" Ryan asked, but I thought I understood.

"You had a relationship with him, with Larry?" I guessed. That would mean Liz at the diner had been right.

"A *relationship*? Hardly." Chris tapped a cigarette out of the packet, lit it, and took a deep drag. "He rocked up here one day, looking for a job. He said he knew the business inside and out, so my mother hired him. Right from the get-go, we got along real well. Anyway, after a week or two of accidentally bumping into him and brushing against him as we squeezed between the shelves, I asked him if he wanted to go to the drive-in. There was one on the outside of town back then. It's a factory now." He puffed on his cigarette. "We packed a few beers and went in that great big car of his—"

"A Ford Thunderbird," I said.

"If you say so. We went to see *Meet Joe Black*. I mean, Brad Pitt, am I right?"

I nodded; he was right.

"And when the movie began, I slid over and started to, you know, make a move. I mean, I thought we were on the same page."

"But you weren't?" Ryan asked.

"Larry. Freaked. Out," Chris said. "Totally lost his mind. He shoved me off him so hard I banged my head on the window. I asked him, 'What's your problem?' He stares at me with this disgusted, angry expression and says, 'I'm not a queer.' So I said something like, 'Hey, don't knock it 'til you've tried it,' trying to make a joke to defuse the tension, you know? But then he hit me, punched me right in the face, giving me a hideous black eye, and pushed me out of his car before he took off. Just left me there to find my own way home, can you believe it?" He took another drag on his cigarette. "I got to the store early the next morning, so I was there when he arrived. I told him to fuck off and never come back."

"And he did?" I asked.

"I never saw him again. Which was just fine by me, let me tell you. Guy was off his rocker."

Chris didn't know anything more about Larry or where he'd gone after he left, so we thanked him and went to a restaurant down the road for lunch. Over lobster rolls, Ryan and I discussed what we'd learned and what it might say about our suspect-in-chief. After the way that pendulum had swung, I'd hoped we'd discover some real information in Woodbridge, and I guess we had. But knowing that Larry had lived and worked there very briefly was not the sort of information that led anywhere fast.

After lunch, we set off for Halliwell, a bigger town about an hour east of Woodbridge, to check out the second fabric store on my list. Ryan snagged the last parking bay in front of Sew Pretty, squeezing in between a monster SUV parked over the line and a Heavenly Haberdashery delivery van decorated with cherubs trailing ribbons and lace. Ryan followed me up the stairs to the store, and turning to ask him a question about something, I caught him checking out my rear end and promptly forgot what I'd been meaning to ask.

Inside, the store was modern and brightly lit with a specialty section dedicated to quilting. I waited beside Ryan, resisting the urge to step back and check out *his* butt, while a delivery man in a uniform and cap branded with the same cherubs as the van completed some paperwork and asked if he could leave a stack of pamphlets on the counter. When he left, the manager — Maria, according to her nametag — asked us how she could help. Looking for something to purchase in the hope that this would buy me time and a little goodwill while I asked my questions, I chose the first thing that caught my eye — an embroidery kit with a design of interlinked Gemini twins stamped on the fabric.

Ryan and I chatted to the manager about her store and slid in a few questions about Larry and Derek Kehoe, but while we learned that her business was doing well and that she ran quilting classes and had an online store which promised forty-eight hour delivery to anywhere in New England, we learned nothing about our suspects. The store was new; she'd started it from scratch in 2015.

"I wish we'd found out more today," I said as we went back to the car. "A full name and forwarding address would've been nice."

"A lot of the process of investigating is ruling out what *isn't*," Ryan said.

"I guess so. At least we know Larry came to this area, that he drove a Thunderbird like the one I saw in my vision, and that he had another violent altercation — a homophobic one at that. It's really looking like he's our guy."

As for Derek Kehoe, we'd found no trail of him and I couldn't resist the growing belief that he was gone, as dead as his poor mother.

The day's investigations were done, so we followed Google's directions to the B&B where I'd made a reservation for us to stay overnight. Our plan was to check out the last store on our list the following morning because it was the only one open on a Sunday and it lay on the route back to Pitchford.

Swallows' Rest was a mid-sized bed-and-breakfast decorated in modern country style. The receptionist welcomed us with a smile and a teeny glass of sherry, and while we checked in, she asked if we'd be going out for supper or if we wanted her to pack us a picnic basket.

"There's a lovely spot a little way into the woods out back, and the ephemerals are beautiful this time of the year," she said.

Ryan and I agreed that the picnic option sounded good. After a day spent mostly driving, neither of us felt like getting back into the car to find a restaurant in town.

"I'll have the basket ready by six o'clock. Okay, so here are your keys." She handed us each a set, and to me, she said, "You requested rooms seven and nine?"

Ryan stared glumly at his keys, then directed a disappointed gaze my way. "You booked two rooms?"

"Seven and nine are adjoining rooms," the receptionist said in a bright and breezy voice. "Now, the big key on each ring is for your room, and the little one, here" — she tapped a smaller key on each ring — "is for the interleading door between them." She gave us a knowing smile and said, "We hope you enjoy your stay here at Swallows' Rest!"

– 36 –

That evening, we walked down the path into the woods, Ryan carrying the food basket and me carrying the wine, glasses and picnic blanket. It was a fine evening, warm without being hot. The ground was dry, but there must have been a stream or a pond somewhere nearby because spring peepers were in full chorus, their high-pitched calls sounding like the ringing of distant sleigh bells. The trees wore a haze of fresh green leaves and buds, and wild leeks as sharp as green blades in the brown soil added sweet oniony notes to the earthy smell of the forest.

Above, birds trilled and chattered, but my gaze was drawn to the ground. I was mesmerized by the exquisite ephemerals. Every year in early spring, the delicate spring wildflowers bloomed in a riot of color from the forest floor, luxuriating in the days of full sunlight before the ash, oak, maple, and birch trees got their full canopies of leaves and covered the ground in deep shade. We pointed out the blooms we recognized: blue cohosh and delicate Dutchman's breeches, the virgin white of bloodroot and starflowers, and the bright yellow of trout lilies and marsh marigolds. Ryan, who recognized more species than I did, showed me the elusive Jack-in-the-pulpit, a hooded and striped tubular flower of blood red and deep green, and insisted I smell red trillium. I drew my nose back sharply from the heart of the flower, where a longhorn beetle rubbed its feet together.

"Ugh, it smells like a wet dog," I said.

He chuckled. "That's why it's also called stinking Benjamin. The smell is what attracts the insects."

Palest pink spring beauties and clusters of tiny heart-shaped squirrel's corn embroidered the clearing where a wooden picnic table and benches sat surrounded by a circle of mossy rocks. In another month or so, after their brief spring splendor, all the flowers would go to seed and die back. Underground, their roots and bulbs would lie dormant and invisible until the next spring, like buried bodies awaiting resurrection.

Ryan unpacked our supper onto the table, while I spread the blanket and poured the wine. When we'd laden our plates with slices of rare roast beef, dill pickles, and tomato-and-basil salad with bocconcini, we sat on the blanket in the softening light of dusk to eat.

"No more talk of killers tonight," Ryan said.

"Agreed." I clinked my glass against his.

We spoke instead about ourselves. I told him about how I'd started studying pre-med after high school, then flunked out and spent a year in South Africa, working in wildlife conservation, before returning to Boston to study psychology. I wanted to know more about his family.

"Tell me about them," I said, spreading whipped butter on a slice of sourdough bread. I took a big bite.

"Well," he took a sip of wine, "you know my ex-wife is a chef in Austin."

I nodded, and he brushed a crumb from the edge of my mouth. My skin tingled where he'd touched it.

"My father died when I was eighteen," he said, and I winced. "But my mother's still alive and kicking. She lives in Atlanta with her new husband and works as a receptionist in my younger brother's practice."

"He's a lawyer? A doctor?"

"A dentist."

"Okay. Wow." I kept my face politely neutral, but I'd never been able to understand why people chose to go into dentistry. I could think of nothing worse than working in a place that smelled of antiseptic, oral rinse, and fear, and greeting reluctant patients to the background sound of whining drills — and the occasional scream, too, probably — unless it was rooting about in people's rotten mouths. I figured psychopaths might be drawn to a career where they could coolly drill holes into people under the risk of being bitten. "What did your father do?"

Ryan, who'd been swirling a slice of tomato in olive oil and balsamic vinegar, popped it in his mouth. When he swallowed, he said, "It's my turn to ask."

Avoiding the question?

"Hit me," I said.

"What was it like being an only child?"

"Okay, I guess. You get more attention from your parents, though I'm not sure that's always a good thing." I took a large sip of wine and held out my glass for more. "I wasn't meant to be the only kid."

"No?"

"There were a few miscarriages before me. I get the sense that's when my mother began to get all superstitious and into metaphysical things. She was desperate to have a baby, and if crystals or affirmations or reiki might help, she was prepared to give them a whirl. Hell, reading between the lines of what my father has told me, she probably would've sacrificed a goat on an altar at the full moon if she thought that would do the trick."

I bit into a tangy pickle while Ryan studied me for a long moment.

"And then you came along," he said.

"Ta-dah!" I said, flinging my hands out and accidentally sending the pickle flying into the woods. "The miracle baby."

His lips curved into a smile that melted the last shard of ice protecting my heart. "I'm glad you made it," he said.

We sat in silence for a while, listening to the night sounds and watching the light fade. Ryan finished his cold beef, and I traded the rest of mine for his pickle. Then while he filled our glasses with the last of the wine, I opened the Tupperware containing dessert. Inside lay five Rice Krispie Treats.

"Oh my." I lay back on the blanket and bit into one. Salted caramel with the perfect level of chewiness. "I know I died once before, but I think I just now finally made it to heaven."

Ryan lay down beside me, smiling at the relish with which I devoured my share of the chewy treats.

When only one remained, I attempted a fake out. "Look there. Is that Orion's belt?" I said, pointing with one hand at a few stars in the darkening sky while I surreptitiously slid my other hand over to the dessert container. I guess a suspicious nature and quick reflexes were part of Ryan's cop skillset because he made a preemptive strike, snatching the last treat before I could.

"No fair!" I complained.

He held it out for me to bite but pulled it back just when I came close.

"Playing games, now?" I said in a false huff.

"No games. I just want you to come and get it." His voice was lower and huskier, and his eyes had darkened.

I inched closer to him, more interested in tasting him, now, than the crispy treat. Pushing myself up on one elbow, I slowly closed the distance between our lips, then gasped when he quickly pulled me close and returned my kiss with interest. He tasted of marshmallow and salt, and he felt solid beneath my hands and warm against my body. I deepened the kiss, then shivered as a pool of cold air surrounded me. Was Colby here again? Did he object to someone else being in his spot? I clambered over Ryan and lay on his other side.

Ryan gave me a puzzled smile. "What?"

"I just feel more comfortable here," I said, but if I'd thought that switching places would be enough to placate Colby, I was wrong. The smell of cola lip balm permeated the air, though Ryan didn't seem to notice it, and the cold intensified.

I was growing annoyed. I'd been enjoying the kiss with Ryan, just as I'd enjoyed making out with him on the couch in my loft. It felt like the sexual part of me was finally coming out of its grief- and depression-induced hibernation. Yes, I'd been with a couple of men since Colby died, mostly in an experiment to dull the pain, but I hadn't been with anyone I cared about.

I hadn't felt particularly *present* with them. I may have stripped off my clothes, but I'd kept my emotions locked up tight inside, and perhaps because of that, I hadn't much enjoyed the sex. Now, with Ryan, I did feel fully *here* and in the moment. I liked and trusted him. I wanted this, and I was going to have it, dammit.

I tugged him closer, and he moved one leg over my hips, pressing himself against me as we kissed. I reveled in the taste of his mouth and the feel of his hands moving over me. My breathing quickened, and an ache pulsed deep in the pit of my belly.

"Ouch!" Ryan sat up, rubbing his head.

"What?"

"A pinecone just hit me on the head."

Enough, I thought. *Time to tackle this.*

"Could you just give me a minute?" I asked Ryan.

He stared bemusedly at me, but I got to my feet and stalked off deeper into the forest, enveloped by an invisible cloud of cold and cola.

"Colby," I said when I was out of earshot of Ryan, "this has to stop."

I looked around, perhaps hoping for a glimpse of him, golden and glimmering between the trees. But of course, there was nothing.

"I loved you. I still love you, and I always will." I swallowed the lump in my throat. "But that's in my other heart, the one that belonged to you, the one that stopped. I'm a different person now." How could I explain this so that he understood I cared deeply about him but that I also wanted to be free to live my life? "We were like ephemerals, you and I. We bloomed, and for a little while, it was so beautiful. It was perfect," I said, my throat tight and my voice hoarse. "But then it was over, and we were gone. *You* were gone."

Not gone.

"Okay, not gone but not fully here either. Oh, Colby, it's great how you look out for me, but I don't think this is where and how you're supposed to be, bound to me in a kind of limbo. I think your … existence … would be better if you, you know, moved on." I sighed, wiping my eyes on my sleeve. "Just let go of me and move on to where you're supposed to be."

No.

Always and forever.

Keep you safe.

"That part of it's okay, I guess," I said, wondering if I was being selfish. "But throwing pinecones at Ryan's head?"

I felt rather than heard his laughter.

"He's a good man, Colby. And he's *here*. You need to let me have this part of my life."

I listened, but he didn't respond.

"All I'm asking for is a bit of privacy, okay?"

Silence.

"Come on, Colby. Do you seriously want to spend your existence being an interfering voyeur?"

For a moment, there was nothing, then I felt a gentle stirring of the air, like an intake of breath, and he was gone. I could feel it. I made my way back through the night to Ryan, tripping over roots and rocks, and went straight into his arms to pick up where we'd left off. This time, there was no cold, no cola smell, and no falling missiles.

After a long while, Ryan sat up, batting at the midges that had discovered us. "Should we continue this indoors?"

"I … um …"

"Hey" — he held up his hands — "zero pressure. But I feel obliged to confess something."

"What's that?"

"I am in like with you, Garnet McGee."

My shoulders relaxed. He was staying true to his promise to go at my pace. So what the hell did I want that to be? I hesitated, feeling like I was standing at a line just as scary as the one around the well house in Crowbury, and then I cleared my throat and spoke.

"Then I guess I should tell you, Ryan Jackson, that I'm in like with you too."

— *37* —

We walked back to the B&B, holding hands, and after exchanging long looks while standing at our doors, we each went into our own rooms. As I got ready for bed, I snuck repeated glances at the interleading door, hoping it might open. I showered, discovering I had the last crispy treat mashed into my hair, and put on the courtesy robe I found hanging in the bathroom. Then I checked the door to Ryan's room again. Still closed. I brushed my teeth and hair and glared at the door before flopping onto my bed and trying to make sense of my confused feelings. Eventually, I bounded off the bed with a string of curses, walked over to the interleading door, and wrenched it open.

Ryan, wearing only a fluffy white towel around his waist, was standing next to his bed. I took in his damp, tousled hair and his bare chest. Colby's build had been lighter and the hair on his chest golden. Ryan had a bigger build, and his hair was black. He wasn't a perfectly handsome boy like Colby had been. He was a grown man, real and solid and waiting for me. With a tiny sigh, I severed my tether to the past, stepped over the threshold and into the room, and then stood on the spot, feeling vulnerable and exposed, not knowing what to say.

"I … I can't sleep," I said, sounding tough, almost belligerent. "My room is …" I glanced back over my shoulder, casting about for an excuse. The room was lovely, decorated in soothing dove gray and white with an elegant orchid of palest pink. My gaze fell on that sole instance of color, and I turned back to Ryan. "My room is too pink. It's pink all over. It's like being in the belly of a whale."

"Well, we can't have that now, can we?" he said, a smile teasing the corners of his mouth.

"No," I said. "No, we can't. Because it might make me all anxious."

"Well, we definitely can't have *that*." He ambled over to the main light switch and flicked it off. Now the room was lit only by the muted glow of the bedside lamp. Ryan tugged back the bedclothes and looked from the exposed sheet to me, his eyes full of questions.

"But I don't know if I should be here, either," I said.

"I see. And why's that?"

"If I come into your room like this" — I walked over to him, my bare feet moving from the hard wooden floor to the softness of the rug beside his bed — "then we'll go full throttle — all cylinders, full torque and maximum horsepower."

"And you don't want that?" he asked, his brows drawing together.

I help up a finger. "Now, I didn't say *that*."

His expression cleared. "I stand corrected."

"I'm cool with bedsprings getting broken, just not, you know, hearts."

"I see," he said, nodding slowly. "Then I guess it would be okay to do this?" He planted a chaste peck on my cheek.

"Yeah, no, I don't think any harm could possibly come from that," I said.

"But I probably shouldn't do this," Ryan said, edging my robe off one shoulder and kissing the skin there, which goosebumped in response. "Or this." He freed the other shoulder and nuzzled it, too, for long minutes.

I drew in a ragged breath. I'd never imagined that my shoulders were erotic zones. "And I probably would be safe with this?" I said, moving my lips to his dimple, kissing it, and breathing in the fresh soapy scent of him before grazing my lips over the sandpaper stubble of his jaw. "But this might be a little risky?" I murmured against the pulse at the base of his throat while my hands ran down the muscled slopes of his arms and chest.

The moan of complaint he gave when I pulled back turned into a sigh of pleasure when I opened my robe.

He took a step back to take in every inch of me. "My, my, my …" was all he said, but the rasp in his voice and the heat in his glance was enough to make me feel beautiful.

"It's not at all safe to look at me like that," I whispered. "And if you were to touch me here and here" — I took his hand and trailed his fingers down my chest, between and over the curves of my breasts — "then that would be downright dangerous."

"Playing with fire," he agreed, leaving a hot line of kisses where his fingers had touched.

"And you really shouldn't—" I began but lost the words as

his lips found a nipple and drew it into his mouth.

The gentle, insistent tugging stole my breath. My head fell back when he moved his mouth to my other breast, and I clung to his shoulders for support as all the hard, icy pieces of me melted.

"And under no circumstances should you move your hands lower," he said hoarsely.

I slid my hands down to his hips, slipping my fingers under the towel at his waist and tugging. The towel fell away, and we came together, skin on skin, with his mouth claiming mine and my hands sliding around his neck, fingers reaching into his thick hair. He deepened the kiss. I shrugged out of my robe, and we fell onto the cool sheet of the bed, limbs tangling, hands exploring, mouths tasting. The ember of my desire fanned hot, moving down my body and up into my heart. I slipped into mindless pleasure, beyond thought or fear, whimpering in wordless need, craving his weight on my body, needing him inside me.

He balanced on his elbows, cradling my face in his hands, and looked deep into my eyes. His own were darker now, the color of thunderclouds just before the storm. He held my gaze as he moved into me with agonizing slowness. I lifted my hips, wrapped my arms around him and, dug my fingers into the bunched muscles of his back, dragging him down, welcoming all of him into me. He groaned and, unhinged by pleasure, I surrendered any remnants of control to our bodies and to him and to the now of our rhythm. Afterward, sated and sticky, I curled up against him and drifted into a dreamless sleep.

It was only in the morning when I yawned, stretched myself

awake and planted a secret kiss on Ryan's taut butt while he still slept, that I realized what was wrong, what was missing. I felt no sense of detachment, no disconnect, no urge to pull on my clothes and sneak out before he woke up and never see him again.

And it terrified me.

– 38 –

Sunday, April 29

I left Ryan sleeping, and after showering and changing in my own room, I went down alone to have breakfast, feeling on edge. If the sex had been bad, or even mediocre, if I'd felt self-conscious or he'd been an ass in any way, I'd totally know how to handle things. But the problem was bigger than that. Our night together had been terrific, which meant I was in unfamiliar territory. What would happen if things went downhill from here? What would happen if they *didn't?*

Ryan joined me at the breakfast table as I was anointing my eggs with Tabasco sauce. "Great morning, isn't it?" he said, grinning like a man who'd got it all the night before.

I eyed him warily, nervous he was about to get all sappy with me.

Instead, he said, "Pretty cynical life philosophy you've got there, McGee," and gestured to my T-shirt, which read *If you're happy and you know it, no, you don't.*

Damn. He probably thought I'd worn this as some kind of

message about our night together, when in truth, it had been the only other top I'd packed.

"It's my mother's fault. I was never like this 'til I was born," I said, but it sounded more self-conscious and stilted than funny.

"Are you okay? Something wrong?"

"No, I'm fine."

He didn't push it. Perhaps he guessed that I felt overwhelmed by the intimacy and was petrified by any thought of commitment.

On the drive south to Newhurst, home of the last store I wanted to check out on the trip, we didn't speak much. I sat on my hands to keep from tearing at my nails with my teeth, and Ryan turned on the radio. This time, there was no static. When we pulled up at the strip mall where a fabric store sat between a Dollar General and a salon that went by the name of The Call of Beauty, Ryan asked if I minded going in alone. Officer Ronnie Capshaw had left him a voicemail earlier, and he needed to call her back.

"I'll wait for you here at the car, okay?"

"Sure."

Fine Fabrics, I discovered as soon as I set foot inside, was anything but. It was a dark, cramped store that smelled musty and didn't look very successful, but it was hard to tell if that was due to the dusty shelves of scant stock or the unfriendly man behind the counter. Middle-aged and pasty-white, with a paunch spilling over his belt, he wore the remains of his black hair scraped over his head in an oily combover. I wandered around the store while he tried his best to be unhelpful to the male couple he was serving.

"Sorry, no orange ribbon," he told them.

Stepping around a revolving stand of dressmaking patterns, however, I discovered shelves haphazardly stacked with hundreds of rolls of ribbon. I picked out three in various shades of orange and walked back to the front of the store to place them on the counter with a laconic "Here."

The two customers thanked me, but they were clearly not fooled by the storekeeper's exaggerated expression of surprise.

"You know what I think, Louis?" the shorter man said.

"That we should take our business elsewhere?" his partner asked.

"You know me so well."

As they left, the man behind the counter mumbled something about not wanting business from their type anyway.

"What type is that?" I asked loudly, though there was no one else in the store to hear my challenge. "Black or gay?"

He gave me a bored look and sighed. "Can I help you?"

Taking a step back from the Satan's fart that was his breath, I pointed at the shelves on the wall behind him where his stock of buttons was stored, every type in a separate glass bottle. "Quite a collection you've got there. You got a thing for buttons?"

"I sell them. You want to buy any?"

I scanned the display, searching for ones like those I'd seen and held. "Can I see those wooden ones?"

He grabbed the bottle and plonked it on the table in front of me. I opened the lid, half expecting to get a vision, but nothing happened, and the buttons inside were nothing like the ones Singh had let me hold.

"Why do you display them in bottles?" I asked.

He eyeballed me like I was stupid. "To keep the dust off them. You want some or not?"

"Yes. Three of these and two of the square yellow ones over there," I said to keep him busy while I asked my questions. "Did you ever have a young man working here by the name of Larry? This would have been sometime in the late nineties."

Did his shoulders tense, or was it my imagination?

He turned back to me and rang up my purchases on the cash register. "Anything else before you go?"

"He had dark hair and would have been in his mid-twenties at the time. Drove a Ford Thunderbird."

The man tossed my packet of buttons in front of me and held out his hand. "Five fifty."

"Well?" I pressed. "Do you remember anyone like that? Or did you ever know a man called Derek Kehoe?"

Scowling, he placed both his palms down on the glass counter, leaned forward, and got in my face. "Lady, you're beginning to piss me off."

The atmosphere in the store, unfriendly to begin with, now felt unsafe, not to mention unsanitary, given his fetid mouth odor. I was aware that I was alone with a menacing man who refused to answer what should have been a perfectly easy question. Was it possible that *he* was Larry? I cocked my head, listening for a message from Colby because he always warned me when I was in real danger. I sensed nothing, so that must mean I was safe. Then again, maybe Colby had taken my plea to move on seriously.

I walked to the door of the store, stuck my head out, and was relieved to see Ryan leaning against his car, eyes closed and soaking up the sun. That satisfied smile was still on his face.

"Chief!" I yelled, and when he opened his eyes, I beckoned him to the store.

When he stepped inside, I told the storekeeper, "I'm Detective McGee, and this is Police Chief Ryan Ja— Jameson."

The storekeeper sneered. "I don't believe you."

Ryan pulled out his police ID and flashed it at the man, keeping his surname covered with a strategically placed thumb.

"This man is refusing to cooperate in our investigation, sir," I said.

"Well, we can't have that now, can we?" Ryan growled, and I bit my bottom lip to keep from laughing at his repeat of the previous night's words. "We don't like uncooperative citizens. We wonder what they're trying to hide."

I nodded like a toy dog in the back window of a car.

"I'm not hiding anything!" the man protested. "Where's *her* ID?"

"In the car. Where's yours?" I demanded.

Reluctantly, he found his driver's license and handed it over to us. Joshua Gage, born November 3, 1968.

"Now, Mr. Gage, perhaps you'd be kind enough to answer my officer's questions," Ryan said.

The man nodded, but his answers were short and sullen. No, he had never had any guy called Larry working for him nor any Derek Kehoe either, he said. He'd been running this store since 1997. What kind of car had he driven back then? A Chevy truck, that's what. A Thunderbird? Hell, no. Did he *look* like a dickhead?

I so wanted to answer that question, but Ryan tugged me outside.

"What an ass wipe," I said when we reached the car.

"True. But if he knows anything, he's not telling. Besides, your fight isn't with him," Ryan said dryly.

I didn't respond to this, scared to ask what he meant in case he said I was fighting myself or some other such entirely too perceptive observation. Back on the highway headed southwest to Pitchford, I asked, "Could that driver's license have been fake?"

"It didn't look it. But it's not impossible, I guess."

I picked at the edge of a nail. "What a strikeout this weekend's been."

Ryan glanced at me, a small frown between his eyes. "Surely not the *whole* weekend?"

There it was. We'd reached the awkward discussion stage.

"About last night …" I began.

"Oh, this is going to be good," he said. "Okay, let's have it."

I put my head down and stared at my hands, trying to figure out what it was I wanted to say. That it had been marvelous or that it had been a mistake? That it had been marvelous *and* a mistake? That I wanted to know what was going to happen now, but I truly didn't know *what* I wanted to happen now? That under my sassy, cynical exterior, my heart was still fragile?

What I eventually said was, "Honestly, I don't know." I looked over at him, trying to guess what he felt.

He met my gaze and held it. "Me either," he said eventually. Then a slow smile spread across his face, dimpling his right cheek. "Though I am certain about one thing."

"Oh yeah? What's that?"

"That bumping uglies with you was *fun*."

I laughed, relieved at the release of tension. "Well, you know what that means, Chief?"

"I'm listening."

"We'll just have to do it again sometime."

– 39 –

During the next few days, there were no new developments in the relationship between Ryan and me. If he'd called me every day, inundated me with messages signed *xoxo*, sent flowers, or wanted to immediately pick up where we left off in Halliwell, I would've spooked like a skittish filly and pranced away to a safe distance. But Ryan was like a freaking horse-whisperer, holding his peace and keeping his distance, waiting for me to calm down, come closer, and sidle back up to him. Which, of course, I did.

I was aware of the absence of Colby. On Tuesday evening, when Ryan and I went for a drink at the Tuppenny Tavern, a woman sat down on the barstool to my left just as if it was as empty as it looked. A glance in the mirror behind the bar confirmed my expression to be one part wince, one part frown and two parts sad smile. If I was a cocktail listed on the Tuppeny's specials board, I'd be called *mixed feelings*.

On the one hand, it was a relief not to be juggling the

demands of two men and hiding Colby's "visits" from Ryan. I'd never mentioned to the new man in my life how I sometimes heard Colby speaking to me or felt his presence. It sounded too crazy, and I figured it would throw a real wrench in the works of my relationship with Ryan. Who would want to be in a love triangle with a dead boyfriend? So it felt good not to have to hide that anymore or to make excuses about falling paintings, and I was pleased that Ryan and I would be able to enjoy each other without supernatural opposition. Mostly, I was truly happy for Colby, that he'd "moved on." I wasn't at all sure what that meant, but I hoped that there were better things to do on the other side of the veil than hang around your old girlfriend.

And yet, I also felt bereft, like there was an empty space somewhere inside me. I hadn't realized how much I'd gotten used to Colby's comforting presence these last few months, but now I missed it. It was a loss, not on the same scale as the grief I'd felt when the flesh and blood Colby had left me but still a loss.

There were no new developments in my Button Man investigation, either, despite the fact that it engrossed my mind even as I knocked Henry's tax receipts into shape and entered his data into the complicated financial software. Ryan and I had found out a couple of things on our trip to New Hampshire but nothing specific enough to take to Singh or even to Washington. If the Button Man kept to his pattern, then in just four days, he would take and kill another Jacob or Antoine or Denzel. And another mother or father or partner would be left with empty arms and a heart full of pain, regret and guilt.

It was maddening to realize that, unless some miracle happened, I wouldn't be able to stop that from happening.

I hoped the FBI was having better luck with their investigations than I was. The news channels updated their countdown widgets daily, but they weren't reporting any new developments. Was that because there were none or because the FBI was holding back on sharing the latest? A hotline had been set up for tips but, as the frustrated-looking journalist reporting from the Nash Forest site said on the morning news, "We want answers, yet all we have is more questions."

Tell me about it, buddy.

I had added Joshua Gage, the foul-smelling jerk from the last fabric store, to my list of suspects. He was the age Larry the Lodger would be now, plus he had dark hair and was clearly homophobic, which would fit someone who went around murdering gay men. But when Ryan ran the man's name through his systems, he found nothing suspicious. Short of checking out every other fabric store in the nation — and there was no guarantee that either Derek or Larry had even continued to work in the industry — I had no idea what more I could do or where to start doing it. The answer came via my mother.

That Wednesday night, I went over to my parents' place for our usual weekly family dinner and gave them an abbreviated version of my trip north. Not wanting my mother to start planning a wedding, I didn't mention that Ryan had accompanied me, let alone that we'd spent a night together, and I also didn't tell them about what we'd learned at the first store or about my misgivings about the man in the last one. I simply said that the whole trip had been a bust.

"But I did bring you something," I told my mother, giving her the paper bag with the embroidery kit inside it.

My mother's pleasure turned to perplexity when she examined her gift. "This is very kind of you, dear, but I don't do needlework. And I'm not a Gemini, you know."

"I thought you could sell it in your store."

"Now, that's a good idea! Did they have more? For all the star signs and maybe of fairies and angels too?"

"Maybe. I didn't check, to be honest."

"You left something in the bag." My mother pulled out two flyers that the friendly woman in the second store must have slipped in with my purchase. "This one is for a farmers' market in Halliwell. Not much use to us. I'm not going to drive two hours to buy an organic rutabaga, am I? But *this* one looks like fun. The annual Fabrics and Finery Convention is happening this weekend in Montpelier! They're going to have stalls with all kinds of fabrics and haberdashery, plus textile crafts, and even talks by experts on all sorts of interesting subjects. I'll bet I could get any number of wonderful products for the store there!" She glanced at my father. "I assume you won't want to go with me?"

"Correct."

My mother turned to me. "And now *you're* going to say you have no interest in these things, too, aren't you?"

"On the contrary," I said. "You had me at haberdashery."

"*Really?*" My mother gave me an incredulous stare.

"Truly. I'm interested in that kind of stuff." And in the people who sell them. "Let's go on Friday. That's the first day, so they'll have a full selection of stock. I'll ask Henry for the day off, and we can drive up bright and early."

My father was not fooled by my newfound interest. He gave me a narrow-eyed glance that told me he'd guessed why I wanted to go to the convention. "I wish you would drop this. It could get dangerous."

"It's a haberdashery convention, Dad. Honestly, what do you imagine could possibly go wrong?"

– 40 –

Friday, May 4

It was after noon by the time we reached the hotel in the center of Montpelier where the convention was being held, and it took a good while to find parking, because apparently, this kind of thing was huge in a way I'd never imagined.

In a vast exhibition hall, passionate crafters demonstrated beading, quilting, weaving, spinning, lacemaking, and needlepoint, while fabric sculptures and yarn hangings decorated the walls. The entire ballroom next door was filled with stalls selling every kind of fabric under the sun, plus enough supplies to sew, knit, crochet, cross-stitch, macramé or patchwork your way to the moon and back.

"This place is jammerpacked," my mother said.

She was right. There were hundreds of exhibitors and vendors, each wearing a nametag lanyard and convention branded ball cap, and throngs of visitors milled around, inspecting and buying the wares. I decided to search systematically, starting on the left-hand side of the huge room and going up and down the aisles, looking at each stall until … what? Until I got a feeling or a flash?

"Come on. Let's do this," I told my mother.

As we walked, she marveled over the goods on sale while I checked the faces and lanyards, dismissing all the women, and any man who was too young or too old to be Larry. I soon grew frustrated with our slow progression, however. My mother wanted to stop and check out every other display, while I was a woman on a mission.

"Let's split up so we can each do our own thing," I suggested. "I'll call you later, and we can meet up for lunch."

"I didn't bring my phone, dear, so we'll have to agree on a time and place," she said.

"One thirty at the entrance to this hall. We'll go for lunch together," I said. "I saw a hotdog vendor back there somewhere."

"Have fun," she said and happily made her way back down the aisle to a stall specializing in applique kits.

I forged ahead, weaving between booths selling supplies for mysterious things like tatting and lucet and crewelwork and stopped at a stall manned by someone who fit my criteria: male, middle-aged, dark hair. He wore a cardigan with a colorful parrot patch and large silver buttons.

"Hi! What is, um" — I stepped back to read the sign on the front of his stall — "stumpwork?"

While he raved about the unparalleled loveliness of raised embroidery and 3D effects. I examined him closely, noting that he wore a wedding ring and seemed to use his left and right hands equally. From my vision, I was pretty sure the killer was left-handed. I sensed no darkness or danger from this man, but then I hadn't touched him yet.

"Fascinating! Especially the bit about padding and puffing," I said. "So, have you been in this business long, Mr." — I checked his lanyard — "Schmidt?"

Ruth from the diner had thought Larry's name was something common like Smith or Jones; Schmidt wasn't that far off.

"Oh yes, for the last twenty years! But I'm not really in the business. I'm just the chairman of the local chapter of the United States of Stumpwork. Would you like to join?"

"Uh, not just yet." I was trying to think of a way to touch his hands and perhaps the buttons on his cardigan too. In the end, I just clasped my own hands around his and squeezed, saying, "But it's been great meeting you. Oh, look at these lovely old buttons. May I?"

I grazed my fingers over several of the buttons, but as when I'd grasped his hands, I felt and saw nothing extraordinary.

"If it's buttons you're after, check aisle H," he said helpfully. "Got every kind you could want there."

I threaded my way through the room, dutifully giving every stall the once-over even though I itched for Aisle H. Perhaps it was just the power of suggestion, but I felt a tug toward the center of the hall, as if my extra sense had already detected something there and wanted me to close in on it. I took a deep breath as I turned into the top end of the aisle. The pull was stronger now. I felt it as a vibration, like a plucked violin string inside me. I tried to walk slowly, to check each booth methodically, but my feet picked up speed and hurried me over to a double-width stand where a cluster of shoppers were bent over a magnificent display of buttons.

Peering between the women grouped in front of me, I studied what I could see of the man behind the stall. He was middle-aged, of average height and build, and the hair peeking out from under his cap was dark brown. When he gave a shopper her change, he used his left hand. My breathing quickened.

The customers moved off, and I stepped up to the table, glancing down at where the man was fiddling with a framed display of embossed brass buttons that might have come from a military uniform. Both his hands were as unmarked and undistinctive as the hands in my visions. He wore no wedding ring, but rings could be removed, and besides, I'd "seen" the killer's left hand both with and without a ring. He was wearing smart black pants and a blue-and-black plaid button-down shirt and his nametag lanyard hung over his chest, but it was turned the wrong way.

When he looked up from the display, I gave him a friendly smile and said, "Hi. What an amazing collection of buttons you have!"

He returned my smile. "If you want buttons, I'm your man."

"You know, I think you just might be," I said slowly.

"Do *you* like buttons, then? Do you collect them?"

"It's probably fair to say I'm downright obsessed with them."

He spread his hands wide over his table as if to say *what's not to like?*

"Have you always been interested in them?" I asked, touching buttons here and there on the table to see if I could sense anything.

"For a while now." Fetching a packet of pearl-white buttons from a box of stock behind him, he added it to his display. "If you're a koumpounophile — a lover of buttons — then you should come to my talk this afternoon. It's all about buttons."

"That sounds fascinating," I said.

"It starts at two o'clock in the Bison Room."

I made gun fingers and clicked twice. "I'll catch you there for sure."

A short woman who'd been waiting impatiently to be served reached over and picked up the framed buttons. "Are these for sale?" she asked in a nasal voice.

"I'm afraid not," he said.

He took the piece out of her hands and laid it back in its spot, front and center of the table. As he leaned forward, his lanyard swung out. I bent sideways and craned my neck to try to read the name, but he straightened before I could see it, and once again, the blank side faced up.

"Why do you have them on the table if you refuse to sell them?" the woman demanded.

"As a reminder," he told her.

"Of what?" she said rudely.

I also wanted to know.

He paused for a second, as if assessing whether he wanted to tell this entitled person something that was clearly personal. But I guess he knew the customer was king because he finally answered, "Of my time in combat."

The woman's eyes widened, and her mouth formed an O. Then she nodded, shook her head, and tutted. "You were in the military? Well, then I understand perfectly. Thank you for your service, sir. Thank you!"

She launched into a long explanation of where and when her own sons had served, while I pretended an interest in more of the wares on the table. When the woman finally left, having bought nothing, I pointed at a packet containing an assortment of buttons.

"I'll take those, please." I got no reading off the packet or the change he handed me and had no further excuse to stand there, but I decided to try one more ploy before I left. "Your nametag is flipped around," I said, trying to sound casually helpful rather than suspiciously excited.

"Oh," he said. "Thanks." And then he turned it around.

– 41 –

Lawrence Johnson.

The two words printed on the nametag set my heart racing and my mind spinning. The nickname for Lawrence was Larry, and Johnson was close enough to Jones. It was *him.* The seemingly mild-mannered man standing in front of me was Larry the Lodger, a.k.a. the Button Man. This was the man who'd wrapped a garotte around Jacob's neck and tightened it until the life drained out of him. This was the man who'd stitched Jacob's lips closed, added a button for extra effect, and then dumped his remains in a shallow grave far from home. This was the man who may well have killed Derek Kehoe.

I must've been staring because he gave me concerned look and said, "Are you okay, ma'am?"

"Yes. Yes, I'm fine. I just … thought of something I need to do urgently. But I'll see you later at your talk, for sure," I said.

I turned and had my phone out to call Singh before I was ten paces away. I figured Washington wouldn't be allowed to come on the strength of my intuition without his senior agent's permission, so I might as well contact Singh directly. Surprisingly, he answered.

"It's me. Garnet. I'm at a fabric convention in Montpelier, and he's here! The Button Man is here."

"What are you talking about?"

I backed up and explained. "The Kehoes — the family who owned that farm with the well outside of Crowbury? They had a lodger named Larry. He drove a Ford Thunderbird, the same car I saw in my vision with the victim who was hitchhiking. He worked in at least one fabric store in Woodbridge, New Hampshire. And there's a man here, one of the stallholders, whose name is Lawrence Johnson. Lawrence — like Larry, see? He's the right age, he's left-handed, and he's all about buttons. That's what he's selling at his stall, and he's even doing a talk on them later. It's him. I *know* it!"

Singh's reaction to my excited babble was distinctly underwhelming. He pointed out that there was no evidence to tie my guy to the crimes.

"That's only because you haven't investigated him, yet. Please just come and see him, ask a couple of questions," I begged and gave him the name and address of the hotel. "His talk starts at two o'clock in the Bison Room. If you leave Rutland now, you'll still be in time to catch him before the end of it."

"I'll see what I can do," Singh said with zero enthusiasm.

"That's a yes, right? You *are* coming?" I said, but I was speaking to dead air.

Impatient and anxious, I hurried to meet my mother at the

food stalls. I warned her we didn't have long because I wanted to attend a talk starting at two. We bought lunch — hotdogs with onions and fries from one of the food stalls — and my mother rambled on about the vendors she'd found who'd be able to supply her with tree of life embroidery kits and ying-yang symbol applique sets.

"And just take a look at this beauty!" she said, opening the largest of her shopping bags to show me the magnificent homemade quilt she'd purchased. From the way she asked whether I liked the design of geometric sunflowers, I suspected it would be an upcoming birthday or Christmas gift for me.

"Lovely," I said absently.

I wanted to go back to Lawrence Johnson's button stall and take a picture of him but was afraid that if I showed too much interest, it might make him suspicious. I was too distracted to finish my food — an occurrence so rare that it had my mother feeling my forehead to test for a fever.

"I'm not sick. I'm just—" For a moment, I considered filling her in on the picture. But when I imagined how she'd react — lots of excitement, too many questions, and the possibility of saying or doing something that would put my suspect on his guard — I decided to keep it to myself. "You know, eager to hear the talk. It's about buttons."

"Oh, well then of course you are, dear," she said, patting the back of my hand indulgently.

I dumped the remains of my food into a trashcan, and we headed to the Bison room. Visitors were already streaming into the venue, but we waited outside while I searched face after face for Agent Singh, even though I knew there was no way he could be there already, even *if* he'd decided to come. I told myself that he was on the way, that he might be an asshat, but he was also a dedicated investigator who would want to check out this lead. Surely, he was.

When the crowd entering the venue thinned down to a few stragglers, I saw posters advertising the talk sitting on tall easels beside the doors at each of the two entrances to the room. They displayed a photograph of the speaker, along with the title of the talk: *Buttons: Milestones and Meanings* by Lawrence Johnson.

I called Singh again, but this time he didn't answer. I left a voicemail reminding him that the killer was due to strike in two days' time. "Even if we do have his name and can find out where he lives, there's no guarantee he'll go home after this," I said. "He might be planning to go straight from here to someplace we don't know about and then what?" I took a photograph of the poster and sent that to him. Even if he hadn't left his office yet, he could still get here before the end of the talk if he broke a few speed limits.

An amplified voice drifted out of the room. The talk had started. Right now, someone was probably introducing Lawrence Johnson, Button Man.

"We need to go in," I told my mother.

"I think I'm going to sit this one out, dear. I have a horrible headache from all the noise and bustle, and a quiet sit-down is just what I need." She indicated a bench near the far door of the venue.

"Oh. Um, can you keep a lookout for Singh?"

Her eyebrows rose. "Special Agent Ronil Singh is coming?"

"Yes. Maybe. I mean, he's interested in learning more about buttons, too, so I told him about this talk."

"I'll keep my peepers peeled!" she said excitedly. Lugging the big bag containing the quilt and her other purchases, she headed over toward the bench

"Send him in as soon as he arrives," I called after her, then entered the room via the door closest to me.

The Bison Room was surprisingly big and almost full. Who'd have thought so many people would be interested in buttons? I grabbed an aisle seat in a row near the back, where I could keep an eye on both entrances and see Singh as soon as he arrived. Which he would. He had to.

On the stage, the master of ceremonies was wrapping up his introduction of Johnson. "— an expert in the field of buttons and who also owns a wholesale supply business. So, ladies and gentlemen — and there *are* a few thorns among the roses here today, I see, ha-ha — it is with great pleasure that I welcome our expert speaker, Mr. Lawrence Johnson."

The man I was sure was the prey I'd been hunting stepped up to the podium, waved a hand to acknowledge the applause, and clicked a presentation into life on the screen behind him.

"We all have a history," he said.

Some of us more than others, Larry, I thought.

"And buttons are no exception."

Johnson pressed a clicker, and I swore under my breath when I saw the slide that appeared on the screen. It was a photograph of a young man in a black bomber jacket and jeans, slouching against the side of a car. The picture had been taken from a distance of perhaps twenty yards, so I couldn't make out the man's facial features too clearly, but I *could* tell that the car was a dark blue Ford Thunderbird. I swore again.

"Do you *mind?*" the woman seated next to me complained.

I fumbled in my handbag for my camera while Johnson said, "Thankfully, I've changed a lot since then. I no longer wear stonewashed jeans, for one thing."

There was a smattering of laughter from the audience. My fingers brushed a smooth glass surface, and I closed them around my phone.

"Buttons, however, still look a lot like they did thousands of years ago," he said. "The earliest known button dates back five thousand years and—"

I brought my phone up, activated the camera, and took a pic of the screen just as Johnson changed to the next slide.

"It was made from shell and was found in the Indus Valley, where modern day Pakistan is."

Heart thumping, I checked the photographs on my phone.

$$- 42 -$$

Gotcha!

The photograph of the slide was slightly blurred, but it was still possible to make out the car model, although because of the angle of the original photograph, the license plate wasn't visible. I forwarded the image to Singh. That was proof that not only did details about Lawrence Johnson match my vision, but they also corresponded with what was known about the man who'd lodged with the Kehoes.

Johnson was now taking the audience through the history of buttons, explaining how they'd originally been made of shell, bone, animal horn and metal, but that they'd also been manufactured from more unusual materials such as stone, compressed paper, glass, ivory, and even a substance called vegetable ivory — the hard white endosperm of certain palm trees. Ordinarily, I would've found this all fairly interesting, but my attention was divided between checking my phone and the doors — where *was* he, already? — and having an internal conversation with Johnson about the type of buttons he personally favored.

How about plastic buttons in dark green, huh? Or wooden buttons threaded with black twine? Show us some photos of those, why don't you?

Instead, he showed pictures of ancient buttons that had originally been used as ornaments and seals, and said that the first usage of buttons as fasteners for clothes emerged in Germany in the thirteenth century.

What about fastening lips? When did that usage emerge, you sick, twisted excuse for a human being?

"These days, of course, the world mostly uses mass-produced plastic buttons, over sixty percent of which are produced in China."

What buttons are you using these days? Whose lips are you sewing?

"Still, it's good to remember the days when a button could be a miniature work of art, like these gold-and-enamel beauties with diamond edging, created by the Russian artist Peter Carl Fabergé — yes, he of the famous eggs — which today are housed in the Cleveland Museum of Art."

I scanned the doors again, then my phone, and chewed on a fingertip.

"And I would be wrong not to mention even more exotic uses. For example, this ring from medieval Italy has a hollow core to hold poison, which could be surreptitiously tipped into an enemy's wine at the feasting table."

You would *like that detail, wouldn't you, you freaking psychopath.*

"In World War II, some Allied agents were issued these buttons" — he flipped to another image — "which, as you can see, contain a miniature compass! And in our own century, hollow buttons have been used to smuggle drugs and diamonds."

Overcome by impatience and anxiety, I slipped out of my seat and headed for the nearby exit, while Johnson told his audience about koumpounophobia, the fear of the sight, smell and feel of buttons. I pushed the heavy door open and stepped outside, closing it softly behind me, then marched over to where my mother was keeping watch by the other door, her handbag on her lap and her shopping on the bench beside her.

"He hasn't arrived?" I asked.

"Not yet," she said.

"Dammit!"

Angry, I slipped back inside the room, where Johnson was now talking about a topic I was keenly interested in hearing — his take on how buttons had assumed a meaning greater than the sum of their limited parts in language and culture.

"Not only do buttons bind separate parts together," he told the audience, "but they can signal personal aspects about us."

As he listed characteristics, he flashed images of different buttons on the screen: style (a furry animal-print novelty button); status (vintage pearl and gold buttons); national identity (green buttons in the shape of shamrocks); hobbies (a soccer ball button), and age and sex (pink teddy bears). I leaned forward when he explained that buttons could even reveal our personal ethos, but the picture he displayed was merely one of a silver button with the three hear-no-evil, see-no-evil, speak-no-evil monkeys engraved on it.

"Buttons have found a way into our language too," Johnson said. "For example, if you're pretty in a dainty way, then you're cute as a button. And if you corner someone to discuss a hot button issue, then you've buttonholed them."

This was more interesting.

"You can be buttoned down or buttoned all the way up—"

Or you can button your lip? Is that what you did to Derek, you vile psycho?

"—and if you're fully aware of what's going on, you're said to have your finger on the button. You might have a cute button nose, but if you annoy someone, you're said to be …?"

He paused, cupping a hand behind one of his ears, and someone from a row near the back shouted, "Pushing their buttons!"

"Correct! And when you want to sleep longer, what do you do?"

"Hit the snooze button," a woman in the row behind me called out.

"And if you're smart and alert, then you're …?"

"Bright as a button!" a few people responded.

Johnson smiled and nodded. "Right on the button!"

The audience laughed, clearly enjoying the game.

I couldn't stand the hilarity or the chasm between the humorous, urbane fellow he pretended to be and the reality of who he truly was. Out of everyone in this audience, I alone knew what he'd done. Never had sitting and doing nothing felt so intolerable. I wanted to run down the aisle and tackle him at the knees, to knock him unconscious with something heavy and sit on his chest until the cops arrived. I wanted justice. No, I wanted *vengeance* for funny, daring Jacob Wertheimer and for all the other young men — possibly even poor, sad Derek —

whose lives Johnson had snuffed out to satisfy some sick urge or fantasy.

"Well, ladies and gentlemen, that brings me to the end of my presentation. We have a little time left for questions, if anyone has any," Johnson said.

A woman near the front asked about the ethics of using ivory and tortoiseshell to make buttons. I checked the door — still no sign of Singh. I checked my phone — no messages. I let out a deep sigh of disappointment. It looked like he wasn't coming. I was desperate for Larry to be taken in for questioning today, but now it seemed like that wasn't going to happen.

"But I don't see the harm in repurposing old buttons made of those substances," Johnson was saying. "After all, the creatures are already dead."

And you enjoy killing creatures, don't you? Even Derek's innocent little cat!

"So, in a way," Johnson said, "if you appreciate and wear those buttons, you're giving meaning to their deaths, aren't you?"

And what meaning did you give to the deaths of all those young men, you utter and complete bastard?

On the remote chance that Singh was waiting outside the room, ready to nab his suspect, I took a photo of Lawrence Johnson using the highest zoom on my phone camera and sent it to the agent so that he would know the suspect the moment he saw him. Meanwhile, Johnson replied to a question about whether he thought buttons would still be around a hundred years from now, and then the MC said he'd allow one final question. A *final* question? I checked the time display on my phone. According to my calculations, there were still fifteen minutes to go before the end of the presentation.

"We have to finish a little early because Lawrence has a flight to catch," the MC explained.

A flight? *Shit.* He was going to get away. I'd tracked him down, and now he was just going to walk out of here, and the day after tomorrow, another man would die. I needed to delay him as long as I could. When I raised my hand, Johnson acknowledged me with a smile of recognition. Here was the button-obsessed woman from earlier at his booth, his expression said. He pointed at me.

"That was a fascinating talk, Mr. Johnson. Thank you so much. Especially the part about … um … the poison rings. I really found that so interesting and … er … unusual. And the hidden compasses, I mean, wow!"

He glanced at his watch and asked, "Do you have a question?"

"Yes. Yes, I do." At that moment, my mind went blank. The only answers I wanted belonged to questions I couldn't ask without tipping him off. Finally, I settled for "Do you think buttons will survive zippers and Velcro?"

"They have so far," he said with a light laugh.

I checked both doors. No FBI agent. "And can I also just ask—" I began.

But the MC cut me off, saying, "Sorry, we really are out of time." He thanked his speaker, the audience applauded, and then with a last wave, Johnson walked up the aisle toward the far exit.

I groaned in frustration, not knowing what to do. Along

with the rest of the audience, I stood up, then I began pushing my way through the throng in the aisle, heading for my exit and hoping against hope that Singh — and Washington, too, maybe — was waiting outside to apprehend Johnson. I exited the venue to find myself in a lobby now packed with convention goers. Standing on tiptoes, I scanned the crowd but saw no police or FBI presence at all.

I did, however, spot a flash of black and blue plaid at the far exit. Johnson had been cornered by someone determined to have a last word with him. When he shifted slightly, I saw that, of all people to be waylaying him, it was my *mother*. What the hell was she doing? I began weaving through the crowd, keeping my gaze fixed on the odd couple ahead. I saw her lay a restraining hand on his arm, and a sense of dread bloomed in my stomach like a dark, poisonous flower.

As though she could feel my dismayed gaze on her, my mother looked up, saw me, and waved. Pointing at me, she leaned over to tell a smiling Johnson something. Just that I'd attended his talk because I was super interested in buttons? Or that I was a psychic private eye investigating murders in which the serial killer had left buttons with his victims? I began to move quicker, pushing past people. No time for apologies now. My mother half-turned to point at the hotel entrance, then held her hands up in a shrug. I could almost hear her saying, "We were hoping the FBI agent investigating the murders would attend your talk, but it looks like he didn't come. I wonder why?"

Johnson turned his head to meet my gaze while my mother kept spilling the beans, and I saw the indulgent smile fade from his face. He *knew*. And in that moment when he comprehended the danger, he grabbed my mother's elbow and dragged her off with him.

What?

"*No!*" I screamed. "Stop him. Stop that man!"

Galvanized into panicked action, I barged through the crowd, throwing elbows and shoving people aside. I caught a glimpse of them headed toward the main entrance of the hotel. Johnson was keeping his hold on my mother while she stumbled along beside him, her shopping bags bouncing against her side.

"Stop that man! Help!" I screamed.

Two men in security uniforms stepped in front of me, blocking my way.

"Let me *go!*" I tried to sidestep them, urging them to hurry. When one grabbed my arm, I wrenched it free and pointed at the hotel entrance. "That man is kidnapping my mother!"

One guard spoke into his walkie-talkie. "Seal the exits. Repeat, seal all doors!"

The other, moving with infuriating slowness, turned to stare where I'd pointed. "What man?" he asked.

Lawrence Johnson and my mother were nowhere to be seen.

– 43 –

My mother is gone. *The Button Man got away.*

I sat cross-legged on my bed in my old bedroom in my parent's house, staring blankly at the wall, reliving that moment earlier in the afternoon when Lawrence "Larry" Johnson had dragged my mother off.

My mother is gone. The Button Man got away.

The words raced around inside my mind like greyhounds on a never-ending track.

More than twelve hours after she'd been kidnapped, my mother was still missing. Despite every law enforcement agency being on the alert, no one had spotted her. Or him. I understood why he might've taken her. Maybe he'd feared the authorities were waiting outside the hotel, and she could be the hostage that ensured his getaway. But why had he *kept* her? The only reason I could think of was me. He was holding her to keep me in check, in case he needed leverage.

I opened the bottom drawer of my nightstand. All the equipment I needed was still there, waiting to be called back into use. I'd used it in those bleak months after Colby died, but

I'd deliberately left it behind when I moved to Boston, hoping to shake the horrible habit. And when I moved some of my old belongings to the loft above Henry's Mason's garage, I had again chosen not to take it with me. But I hadn't gotten rid of it either. Maybe I, too, had anticipated a time when I'd need some leverage against myself. I peeled off my socks and let my fingertips trail lightly over the sole of one foot, hunting for a raised ridge, a rough edge, a filament of skin.

Singh and Washington had arrived together, twenty minutes too late. When they came over to where local cops were taking my statement, Washington explained that they'd been delayed by a multi-car pileup on I-89 outside Montpelier. He then gave my shoulder a sympathetic pat and told me they were doing everything possible to try to find my mother. Singh offered no words of comfort; his face was thunderous, and a tic pulsed in his cheek. I knew he was furious that, against his instructions, I'd involved myself in the case again. But I, too, was full of anger, and mine was fueled by uncontrollable fear and panic.

I turned on him and demanded, "If you knew you'd be late, why didn't you alert local police? They could've gotten here in time."

"Because I don't mobilize law enforcement agencies based on the hunch of some self-proclaimed psychic!" he snapped.

"Turned out my 'hunch' was *right*, though, didn't it?" I snarled.

Singh's mouth curled in contempt. "Oh, my bad! I didn't realize you'd had a premonition about your mother being kidnapped."

That hit home. But my only defense was to attack, so I yelled, "Your stupid lack of trust in me is costing us. It's risking lives!" I was only just holding my tears at bay.

The two police officers had been looking from me to Singh and back again, tracking the volley of shots. When the agent, his face tight with fury, took a step toward me, they fell back a few paces and pretended an interest in their notepads.

"*A*, there is no 'us,'" he said in a voice icy with barely controlled wrath. "And *B*, it is your stupid *trust* in yourself that is risking lives. Your mother's, for one!"

At that, my tears spilled over. Regret, fear, anger, shame, humiliation — I felt them all. Looking disgusted, Singh told Washington to take my statement.

"And when he and the Montpelier police have finished with you, go home," he told me. "Go home and stay there. Do not contact me or anyone at our agency. Keep your interfering nose out of this investigation, or I will allow myself the great pleasure of arresting you for obstruction of justice myself."

He'd stalked off, and shaking with rage and terror, I'd jumped through all the official hoops necessary before being given the go ahead to leave.

Now I picked at the ball of my foot, raising a tiny shred of skin. Gripping it with my old purple tweezers, I pulled down slowly and steadily. It was important to get just the right tension and speed. Pull too hard or too fast, and you merely succeeded in breaking off the tiny edge. And where was the satisfaction in that? Where was the pain?

I so desperately wanted someone to blame. Someone other than myself. I wanted to believe that if Singh had left earlier, arrived sooner, or trusted me more, then Johnson would've been apprehended, and my mother would now be safely back at home, making us chamomile tea after the day's excitement.

The thin filament of skin peeled off in a satisfyingly long strip. I laid it on a Kleenex on the bedspread beside me and stared at the raw band of flesh now exposed — pink, with a small jewel-bright drop of blood just oozing at one end. Pretty in its own way. The first piece was always the hardest — finding the place to begin, getting the movement just right, and feeling the first shock of pain — but the second was always easier. With the tweezers, I pinched at the edge of skin beside the peeled strip and tore down, holding my breath against the burn.

Why hadn't I anticipated what had happened? How could I not have foreseen the possibility of it? Yes, I'd never been able to see the future — my stupid "talent" was only good for seeing the past — but I should've *thought* ahead, realized that my mother, who always wanted to be helpful and didn't know that I suspected Lawrence Johnson of being the Button Man, might've tried to detain him for a minute so that I could have a word with him, or she might have wanted to let him know that he could be able to help out the FBI with his button expertise.

I was to blame for what had happened to my mother, for what might even now be happening to her. Why had I let her go to the damn convention with me? I'd known after our unsettling experience at that creepy house in Hucknall that it was stupid, reckless even, to take her with me on my investigations, and yet, I'd done it again. I'd welcomed her company on the trip, and ignoring my father's warnings that it could be dangerous, I'd exposed her to a man who was deadly.

I peeled another shred of skin, laid it beside the others on the tissue, and watched a trickle of blood traverse the wrinkled surface of my foot.

If only I'd told her why we were really there. I hadn't trusted her not to say or do something stupid, but I was the one who'd been stupid. If she'd known who I suspected Johnson to be, she would never have approached him. I was always holding back from trusting others, rationalizing that I didn't want to impose on them, while deep down believing I couldn't rely on them. It was inexcusable hubris, as though I alone knew what to do in any situation, as though I could handle any eventuality by myself. And look what my desire for self-reliance and my fear of being let down had resulted in now.

When I'd gotten home, I checked the medicine cabinet in her bathroom and found her blood pressure and blood thinner medications still there. She hadn't taken them with her — why would she? — and the situation she was in had to be cranking up her blood pressure. Was she even still alive?

I tore another strip, wider, deeper, to block out the thought, to pull me back from the torment of what-ifs and if-onlys and anchor me in the here and now of my pain. I was an idiot and a bad daughter. My mother was kind, thoughtful and loving. She only ever meant well. Any problems in our relationship were my fault. I was too easily irritated, too keen to avoid spending time with her, too intolerant of her enthusiasms and eccentricities.

If she comes back safely, I'll be a better and more loving daughter, I promised whoever might be listening in the universe.

I dabbed at the bloody bottom of my foot and then twisted the top off an old tube of iodine ointment, wishing I could cleanse myself of guilt as easily as I could disinfect my foot. The distinctive smell took me back to my darkest periods of grief, but the searing sting when I anointed my flayed flesh brought me right back to the present.

Back in Montpelier, I'd begged Washington to hold off on calling my father. I needed to be the one to break the news, and I needed to do it in person. I'd left as soon as I could and driven home with my head swirling and my heart in my throat, constantly checking my phone for any updates.

It was dark by the time I'd arrived at my parents' home and went inside. My dad was in the living room, reading a book, and he greeted me with a smile. I tossed my jacket onto the couch, and the crystals in its pockets spilled out onto the cushions. The news, so terrible, was impossible to speak, and yet, I had to say the words, had to repeat them when he failed to understand the first time. I watched how his face drained of color, how his fingers tightened on the arms of his chair, how his mouth opened to speak the recriminations he must be thinking — *this is your fault. I told you to stay out of it. I knew something bad was bound to happen. Your mother's probably dead in a ditch somewhere, and you're to blame!* — and then closed again, with the unuttered words ghosting the space between us.

I apologized, but the inadequate phrases floated away like chaff in the air while the substantial facts of what had happened and what might yet happen fell like threshed grain and remained. I poured us both a scotch and sat in silent vigil with my father.

I opened the door for Ryan when he came but heard nothing of what he said because it wasn't news of my mother. There *was* no news of my mother. Ryan sat with us for hours, holding my hand, bringing my father and me hot drinks, making toast and insisting we eat it. When Ryan left at midnight, my father had shaken his head at my pleas for him to go to bed, and I'd trudged upstairs alone. To my old room, my old habit.

Now I stared at the thin ribbons of skin laid out on the tissue beside me and, rearranging my legs so that the rough heel of my left foot was now uppermost, began peeling again, welcoming the pain.

My mother is gone. The Button Man got away.

– 44 –

Saturday, May 5

Dawn broke, oblivious to my misery, which craved the comfort of darkness. Birds sang, and the sun hauled itself over the horizon for the millionth time. Somewhere, a dog barked, a newspaper landed on a garden path, and flowers turned their faces to the light. I was holed up in bed, fighting a hangover and bracing myself for bad news. I'd spent the night wrestling with my duvet, punching my pillows and beating myself up.

Eventually, driven by caffeine deprivation, I went downstairs, wincing with every step. My father was already at the kitchen table, hollow-eyed from lack of sleep and hunched over a cup of coffee. I was pouring myself one when the kitchen telephone rang. I hesitated, both needing and dreading to hear the news, then picked up the receiver with an unsteady hand.

"Hello, dear. It's me."

"Mom? Mom, is that you?" I asked.

My father stood up, his eyes wide and a hand over his heart.

"Yes, dear, it's me," she said.

"Are you okay?"

"Safe and sound in one piece!" she said, sounding tired.

My father snatched the phone and began asking questions, while I sagged into a chair, blowing out a long breath and wiping a trembling hand over my eyes.

A few minutes later, my father hung up and turned to me. "She's safe."

"How? Where?" I said weakly.

"Seems he just let her go, and a motorist found her this morning, walking along the highway outside of Hardwick. She said something about giving her statement — I don't know if she already has or if she still needs to — and then they'll bring her back to Pitchford."

We stared at each other for several moments, saying nothing, communicating everything, and then we embraced, crushing each other tightly as we sobbed our relief. After an interminable ninety minutes, Ryan's car pulled into the driveway.

"They must've taken her to the police station," I said as I bolted to the front door. Outside, I ran to the car and hugged my mother, where she still sat in the passenger seat, telling her that I was sorry, that I loved her, and that I would be a better daughter in future.

"Goodness gracious, dear. Let me get out of the car before you drown me in tears!"

I helped her out, noticing the smears of dirt on her pale face and the circlet of bruises around her frail, blue-veined wrist. Still apologizing, I clung to her, needing to feel the solidity of her small frame in order to believe that she was truly home and safe. She patted me on the back, reassuring me that it wasn't my fault and comforting me like I was a little kid. I dashed my tears away, feeling bad. It wasn't her job to console *me*. I'd studied the circle of support. Compassion and reassurance were supposed to flow to the victim. I stepped back as my mother was swept up into my father's embrace, and I watched him gently escort her inside the house.

"Thank you," I told Ryan.

"Don't thank me. I had nothing to do with it." He looked grumpy at the thought.

I followed my parents into the living room, where my father settled my mother comfortably on the couch after brushing the spilled crystals from last night onto the carpet. Before he covered her legs with a blanket, I saw that her knees were scraped and bruised, and a scabbed scratch ran the length of one calf. She was missing a shoe, and her bare foot was wrapped in a bandage.

"Do you want a drink?" I asked. I knew I did.

"A cup of tea, please, dear. With *two* spoons of sugar."

"I'll get it," my father said and disappeared into the kitchen, where I suspected that he would have a good cry.

"Are you all right, Mom?" I asked. "Really all right?"

"Of course I am," she said. "Just a bit scratched and bruised."

"Did he hit you?"

"No, no. Nothing like that. But he did push me out of the car, and it was rolling at the time, though only slowly, so I got a little banged up. Goodness me, what a night!"

My father returned and tenderly wiped her face clean with a damp washcloth. He pressed his lips against her forehead and held the contact until the kettle whistled in the kitchen. "Tea," he said and left.

"So he just let you go?" I asked my mother.

"Well, no. I talked him into it, or should that be *out* of it? I explained how he was stacking up some very bad karma by picking on an innocent old lady, and told him he needed to think very carefully about his actions because he was under the baleful influence of Mercury in retrograde, although, to tell the truth, I don't actually know if Mercury is currently in retrograde, and I certainly couldn't be sure last night because my head was all in a muddle with worry. Anyway, I must've gotten through to him because when I began telling him about Saturn, that's when he opened the door and shoved me out."

I exchanged a glance with Ryan, feeling a hysterical and entirely inappropriate urge to laugh.

"He even tossed my purse and shopping bag out after me and then roared off, leaving me in the absolute middle of nowhere! I was shocked because until he started the senseless rambling, he'd seemed like a nice enough man. But really, he was a wolf in sheep's skin."

"Clothing," I said absently.

"What's that, dear?"

"It's 'a wolf in sheep's clothing.'"

"That can't be right, dear. Sheep don't wear clothing."

"They don't wear skins either," I said irritably. Crap. Fifteen minutes in, and I'd already broken my resolution to be more patient with my mother.

"Like a wolf in sheep's wool then," she said.

My father brought in a tray with a cup of tea, a plate of cookies, and the two amber bottles containing my mother's medications. When she took her cup, it rattled on the saucer. She was putting on a great show of bravery, but clearly, she was more affected than she wanted us to see.

"What did you do then?" I asked her.

She took a long sip, sighed, and said, "Nothing I *could* do. I was on a dirt road with no buildings or lights in sight and no idea which direction to go. So I just found a tree and went to sleep under it, wrapped in my lovely quilt that I bought at the convention."

"Oh, Crystal," my father said, his face pinched with distress.

"Yes, it wasn't the most comfortable night I've ever had." She took another sip of tea. "But morning always comes after the darkest dark, and when it did, I used my quartz necklace to divine which way to walk. When I got to the main road, I flagged down a car. The lovely driver, a nurse on her way to her morning shift, took me straight to the police station, and everything happened rather quickly after that. Everyone was so kind."

She finished her tea. My father immediately poured her another and urged her to eat a cookie. Color was returning to her cheeks, though her face was still drawn with exhaustion.

"Can you tell us what he said, the man who kidnapped you?" Ryan asked.

"At first, he didn't say much. We drove around for what felt like hours while it grew dark, but I think it's fair to say I did most of the talking."

That, I could easily believe.

"After a while, he told me to button my lip. And he said it so fiercely that I really thought I ought to. Then we drove around in silence for a while, but I could tell he was very upset, and eventually, he started muttering to himself."

"What did he say?"

"Nothing that made much sense to me. Duty and punishment and whether it would spoil it to kill me."

My father pushed the plate of cookies closer to her. "Spoil what?"

"Spoil the fantasy," I murmured.

"I thought I might be toast there for a while," my mother continued, "but Michael was protecting me, of course."

"Michael?" Ryan asked, surprised by this mention of a new person.

"The archangel, dear," my mother explained kindly.

"Ah, I see." Ryan, bless him, kept a perfectly straight face.

"And he granted me a miracle, too, now that I think about it! Oh dear, I clean forgot to tell the nice police officers in Montpelier about it."

"About what?" I asked.

"That I got something of his!" From the depths of her bra, my mother drew out a small object and held it up for us to see. I gaped at the black-and-gold class ring between her thumb and forefinger.

"How the hell did you get that?" I said.

"It was dangling from a chain on the rearview mirror in his van. When he started pushing and shoving me, I grabbed whatever I could to hang onto, including the mirror. The chain snapped, and it came off in my hand. Maybe you can get fingerprints off it?"

I glanced at Ryan, who cocked his head in a way that said he thought it was unlikely. Whatever prints might have been on it, they'd be smudged after her handling of it and a night spent nestled against her bosom.

"Give it here," I said. A lab might not get anything off the ring, but maybe I could.

– 45 –

I held the black-and-gold ring between my palms and closed my eyes. Darkness yawned like a hungry void, beckoning me into its endless hollow. Fighting the heaviness constricting my chest, I drew a deep breath and moved forward into the foul abyss.

There's light, but it's shady.
Daytime in the woods.
In the distance — a blurry outline of buildings with a faint smudge of red.
A man grunts. He stands behind another man, arms wrapped around him. A macabre embrace.
He drags the slumped torso backward. It's a dead weight. The head lolls facedown on the bloodstained shirt, and the heels rake twin trails through the mud and leaves.
In a place of deeper shadows, a shallow trench lies waiting in the earth, and a shovel rests against a tree trunk.

He slumps to his knees and shoves. The body topples into the grave, landing on its back with a dull thud. The man pants, catching his breath, then heaves the legs into the hole too.

The muddy, bloody face gapes blindly at the trees and sky above.

You shut your mouth, the man says. But the corpse does not obey.

He grabs the shovel and slams it under the chin. Teeth click together, then the jaw falls open again.

The man curses, leans across, and wrenches a button off the dead man's bloody shirt, and jams it into that yawning mouth. You'll stay buttoned up for good now, he rasps.

He stands and shovels dirt, covering the face and the bloody smile across the throat.

He feels calm. He made the problem go away.

Gasping, I clawed my way back to the light and to the present.

"Larry *did* kill the Kehoe boy. He killed him and buried his body in the woods by that farm in Crowbury!"

Ryan stared at me with wide eyes. "You saw it?"

I nodded. "It made his 'problem go away.'" I sketched air-quotes around the words.

"He said that to me too," my mother said unexpectedly. "I remember now. He was muttering about rules and vows, and saying he'd make the problem go away and then *he'd* be satisfied and proud of him."

"He?" I said. "He, who?"

"I don't know, dear, do I?" she replied and yawned widely.

"Can we just go back to his vehicle for a moment? Did you manage to see what kind of van it was?" Ryan asked my mother.

"A white delivery van, but don't ask me the make or model or registration number because as I told the police, I don't know. I *did* see that it had angels on the side," she said, sounding proud of her observational skills. "Of course, as soon as I saw those, I knew I was under divine protection and I'd come out of it in one piece eventually."

Ryan made a sound of surprise, and a strange expression crept over his face. "I've seen that van before," he said.

"*What?*" I said, stunned. "Where? When?"

"You've seen it too!" Ryan told me. "It was parked outside that store, the second fabric store we went to, the one in Halliwell. Remember?"

I did. "Heavenly Haberdashery!" I gasped, seeing again the white van with floating cherubs twirling ribbons on the side. "But that means … that means …"

"It means we saw *him* too. Yeah! Our focus was on the storekeeper, but *he* was there. He was the delivery man in the uniform and cap, dropping off the flyers advertising the convention where he was due to give a presentation on buttons."

"Of course!"

I'd assumed the killer might have worked in a fabric store, but he could just as easily have gone into a business that *supplied* those stores with what they needed. It would keep him mobile, traveling the highways and trawling for victims. Hadn't I read how psychopaths got restless and loved to drive? Even the FBI's original profile had said that their unknown suspect might be something like a trucker or travelling salesman. I'd been so blinded, so stupid.

Ryan stood up. "That store, what was it called?"

"Sew Pretty," I said, still reeling from the realization that I'd practically bumped into Johnson before the conference. "Spelled S-E-W."

"I'll call the FBI Montpelier police and give them a description of the van," Ryan said. "Maybe they can get more information from the store about their haberdashery supplier."

He went outside to make his calls, and I turned back to my mother. "Larry — Lawrence Johnson, the man who kidnapped you — did he say anything about where he was headed? Did he mention where he lived?"

My father said, "That's enough, Garnet. Can't you see how tired your poor mother is? She needs to rest."

"I'm sorry, Mom. I really am," I said earnestly. "I know you've probably already answered these questions and you must be worn out, but this man is a killer, and he's due to kill his next victim tomorrow."

My father pressed his lips together angrily, but my mother patted his hand. "Let her ask her questions, Bob. I'd like to help."

"Could you see where you were going, where he was driving?" I said.

"No, I didn't have my glasses on and didn't want to try to get them out of my purse in case he thought I was reaching for a gun! I can only thank the goddess that when all was said and done, I'm a woman."

"What do you mean?" I asked.

"Well, just before he threw me out of his van, he said, 'Real men don't hurt women.' Just like that!"

"But real men do hurt men?" my father asked, sounding outraged.

"It'll be one of his rules," I explained. "That he only kills gay men."

"I need to visit the bathroom," my mother said.

My father insisted on accompanying her, and not knowing what else to do, I made a pot of coffee and another of tea. We were all drinking fresh cups when Ryan returned to the living room, looking puzzled.

"Did you get ahold of Singh?" I asked.

"Yeah. They've got addresses for Johnson's house and business in Concord, and they're going to descend on both places simultaneously, even though he probably won't be going near either, now."

"Any other developments?" my father asked.

"They lifted fingerprints off the podium and microphone and from Johnson's stall at the convention," Ryan replied. "And they checked them against the IAFIS database."

"They got a hit?" I guessed.

"There's a Lawrence "Larry" Johnson in the system. Seems your lodger was arrested for credit card fraud in New York in 1994."

"Yesss!" I punched the air in victory.

"I'm not surprised to hear he was a crook too," my mother said.

"But there's a problem," Ryan continued. "The prints on

file for Lawrence Johnson don't match the prints of the man who lectured on buttons at the convention. Those prints got no hits in the system."

"I don't understand," I said, feeling deflated. "How's that possible?"

"Could be an error at the lab, I suppose. It *was* a rush job. They're going to check again."

"I hope they find him soon," my mother said. "Judging by last night, he's not right in the head and likely getting worse by the minute. Good gracious, but he was agitated! Sweating badly and slapping his forehead over and over again. Which, I don't mind telling you, I really didn't think he should've been doing. Not when he already had that dent. So I told him—"

"Dent? What dent?" I demanded, feeling suddenly cold.

"A little hollow, just here." My mother touched the hairline on the right side of her forehead. "I saw it when his cap came off."

– 46 –

My mouth fell and my scalp tightened. Had I gotten it all wrong? Again?

"Garnet?" Ryan asked.

He didn't understand the significance of what my mother had just said because I'd never told him about the dent. I'd forgotten all about it until now. Saying nothing, I stared down at the ring in my left hand. It lay on top of the old silvery scar that was my reminder of the day I'd searched for Colby, the day he'd turned up dead. I scooped up a handful of the crystals from the carpet and, holding them in my right hand, closed the fingers of my left around the ring. I shut my eyes and bent over my hands, doubling down on my efforts to see more.

When the image of the man and the corpse returned, I pushed my mind back beyond it, further into the past, deeper into the silent darkness.

Thin early-morning light.
A man in stained overalls slouches against a red barn
wall, sucking on a bottle of beer and eyeing the younger

man who stands before him, twisting a hat in his hands.

I have a fair idea what must of happened, the slouching man says. It came to me last night. I've been asking your mother for the deed to this place. But she says she doesn't have them, and I believe her. I know she'd give them to me if she had them. Hell, she'd give me anything I asked for. He smirks.

The younger man grips the hat tighter, his white knuckles standing out against his dirty skin.

She said there was some hold up with the old man's estate, that she was waiting on the death certificate from his family in New Hampshire. So I volunteered to drive up there and go get it. Helpful, like. Next thing, she's mighty upset and begging me not to go. So I got to thinking, why would that be? And you know what I came up with?

No, the youth says. No, I don't.

I think she doesn't want me asking difficult questions of the old man's family, if he even had any. I think there ain't no death certificate up there. And you know why that is? He points the bottle at the young man. Because the old man never left this here place. You could say, he bought the farm.

He laughs and puts a hand up to shield his eyes while he scans to the left and the right. Where do you think I'd find him if I went looking? Under the barn floor, under a tree in the woods … at the bottom of the old well? Yeah, I figured that would be a real good place to dump the old man, and I was right.

The youth says nothing, but his face tightens as he stares down at the weeds growing in the dirt.

The man downs the last of his beer and tosses the bottle aside. Did you do it? Or was it your momma? Wouldn't surprise me none if it was her. Scrawny bitches like her are always stronger than they look.

What do you want from me, the younger man asks dully.

The deed to this place.

We've got no deed.

Well, you must have some cash stashed away from the sale of the store. And you're a hard-working fella. You'll make more as the years go by. As long as you keep mailing me checks every month, no one needs to know what happened to grandpops. But if you don't, well then, you'll have a real problem right soon.

You're the problem. I want you to go away.

And I'm happy to oblige, boy! There's nothing keeping me here.

The younger man nods slowly. Okay. But then you've got to go directly. Today.

Fine. I need to collect on a bet or two in town, and while I'm there, I'll take my leave of the good folks of Crowbury. I'll be back here this afternoon for the money. He waves, and the ring on his finger flashes in the sunlight.

I opened my eyes, blinking hard and shaking my head to clear it. My mother, father and Ryan were all staring expectantly at me.

"I've been hunting the wrong man," I said softly. "The right name but the wrong man. Or is it the other way around?"

"What do you mean?" Ryan asked urgently.

"It wasn't Larry Johnson who killed all those men."

"I'm so confused," my mother said. "You said it was him. If *he* isn't the murderer, then why did he kidnap me?"

"The real killer," I said, "is the man who *calls* himself Lawrence Johnson."

My father was also looking perplexed. "There's a difference between those two?"

"And I think I have an idea where he might be headed."

"You know who the killer is?" Ryan asked. "Where he is?"

"Do I *know*, like know for sure?" I shook my head slowly. "Nope. It's just a hunch, that's all. So if you're going to suggest I call Singh, don't."

"Would it matter so much if you called them, and then it turned out to be a false alarm?" my father asked.

"It's not the embarrassment of being wrong that I'm worried about." I was well over that. I'd had lots of practice dealing with my mistakes. "It's that they simply wouldn't come, not on the basis of a mere guess."

Ryan nodded grudgingly; he knew I was right.

"Plus, Singh will arrest me if he knows I'm still nosing about. I need to go check it out myself first," I said. "I'll call him if I find anything."

I stood up and grabbed my handbag, ignoring the vociferous protests of my parents, who both believed this was sheer folly — my father because it might be dangerous and had I learned nothing, my mother because it was positively foolhardy to rush off into the unknown without first reading the cards for celestial guidance.

Ryan stood up, too, and for a moment, I thought he was going to block my path. But instead, he said, "You're not going alone. I'm going with you."

My mouth opened, an automatic protest on my lips at both the order and the peremptory tone. I didn't like being told what to do, not by anybody. And hadn't I just spent most of the last twenty-four hours regretting bringing someone else into my investigation and swearing never to endanger anyone again? Then again, as he himself had once said, Ryan wasn't just anyone. He was a cop; he could take care of himself. He would probably even take care of me. When I'd fallen through the trapdoor at that barn, I'd learned for myself that it was crazy-stupid to walk into potential danger alone. I trusted him, and more than that, I actually *wanted* him by my side through this.

Ryan had his hands on his hips and was glowering at me. His change of expression when I merely said, "Okay, sure," was comical. He hadn't expected me to give in so quickly.

"On one condition," I added quickly.

At once, he looked wary. "Oh yeah? And what's that?"

"You bring your gun."

$$- 47 -$$

We went in Ryan's car. It was faster, and after my sleepless night, I was too tired to drive. I wasn't too tired to eat, however. At my mother's insistence, my father had sent us off with packed sandwiches and a couple of cans of Coke. As tense as I was, I shouldn't have been hungry. But anxiety always gave me an appetite, as did boredom, exercise and anger. Life, really.

As soon as we were on the highway headed north, as per my directions, Ryan said, "Explain everything."

"The Button Man," I said, "is Derek Kehoe, son of Mary Kay and grandson of Marvin or Mervin Kehoe."

"It's the *boy?*"

"He was only a few years younger than Larry." I ate my ham sandwich, mulling over what I'd seen and how it connected to what I'd learned. "I was so used to viewing him as the tragic victim — which he *was* — and the sweet little boy that girls and teachers loved that I never really considered him seriously as the killer, especially after what we found out about 'Larry' having worked at that store in Woodbridge and assaulting the guy there. Derek's trail just went cold and all signs seemed to point to Larry. But it was all there," I said, thinking of Derek's childhood, the abandonment, abuse, and head injury.

"So who was Larry Johnson, then?" Ryan asked.

"Just a drifter and a grifter, I guess." I handed Ryan a sandwich half. "He was a fraudster who hustled and exploited lonely women and maybe cheated at cards. But when he progressed to blackmail, that's when he met his end." I told Ryan the details of the altercation between Larry and Derek that I'd witnessed in my vision. "Larry said his goodbyes to the people in town, who would then think nothing of it when he disappeared, and returned to the farm, expecting to get a nice, fat package of cash. But Derek had other plans for him."

"How old would Derek have been then?"

"About nineteen or twenty, I think. Old enough to take on Larry, anyway, especially if he'd been drinking since the morning, which it looked like he had in my vision."

"So Derek Kehoe murdered Lawrence Johnson."

"That's what I believe, yeah. He slit Larry's throat and buried the body in the woods at the back of the farm, where no one was likely to come across it. But he must've kept Larry's belongings — his class ring, definitely, and some form of ID at the very least, like his driver's license or social security, if he had one. And, of course, the Thunderbird." I popped the tab on my can of soda. "He would've needed to hide that from his mother."

"You don't think she knew?"

I took a long swallow, considering. "I can't be sure, but I don't think so. I'm guessing she loved Larry, or thought she did, and wouldn't have wanted him harmed. And with her pitiful self-esteem, she would've been all too ready to believe that yet another man had run off and left her. When she killed herself, there was nothing keeping Derek on the farm any longer."

"Then he took on the identity of Larry Johnson," Ryan said.

"I reckon he would've been keen to shed his horrible past, leave that good-for-nothing farm behind, and make a fresh start. So he became charming Larry Johnson, the guy with the cool car and class ring. Maybe that wasn't immediate, maybe it took time to assume that personality, but either way, poor pathetic Derek Kehoe was no more."

"Hmm." Ryan braked hard to avoid crashing into the back of a truck taking a turn without signaling. "Except that wherever we go, that's where we are."

"Exactly. So Derek left Crowbury and, at some stage, maybe even immediately, went to Woodbridge and got a job at that store there under his new name. Maybe he overdid the charming act, and that's why the guy there got the wrong idea about him."

"You don't think Derek Kehoe's gay?"

"I don't know," I said. "Maybe, maybe not. I do know that his grandfather had drilled it into him that he mustn't be a pansy or a sissy. It's not a huge leap to imagine Derek taking on his grandfather's homophobic attitudes and then lashing out at that guy at the drive-in when he made a pass."

"And after that, he went … where?" Ryan asked.

"I don't know that either," I admitted. "Perhaps that's when he started his haberdashery supply business, using the Ford until he could afford a van. I saw the Thunderbird in my vision, which makes me think that in the early days, he would have been cruising the highways of New England in that car, picking up hitchhikers, runaways, seasonal workers, and maybe even sex workers."

"And killing them." Ryan's hands tightened on the steering wheel.

I nodded. "I imagine it would've been much later that Lawrence Johnson became the respected expert on buttons and the owner of Heavenly Haberdashery."

"What's your theory on motive?" Ryan asked. "Anger, control, the thrill of the power?"

"All of that, yeah. And maybe more," I said, thinking of what I'd seen in my visions. "The stitching of their lips — pushing a needle into and out of the flesh — that's a kind of penetration."

"That's a bit far-fetched, isn't it?" Ryan said.

"Well, it is Freudian," I said. "He saw penises in everything."

I didn't think it was a stretch to see Kehoe thrusting his thumb in and out of the still-warm mouth of a dead man as a kind of fellatio or rape, though whether that impulse had originated in sexual desire or the desire for power and dominance — a need at the core of rape — I couldn't tell. The problem with my visions was that I saw only narrow slivers of time. I didn't know what all might've happened before or after Kehoe killed his victims.

We rode in silence for a few minutes. The afternoon sun was warm on my arms, but inside, I felt cold, thinking about

Kehoe refining his methods, executing his fantasy, and hiding the remains of all those lives. My phone signaled an incoming text message, and checking it, I saw that it was from Deaver. "Not again," I muttered, expecting another request for more information on the serial killer case. Deaver might just be a harmless psychology professor, but that didn't make him any less of a nuisance. This time, however, it was him giving me the update.

Have you seen the news about them finding a match for the bones in the Nash Stream Forest?

The last news I'd read on the investigation was that two sets of remains from the mass burial site remained unidentified. I'd had more important things occupying my time in the last two days than staying on top of news sites. I opened a browser on my phone and after checking my news app, I let out a sound of surprise when I read a post with the headline *New Development in Nash Remains.*

"What's up?" Ryan asked.

"Remember how Singh refused to tell me what they found in the well at the Crowbury farm? Well News24 is reporting that it was a couple of smaller human bones plus a scrap of fabric with a buckle on it," I said, excited by what I'd read. "And the unidentified, incomplete remains found in the Nash forest?"

"The bones and fabric from the well are a match for that?" Ryan guessed.

"Right in one. That body is Kehoe senior's. It's got to be!

That's why that set of remains didn't match the others in terms of age or date of death. Kehoe was older, and he died sometime in the mid-nineties. And I'm guessing he *did* die in the well. That's why I sensed death there."

"So sometime afterward, Derek Kehoe must've moved his grandfather's remains to the forest in New Hampshire," Ryan said.

"Yeah. I wonder why he did that," I said.

"It must've been done many years later. The body was probably skeletonized, and a couple of bones fell off when he removed it from the well."

"And his clothes would've been disintegrating, too, so that's why fragments of them were left behind. I'll bet the fabric and buckle are from the overalls I saw him wearing in my vision. And the button!" I exclaimed, connecting another series of dots. "That rusted metal snap button Singh brought me to touch, that must've been from the coveralls too. The body didn't match the usual victim profile. That's why he wanted me to read it and get a feel for whether it was the same killer."

I read to the end of the article and checked a few more news sites. There was coverage of the kidnapping of a woman from a hotel in Montpelier, and one site had already reported the news of her safe return, but it seemed like neither the FBI nor the cops had alerted the media to the fact that the kidnapper was also a suspect in the Gay Slayer case.

"They're reporting the FBI as saying they have several new leads and are hopeful of making an arrest shortly." I bit a hard ridge of skin on the side of a fingernail. "I hope that's true. I truly hope they're closing in on him."

Ryan cast me an appraising glance. "Do you think they are?"

I considered for a moment. "I have a feeling they'll be searching New Hampshire for him. But I think he's going to ground," I said. "He's going home."

– 48 –

The sun was setting by the time we took the turnoff to the old Kehoe farm. Ryan pulled over on the dirt track, killed the engine, and said, "We need to discuss our plan."

"A plan, right!"

"Give me an idea of the layout of this place."

"I can draw it for you," I said. "Do you have some paper?"

He handed me a leather-bound notepad with a pen in a holder on the side, and I sketched a map of the dirt track, the house, and the outbuildings beyond.

"We'll have to search them all," Ryan said. He parked the car across the dirt track between a dense thicket of bushes on one side and a huge tree on the other, blocking the easiest way out.

I gave him an approving nod. "Good thinking."

"Speaking of good thinking," Ryan said, "I think you should wait here until I've checked this place out."

"Like that's going happen," I said and got out of the car.

Ryan followed suit, closing his door with a soft click. "Stay by my side," he said softly, and we set off in the direction of the farmhouse.

It was difficult to keep from whimpering with every step. My feet were still raw and tender, and it hurt to walk. If I got through this, I swore to myself that I would get professional help for my excoriation disorder. After a few steps, I discovered that walking on the outside edge of my feet hurt less. The only problem was that Ryan noticed my odd gait at once.

"What's up?" he asked.

"Nothing, I just um … I just have a splinter, I think."

"In both feet?"

"Over there." I pointed ahead to where the dilapidated old house had come into view. The half-collapsed porch roof and broken windows gave it the appearance of a face leering at us. As we drew closer, sticking to the deep shadows on the side of the track, we saw the barn behind the house, a hulking presence against the dimming sky, where swallows or perhaps bats darted in swift black arcs. As before, a heaviness settled in my chest, and nervous dread filled my stomach.

Tripping on a protruding piece of rock and landing hard on my mangled right foot, I hissed in pain then crept up to the house in a hunched and painful trot, heading for the porch steps. But Ryan whispered an order to stop. I crouched, waiting, while he drew his gun and peered into the front windows. When he gave me the all-clear, I climbed the stairs behind him, both of us keeping to the sides to minimize any telltale creaks.

The front door listed on its hinges, leaving enough space for us to get past. Had the FBI left it open when they finished searching this place weeks ago? Or had the killer visited more recently? As soon as I stepped inside, I could tell that the Button Man wasn't in the house, though it seemed to me that Mary Kay and old man Kehoe lingered in the shadowed corners, faint memories rather than ghosts.

"He's not here," I told Ryan, but he still searched every room and possible hiding place.

I walked directly to the back door, already feeling the pull of the barn.

No.

Colby was back. I felt a surge of comfort, even though his presence meant I was most likely in danger.

"Nothing," Ryan said, joining me in the kitchen. "And no sign of another vehicle that I can see."

"He's in the barn. I can feel it."

"He's there? Like, right this moment?"

"Yes."

I sensed Derek's presence with every alert fiber of my being. The round barn with its peeling red paint and rotting roof thrummed with the presence of the man I'd come to confront, and my very cells vibrated in sync with that frequency. My fatigue slipped off me like shed skin, and energy surged from my core. I reflected on how ironic it was that the more I connected with those who'd passed on, the more I flirted with my own death, the more I felt wonderfully, vitally alive.

I opened the back door of the house and began the walk, which seemed an inevitable move in a chess game that had started months ago when I touched that rib bone and first sensed the darkness. All my steps since, even the false starts and dead ends, had led me ultimately and inexorably to this moment. The magnetic pull drawing me to the barn increased as I drew closer.

It became so strong that in my thrall to it, I no longer felt the pain in my feet and only dimly heard Ryan ask, "What's that?"

He was pointing at the sloped ramp on the side of the barn.

"It goes to the hayloft above the barn," I said.

"Wait here," he said, positioning me behind a stack of old tires near the ramp. "I'll check the main level of the barn."

"Okay, sure," I said, though I had no intention of waiting anywhere. "Watch out for the trapdoor."

Ryan clearly thought that if Kehoe was here, he'd be in the main level of the barn. That's why he wanted to check it out for any danger first. But I could feel that wasn't where Derek was. I waited until Ryan, gun in his hand, disappeared around the side of the barn, and then made my way to the base of the ramp. With every step I took up the incline, my feet moved more surely, my heart hammered faster in my chest, and the awareness of my prey grew stronger.

No, Garnet!

Ignoring Colby, I slipped through the open door at the top of the sloped drive and moved inside. At the edge of the hayloft platform stood the man I'd thought was Lawrence Johnson, but the neat, tidy button expert was gone. He still wore the black-and-blue checked shirt, but now it was crumpled and stained with dirt. His hair lay lank with grease against his putty-pale skin, the long bangs only partially obscuring the evidence of his old head injury. His eyes burned with an emotion closer to exhilaration than fear.

"Hello, Derek," I said gently.

A look of surprise rippled over his features, followed by a moment of recognition.

"You!" he said.

"Yes, me."

He glanced back over his shoulder at the gaping circle of space at the core of the barn, looked over the edge down at the barn floor below, and then back up at me. His eyes narrowed, and I felt rather than saw him tense his body. With no time to protest or run, I braced myself for the impact of his charge. But instead of hurling himself at me, he simply stepped off the edge of the platform and disappeared.

— 49 —

A thud and a grunt sounded from the barn floor below.

Shit! I sure as hell had *not* expected that.

I ran to the edge of the platform and peered over. Kehoe had landed directly on top of Ryan.

"Ryan!" I yelled in terror. "*Ryan!*"

When he didn't move, I told myself he'd merely been winded or knocked unconscious, but I needed to get down there and check to see if he was okay. I didn't dare make the leap. It was a good twenty feet to the barn floor. The heavy chain with the hay hook hung from a nearby beam. I could grab that and inch my way down. But even as I considered whether my upper arm strength would be sufficient to stop me from falling, Kehoe reached for the firearm lying a few feet away from Ryan's unmoving hand. So much for the chain idea. Kehoe would shoot me where I dangled.

I sped out of the hayloft, jumped off the sloping drive, and fell to the ground. I leapt back up, frantic to check on Ryan. I couldn't just rush blindly into the barn, though — Kehoe might freak out and shoot Ryan. Or me. I spun in an agitated circle, looking for help, for ideas. What to do? Think! Remembering my phone, I called Singh. *Answer*, I willed him. *Answer the bloody phone.* The ringing continued uninterrupted. *Just for once in your precious, patronizing life answer the damn phone, you utter asshole!* The call clicked over to voicemail.

I muttered a frantic message. "This is Garnet McGee. I'm at the Kehoe farm outside Crowbury, and the killer's here. Do you hear me? He's in the barn, and he's got a gun. There's an officer down. And I don't know what the fuck to do. Just get here! Now! Before—"

A beep cut me off. I shoved the phone back into my pocket and crept around the curved red walls, down toward the main level of the barn. Another idea, an obvious idea that should've occurred to me immediately, hit me. I should call Washington. Surely, he would answer? But even as my right hand moved around to my back pocket, Derek Kehoe stepped out of the barn, pointing Ryan's gun at me.

"Put your hands where I can see them!" he ordered.

Shit. I did as I was told.

"Come inside the barn, where your friend is waiting for you. And move slowly."

"Okay," I said, trying to keep my voice calm. "But don't shoot, okay? I'm not armed."

No, no, no!

Keeping my empty hands stretched out in front of me, I edged past Kehoe into the twilight gloom of the barn.

"Go over there." With the gun, Kehoe waved me toward the spot where Ryan sat slumped, head on his chest, against one of the wooden poles that supported the hayloft overhead. His phone lay in pieces beside him.

Walking backward so Kehoe wouldn't see my own phone in my back pocket, I moved to Ryan. When I reached him, I saw that his hands were behind his back, handcuffed around the pole.

"Sit down next to him," Kehoe said.

As I sat down cross-legged in the dirt, Ryan began coming to. Raising his head as if it weighed a ton, he focused his gaze on me.

I rubbed his face gently, leaning close to whisper, "I've called Singh." Then out loud, I said, "Ryan, Ryan! Are you okay?"

"No talking!" Kehoe barked.

Ryan nodded grimly. His lip was bloody, and his expression was a blend of pain and fury, but he was conscious and didn't appear to be seriously injured.

Kehoe glanced through the open door at the deepening darkness outside. "You," he said to me. "What's your name?"

"Garnet."

"*Garnet?* Well, Garnet, come light this lantern here."

I took slow steps to the oil lantern, which sat on the ground beside the heavy chain with the hay hook, desperately trying to come up with an idea of how to use this opportunity to Ryan's and my advantage. Kehoe backed up as I drew near, so I wasn't able to rush him. Throwing the lantern at him wouldn't incapacitate him, even if I did manage to hit him. I knelt, lit the wick, dropped the box of matches beside it as he instructed, and stood up again. There was no point in toppling or tossing the lit lantern — it would make this tinderbox of a barn go up in flames, trapping Ryan in the inferno. So I went back to sit next to Ryan, frantically running through possible next moves in my mind.

I needed to play to my strengths, which were more psychological than physical. And I needed to get Kehoe talking to buy time for Singh to send help. *Please let Singh check his messages, even though it's a Saturday evening. Please.* Behind my back, I reached for Ryan's fingers, welcoming their comforting squeeze.

But Derek Kehoe didn't want us comfortable. "Hands in front, where I can see them!" He moved back to stand beside the lantern, and the flickering light cast strange shadows over the bland features of his face.

I let my hands lie limply on my thighs, but Ryan shifted impatiently, yanking against the wooden pole a few times, though neither it nor the handcuffs were going to give way. I placed a hand on his thigh and rubbed it back and forth, telling him with my fingers to take it easy.

I hoisted a gentle smile onto my face and directed it at Kehoe. "I can understand why you'd want to be able to see, Derek, why you'd want lots of light. The dark must be hard for you, especially in this place."

"What do you mean?" he demanded, frowning.

"I know what happened to you, Derek, what your grandfather did. What he did to your mother." I spoke slowly and kept my tone sympathetic.

He sneered at me. "You know nothing. No one knew."

"And I know what happened here in this barn, how your grandfather locked you in that cage in the cellar below us and left you there in the dark," I said.

Kehoe's face tightened, and the hand at his side bunched into a fist. Traumatic memories, no matter how hard people tried to suppress them, were never far below the surface.

"And I know how he punished you with buttons," I continued. "How he made you kneel on them when you were just a little boy. That must've hurt so bad."

Kehoe's bottom lip extended a bit, and he blinked several times. Then he seemed to push down the vulnerable feelings that threatened to rise. Straightening his shoulders, he jutted out his chin and said, "You get used to the pain after a while."

I arranged my features into a compassionate expression, thinking through the implications of what he'd just said. "After a while, it didn't work as well as a punishment?"

Kehoe nodded.

"So he had to find new ways, crueler ways?"

A ripple of distress crossed Kehoe's face. Was he recollecting memories even more disturbing and painful that the ones I'd seen?

"That's what you meant at the conference when you said those framed brass buttons were a reminder of your time in combat," I said. "You kept them from when you were a child, didn't you?"

Kehoe nodded slowly.

"You weren't in the military, but you were at war — with your grandfather."

"Yes," he said and then, surrendering to the irresistible lure of my understanding and empathy, began talking about the trauma and terror he'd bottled up for so long. "If I talked back, he'd make me hold a button to my mouth." Kehoe held an index finger up to his lips in a shushing gesture. "It doesn't sound so bad, but it is when you have to do it for hours. Your arm aches, and your finger gets stiff and goes into spasm. But you better not move, or you'll get worse. He'll make you put the buttons *inside* your mouth, lots of them sometimes, and hold them there."

I made a sound of sympathy. "You were scared you might swallow them."

"He counted them, before and after, to make sure I didn't."

"Were you frightened you might choke on them?" I said. "Can you still remember the feel of them on your tongue, on your cheeks, clicking against your teeth?"

I could feel Ryan's curious gaze on me. He must know that I was stalling for time, but did he understand that I was trying to regress Kehoe to a less dangerous, more childlike state? Could he tell that it was working?

Kehoe ran his tongue around the inside of his mouth as if the metallic tang of a brass button still lingered there. "I can still taste them."

"And you weren't allowed to cry, were you?" I said.

"Grandpa said crying was for sissies. For girls. If I cried, he put me in the cage."

"And that was so scary down there in the dark."

"One time, he said he was gonna get one of my mother's needles and sew my mouth shut with tomato twine. 'That'll teach you a lesson. That'll stop your blubbering for good!' That's what he said."

"So you had to keep quiet. You had to button your lip."

He nodded. "I had to learn control."

"Ah, you were such a brave little boy, all alone in the cage in the dark." Sweat was trickling into my eyes. I wiped my face on my arm, moving slowly so as not to startle him.

Ryan spoke into the silence. "Man, you must've hated your grandfather."

"I didn't! I didn't hate him. I loved and respected him!"

Even after what he did to your mother? I wanted to ask but didn't. I wanted him to regard me as an ally. So instead, I said, "You needed your grandfather too."

Kehoe rubbed the toe of his shoe in the dirt beside the lantern, muttering, "Without him, where would we be? How would we survive?"

"That's what your mom said?" I guessed.

Ryan drew a breath as though about to say something — perhaps that Kehoe must've hated his mom, too, for not protecting her son — but I cut in quickly. "She wasn't brave and strong like you were. She wasn't strong enough to stop your grandfather. *You* had to do that, didn't you?"

– 50 –

Kehoe watched me uncertainly, his left hand clutching the firearm, his right rubbing the base of his spine. Had he hurt his coccyx in the fall? Good. I hoped it hurt like hell.

"That's why you pushed your grandfather into the well?" I said.

"I didn't push him. He *fell*. It was an accident!"

Ryan made a soft sound of disbelief, but I said soothingly, "I understand, Derek. You were just trying to make him stop, and then he fell."

"He wouldn't stop. He kept shouting at me," Kehoe said, dashing a hand across his forehead to wipe hair out of his eyes, revealing the shadowed dent at his hairline. "He always shouted at me."

"Saying cruel things, calling you ugly names." In the flickering lamplight, it was hard to tell, but I thought I saw the shine of tears in Kehoe's eyes. "You *had* to push him back. And then when he fell, he was so angry that you had to leave him down in the well, didn't you?" Phrasing my accusations as questions softened them. Another therapist's trick.

"I only meant to leave him there for the night. To teach him a lesson. You have to stay there until you've learned your lesson!" Was he repeating what he'd said to his grandfather or what his grandfather had told him on so many occasions? "But when I went back in the morning and slid the well cap off and dropped the ladder, he didn't come up."

"Maybe you thought he was playing a trick on you?" I suggested. "He wanted you to go down, and then he'd leave *you* there."

"Yeah. But I went down and checked anyway because I loved him!" He directed the last part at Ryan.

"And he was dead?" I said. "That must have been so awful for you."

"It was an accident. That's what momma said. Just an unfortunate accident." Kehoe's bottom lip trembled.

"Killing Larry wasn't an accident though, was it?" Ryan accused, his tone tough and mean.

Was he playing bad cop to my good cop in order to keep Kehoe off-balance, to keep him talking? *I* wanted to keep Kehoe calm; I hadn't given up hope of talking our way out of this, so I shot Ryan a look and, turning my head so Kehoe wouldn't be able to see, mouthed, "Trust me."

Ryan gave me a small reluctant nod.

"That was his own fault," Kehoe spat. "When boys are bad, they have to be punished. And he did bad things. He hurt my mother! He was a problem, and I had to make him go away."

"How did it feel?" I asked.

Kehoe smiled, his dark eyes glinting in the yellow light of

the lamp. "It felt *good*," he said, drawing out the last word.

Ryan squirmed uncomfortably, no doubt thinking it would feel good to drive a fist into Kehoe's face, but said nothing.

Keeping any hint of judgement out of my voice, I asked Kehoe, "Good in what way?"

"Like I'd fixed something that was wrong." His smile widened. "Like I was in control for the first time in my life."

"Yeah, I can understand that. So were those other young men problems too? Or were they bad boys who needed to be punished?"

"They were wrong," he snapped.

"Wrong how?" I asked, trying to keep my tone soothing.

"They liked other men. That's not right. It's bad. Unnatural. Grandpa said so."

Ryan sighed in exasperated contempt. I knew it must be killing him to say nothing.

"Grandpa believed men should be men," I said to Kehoe. "And you wanted to be a real man, just like your grandpa wanted you to be."

Kehoe nodded. "Just like he was."

It took all my self-control not to tell this pathetic excuse for a human being that the toxic masculinity his grandfather had embodied was anything but manly. "You never had sex with them, did you?" I guessed. "The young men you gave rides to."

His face contorted into a rictus of disgust and fury. "I'm not one of *them*."

"No, no," I said quickly. "Of course not."

"I'm straight! I like women. I was married once. I'm not some kind of disgusting freak!"

Biting back a dozen hot retorts, I merely said, "You're not like that."

"No." He sounded irate that I might ever have considered it. "*I'm* normal. *They're* disgusting."

"They should've kept that part of themselves buttoned up?" I said.

"That's right. We can't all just have what we want. What if I'm in a jewelry store and I really want a Rolex? I can't just steal it, can I? Because it's wrong to steal."

"Is that how your grandfather explained it to you?" I asked. "That it's wrong for a man to love another man?"

He nodded several times. "Maybe they can't help what they feel, what they want. But they do have a choice about what they do, and they made the wrong choice. So I had to stop them."

"Once they were dead, they couldn't say or do the bad things anymore," I said.

"That's right." He was calming down, feeling understood.

"And you sewed their lips shut because …?"

"To keep them closed," Kehoe said like it should be obvious. "Buttoned up, like grandpa wanted. It was my duty. Though sometimes" — a sly smile crept over his features — "doing your duty can be a pleasure. The purest kind of pleasure."

I wanted to throw up. I'd felt pity for Derek Kehoe, for the boy he'd been and the pain he'd suffered. Now, I merely felt sickened. I couldn't show him that, though. "You were just doing your duty," I said. "Perhaps even God's work?"

Kehoe snorted. "There is no God. I was doing my grandfather's work, like I vowed I would."

"You made your grandfather a promise?"

"Yes, after I— After he died. I promised him I would be good, that I would make it up to him by doing what I knew would make him proud of me."

I'd had him so wrong. Wrong name, wrong job, wrong motives. Derek Kehoe hadn't killed for the thrill of it — or not primarily anyway — and certainly not from motives rooted in lust. Yes, he'd gotten off on the power and the control. And yes, perhaps beating and killing his victims allowed him to vent the deep rage the helpless boy had felt toward the adults who'd abused, abandoned and betrayed him. But primarily, he was a mission killer. He'd internalized his grandfather's beliefs about what it meant to be a man and murdered young gay men because their sexuality was forbidden by the patriarch's rules.

Derek had never really gotten free of this place, of his grandfather's abuse and toxic attitudes. He'd merely kept it all buried inside, where it had festered and putrefied until he felt compelled to act.

In one of my visions, I'd sensed that the killer wanted to be like his victims in some way. Now, I thought I understood why. Derek had loathed them for their sexuality and judged them to be less worthy as human beings because of it, but perhaps he'd also envied their freedom, their courage to be themselves and live their lives with integrity and honesty, when he'd still been living under the thumb of the twisted man who'd ruled his life. And he'd somehow decided that he could atone for his guilt in killing his grandfather by enacting that man's bigotry in the form of real-life death sentences.

"How did you know which of those young men were the

kind your grandfather hated?" I asked Kehoe.

"Mostly, I just knew."

"Oh, for God's sake," Ryan said, apparently unable to stay silent any longer. "Next thing you're going to say is that it was their fault for making a pass at you."

Kehoe glared at him, but I said kindly, "Don't mind him, Derek. You can tell *me*. I'll understand."

He sniffed as though feeling hurt, and I had to bite down on my lip to keep from telling him that *he* wasn't the injured party here. Making a show of speaking only to me, he said he could usually tell when men were gay, and when he wasn't sure, he checked. He'd make a pass at a guy just to see how he reacted. If the guy tolerated his advance or responded, his number was up.

As he spoke, I found myself imagining the scene, seeing him as he cruised up streets and down highways in the Thunderbird, searching for his next victim. It was like I was beside him in the memory, hunting along with him.

He's humming along to a tune on the car radio when he spots a young man in a sky-blue shirt, standing on the side of the highway with his thumb stuck out. He pulls the Ford over, rolls down the window, and smiles. "Want a ride?"

The young man gets into the car, grinning at his luck. This driver seems safe enough, and the wedding ring is reassuring. Just a family man out for a drive.

Kehoe makes a move, and when it's not rejected, he flips his switch, beats up his passenger, and somewhere — in the car, in the woods, in his house — takes time to enjoy the intoxicating control he has over the young man before he kills him. It's ecstasy having this much power. Nothing else has ever come close. Then he shoves a button into the dead man's mouth or sews the lips closed with the button stitched on dead center and gets rid of the body.

He's done his duty and buttoned up the man permanently. Grandpa would be so pleased. He'd say it was a fitting punishment.

Afterward, he feels wonderful. It's the best high ever, bliss. He's a good boy. A powerful man. He's atoned for what he did to Grandpa. That night, he sleeps deeply, his conscience clear, his body relaxed, his fantasy sated. But all too soon, the tension begins to build again, and the guilt resurfaces like stinking fumes from a manure cellar.

He resists as long as he can, living on the meager joy of memories, the pale imitation of fantasies, while the compulsion grows and grows until he has *to get back in his car and onto the highway, and start the hunt all over again.*

– 51 –

I shook my head to clear the imagined images. In front of me stood the killer, still rationalizing his behavior by defending the indefensible. A few times, he said, he'd made a pass at the wrong person and gotten beaten up for his trouble. And he hadn't defended himself because those men were in the right, weren't they? They were real men. Twice, he'd been robbed by straight men, but he hadn't hurt them because they, too, weren't bad.

"Grandpa wouldn't have wanted you to hurt *them*," I said.

"Exactly," he said.

"Why did you move your grandfather to the forest?" I asked.

"I didn't like to think of him down there in the well, all alone. I don't think he would've liked it." A show of the old fear crossed his features. "I was living in New Hampshire by then, and I'd found that lovely spot, so I decided to bring him there. It was the right thing. I could visit him there."

"It was like a shrine."

"That's the word!" he said. "I could bring him my work,

like offerings. And I could start fresh, regain control."

"I don't understand," I said.

"I'd been doing it more often as the years went by, taking out more and more problems," he said casually, as though describing taking out the trash.

I remembered how the number of his known and suspected murders had escalated in the late 2000s.

"And I was getting a little … reckless. So once I had grandpa all settled, I decided that from then on, I'd do just one a year."

"On May sixth?"

Once more, Kehoe's face creased into an unsettling smile. "Grandpa's birthday. I thought it would be a way to honor it, fixing a problem and burying it there where he could see my work. A nice tribute to him."

I wanted to yell at Kehoe, to tell him he was crazed and vile and evil, but I cleared the words from my throat and made myself to speak calmly. "When did you move him?"

"In the spring of 2010."

"So," I said, trying to remember the dates of the recent murders, "Denzel Harris would've been the first man you buried there. And the last man before that was the one you left near the quarry outside of Pitchford."

Kehoe shrugged.

"His name was Jacob. Jacob Wertheimer."

"If you say so," he said indifferently.

I wanted to hit him. My hands closed into fists, and a cold rage swamped me. "I was the one who found his remains, you know?"

Kehoe's eyebrows rose in surprise. "That's why you're so interested in me?"

"Yes. I wanted to find you because I found him. I held one of his ribs in my hand."

Kehoe's eyes glittered with avid curiosity. "And what did that feel like?"

"Bad, Derek. It felt very bad."

He grunted. "You know what feels bad to me? Knowing I can't go back and visit my grandfather now. Knowing that he's lying on a cold steel table in a mortuary somewhere."

"That must be hard for you," I said. "I'm sorry, Derek." Though I didn't feel it, not at all.

"Sorry? For *him*?" Ryan gave a humorless laugh and although he said nothing more, his expression as he stared at Kehoe was one of unmistakable contempt.

Kehoe's face, which had softened in response to my compassion, now twisted in fury. He marched over to Ryan and kicked him in the ribs. Ryan grunted and slumped over.

"Derek, please don't. Please," I begged.

Kehoe's nostrils flared, and he landed another kick on Ryan's hip, but at my continued pleading, he spun around and walked away. Back beside the lantern, he rocked on his heels for a few seconds, contemplating Ryan, who was sucking in shallow, painful breaths. I stayed still, afraid any movement might tip Kehoe into uncontrolled fury.

At last, he spoke. "Say you're sorry," he said to Ryan, and I tensed.

Ryan raised his head and looked Kehoe in the eye. "I am truly very sorry," he wheezed, and I released the breath I'd been holding. But then Ryan added, "I'm sorry for the poor people you hurt and killed."

Kehoe's lips curled, and he nodded as if he'd been expecting that sort of response. "I've had enough of you. You're a problem I need to fix," he said. Then he raised the gun and pointed it at Ryan.

"No!" I screamed, and at that moment, my phone rang.

Kehoe looked disoriented for a second. He patted his pockets with his free hand, searching for the ringing phone. When I started to get mine from my back pocket, he yelled, "Let it ring!"

"But—"

"Let it ring!"

For a moment, I debated, flipping through the permutations of what might happen if I reached for it anyway.

Leave it. Danger!

It was agonizing to do nothing but listen to Colby's warnings and the sound of my phone echoing in the barn. The noise stopped. Seconds later, it started again. And again, I did nothing. When it finally stopped ringing and stayed silent, Kehoe ordered me to stand up.

I got to my feet, and he said, "Take that phone out with one finger and thumb. Don't try anything!"

Hole.

I fished the phone out of my back pocket, wondering what Colby meant.

"Now bring it here."

Hole.

"Slowly," Kehoe said, keeping the weapon in his left hand trained on me.

Open hole. Behind!

I grasped what Colby was trying to tell me, and as I drew closer, I started to toss the phone to Kehoe, planning to aim high so he'd have to step back.

But he uttered a sharp "No!" then added, "Just hand it to me. No fast moves."

Slowing my steps, I glanced left and right. Old shreds of hay were underfoot, the hoe lay about five yards away, and the hay hook and chain were hanging near the lantern on the floor. I transferred my phone to my left hand and held it slightly out of reach of Kehoe's empty right hand. Then, in the split-second when his gaze flicked to the phone and he reached out to snatch it from my grasp, I seized the heavy chain with my free hand and swung it at him with all my strength. He stepped back quickly, so it only brushed against him, but those few steps were enough. With a short scream, he fell through the open trapdoor into the manure cellar.

"Good job!" Ryan said, but his relieved tone changed when I made to follow Kehoe down the hole. "Stop! What are you *doing?*"

"It's not that big of a drop," I said.

"Are you insane? He has a gun! You'll be a sitting duck."

"Oh," I said, feeling stupid. "I'll go around then." I gestured to the barn door.

"He'll still have the gun!"

I knew Ryan wanted to protect me. Making sure I stayed safe was the reason he'd insisted on accompanying me on this trip. He'd be feeling mad and miserable that he'd so far failed to do so.

"Garnet, listen to me, *please*. You'll get yourself killed."

"I can't just let him get away, Ryan."

"Wait here with me until help arrives."

Stay.

"We don't even know if help *is* on the way," I pointed out, inching my feet toward the barn entrance. "And if he gets away now, we might never find him again."

Back when Ryan and I had played darts at the Tuppenny Tavern, he'd urged me to stop overthinking things and trust my instincts. At that moment in the barn, my instincts warned me that the Button Man was about to escape.

"Don't go!" Ryan yelled, fear for me making him angrier than I'd ever seen him.

Don't go! Stay!

How funny that the one time the two men in my life were in agreement, I couldn't oblige.

I'm sorry, I thought to Colby. To Ryan, I said, "What would you do if I was the one tied up and you were free?"

As I ran out of the barn, I could've sworn I heard his teeth grinding.

$$- 52 -$$

I raced out of the barn and sped around to the outside entrance to the manure cellar. The double-wide doors were ajar, a silent invitation for me to enter, but taking a page out of Ryan's cop book, I took a moment to peep through a chink in the wall and immediately solved the mystery of the missing van. It was parked inside the cellar, where no doubt, he'd hidden the Thunderbird, too, all those years ago.

I so did *not* want to go into that dark place with its even darker memories. And I did not want to confront the armed serial killer hiding inside. Why did I keep finding myself doing the very things I feared most — going into murky, rat-infested holes, trusting people, daring to care again?

Stay. Stay safe. Danger!

Yeah, okay, Colby. I heard you the first time.

Spying a rusty tire iron leaning against the outside wall, I grabbed it. It felt good to have something heavy in my hands. Working on the assumption that if Kehoe took a shot, it would be aimed at my head or chest, I got down on my hands and knees and, keeping low to the ground, crawled through the gap between the doors. I paused to listen. Above the rustlings and skittering of little creatures, I heard something else — labored breathing.

As my eyes adjusted to the dark, I spotted Kehoe. He was lying down, perched on his right elbow, just outside the square of golden lantern light shining through the open trapdoor above. One of his feet was bent at an impossible angle. That was the good news. The bad news was that the hand holding the firearm pointed directly at me, was steady.

"Derek?" I said in my soft, sympathetic voice. "It looks like you've broken your ankle. Why don't you let me call for help?"

"Stay where you are, or I'll shoot," he said.

I could hear pain in his voice but also determination. He wasn't kidding.

"Okay, but I'm just going to stand up. Is that all right?" I got to my feet slowly, but so did he, grabbing a nearby rake and using it to pull himself up.

"Throw that tire iron away," he said. "Throw it outside."

Since I wasn't within striking distance, my weapon was useless against his firearm anyway, so I flung it out the door, then took a small step toward him.

"Stop! I don't want to kill you." He sounded sincere.

"I don't want you to kill me either," I said. "But, Derek, we've got ourselves a situation here, don't we? What's your plan?"

He flipped the rake upside-down and, using it as a crutch, hobbled sideways toward his vehicle. "You're going to stay right where you are. I'm going to get into my van and leave."

We were so close to taking him down, and now he was just

going to get away? Drive out of here and kill another young man tomorrow? Not if I could help it. I looked around, searching for a weapon, but saw nothing useful.

He edged closer to the van and opened the driver's door. "Just stay where you are," he said.

But I took another step closer, and he lifted the pistol and fired a shot at me. It missed but not by much. Ears ringing from the bang, I ducked behind one of the stone pillars, panting as if I'd just run a mile. Shit. I hadn't expected him to actually shoot at me. Now what?

"Derek?" I called. "Don't kill me!"

"Just stay where you are, and I won't," he yelled back.

I heard car keys jingling and peeped around the pillar. He was struggling to climb inside his van. I was running out of time to stop him.

"I don't kill good people," he said.

"Yes, you do, you shithead!" I yelled in frustration and saw him flinch as though my last word was the blow of a baton.

That was when I got the idea. I *did* have a weapon, a very powerful one. Could I bring myself to use it, though? It would go against all my training — against my very nature — to strike at his deepest wounds. Not the broken ankle or the sore back, but those old, primal injuries, the ones in the very core of him that had never healed. I had no option. I either had to attack now or let him escape.

Holding my hands above my head, I stepped out from behind the pillar. Kehoe's head snapped around, and he raised the gun again.

It was a relief to finally allow my face to show my contempt.

In a cold, hard voice, I said, "Your grandfather was right, Derek, wasn't he? You *are* a shithead."

"Shut up!"

"You were never your own man, just a shadow of him."

"I'm warning you!" he yelled, but his voice was higher, and the hand pointing the gun at me shook a little.

I shook a little too. I'd never been this cruel, not to anyone, but now I forced myself to find more vicious words to hurl at him. "Worthless and unlovable, that's what you are. Your mother knew it. That's why she couldn't even be bothered to keep herself alive for you."

"No, I—"

"Useless. You couldn't stop her from killing herself, and you didn't protect her from the men that used her. What kind of a son *were* you?"

His face crumpled, and his grip on the rake slackened.

"You were never strong. And brave? Don't make me laugh." I swallowed the bile of self-disgust that burned my throat and kept attacking. "You took your anger out on a helpless little cat because you were too weak to stand up to your grandfather, too weak to take him on man to man."

The rake fell from Kehoe's grasp, and he swayed, his balance now precarious.

"And what did Grandpa do to your mother, Derek? What did he do with her when he was angry and you were kneeling on buttons? Did he take her to his bedroom, get her to fix his mood there?"

Kehoe held out his hands as though he could fend off my words. "He never! He never did that!" The gun sagged in his hand and his chest heaved as he gasped.

"I think he did, Derek. And you never did anything to stop him. You just let her get hurt over and over again." I edged closer and saw that his bottom lip was trembling. "Mind you, she didn't protect you either. Maybe she didn't think you were worth it."

"I was. I was a good boy."

"No, you weren't. You were a bad boy." Another step. "Your grandpa knew the truth about you. You're just a sniveling little coward!"

He flinched, drawing his shoulders in as though cringing from a coming blow. I was getting there. Standing as tall as I could, I summoned all the harsh, brutal words I knew his grandfather had used against him.

"You're a filthy little shit who still wets the bed!" I said, my voice cracking.

"No, Grandpa!"

That shook me. He'd merged me with his original abuser. I'd reactivated his abuse, and he was right back there, reliving it. I was crossing all my boundaries, betraying my beliefs, but there was no time to hate myself for breaking another human being like this. The guilt and self-recriminations could come later. Right now, I had to press my advantage.

Speaking in a rough, deep voice, I said, "Get down on your knees, boy."

Half to my surprise, he did.

"You kneel on those buttons until you learn your lesson. Until you learn some self-control."

Kehoe was crying now, hard sobs that shook his shoulders,

but he made no sound. I closed the distance between us and kicked his hand, sending the gun into the inky depths of the cellar.

"Button your lip, boy, or I'll do it for you."

He nodded frantically, silently.

At that moment, he looked so much like a hurt little boy that I almost forgot the horror of who else he was, what he'd done. I wanted to hold him, to rock him in my arms and assure him that everything was going to be alright. That he *was* a good boy. But I couldn't. I couldn't risk him coming out of this child ego state and becoming the cold killer again, so I shed any remnants of mercy and made myself become his tormentor.

"You've been a bad boy, and you know what that means?"

His panicked eyes were wide and white in the darkness.

"It means the cage," I snarled. Had those words come from me, or *through* me?

"No, Grandpa, please!"

"Get into the cage like the filthy little animal you are!" I bellowed.

Whimpering, he turned onto his stomach and crawled on his belly, using his good leg to push himself inch by inch across the dirt, back into the gloom where the cage was, back into his worst memories. I walked behind him, whipping him on with ruthless words, increasingly unsure where I ended and his grandfather began. When he crept into the cage, I slammed the door down with a grating screech and jammed it shut with the rake.

He screamed and bayed. He rattled the bars of his prison, begging to be let out, promising to be a good boy, a real man.

I staggered over to a nearby pillar and slid down weakly against it. My own deep sobs joined his in a discordant chorus of misery. What had I *done*?

"Garnet! *Garnet!*" Ryan was shouting from above. How long had he been calling me? How long had I, too, been absent from this present?

"I'm okay," I called, then mumbled softly to myself, "I'm okay." Just too exhausted to move another inch. Just dirty, outside and in. Just hating myself for crushing another human being. I was chilled that, even in self-defense, I'd been capable of doing such a thing.

Safe! Mine. Always and forever.

Colby's voice was loud and fierce in my head. Above me, Ryan was still shouting, demanding to know what was happening, whether I'd been shot. In the cage, Derek's howling and wailing subsided into hoarse whispered pleas. Then he curled up into a tight ball, and his high-pitched keening sliced through the night, and through me, until it was drowned out by the wail of approaching sirens.

— 53 —

Sunday, May 6

The chair to my left was empty, but then, so were most of them. Six o'clock on a Sunday morning wasn't the busiest time of day for a police station. In the corner of the waiting area, a drunk was sleeping off his bender, while a cleaner pushed a broom around the floor, sweeping up the dust and detritus of the night before and filling the air with the sharp scent of Pine-Sol. Somewhere, a phone rang, and a door slammed.

The media was already gathering outside, hungry for more details, but inside the Montpelier Police Department, most of the hustle and bustle came from cops and FBI agents. Ryan and I had given our statements, answered a thousand questions, and dozed in our hard plastic chairs, waiting for permission to leave. Half an hour earlier, Ryan had excused himself. I figured he was going to try to find some painkillers for his bruised ribs and aching head, but instead, he'd returned with a Big Mac, fries, and a tall cup of hot chocolate. It was probably the most delicious meal I'd ever had. The burger and fries were hot and salty and comfortingly bland, and the drink was tooth-achingly sweet.

"You're a fine man, Chief," I said and leaned against him, welcoming the weight of his arm around my shoulder.

Tyler Washington, now in one of the station's back offices with Singh, had spent time with me in the night, listening to my account of what had happened, writing up my statement, and thanking me for helping to apprehend the killer. It felt good to have used my gift — and my brains — to track down the Button Man, to be the reason why he was now in an interrogation room or perhaps a holding cell inside this building and no longer out there killing innocent people. There was satisfaction in knowing that my gift had practical value and that I could do some good in the world, that I'd helped bring about justice for Jacob and all the other victims.

But I was less pleased about what I'd had to do, who I'd had to become, to take down Derek Kehoe. I'd hunted him, and when I had him in my sights, I'd taken the shot, using my words as bullets. What I'd done to him — reopening his wounds, deepening them — had been abhorrent, a kind of soul murder, and I'd spent much of the night wondering if I could possibly have done things differently. Letting him go to kill another man hadn't been an option, but it probably would've been kinder to have shot him.

The TV mounted in the corner of the waiting room was tuned to a news channel, and when they cut to a reporter covering the serial killer story, I got up and turned up the volume. The drunk startled awake with a grunt, mumbled something incoherent, and then subsided back into soft snores. I watched the news coverage of "The Gay Slayer" with growing cynicism. Knowing almost nothing about the killer or his crimes hadn't stopped them from compiling inaccurate reports, and they were still tossing around simplistic theories about Kehoe — that he was gay or schizophrenic or part of a cult.

"I guess 'Man raised in dysfunctional, abusive family and societal culture of toxic masculinity attempts to police men with non-normative sexuality in an a futile and murderous attempt to win approval from his long-dead abuser and atone for his guilt in killing him, while channeling the rage and helplessness he experienced in repeated childhood trauma into deadly violence so as to try feel powerful and compensate for his insecurities' doesn't make for as click-baity a headline," I said.

"Welcome to the wonderful world of how the media reports on law enforcement and murder investigations," Ryan said tiredly.

"I mean, I know he was a victim, abused and damaged in so many ways …"

Ryan yawned. "But at the end of the day, it was still a choice he made, not a destiny cast in stone. Nobody forced him to kill."

I closed my eyes and rested my head against the wall. "Why do people have to judge others for being different? Why are people so scared of those who don't look or act or sound the way *they* do that they feel entitled to end them?" I sat up straight and glared at the TV, though I no longer really saw it. "And it's not just crazed killers who try to shut down others. Everyone's got an opinion on someone else and feels like it's their duty to tell them how to live their lives just because they don't like having to deal with someone who deviates from the norm. Or because they're afraid of it, or don't believe it's real. Why can't the world just let people be who they are?" I was close to tears.

"Are we still talking about Kehoe?" Ryan asked gently.

I bit down on the rim of my cup, leaving indentations in the curled cardboard and thought about Ryan's comment. I felt a sudden rush of love for my parents. For all her frustrating foibles, at least *my* mother believed in me and my abilities. And my father loved me enough to allow me to become whoever and whatever I wanted, even when that was something he didn't understand and wasn't fully on board with.

Remembering how close that bullet had come to killing me, I resolved again to improve my relationships with them. Life was fragile. No, scratch that. Life was robust and tough and determined. But it was also impermanent, and good parents were worth holding onto. As were good men, I thought, tightening my hold on Ryan's hand.

Outside, dawn was staining the sky with ruby and scarlet streaks. I wanted nothing more than to go home to Pitchford, shower until the hot water ran out, and fall into my bed to sleep for a week. Even the prospect of doing more filing for Henry, while arguing with him about my odd eyes, sounded appealing.

I was eating the last of my burger when Singh emerged from a back room and walked down the hallway toward us. His tie was loose, his collar open, his jaw unshaven, and he wore a nice shade of purplish-blue under his eyes. So the man was human, after all. Good to know. Stopping in front of us, he stared down at me with an unfathomable expression. His fingers played with a set of keys while his mouth opened, closed, then opened again. He said nothing, but finally, he gave me a nod. I don't know if I imagined it — I *was* tired enough at that point that hallucinations were a distinct possibility — but I thought I detected respect in that nod.

He left via the staff exit — a glass door opening to the side of the building — and a police officer came to tell us we were free to go.

"Finally!" Ryan said, but I made him wait until I'd eaten my last fry and drunk the last of my hot chocolate.

Licking salt off my lips, I shoved the trash into the brown bag, squashed it into a rough ball, and lobbed it into a trash can on the other side of the room. "She scoressss!" I said.

Ryan was impressed. "You're a lot better at junk food sports than darts."

"I've had way more practice."

As I stood up, I heard a noise coming from down the hallway. Turning around, I saw Derek Kehoe. The shackles around his ankles and wrists were connected to a chain around his waist, and he shuffled along slowly, escorted by an armed guard of four officers. As he drew closer to us, his eyes sought mine, and there was something wild in his gaze. The tortured boy was gone; the urbane button expert was no more. In their place was a man burning with hatred.

"You think you got me good, don't you?" he said, his hoarse voice sounding almost amused. "You think you're saving lives."

I couldn't speak, couldn't move. The savage light in his eyes pinned me on the spot.

He stopped when he drew level with us, resisting the tugs on his elbows to move him to the side exit, where his transport waited.

"Well, I've got news for you." He took a fettered step toward me.

Careful! Colby warned as Ryan tugged me back.

"I'm not alone," Kehoe whispered. "There are more of us."

Then he turned and hobbled away, stepping out into the scarlet glow of dawn.

"Red sky at morning," I murmured, watching him go, "shepherd's warning."

Dear Reader,

I hope you enjoyed this novel! If you did, I'd really appreciate it if you'd leave a review, no matter how short, on your favorite online site or book club, or on Goodreads. Every review is valuable in helping other readers discover the book.

Visit my website (www.joannemacgregor.com) to join my VIP Readers' Group and get my monthly newsletter, with advance notice of my latest releases, competitions, giveaways and offers for free review copies, as well as a behind-the-scenes peek at my writing process. I won't clutter your inbox or spam you, and I will never share your email address with anyone.

I'd love to hear from you! Come say hi on Facebook (@JoanneMacg), Twitter (@JoanneMacg) or Instagram (joannemacgregor_author), or reach out to me via my website (www.joannemacgregor.com/contact) and I'll do my best to get back to you.

- Jo Macgregor

Other books for adults by this author

The First Time I Died
The First Time I Fell
Dark Whispers

Acknowledgements

My thanks to my editor, Chase Night, and to my fabulous beta readers, Emily Macgregor, Nicola Long, Edyth Bulbring and Heather Gordon for all their invaluable feedback — I'm so sorry you always get to read my books in their raw, unfinished state! I'm also grateful to my expert Vermont reader Cameron Garriepy and to Dr. Stephanie Erin Hart for helping me with the medical details. You all help improve my writing immeasurably, and I deeply appreciate each one of you!